PRAISE FOR
THE FATE'S THREAD SERIES

AMAZON EDITORS' BEST BOOK OF JUNE 2024   SCIENCE FICTION & FANTASY

"The tastiest treat for fantasy lovers. Following the perfect drama between two sneaky immortals, *The God and the Gumiho* glows with its supernatural antics and sumptuous world."

—Chloe Gong, #1 *New York Times* bestselling author of *These Violent Delights*

"Korean folklore, murder mystery, and a quirky love/hate story combine in this highly entertaining novel. *The God and the Gumiho* is one of a kind!"

—Juliet Marillier, author of the Sevenwaters and Blackthorn & Grim series

"Enchanting fantasy . . . With an intoxicating mix of action, mystery, and deliciously angsty romance, this reads like the most bingeable K-drama. Readers will be riveted."

—*Publishers Weekly* (starred review)

"This spellbinding dive into the supernatural realms of South Korea seamlessly blends Korean mythology with contemporary urban fantasy.... [Sophie] Kim's adult debut marks her as a talent to watch. With its blend of romance, mystery, and supernatural intrigue, *The God and the Gumiho* is sure to enchant readers."

—Booklist

"An action-filled contemporary fantasy based in Korean mythology, featuring morally gray characters and a little heat."

—*Library Journal* (starred review)

BY SOPHIE KIM

Fate's Thread
The God and the Gumiho
The God and the Gwisin

Talons
Last of the Talons
Wrath of the Talon
Reign of the Talon

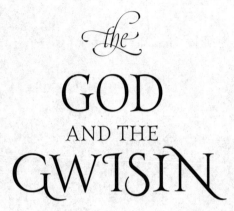

the GOD AND THE GWISIN

~ BOOK TWO OF FATE'S THREAD ~

SOPHIE KIM

NEW YORK

Del Rey
An imprint of Random House
A division of Penguin Random House LLC
1745 Broadway, New York, NY 10019
randomhousebooks.com
penguinrandomhouse.com

2025 Del Rey Trade Paperback Original

Copyright © 2025 by Sophie Kim

Penguin Random House values and supports copyright. Copyright fuels creativity, encourages diverse voices, promotes free speech, and creates a vibrant culture. Thank you for buying an authorized edition of this book and for complying with copyright laws by not reproducing, scanning, or distributing any part of it in any form without permission. You are supporting writers and allowing Penguin Random House to continue to publish books for every reader. Please note that no part of this book may be used or reproduced in any manner for the purpose of training artificial intelligence technologies or systems.

Del Rey and the Circle colophon are registered trademarks of Penguin Random House LLC.

Library of Congress Cataloging-in-Publication Data
Names: Kim, Sophie, author.
Title: The god and the gwisin / Sophie Kim.
Description: New York: Del Rey, 2025. | Series: Fate's thread; book 2 |
Identifiers: LCCN 2025006665 (print) | LCCN 2025006666 (ebook) |
ISBN 9780593599686 (trade paperback; acid-free) | ISBN 9780593599693 (ebook)
Subjects: LCGFT: Fantasy fiction. | Novels.
Classification: LCC PS3611.I4548 G64 2025 (print) | LCC PS3611.I4548 (ebook) |
DDC 813/.6—dc23/eng/20250228
LC record available at https://lccn.loc.gov/2025006665
LC ebook record available at https://lccn.loc.gov/2025006666

Printed in the United States of America on acid-free paper

randomhousebooks.com

1 3 5 7 9 8 6 4 2

Book design by Ralph Fowler

Book team: Production editor: Michelle Daniel · Managing editor: Paul Gilbert · Production manager: Chanler Harris · Copy editor: Madeline Hopkins · Proofreaders: Debbie Anderson, Jill Falzoi, Barbara Greenberg, Rebecca Maines

Adobe Stock illustrations: Larisa (rope with knots), Ivantsov (night sky), Gstudio (crescent moon)

The authorized representative in the EU for product safety and compliance is Penguin Random House Ireland, Morrison Chambers, 32 Nassau Street, Dublin D02 YH68, Ireland. https://eu-contact.penguin.ie

For my mother.
Mom, I look up to you more
than astrologers look up at the stars.

The ship on which Theseus sailed with the youths and returned in safety, the thirty-oared galley, was preserved by the Athenians down to the time of Demetrius Phalereus. They took away the old timbers from time to time, and put new and sound ones in their places, so that the vessel became a standing illustration for the philosophers in the mooted question of growth, some declaring that it remained the same, others that it was not the same vessel.

—Plutarch, *Plutarch's Lives*

AUTHOR'S NOTE

Ahoy there!

I'm thrilled to see you've returned for another adventure. The perennially grumpy (and caffeine-deprived) Detective Seokga, as well as other characters both startlingly familiar and wonderfully new, eagerly await your boarding upon the SRC *Flatliner*. Monsters, magic, and mayhem await, along with a hearty dash of whodunit and, of course, romance.

So very much of it.

Yet before you step foot onto this esteemed cruise ship and are carried through the churning currents of the underworld's river, please do humor me as I don my captain's cap and commence my own twist on a safety briefing. After all, these waters can be tricky—even dangerous—if not properly navigated.

The God and the Gwisin is in no way intended to be a guide to traditional Korean mythology. As in all my books, I have taken significant creative liberties. It is a belief of mine that retellings keep stories alive and spark interest in the original lore. It is also a belief of mine that in order to retell, an author *must* understand the original cultural context of the stories they work with. Please rest assured that I have carefully researched the traditional tales of my heritage and the centuries of history that inspired them.

With that said and done, welcome to your vacation upon the SRC *Flatliner*! I dearly hope that you enjoy your stay.

All aboard!

(And remember to mind the rails.)

the GOD AND THE GWISIN

CHAPTER ONE

KISA

Seoul, 2018

T<small>HE GLITTERING BEHEMOTH</small> that is Seoul's Shamanic Hospital towers above the city's streets, lording over its nightlife with a certain smugness only a building of great esteem can possess. Within this pillar of cold steel, steadfast concrete, and sparkling glass lies a world of bustling paramedics, striding doctors, a symphony of mechanical beeps and white-tiled floors that somehow remain pristine even as creatures and mortals alike are wheeled through the winding halls on gurneys.

Up and up the hospital stretches, pulling itself toward the night, where dark gray clouds smudge the rich navy sky and where a young woman sits underneath the stars and kicks a foot in a calculated motion over the edge.

She has carefully tied her hair back in a low bun, but wisps of dark, mocha-colored curls escape their band and brush against her cheek, accompanied by a cold kiss of wind. The young woman wonders, feeling rather detached from it all (a side effect, no doubt, of pulling twenty-four-hour shifts in the Magical Maternity Unit), if another gust would be enough to knock her over. Enough to send her fluttering down like an autumn leaf from a tree, crumpling on the ground below.

She sighs, leaning her cheek against the knee of her propped-up leg and staring down at the crawl of traffic below.

Yoo Kisa is utterly exhausted with her life. Exhausted from the long shifts with her hands fumbling for the slippery skin of a newborn, the eternal sleeplessness and concerning dependency (addiction, really) on fruity energy drinks and flat whites. Exhausted from being a shaman.

Perhaps, she thinks wearily, she should have specialized in something other than magical medicine. Her former New Sinsi University (Magical Division, of course) classmates seem to be doing well, from what she can decipher through the smiling posts on social media. Yuna, her old roommate, is the city's top glamourist—and paid in the hundreds of thousands. Jinny, Yuna's sister, has fulfilled her lifelong dream of being a god's assistant, running errands for none other than Yongwang the sea god himself and even residing in Okhwang. Kisa's rival Kim Dae, with whom she was always competing for top marks in the specialty, now works in Hallakkungi's flower garden and is part of the flower god's prestigious botanical research team, which is famous for their contributions to pharmacology. None were foolish enough to go directly into magical medicine. It's at least ten times more difficult, more dangerous, than mortal medicine—the dissimilar internal anatomies of dokkaebi versus imoogi, versus gumiho versus demigods, is only one example of the many, *many* differences.

Oh, taking this job so soon was a grievous error on her part, a flaunting of her own brilliance. Yoo Kisa, top of her NSUMD class. Yoo Kisa, a prestigious doctor, diving into the hospital mere minutes after graduation. Practically unheard of for a twenty-two-year-old shaman to skip the additional four years of medical training, but Kisa was just *that* good. One of her professors had fondly referred to her as the "nucleus" of NSUMD's graduating class of 2017. A powerhouse.

And it's true.

NSUMD is renowned for taking "prestigious" and "cutthroat" to another level entirely. In any mortal university, sabotage would have been frowned upon. In the Magical Division, it had been *encouraged*. Kisa is unable to count the number of times her laboratory experiments had been tampered with... or the number of times she'd returned the favor in full. There was no punishment for physical altercations, either. Shamans were in constant competition with one another, egged on by their patron deities. The gods may not be able to fight amongst themselves, or do anything to disrupt Okhwang's inner harmony, but their shamans? Through their shamans, the gods can be as nasty as they please.

Yet despite it all, Kisa did more than succeed. She *excelled*.

She could read a massive tome on history within four days and write a dissertation on the subject within three weeks. Her hand flew up in every class, and she received nothing less than top marks every semester. Channeling the power of her patron goddess, Samsin Halmoni, is something Kisa is remarkably adept at. A good mother heals, after all—chicken noodle soup, bandages, kisses on the head—and for Kisa, who had longed to be an obstetrician since her own mother died in childbirth, connecting with the goddess of childbirth comes smoothly, and so does channeling Samsin Halmoni's magic into her work.

The flesh of a mother can knit itself back together underneath Kisa's touch. A baby born on the brink of death can be revived, can transform into a wailing infant, flushed and healthy.

Kisa is also one of the leading experts on fetal congenital heart disease, able to detect what the machines sometimes cannot, able to perform the necessary surgeries with skilled hands that never falter, never fail. Yet there's a catch: She cannot heal mortals. Kisa can heal only creatures, those who believe in the power of the Korean gods.

And that restriction *hurts*. She aches from it—and for something... *more*. She knows not what—just that there's a startlingly *new* feeling of emptiness within her today, a dark, gaping void waiting to be filled.

Perhaps it's from skipping her usual order of a flat white this morning in favor of a few more treasured minutes of sleep. The lack of caffeine has certainly done her no good.

Kisa inhales a deep breath of night air but is unable to clear the taste of antiseptics and the surgery room from her lungs. Her head still throbs from the emergency C-section she'd had to give a petite haetae woman. Haetae are notoriously hard to deliver, the guardian creature's wary streak beginning in the womb. Sometimes the babes are too cautious to even want to come out into the world of danger. Kisa swallows hard.

How long has it been since she left the hospital? Days? Weeks? Ever since the hospital cut their staff numbers, she's been working herself until she falls from the brink of exhaustion and has no choice but to pull herself back up. Kisa's vision blurs with tears. It's not that she doesn't love what she does, or that she no longer feels the surge of triumph when she delivers a happy and healthy child. It's that she's so *tired*.

Nobody knows she's up here.

It would be so easy to slip away... to finally rest...

Kisa chews on her bottom lip. A flicker of red intrudes in her vision and she grimaces, pointedly not looking at the red thread that tied itself around her left pinky finger hours earlier, wrapping itself around the little finger in an intricate floral pattern almost reminiscent of a mugunghwa.

It's no surprise, really, that she's seeing things. It's the stress of it all, affecting her nervous system, increasing her vulnerability to hallucinations. Because there's no chance the thread, the one trailing down the building, winding into the streets below, is real.

She's seeing things. Feeling things.

Oh, yes. Kisa can somehow *feel* the smooth cord wrapped around her skin just as she would any real thread. Yet unlike real threads, this one won't come off. It appeared this afternoon, right when Kisa was creating the C-section's first abdominal incision. She nearly startled, but regained control of herself, conscious of the repercussions of any jerky movement on her patient.

"Go away," Kisa whispers now in English to the hint of red she can still see. Obviously, it doesn't reply. It doesn't reply when Kisa pleads to it in British-accented Korean, either.

Yet the hairs on the back of her neck still prick up. A slow trickle of anticipation crawls down her spine, and her limbs suddenly feel heavy with dread. Something has been decided, she senses. Something has been etched into stone, and there is nothing she can do to stop it. It's life-changing, life-altering . . .

Life-ending. A knife to cleave twenty-two years in half.

Her spine stiffens. As it begins, Kisa sucks in a shallow breath, tasting something bittersweet at the back of her throat. It reminds her of her stepmother's fixation with anti-aging creams. She stares down at the city below, heart thumping. It all happens so fast. Kisa doesn't even have time to open her mouth, to scream a plea to her goddess.

For in an instant, her body is sliding off the roof and she is, for a perfect, brilliant moment, weightless and hovering over Seoul. But then gravity grabs her by the ankle and tugs her down, yanking her past rows and rows of gleaming glass windows all stacked upon one another, laughing as it hauls her toward the ground in a perfect swan dive.

Kisa closes her eyes.

It's over soon enough.

CHAPTER TWO

SEOKGA

New Sinsi, 2025

THE ONLY PART of Seokga's sessions with the venerated Dr. Jang Heejin he truly dislikes is when, halfway through the session, the grandmotherly shaman-turned-deity-psychologist inevitably asks him how his inability to find Hani makes him *feel*.

When she first asked him that, approximately two days after the Red Thread of Fate appeared, Seokga had fixed her with his cold green glare, leaned in close to the aging therapist, and demanded (in a voice sour enough to curdle milk): "How do you *think* that makes me feel, you stodgy old crow?"

Dr. Jang hadn't even bothered with the pretense of writing something down in her ever-present leather-bound notebook. Instead, she snorted. It had taken Seokga aback enough that he'd finally (and begrudgingly) begun to trust the doctor Hwanin had assigned to him back in 1992 when he reclaimed his godhood in full (to make sure he didn't "snap" again, as his brother so aptly put it).

Since letting Dr. Jang into his mind, Seokga has discovered he has a plethora of daddy issues, an avoidant-dismissive attachment style (for everyone besides Hani, of course—it seems that she was the exception to everything), and a boatload of trauma from watching the love of his life die in front of him with his hand around the hilt of the dagger that killed her. Fun. And since beginning to treat Seokga some thirty-three years ago, the good doctor has gone significantly grayer. Although Seokga would very much like to take the credit for that, shamans *do* age. At a slightly slower pace than mortals, yes (a sign-on bonus from their patron deity), but they do wither, acquire depressing wrinkles, and ultimately die. He's loath to admit it, but other than the storm-cloud gray hair, Jang looks rather sprightly for a seventy-something-year-old.

"Seokga?" Dr. Jang prompts expectantly. Now, seven years after the red thread first appeared, Seokga just rubs his eyes in exhaustion. He's tired, bone-tired, and even the large iced coffee currently perched on the table between himself and Dr. Jang isn't helping. "I just got back from Antarctica," he replies hoarsely. His voice is always raspy, but the bitter winds hadn't helped. At all.

"Antarctica," Dr. Jang repeats. Her warm brown eyes, lined with wrinkles, show no emotion save for a calm neutrality that Seokga has grown to appreciate. She tilts her head, and the autumn sunlight from the circular window behind her illuminates her permed gray hair. "You thought Hani would be there?"

Seokga grits his teeth, glaring at the long Red Thread of Fate attached to his pinky. Nobody can see it but him. It's tangled, twisted, and has so far led the trickster on a wild goose chase all around the world. For a blessed handful of hours after it had appeared, the red thread seemed to have been bringing him to Hani—a clear, straight line with neat turns. Imbued with a lightness and filled with a pure, sparkling *cheerfulness* that he hadn't felt since before Hani's life sputtered out in front of him in that cursed warehouse, Seokga had called Dr. Jang almost immediately, bursting at the seams with the need to tell somebody that everything in his world—*everything*—was going to be right again. *Seoul,* he'd panted out loud to the kindly doctor as he leaned heavily on his cane. It was leading him to Seoul. But a few hours after night fell, it was like the damned thing had stopped working. It ran him in circles until it tangled itself, brought him to one place only to twist back and head toward another, and was an overall useless piece of string.

In hindsight, his joy is humiliating. As is his happy-go-lucky phone call to Jang. How dare she have witnessed him *cheerful*? He's been working hard to compensate for it ever since by being exceptionally miserable. And it's easy to do.

If Hani is anywhere on this world, he should be able to find her. Why can't he find her?

"It kept yanking down," Seokga now explains to Dr. Jang, who nods in sympathy. "Antarctica is . . . down. But there was nothing there except for penguins and fish and ice." His lip curls. He'd hated the foul, squawking things, but Hani would have loved the penguins. She would have thought they were adorable, and probably would have named each and every one something ridiculous. A familiar ache lodges itself in his chest, and Seokga takes a hasty slug of Creature Café coffee.

He wonders if Hani's reincarnation—wherever she, or he, is—would name the penguins, too. *It's fine if they wouldn't,* he tells himself. It's fine if they're different from who they were in their past life, his Hani, his love. It's fine. It's fine. Seokga can't, and won't, expect Kim Hani to be as she once was at the other end of the thread.

But you want her to be there, a cold little voice whispers back to him. *Waiting for you. The woman from the nineties. The mischievous gumiho. You don't want anyone else.*

Seokga swallows hard and stares at Jang's desk as he shoves those bitter doubts away. He won't let himself think about it. Not until he finds Hani. Not until he finds her. All he wants to do is *find* her—

Dr. Jang leans forward across the polished wooden surface, face serious. "Seokga," she says, and he's half-terrified she'll try to reach for his hand or otherwise comfort him. He has developed a serious aversion to *comfort*. The one time that Hwanin tried to hug him after a frustrating trip to Australia that yielded nothing, Seokga had nearly jumped out of his skin.

"What are you doing?" he'd hissed at Hwanin.

His brother had made a noise of disbelief. "I was going to hug you—"

"Do it slower next time, then," Seokga replied, hastily backing away. "I thought you were going to murder me."

"That's my line, brother, not yours," Hwanin replied, lips quirking.

Seokga doesn't want pity. He just wants Hani.

But Dr. Jang doesn't reach for him. Instead, she regards him somberly. "You're burning yourself out. You're exhausted, and I am seriously concerned about what will happen to you if you keep working yourself like this."

He stares fixedly at the pictures and accolades on the wall. Her son and daughter-in-law, grinning with their seven-year-old child in a park, the picture of a perfect, happy family. A BS in psychology from New Sinsi University, and a BA in shamanism. A PhD from New Sinsi University, Magical Division in deity psychology. Newspaper clippings of her practice, a cozy office conveniently next to a Creature Café, with headlines applauding her work supporting the pantheon. She's done a remarkable job reforming him into a god who doesn't *overly* obsess about staging coups. Seokga wishes she'd been around when his father, Mireuk, had what

Dr. Jang has called in past sessions a "psychotic break" and created all the evils of the worlds.

She might have been helpful.

"I know you miss Hani, Seokga," Dr. Jang continues, "but some time off is minuscule compared to the amount of time you have to search for her. And . . ." She hesitates, shifting in her seat. "Well, Hani can find you, too, dear. The thread *does* go both ways, after all."

Seokga rips his gaze away from the clippings. "She might not know what it is," he says, not letting himself entertain the other explanation as to why they haven't found each other yet. Not considering that she might be running from him. "Statistically, it's more likely she's human than a creature. If she's human, she may not know the stories about the thread." He swallows hard. Hani, whoever she is now, must feel the same pull—the same longing—as he does. The red thread has turned them into magnets aching to connect. Yet he still hasn't found anyone with the wine-brown eyes of his Hani, eyes that Hwanin promised would remain the same in this life.

Thirty-three years.

Thirty-three years of grief and longing. Thirty-three years since 1992, that golden year when a woman with a sly smile and a laugh like the tinkling of bells flounced into his life and sent him falling, head over heels. Thirty-three years since they tackled each other in the bamboo forest, since they shared a tentative kiss on a fairy's mountain, since Hani brought snacks to a stakeout, since she ran her fingers through his hair as he threatened to burn the whole world down, since he held her in his arms . . .

Thirty-three years since the Scarlet Fox died.

Seokga pushes down a hot stab of bitter emotion, anger, and betrayal. He drowns it in another sip of cold, cold coffee.

Dr. Jang sighs. "I'm going to be blunt, Seokga. You're falling apart at the seams. If you don't stop now, you'll be nothing but a husk. Forgive me, but have you looked in a mirror recently?"

He knows what she's referring to. The dark circles under his eyes. The bloodshot corners. Finding Hani has consumed his every waking moment. He doesn't even use *conditioner* anymore.

And the changes go deeper than that, too. Seokga, although he should possess all of his powers now that he is again a deity, is unable to do one thing—riffle through the minds of creatures. Try as he may, something blocks him each time. Something tells him that it's the pressure, the desperation and extreme fatigue, interfering with his capabilities. That should he sleep more than two hours a night, perhaps he'd have no trouble at all.

But he can't stop. He *can't*.

For a time, he was better. Before the Red Thread of Fate appeared, he was excited. Eager. Happy. Playing harmless pranks, wandering the streets of Iseung, eager for the opportunity at every corner. Convinced he would see Hani at any second.

Now he's tired. Depressed. Miserable.

Dr. Jang smooths down her modest black blouse and reaches for the analog telephone at her side, giving him an *I told you so* look that somehow manages to still be kind.

Yet every part of Seokga stiffens as she punches in a few numbers. "Who—?"

The therapist gives him a stern look. "I'm calling your brother. As your doctor, it is within my jurisdiction to prescribe you with something you dearly need."

Seokga frowns, thinking of the meds he's already on—pink pills he takes with his evening coffee at seven each night. "What?"

Dr. Jang presses the phone to her ear. "A vacation."

Tonight, dinner is takeout from Iseung, the mortal realm: deep-fried corn dogs dusted with sugar and drizzled with ketchup and mustard. It is, in Seokga's opinion, an affront to his holy eyes and taste buds. It was Hwanung's turn to bring dinner to the monthly pantheon gathering, in which all Okhwang's gods sit around an overlarge table in Cheonha Palace and "bond."

Oh, Seokga *hates* bonding. He prefers the logistics that come first: the scheduling of Korea's weather with its respective gods, discussion of Unrulies and how the haetae are faring against them, how things are going for Yeomra in the underworld, et cetera. Today's discourse was a particularly riveting discussion of the shamans: Korean family lines blessed with patronage of one deity or another, tasked with performing the minute duties that the gods themselves can't be bothered with (such as the creation and maintenance of glamours, healing the sick, and—at least for Seokga's shamans—causing chaos whenever the opportunity presents itself) . . . And there's also the unspoken obligation of proving their patron deity's superiority over all the other gods. Seokga's shamans have been specifically instructed to seek out Hwanin's shamans and use their shape-shifting magic (generously bestowed upon them by Seokga himself) to change into birds and shit all over their snobby heads.

(Deity shamanism has, clearly, changed since the ancient days. Many still practice the old ways, but Seokga greatly prefers his shamans to practice modern traditions as it's vastly more entertaining.)

He sighs, utterly bored and wishing he was watching his shamans unleash their havoc.

Seokga envies Yeomra right now. Unable to leave Jeoseung, Yeomra joins these monthly meetings by using some bizarre mortal contraption that allows his face to be projected onto the screen at the front of the dining room. That means he doesn't need to eat any of this food. Although right now, Yeomra is watching the proceedings with thinly veiled longing in his black eyes.

Sitting across the low table, pinching one disgusting specimen of corn dog, is Hwanin. The heavenly emperor's blue-black eyes flecked with stars meet Seokga's for a brief moment before his lips twitch and he sets the corn dog down with an air of grim finality. Next to him, his son is happily munching away, looking quite proud of himself for his contribution to this month's dinner.

Seokga rolls his eyes but must admit Hwanung's cheerful little crunches are a nice break from the heavens-shaking fights Okhwang has been riddled with lately. It's rare, nowadays, that Hwanung's mouth is (relatively) shut and not screaming expletives at his father about anything and everything.

Focused on the foul food, Hwanung is also leaving Seokga alone, which is a pleasant change. Ever since Seokga's return, Hwanung has been by equal turns furious with and terrified by him. Many times, Seokga has caught the law god trailing him as if scanning for any sign of wrongdoing to report to his father. Like a few other members of the pantheon (especially Samsin Halmoni), Hwanung has never quite forgiven Seokga for stabbing his father in the back by leading thousands of Dark World monsters into Okhwang and then having the audacity to call the attempted coup "just a bit of fun." He's quite certain that if given half the chance, Hwanung would hurl him back down to Iseung.

Seokga formed this theory after Hwanung explicitly told him that if he was given half the chance, he would hurl him back down to Iseung. The dangerous glint in the boy's eyes had told Seokga he'd meant it. The boy is always dancing with danger—from dating fierce bear-shifters to challenging Okhwang's seasoned warriors to cage fights. He *looks* dangerous now, too: studs in his bottom lip, leather jackets, and hair that is no longer bleached silver like his father's but is instead a shaggy dark purple.

"Delicious," Dalnim snarfles. The usually dainty moon goddess is attacking her food like a lion would its prey. Next to her, her twin, Haemosu, stares in delight as the mozzarella cheese stretches to an impossible length as he pulls the corn dog away from his handsome face.

Seokga and Hwanin may be as different as day and night, but proof of their brotherhood is in the way both deities push away their plates. Hwanin takes a sip from his goblet (although inside, Seokga knows, is another disgusting mortal creation: soda) and pointedly clears his throat. Immediately, a hush falls over the spacious room. Habaek, the river god, falls silent mid-laugh. Jacheongbi, goddess of agriculture, straightens to attention. At the motion, a few pink cosmos flowers woven in her hair flutter to the ground.

Hwanin's throne isn't in here, but it might as well be. Even though he sits cross-legged on a cushion rather than his sovereign perch, he is still the emperor of Okhwang, and the picture of royalty. His silken hanbok of dark blues and silvers matches his eyes and hair, respectively; hair that reaches his chest in an icy curtain. "Thank you, Hwanung, for the lovely meal," says Hwanin, patting the law god on his head. Hwanung scowls, jerking away. His father clearly pretends not to see, but Seokga doesn't miss the flash of hurt in his brother's eyes. It's been there often recently.

"Now that we've all had a chance to, ah, enjoy the food"—Hwanin's composure seems to falter as he meets Seokga's eye, and Seokga pointedly lowers his gaze down to the very untouched corn dog on his brother's plate—"we have some more matters of business to attend to. Specifically, Seokga's *vacation*."

Seokga is very glad he hasn't eaten a bite of food, because if he had, he'd be choking on it. It's been a day since his session with Dr. Jang, and Hwanin has not until *now* mentioned the damnable thing at all. At Seokga's shocked expression, Hwanin smirks, and

Seokga dearly misses the time when he could be at his brother's throat without this useless *moral compass* he seems to have developed holding him back.

It is unfortunate that, since his return to Okhwang, he and his older brother have become almost-sort-of friends, Seokga seethes. (The almost-sort-of condition being there thanks to the role Hwanin played in Hani's death. No matter how hard Hwanin tries to close the gap, Seokga quickly widens it once more.) Nevertheless, the almost-sort-of friendship is unfortunate, because there is nothing he'd like better, in this very moment, than to strangle Hwanin. Dr. Jang's "prescription" isn't necessary and will only hold him back from finding Hani.

"Brother," Seokga growls, some of that old vehemence brimming to the surface. He wraps his fingers around the cane lying at his side, knowing the blade he can unleash by snapping the silver imoogi handle with the right amount of strength. He won't, of course, but the motion gives him a sense of comfort. "You overstep. I don't need, or want, a vacation."

"Oh, dear," sniffs Samsin Halmoni in disapproval. "Is that how you speak to your elders, Seokga?"

Seokga turns his wrath to Samsin Halmoni. "Is that how you speak to your *superiors*?" he hisses back, slitting his eyes. The other deity goes pale.

"You naughty little boy," she whispers. Seokga fixes her with an unimpressed look that's more scathing than any words could ever be.

"Ha!" says Hasegyeong, the cattle god, turning to Jowangshin, goddess of the hearth. "I told you she'd say that at least once tonight."

Jowangshin sighs and passes a few crumpled mortal bills to a gloating Hasegyeong.

Hwanin does not look very bothered at all as he turns to

Yeomra, on the screen. "Go on," he says to the death god. "Tell him what we've decided."

Feeling as though he's about to be told he's been sentenced to death (or worse, thrown from Okhwang *again*), Seokga turns his attention to Yeomra. The death god appears to be sitting in his office, surrounded by the rich black hues of his wallpaper, neat bookshelves, and the cushioned back of his leather chair. The darkness of it all is rather on the nose for the ruler of Jeoseung, but Yeomra himself is anything but.

If Seokga saw Yeomra on the street (which is, thankfully, impossible—the ass is stuck in Jeoseung), Seokga would take him for a young, cocky CEO. A chaebol, perhaps. Yeomra lounges in his chair, the buttons of his dark shirt unbuttoned to show off a hint of his chest, a smarmy salesman's smile on his face. His hair is supposed to look messy, but Seokga has done that very style to his own hair enough to know it takes an *immense* amount of time.

"Seokga," Yeomra says, lifting a hand and waving idly, his silver rings flashing in the light, "nice to see you." He winks, and Seokga sees that his eyelids are smudged with dark powder. He is unimpressed, and part of him suspects that it's Yeomra that young Hwanung is looking to for style inspiration.

"No," Seokga replies, voice as chilly as the Antarctic winds he so recently endured. "It is not. As you well know, Yeomra, I do not like you. At all."

The god's eyes narrow on the screen. "We've decided that—"

"I'm not interested in whatever proposal your egregiously small brain has come up with."

"Seokga!" shrieks Samsin Halmoni, hands flying to her pregnancy bump, as if she can prevent the fetus from hearing his razor-sharp words.

Seokga doesn't apologize. He's hated the death god ever since he somehow missed an eoduksini escaping his realm in the body of one of his jeoseung saja and left Seokga to deal with it—and the consequences. *Hani.* Again, that familiar pain.

Yeomra narrows his eyes. "Right. Well. Your brother told me about your situation. If you need a place to relax—"

"I don't," Seokga snaps nastily, contemplating the ramifications of throwing a corn dog at Yeomra's projection. "Mind your own business, cadaver."

"Seokga!" Hwanung hisses, mouth full. His nephew fixes hateful eyes on him. "Remember your place."

"You're dribbling food down your chin," he clips back coldly.

Hwanung's cheeks redden, and he almost—*almost*—curls in on himself, shoulders slumping. Yet Seokga decides not to feel at all bad as his nephew rolls his eyes a moment later, apparently attempting to muster some bravado from what must be deep, deep, *deep* down in his shriveled little soul.

"Ignore him." Hwanin tells his son, sending Seokga a chiding look. "Continue, Yeomra."

Yeomra shifts in his seat, apparently feeling the weight of Seokga's death glare all the way in the underworld. The leather creaks. "I'm sure you've heard of my masterpiece, SRC." He pauses, as if waiting for praise and applause.

Seokga takes great pleasure in staring blankly at him, although he knows very well what Yeomra's little pet project is. It's been in *Godly Gossip* more times that he can count.

Not that he's reading *Godly Gossip*. Dr. Jang's waiting room is, unfortunately, plastered with them.

And they really know how to write a hook.

SRC. Seocheongang River Cruises. Cruise ships, sailing on the underworld's Seocheongang River, offering one last festive hurrah to the dead guests before they step off for reincarnation. It's a clever idea, Seokga supposes. And a lucrative one. With the way

Jeoseung works, Yeomra has fashioned himself to be more of a CEO than an emperor. Having an entire realm at your disposal and nobody but the dead to share it with leads to boredom. While an emperor can be waited on hand and foot, a CEO must strive to expand. To make their company bigger and better. Thousands of years ago, Yeomra's first act as "CEO" was to employ jeoseung saja—creatures who guide souls down to the land of the dead. Seokga's stomach twists as he remembers Hani's soul slipping into the hearse, leaving him behind as morning sunlight cracked and spilled over New Sinsi.

I swear on Hwanung, god of laws and kept promises, that the sun will shine on us both once again.

What a cruel joke.

Hwanin sighs, jerking Seokga out of his reverie as he looks at his poker face in exasperation. "You're not being very mature," he mutters out of the corner of his mouth.

"Anything to make his fragile little ego squirm," Seokga replies in an icy, quiet undertone.

Yeomra looks like he's clenching his teeth together as Seokga withholds recognition. "I'm offering you a spot on my best ship for the duration of its upcoming cruise," he spits, as if it's being forced out of him. Indeed, his eyes flick momentarily to Hwanin in unconcealed reluctance. "The SRC *Flatliner*."

"It gives me great delight to refuse your offer." Seokga smiles coldly. "I couldn't be less interested in taking a trip on your little boat."

"It's not a little boat. It has *ten* decks—"

"I don't care."

Yeomra sucks on his teeth, glowering although he's sinking lower in his seat. Seokga's *don't fuck with me* grin, he is pleased to note, seems to have a universal effect on both mortals and death deities alike. Smugly, Seokga straightens the collar of his slightly rumpled black trench coat and congratulates himself on a job well done.

Yet across from him, Hwanin catches his eye, and his expression has Seokga's heart sinking before the words even emerge. "Too bad," his older brother says without an ounce of sympathy. "I've already bought three tickets. We leave tomorrow morning."

"I'd rather skin myself alive," hisses Seokga on instinct, and then pauses a moment later, brows knitting together. "Wait. *Three?*"

CHAPTER THREE

KISA

Yoo Kisa had once thought she knew suffering.
But that was before her first turn-around day.

Aboard the SRC *Flatliner,* Kisa hustles down the ship's "I-95"—a long corridor spanning Deck 0, and the main point of travel for loading supplies and luggage on and off the ship. She grits her teeth as she pushes the luggage cart down the humid hall, where even the white-painted walls drip with sweat. One would *think* the dead pack lightly, but alas. It seems Jeoseung's CEO insists the *Flatliner*'s esteemed guests board with every trivial item they could possibly want. Clothing from their past lives. Books. Laptops. Entire TVs. Once, Kisa had the pleasure of loading an entire *liquor cabinet* onto the ship.

She huffs and puffs through her teeth as she reaches the end of the I-95 and passes the luggage cart on to a solemn-faced grim reaper. He's dressed in a smart black suit and a bowler cap, which he tips slightly in greeting before wheeling the luggage through the ship door leading to a lowered metal plank, which will deposit him—and the suitcases—onto the pavement of Port Jeoseung, where the disembarking guests will have the opportunity to bring their belongings with them to whatever waits past Port Jeoseung's terminal. Kisa pants, wiping her brow with a wrist as she lingers by the door, letting a cold kiss of underworld air cool her hot skin.

Death isn't what she thought it'd be. No, not at all. What she's seen so far of Jeoseung reminds her of any congested city: towering buildings, cramped coffee shops, narrow streets littered with newspaper clippings, and a central park. The only differences are that the office buildings display buzzing neon signs advertising themselves as the Department of Afterlife Reincarnation (the DAR, said to have agonizingly long lines), the Courtrooms of Hell Sentencing, and an amalgamation of other equally terrifying yet fascinating company names. The newspaper clippings don't have an obituary column: Instead, they're drowning in announcements of who was reincarnated as what (*Congratulations to Shim Himchan on his reincarnation into a puppy!*) and gleefully gloomy gossip about who was sentenced to what hell and why. The central park's trees are twisted and skeletal, some bone white and others pitch black. And, of course, the city's denizens who visit the coffee shops and wander the streets are very, very dead. Ghosts. Gwisin.

She's a gwisin, too, now. Part of Kisa is still fascinated with this, even after seven years—and she itches to research, to seek into the *why*. Why, for example, has she maintained a corporeal form? It's not her original one, but it might as well be, down to the exact hue of her wine-brown eyes and the heart-shaped birthmark right above her left brow. Is the soul inextricably attached to the flesh? And why does she still breathe? She doesn't *need* to, but her body still unconsciously sucks in the underworld air. A heart even beats in her chest, despite Kisa's status as very much deceased. Her working theory: She exists in the underworld as she *remembers* herself existing in the living realm. And she remembers her heart beating, her lungs working. Oh, if Kisa had access to a lab, she could run so many tests...

"Kisa!" a voice snaps at her back, and she turns—wrenching her gaze away from the miserable black skyline of Jeoseung and the jeoseung saja working the port—to see the cruise director, Lee Soo-min. Soo-min stands in the middle of the I-95, forcing other crew members to squeeze by her as she props a hand on her hip.

In her life, Soo-min was heiress to a technology company before meeting her untimely end at the hands of her money-hungry fiancé. At least, that's the rumor around the ship: Soo-min has stubbornly maintained that she died saving a kitten from a fire somewhere in Itaewon.

It's unlikely. Soo-min is a samjokgu—a three-legged dog-shifter. And samjokgu famously despise cats. Besides, diving into a fire would almost certainly go against Soo-min's fourteen-step skincare routine, the details of which Kisa has been unfortunate enough to overhear at staff meetings.

Regardless of the circumstances of Soo-min's death, however, it's no leap to say that she was probably the most pampered of them all: hence her assignment as cruise director, one of the most taxing occupations on board.

That's the gist of the ship—guests who worked too hard when they were living board the SRC *Flatliner* and are waited on hand and foot by crew members who barely worked a day in their lives. Kisa has appealed, over and over, to Jeoseung's CEO to revoke her sentencing as a crew member to no avail.

"You were idle," she'd been told by a bored-looking jeoseung saja with a clipboard who'd been sent back to inform her of the CEO's decision.

"Excuse me?" Kisa had snapped, certain she had misheard. She'd been exhausted every single day of her life, had worn herself to death in that hospital. It simply wasn't possible that she'd been marked as "idle."

The jeoseung saja rolled his eyes. "Yoo Kisa. Daughter of

Volkov, Natalia, and Yoo, David. Annual income by age twenty-two..." He widened his eyes meaningfully.

"Excuse me!" Kisa drew herself up to her full height, which wasn't very impressive (a mere five foot three) and placed her hands on her hips. "I worked myself to death for that money. Have you ever met *any* shaman who simply *prancercised* through life without a single responsibility? If you're deciding who was idle in their life, I seriously suggest that you rethink your measuring system. In fact, I might suggest a new metric with a focus on the dimensional attributes of nepotism and—"

"I wasn't done. It says here," the reaper drawled, referencing his clipboard, "that you have some built-up karma from your *past life*. Seems you were—and I quote—'one of the laziest freeloading women to exist' and 'exceptionally skilled at robbing ATMs.' Due to an anomaly, you got off easy the last time around... But all bills have to be paid eventually. Be glad you weren't sent to one of the seven hells," the jeoseung saja had suggested as Kisa's jaw dropped. "You'll serve on this ship until the DAR decides you're ready for reincarnation."

"Which will be when?" she spluttered.

A nasty smile. "When your karmic punishment is over."

Kisa is fully aware of past lives, of course, but she simply cannot conceptualize herself as somebody who apparently stole money from ATMs. Rules, thinks Kisa, are the only things that keep society from falling into utter bedlam. She follows them with an almost holy reverence. So the notion that this is karmic retribution for her past life is utter nonsense. How bad, truly, could Kisa have been? It's complete hokum, really.

As are Soo-min's next words, urging her to stop "dillydallying" and get back to work. Kisa clenches her jaw but obeys. If she ever wants to retire from the SRC *Flatliner,* she needs to be on her best behavior.

For the next few hours, Kisa works herself to the bone, as she's done for years now. Yet there is no satisfaction of a safe delivery, no joy upon hearing the wailing cries of an infant. There's only a stack of work that keeps piling up, and up, and up . . . and that perpetually hollow feeling in her chest, that sort of panging ache for something she *still* can't quite put her finger on.

Her old life, perhaps? Before the hospital, before it all crumbled to ash in her hands . . . The misty, rainy mornings at NSUMD, studying in the cavernous library, chewing on the end of her pen and flipping through the thin—nearly translucent—yellow pages of her treasured textbooks. The coffee shop near campus, where creatures clustered and chattered over mugs of macchiato and frappés. Could that be it?

Yet a small voice deep down asks if it's something *else* she longs for. Something entirely different from beloved textbooks and campus cafés. It whispers in half-ignored words that if only she sat down and put her brilliant mind to the psychological puzzle, she'd have it solved within no time. Yet *time* is exactly what Kisa lacks. So this longing . . . Well, the reason for it is still a mystery, just as it was the day she died. She calls it a longing for what she lost and leaves it at that.

There's no time for anything else.

After finishing off-loading the rest of the luggage pile, she grudgingly moves on to her next chore of changing the linens in the Deck 6 cabins alongside a few other girls who normally work in waitressing. It doesn't matter what their usual jobs are: On turn-around day, everybody does everything.

What Kisa wouldn't give to be on her usual shift in the SRC *Flatliner*'s sick bay. Some crew members who die particularly violent deaths (like, for example, falling off a skyscraper) receive treatment the moment they are assigned to the *Flatliner,* so as to not scare away the guests.

None of them are at risk of dying, obviously—the treatments are really for psychological purposes: When a dead soul sees their wounds being treated just like they would be in the world above, their identity becomes less intertwined with the injuries of their death. Thus, their form can return to how they remember it existing before the gunshot, the car crash, the fall, the disease, et cetera. *Restoration,* it's called.

It's dull, tiring work . . . But at least it's *interesting,* to a degree.

As she stuffs the dirty sheets into the wheeled hamper, Kisa jolts in pain, something between a shriek and a swear escaping her lips.

The red thread forever wrapped around her pinky tautens enough to hurt. Kisa gasps, stumbling back. One of the girls worriedly asks if she's all right.

"I'm fine," Kisa murmurs, attempting a smile before hastily wheeling the now-full hamper out into the corridor, heart pounding and finger screaming in agony. As she waits in the corridor for the elevator to take her to Deck 3, where the laundry room is, Kisa does everything in her power not to look at the red floral knot squeezing her throbbing pinky.

In the seven years since her death, Kisa has come to the rather unfortunate conclusion that it is not a stress-induced hallucination at all. She's considering another hypothesis instead: that she is experiencing an extremely rare part of the mythological canon, a physical manifestation of destiny that is meant—in theory—to lead Kisa to her soulmate. It took her a while to form this hypothesis—the red thread, even to shamans, is viewed as little more than a legend. Yet here it is, tied to her finger.

As she gives in and looks at it, it wriggles slightly. Like it's an anxious caterpillar trying to say "hello."

Kisa is quite certain her Red Thread of Fate is faulty. Seeing as she is, one, dead (has anybody ever met their soulmate *after* they died?) and, two, in seven years, it has become incredibly tangled. Perhaps Gameunjang Aegi, the luck goddess, made a mistake.

What a fascinating mistake, though.

There is no end to the scarlet string, which seems to span on forever and ever as matted lines of messy, snarled knots and lumps, winding around corners, curling through the hallways, tangling in on itself before stretching out across the Seocheongang River to a place far away.

She has attempted to study its material to no avail. Whatever its composites, the string is untouchable, and entirely unbreakable. It is no usual thread: no indications of cotton, nor rayon. Both those materials can be neatly severed by scissors rather than passing through them like a ghost. In addition to that, the red thread isn't visible to anyone but her.

Why has it tightened? In all its years of existence, the string has never squeezed her finger like that. Still puzzled, Kisa dumps the dirty linens in the laundry room, where a plump-faced dokkaebi with pointy ears promptly sets to queuing them up for the next line of washing. The vast room of machinery smells like the gallons of detergent used every week: birchwood and lavender. She lingers for a moment longer, letting the rhythmic churning of the industrial-sized washing machines wash over her. Her pinky still feels as if it's about to be sliced off at any moment, but she doesn't let it show. Kisa has become quite good at hiding her pain, burying it under mental recitations of her favorite books, which range from smutty paperback romances to heavyweight volumes on the dokkaebi cardiovascular system.

> Dokkaebi are known to have two hearts, both of which pump blood throughout the body. The right heart is responsible for blood flow to the upper body, while the left heart is responsible for blood flow to the lower

> body. One might be tempted to compare the number of hearts to some cephalopods. However, the dokkaebi's are not branchial, consisting of more than one chamber. When performing a maze surgery on a dokkaebi patient, it is imperative to keep in mind that...

As turn-around day reaches its peak and new guests file on board, Kisa grows more and more troubled. The string has begun to vibrate and—to Kisa's utter shock—begins to untangle itself, straightening into a neat red line. A moment later, it's shaking ferociously... almost in warning.

As if something is coming.

As if something is coming for *her*.

How very interesting, Kisa eagerly thinks, before realizing that she should possibly be quite frightened.

CHAPTER FOUR

SEOKGA

"Subtle," says Seokga, staring through the glass at the mammoth that is the SRC *Flatliner*. He slides down his sunglasses to take a better look, practically pressing his nose to the window. Not that the glasses are even relatively necessary in Jeoseung, where the sky is varying shades of black and gray—and it's so early that the blazing red sun is still hidden. The shades are for a dramatic, brooding sort of effect. Seokga is quite peeved about being here, after all.

"The 'flatliner' bit is Yeomra's idea of a joke," Hwanin says with a sigh, standing next to him on the skywalk that leads into the *Flatliner*'s maw. Behind them, a steady stream of chattering gwisin file past, excited to begin their journey. "He's proud of it."

Seokga says nothing, still glaring with thin lips at the ten-stacked-decks monstrosity, taking in its glittering black hue that reflects the Seocheongang's crimson waters. Indeed, Seokga is so focused on staring at the ship in reluctant admiration that he doesn't notice that the Red Thread of Fate is slowly undulating through the air, untangling itself as it finally, finally—after seven years of disorientation—senses a clear path toward *her*.

"It's not as witty as he thinks it is," Seokga mutters, although his neck has craned, eyes flicking past the sparkling light inside dozens of windows to latch onto the ninth (and second-to-top) deck, where there seem to be a number of pools.

"I agree with Seokga," Dr. Jang says from where she stands next to him, wrinkled hands clutched nervously around her tote bag. For the very first time, Seokga is seeing her in something other than her usual blouses: She's donned a festive Hawaiian shirt for the occasion, and she's even wearing pink flip-flops with little flamingos on them. "It's a bit gauche."

"Indeed," mutters Seokga, staring at the flamingos.

Three tickets. One for Seokga. One for his insufferable brother, who's left his son temporarily ruling Okhwang in his place. And one for his *psychologist*. Apparently, Seokga's "vacation" doesn't entail a break from his sessions with Dr. Jang. It is, in Hwanin's words, *too much of a risk, especially when considering your past* antics, *brother. Remember that time you led Gamangnara monsters into Okhwang?*

So much for having become almost-sort-of friends.

Hwanin shakes his head. Unlike Dr. Jang, Hwanin is wearing his usual attire, earning confused looks from the onboarding ghosts. Seokga rolls his eyes. As much as Hwanin may deny it, Seokga is certain that Hwanin *likes* to be looked at. That he soaks up the attention like a sponge in dishwater.

Seokga isn't surprised. They're brothers, after all. They're bound to have *some* similarities.

Dr. Jang rummages around in her purse before pulling out a mint, looking slightly green. For living creatures, the teleportation trip down into Jeoseung is extremely nauseating, and Dr. Jang is only a shaman. Seokga looks at her in sympathy before Hwanin, clasping his hands together, smiles in a reassuring way to his two companions.

"Shall we?"

"Fine," mutters Seokga. Dr. Jang looks at him with pity, more than she's ever shown in her office. Seokga bristles, suddenly uncomfortable. "You can take the therapist out of the office," he snaps as he follows Hwanin into the ship, "but you *shouldn't* take the office out of the therapist."

Dr. Jang's eyes flicker with hurt and Seokga momentarily feels like a colossal piece of trickster-god shit, but then he's been swallowed by the SRC *Flatliner* and his guilt slips away.

The SRC *Flatliner*'s atrium is startlingly reminiscent of the 1920s' overindulgent glitz and glamour. The floors on which they stand are tiled shimmering slabs of black quartzite, smoky black tendrils stretching out across the wide expanse. Polished to a shine, they reflect the largest chandelier Seokga has ever seen in his extremely long life, its light dappling the lush velvet chairs artfully arranged below. Massive flights of stairs coil up and around the atrium, leading to what is undoubtedly an equally indulgent beyond. Stressed-looking crew members hustle and bustle on the floors above, visible from their heaving torsos up.

"Hwanin's tits," Seokga breathes, taking off his shades. The crowd of passengers seems to think the same. He sees one elderly man staring at the chandelier clutch his chest as if about to have a heart attack.

Dr. Jang, despite being somewhere in her seventies, giggles in unbridled cheer like a schoolgirl. "Quite," she agrees, whatever hurt she felt forgotten in the face of such grandeur.

Hwanin makes a disappointed face at them both. "I wish you wouldn't refer to my ti—my chest like that."

Seokga opens his mouth to reply that it was Hani who taught him that particular euphemism, so he shall never stop—but something very, very peculiar happens first, and a sound embarrassingly similar to an undignified squeak leaves Seokga's mouth before he can stop it.

"Brother?" Hwanin looks as if he doesn't know whether to

laugh or place a hand on Seokga's shoulder in concern. In the end, he does both. Seokga's so shocked that he doesn't even shy away from Hwanin's touch. "Are you . . . ?"

He doesn't hear the rest of his words. The Red Thread of Fate has tightened itself like a boa constrictor around Seokga's pinky, enough that all blood circulation has been cut off and his poor finger bulges in protest. But that doesn't matter. That doesn't matter because the Red Thread of Fate is no longer tangled or twisted as it has been for seven whole years. No, it's . . . it's leading him toward the winding flight of stairs, one perfect line twining around and around before vanishing. It's as if Seokga's heart freezes in his chest for a moment in pure shock, before the ice around it cracks and his heart is suddenly pounding so hard that he's certain it will punch through his ribs, through his flesh and bone . . .

"Hani," he gasps out, legs suddenly weak but always, always strong enough to carry him toward the woman he loves, the woman he lost, the cheerful gumiho with a world of humor and mischief in her wine-brown eyes—the sunshine to his deepest night, the happiness to his immortal misery. "My Hani," he rasps again, vision blurring as he begins to run, following the Red Thread of Fate toward his lost love.

He can feel it, at the end of the thread.

Someone is waiting.

Someone is waiting for him.

CHAPTER FIVE

KISA

Kisa wonders how, exactly, one should wait for their soulmate. For a good moment or two, she thoroughly contemplates posing on one of the sick bay's beds, head propped up on one hand and the other resting on her hip. After a brief attempt, the cot squeaking uncomfortably beneath her, Kisa abandons that idea and instead decides to artfully lean against the clinic's polished-granite front desk, a fixed smile on her face.

Although her heart is racing, she has come to the sensible conclusion that there is no point in running from whomever is attempting to find her. They're attached by a red thread, for the heavens' sakes—there is nowhere she can run, nor hide. So really, the most reasonable thing Kisa can do is to make a good first impression. Currently, she is smiling the smile that has landed her internships and jobs. Very professional, and extremely calculated.

"What are you *doing*?" Her co-worker Kim Hajun is staring at her with abject horror from where he's restocking one of the white medicine cabinets. The former K-pop star looks unsure as to whether he's meant to laugh or to stride over and shake Kisa's shoulders.

Hajun is one of Kisa's only friends on the SRC *Flatliner,* despite having met each other just six months ago. He is one of the newest crew members on the ship, having died in April. Kisa had been the one to Restore him, carefully binding his bleeding inner wrists and treating the slender singer for blood loss.

The true treatment, though, should have been focused on his mind. There was such darkness inside of him, a sort that nobody would ever expect from a boy with such a sweet smile and sparkling eyes. Certainly not even the jeoseung saja in charge of SRC recruitment, who took one look at his file, saw *K-POP STAR* in huge red letters, and plopped him into servitude without a care for the stress Hajun must have been under while alive. Kisa fervently attempted to school herself in the field of psychology with the limited medical journals on board, but she was utterly out of her depth. She is a doctor of flesh and bone, and is terrified of damaging the fragile system of the psyche with indelicate hands. So for now, she can only offer Hajun one thing: friendship.

And it's so easy to be friends with him. Hajun is a gentle, kind soul who has made her time on board so much easier. He's quick at learning medicine: Under her watchful eye, he's becoming a capable ship medic. She likes to think that he's healing, too, away from the pressures of the entertainment industry. He certainly laughs more these days.

"Kisa?" Hajun repeats anxiously.

"Hajun," says Kisa, careful not to drop her practiced smile, "I am in a perfectly natural state of pleasantness."

"You look . . . constipated." He shuts the cabinet and turns back to her, eyebrows high on his delicate face. "And your left eye is twitching."

"*That,*" she retorts, dropping her pose, "is because of *you.*" Kisa shifts from foot to foot nervously, glancing at the medical center's swinging doors that have yet to open. The red thread is growing shorter, tighter. No doubt that signifies that whoever is at the other end is approaching Deck 3. "If you must know," Kisa says with a sigh to a confused Hajun, "I am waiting for my soulmate."

He chokes. Hajun is the only person Kisa has confided in, and although he can't see it, he stares at her pinky where the thread is wrapped. "Right now? The thread?"

"Yes," says Kisa. "The string is growing shorter by what I estimate to be ten inches per every thirty seconds. If each foot represents space traveled, then—"

"Oh, please," Hajun murmurs, but he's smiling softly. "Not the calculations."

She pins him with a glare. Hajun doesn't seem to notice, face suddenly stricken with some realization as he hurries over to her.

"Kisa," he whispers urgently, "what if he's horrible?"

"Thank you, Hajun, that is precisely what I needed to hear right now."

"No, really," her friend insists, grabbing her shoulder with wide, worried eyes. "What if he's one of the dokkaebi? Or an imoogi? Kisa, what if he *shifts into a giant serpent and eats you*? Worse . . . what if he's one of the demons you've told me about? An eoduksini?"

"There hasn't been a recorded eoduksini spotting since spring 1992," Kisa replies factually, although a distinct sweat has broken out on the back of her neck, dampening her bun of curls. They are, after all, in the underworld. Although the eoduksini are kept under lock and key in the Torture Department, it's possible one could slip out . . .

No. She shouldn't let her friend frighten her. Hajun has taken the whole creatures-from-mythology-exist learning curve with about as much grace as a beached whale. Kisa is a respected shaman . . . or she was. At any rate, she is perfectly capable of handling herself.

"What if he's an *inmyunjo*?" wails Hajun, who had nearly shat himself the first time he'd come across one of the winged creatures on board—even though Unruly inmyunjo are nonexistent. "Or a gumiho? What if he steals your soul?"

Kisa is exceptionally conscious that footsteps are now echoing down the corridor's hall, that the red thread is practically *choking* her finger, that she is very possibly about to experience something hardly ever documented in any academic literature—something that will gain her significant conversance regarding a rare phenomenon and, possibly, impressive accolades should she somehow manage to share such valuable knowledge. And Hajun is ruining it. "Please be quiet," she mutters to him. "You're interrupting a pivotal moment in mythos experience—"

Her friend ignores her. Breathing hard, Hajun looks wildly around the clinic's small front room and, before Kisa can stop him, launches himself over the counter and grabs a paperweight. "It's okay, Kisa," he pants. "I'll protect you—"

It's as if Hajun's voice plummets underwater, becoming muted and unintelligible as something—something so very important—*shifts*. She's only experienced something like this once before, this feeling of a great and terrible change . . . The moment before she fell.

It's as if the world is slowing again, as if the opening doors are not blasting open as they truly are, but instead gradually swinging open as a tall figure steps out of shadows, every step a slow-motion montage that causes Kisa's breath to catch in her throat.

Inky black hair stirs softly in the air as the doors begin to shut behind him, lifting upward from a tense forehead where thick, dark brows slant together. The red thread between them begins to glow scarlet, and Kisa wonders for a brief moment if its material is naturally bioluminescent before her thoughts slow to a crawl at the sight of his deep green eyes—as if she is staring into a forest of raw emotion. No eyes that she has ever seen match that shade. Such raw, undiluted color should not be possible. There is something familiar about him, she thinks as a peculiar feeling overtakes her chest. It's an insistent *tug* that makes her gasp, then what feels like an almost mechanical shifting of parts and pieces into place, clicking together to produce an odd feeling of . . . fullness?

Perhaps it's heartburn, Kisa thinks vaguely, still captivated by those eyes. The man opens his mouth . . .

And time is no longer a slow, sluggish thing. Behind Kisa, Hajun is roaring a battle cry—and then the paperweight is flying through the air, a heavy glass orb that smashes into the side of the man's head before either of them has time to react. Kisa gasps as the man stumbles backward, slips on the polished tiles, and crashes to the shattered glass littering the floor.

For a very long moment, the entire sick bay is very silent.

The red thread, almost abashedly, slowly stops glowing and sways awkwardly in the air.

"*Ergggkgggk,*" groans the beautiful man on the ground.

Kisa, jerked out of her reverie, spins around to glare at Hajun. "Did it *look* like he was about to attack me?" she demands. "Really, Hajun—"

The idol runs a hand through his messy ash-brown hair. "Uh," says Hajun, suddenly looking extremely guilty. "I, um, I panicked?"

Gritting her teeth, Kisa forces her brain to launch into doctor mode. She's attempted to form many theories explaining why the dead can feel pain and be injured (rapid soul-adaptation to a hostile environment?), but it seems that it's simply because they are *used* to it and expect to be hurt when struck. If they could turn off that expectancy . . . Kisa pushes aside the thought.

Whatever the reason, this gorgeous—this man is hurt. After forcing her limbs to unlock, Dr. Yoo Kisa hurries to his side, leaning above him. His right temple is bleeding, and shattered glass dusts his dark hair like snow. There is something wrong, something off about the scene, but Kisa is far too frazzled to dissect it. "Hajun," she snaps, "cloth. Now."

As Hajun hurries toward the supply closet, Kisa gently lifts the man's head. To her surprise, he lets her—for some reason, she had been expecting resistance. Perhaps it's due to the intensity of his eyes or the exact curve of his mouth, as if it is used to resting in a perpetual sneer. But the man seems to be quietly stunned as she lifts him, brushing the glass from his hair, checking for any embedded shards. None.

"Can you sit up?" she whispers, voice barely audible. Kisa sits back on her haunches, trying to remain clinical, even as he obeys, gazing at her the entire time. The intensity has blood rushing to Kisa's cheeks, warming them a pale indigo. She's suddenly conscious of the color, ducking away. It's the one thing that seems to have changed from their lives above: Here, the dead always, always have blue blood. Perhaps it's Yeomra's reminder to them, a way to ensure denial is impossible. Or perhaps Jeoseung has no oxygen, and they breathe in something else entirely. It doesn't matter. Perhaps it's her little vanity, but Kisa hates it.

To hide her sudden disconcertion, she turns her attention back to the man's hair. His eyes flutter shut for a moment as she brushes through it again to make sure there are no cuts. Only then does Kisa realize he's trembling, just like a baby bird. When his eyes open again, she finds that she's unable to look away. It's as if, she thinks, they are opposite poles, and he is drawing her toward him despite her best efforts. The red thread rises between them, swirling happily, forming into tiny little ... hearts? The sight is enough for Kisa to blink, breaking the man's soft—yet intense—gaze.

"Kisa? Here." Hajun returns with the cloth and the red thread quickly straightens itself out as Kisa snatches the fabric, presses it to the man's head, dabbing it against the red blood ...

Red blood.

Red. Blood.

"Will I live?" the man asks. His voice is low and raspy. He stares up at her with wide, sparkling eyes.

The cloth falls from Kisa's hand. She didn't notice it before, but she does now—and that means... That means...

He's *alive.*

CHAPTER SIX

SEOKGA

Kisa. Her name is *Kisa*.

And she's staring at him, small mouth agape, curly brown hair a mess as it escapes its band. This close to her, he can count the exact number of freckles on her small nose while, all the while, his heart slams itself frantically against his ribs. She has a small, heart-shaped birthmark above her left eyebrow. He can't look away from it, mesmerized by something that—on anyone else—would be so small a detail, so insignificant, that he wouldn't bother to notice.

It's as if Seokga is existing within a dream, a dream where Hani's long-lashed wine-brown eyes stare at him as if he's an absolute impossibility.

Thirty-three years.

Thirty-three years of desperate searching and she's finally *here*. Hani. His Hani, his gumiho, with her sharp-tongued wit and cheerful, hot-chocolate-loving soul. There is no visible similarity but for the Korean heritage and wine-brown eyes, but—this is *Hani*. Undoubtedly, irrefutably Hani. He feels it in his soul, so powerfully that he trembles.

And she does not know him.

He has found Hani, his best friend, his soulmate, and she does not know him. It is in the way her touch is gently clinical, even when her fingers ran through his hair. Those beautiful eyes have no hint of recognition within them, only a growing puzzlement and something that looks remarkably like a ravenous curiosity.

You expected this, he scolds himself. How many times has he wondered who she might be, clutched by the fear that she'd be different, too different, than who she once was? In the thirty-three years he's waited for her, he's imagined her as hundreds of thousands of people. There was one particularly harrowing nightmare in which Hani's reincarnation was an elderly man with a penchant for passing gas in his retirement home's crochet group. Seokga had awoken screaming and drenched in sweat, the walls of his Okhwang palace shaking with the force of his cries. The explanation he'd muttered to a panicked Hwanin (and the army of fifty warriors the emperor had brought with him to Seokga's residence) had somehow found its way into *Godly Gossip* the very next day.

Humiliating.

And so there is a terrible sort of common sense deep within Seokga, one that tells him that Kisa does not know him. That, really, he doesn't even know *her*. But the trickster still cannot help hoping that as her small hands take his face, she is about to kiss him . . .

No. No, of course not.

Seokga bites back his disappointment as Kisa simply stares at him, brows furrowing, lip pulled in underneath one of her front teeth. "Fascinating," she murmurs, tilting his head left and right, staring at the cut that will soon begin to heal itself over. "I wonder . . . Hajun," she says suddenly to the boy who threw the paperweight. Normally, Seokga would make him regret being born—and assuredly, he will later—but he's in too much of a daze to do anything but send the boy a withering sneer. It's delightful to see how he pales. A sudden stab of envy cuts through Seokga's skin. If they're a couple... "You could have killed him." Kisa passes the cloth to Hajun, who looks even more like he's about to keel over.

"Well," the boy says uncomfortably, "I didn't think he was *alive* in the first place."

Seokga holds his breath before her gaze returns to his.

"You're truly living," she says in accented Korean. British, perhaps?

"And you're... you're dead," he breathes, before the enormity of that fact hits him in full. Suddenly unable to move, Seokga fights to think past the roaring wave of grief as it threatens to consume him. She died. Before he could reach her, she died. How? How did it happen? How... He's vaguely aware that she's saying something else, but he cuts her off before he can think better of it. "When?" he croaks and grabs her right hand, the hand where the red string is tied. "When?"

Kisa blinks. "March twenty-fourth, 2018, eight-thirty P.M., Seoul," she reports factually. "Cause of death: fatal fall from a rooftop."

Seokga nearly chokes as he finally scrambles to his feet. The same day the Red Thread of Fate appeared. She *was* in Seoul. How did he miss her? How did he not find her? Why couldn't he save her? It feels as if knives are tearing him apart from the inside.

Kisa climbs to her feet, as well. "The living typically aren't allowed on this ship," she says slowly. "I'm very curious to know how you've done it. Can you confirm my theory that Jeoseung's plane of existence is merely a designated holding place for the dead: a sort of storage closet with a chute to reincarnation, if you will? Was there a door you came through? Can you confirm this realm could be hospitable to living organisms? Is there actually oxygen?" Her speech has become much faster by this point—Seokga can barely keep up with her. All he knows is that she's using jondaemal, her words so *formal* that Seokga can barely breathe.

It's really all gone, is all he can think, all the memories, all the love and friendship that had bloomed between him and Hani, erased and replaced by fucking jondaemal. An ache shivers through his heart, splintering into a sharp, bitter pain as Kisa continues to speak, addressing him as a stranger. He presses a shaking hand against his chest in a desperate, and thoroughly futile, attempt to keep himself from falling apart completely. "Is the realm's physical or metaphysical structure able to be manipulated to support carbon-based, natural and biotic—"

As her line of interrogation continues, Seokga sucks in a small breath. *You expected this,* Seokga tells himself, but he's beginning to think that he hadn't, that he hadn't at all. "Jeoseung is not accessible to regular living mortals, although it can be to creatures, if they know where to look," he rasps after a long moment once she's finished talking, his mind still whirring, still teetering on the edge of a magnificent mental breakdown. He is speaking automatically, the words fed to his tongue by the small part of his brain that isn't muddled in shock, longing, and grief. "The pantheon, too. I'm a god."

Hajun gasps and slowly retreats to a back room. But Kisa—Kisa looks at him for a long moment, and he has the distinct impression that her brain works like a book, and she's currently flipping through its pages, searching for something. It's almost extraordinary to watch those familiar eyes narrow and widen, to sense the knowledge being riffled through behind them.

"Green eyes . . . *Green eyes.* Seokga," she finally whispers, and his name on her tongue . . . He fights to remain standing upright instead of sinking to his knees like some bumbling fool. "I knew you looked familiar."

His agonized heart stutters, stops, and refuses to restart. "I . . . I do?" he stammers. Inelegantly. "You kn-know me?"

But Kisa, to Seokga's eternal disappointment, isn't throwing herself into his arms and swooning with infatuation while rose petals shower down around them. Instead, she's looking at him as if he is some sort of fascinating insect underneath a magnifying glass. Again, that horrible, splintering pain. "God of deceit, of trickery. Subject of *The History of Deceit: An In-Depth Examination of Prince Seokga's Fragile Ego Throughout the Years* by Professor Lee Mi-young. I had a few critiques on that book," she muses, drumming her fingers on her chin. "The professor was highly biased. Her brother was killed by the eoduksini back in the nineties . . . It was a glaring conflict of interest. Professor Lee unfortunately didn't seem to take the criticism very well," Kisa adds, shaking her head and looking incredibly affronted.

Seokga blinks. If Kisa had access to that blasted novel, to the professor who wrote it, that means . . . that means she's a shaman. But to which god? The entire pantheon knew, for years, that Seokga was searching for a girl with distinctly one-of-a-kind wine-brown eyes. Who kept her from him? Seokga can barely breathe as rage replaces his heartbroken mourning, but his anger falters as Kisa pauses, eyes drifting to the red thread.

Seokga holds his breath, terrified that she'll find him unworthy. That she'll shun him.

Her next words nearly bring him to his knees again. Those damned eyes are suddenly sparkling again as she looks to him, and there's a slight blue flush to her skin. "This is brilliant," she breathes, taking a step closer to him. "Absolutely brilliant."

Do not fucking cry, Seokga warns himself as she clasps her hands together, grinning. Happy tears are for fools.

"Do you mind," says Kisa eagerly, and he notices that her nose scrunches when she smiles, "if I ask some questions?"

Every inch of Seokga is still shaking as he stands in line at the Creature Café located on Deck 8. The SRC *Flatliner* has long since taken off, and the café's glass windows overlook the shimmering red waters of the vast Seocheongang River. The familiar smell of roasting coffee beans comforts him. He knows it's not real: Food and drink here are memories—even ghosts—of food and drink above, generated by Yeomra. There are no caloric benefits from drinking the large iced coffee with one cream and one sugar that Seokga orders at the register, but he doesn't mind. It tastes real, and should he grow hungry, Hwanin and Dr. Jang brought along a grocery store's worth of food in their luggage.

"And for you?" the café worker asks Kisa, punching in Seokga's order and looking bored. Seokga feels a pang of nostalgia, remembering when it was Hani behind the counter, purposefully messing up his order.

"Hot chocolate," Seokga replies before he can stop himself. It just slips out.

"Actually," corrects Kisa, shaking her head, "I'll have a small flat white, please."

Seokga swallows hard, gripping his cane tight. Hani hated coffee. She *loathed* it.

But she isn't Hani, he reminds himself. *Her name is Kisa. It's fine if she likes coffee. She's not going to be the same person that she was in her past life. You know this.*

At least she isn't an old man.
At least she isn't an old man.
At least she—

"Are you all right?" Kisa asks politely, and he realizes that she's staring at him, eyebrows furrowed.

Seokga hastens to arrange his expression into something other than abject horror as the barista passes them Seokga's coffee and Kisa's . . . flat white. "Perfectly," he manages to wheeze. "I am perfectly fine."

Kisa does not look in the least convinced, but leads him to a circular wooden table and sits primly in one of the chairs regardless. "I have to be back at the sick bay in twenty minutes," she says, sipping her drink. Seokga is slightly disappointed not to see a grimace of disgust, as Hani might have made. "Lots of gwisin will complain of seasickness on the first day of the cruise. Our mentor finished her penance on this ship a few months ago, so it's only Hajun and me working there at the moment." She sets down her drink and leans forward. Seokga wants, badly, to brush a stray curl out of her eyes, but refrains with notable effort.

She's his lover and a stranger all at once.

Oh, he's very much struggling, torn between intense feelings of both distance and familiarity. "I'm assuming we're soulmates," Kisa says matter-of-factly. "Threaded soulmates."

He nearly spits out the long draw of coffee he's taken. "Well—I—yes," he sputters, choking. *Great job,* he thinks. *Very smooth. Even better than falling to the floor and saying "errrgkkk."*

"Hmm," Kisa hums, calmly taking another sip. "Why?"

The café hustles and bustles around them, cheerful jazz music playing on the speakers. Meanwhile, Seokga is frantically dabbing at his suit with a napkin and trying not to hyperventilate. "*Why?*"

"Yes. I mean, statistically, apparitions of the Red Thread of Fate are minuscule. I would estimate them to be less than one percent. The last Threaded couple was rumored to be centuries ago, and even then, they were allegedly both gods. I assume you know who I'm referring to?"

"Haemosu and Yuhwa," Seokga mutters, remembering that

particular fiasco. Relations between Haemosu and Yuhwa's father, Habaek, are still frosty at best.

"There must be a reason we're Threaded," Kisa continues, tracing invisible words that look awfully like an entire paragraph on the table with her index finger. "So far, I've come up with a few hypotheses but narrowed it down to the one that makes the most sense logically."

"And that is?" he breathes.

She meets his eyes and cocks her head, frowning slightly. "You knew me in a past life," she says, pausing in her scribbling. "We fell in love, then I died. You were looking for me. The Red Thread of Fate manifested on March twenty-fourth, 2018, which was—coincidentally—the day that I died in *this* life. In accordance with what I know of the red thread, it may manifest at an emotionally fraught time. For example, Yuhwa and Haemosu became Threaded in the middle of running away from her father, Habaek. That's why it manifested on my death day. It could sense . . . something." Kisa takes an idle sip of her coffee as Seokga lurches forward in his seat.

Does she remember? Does she—

"Before you ask," Kisa says primly, "no, I don't remember anything. But I've learned a little about my past life. You seem like the type of person who would fall in love with a woman who is very good at stealing money from ATMs. I based my working theory off that. Although I'm sorry to tell you that I've never stolen anything before." She hesitates. "Also, I did read an issue of *Godly Gossip*, once. When I was ill. Not that it wasn't academically stimulating, in its own sort of way, but . . ." Kisa clears her throat. "You were in love with a gumiho, weren't you? During the nineties' Dark Days?"

Seokga has become aware that he is making a wheezing sound,

and really does try to stop. It is, unfortunately, impossible. "Yes," he manages to whisper.

Kisa nods, looking thoughtful. "So I suppose I was her? Or, she is me? Rebirth philosophy is such a convoluted field. I don't suppose you've heard of the Ship of Theseus problem?"

He shakes his head, trying to steady himself. Trying to breathe.

It's not working.

"It's a thought experiment. Is Theseus's wooden ship, which has all of its parts gradually replaced by stronger timber, the same ship?" Kisa chews on her bottom lip. "Some philosophers say no. How could it be? A ship of pine isn't the same thing as a ship of, say, oak. A gumiho isn't the same as a shaman . . ."

It's as if the floor has dropped beneath Seokga's feet, and he grips the edges of the table as Kisa muses on. *Collect yourself. She's right.*

"But some philosophers say that there are *two* Ships of Theseus. One oak, one pine. Both the same, yet compositely different. It's fascinating, really. What do you think?"

"I think," rasps Seokga, "that I'd need something stronger than coffee to answer that question."

She's so different from Hani. There are no quick jokes, no mischievous grins, no strawberry egg buns on the table in front of them. Hani was always quick, but Kisa's mind is working at such a speed that Seokga feels he cannot hope to ever possibly keep up. And this thought experiment . . . It is sending him into a state of panic. Has he lost Hani completely, after all?

Stop, he orders his spiraling mind as he watches Kisa's eyes dance over his expression. *Stop—*

But it's too late. She's seen his ragged edges peeking out from underneath his façade, the bitter disappointment and confusion. Kisa's own face falls, then blushes blue.

"I'm sorry," she says, clearing her throat. "I didn't think . . ." He watches, momentarily frozen as she scratches awkwardly at the tabletop, seemingly struggling to find words. "You use banmal with me," Kisa finally continues, and Seokga feels a rush of hot embarrassment. He's been using the informal with her, and even though this is not uncommon—he generally speaks banmal with everyone, due to his advanced age and overall superiority—it humiliates him to know that his motive for using banmal, a friendship and love that don't *exist* for Kisa, is so glaringly obvious. "I shouldn't have brought up the ship."

"No," Seokga says after a long moment, in which he slowly and painstakingly glues himself back together. "Thank you for sharing it with me. It's . . ." Horrifying. Depressing. Going to keep him up at night. ". . . relevant. I hadn't heard of it before." *You can use banmal with me if you'd like,* he wants to add, but somehow cannot find the courage.

Kisa nods, blush receding, back to business. "Perhaps we can solve it," she offers and smooths down her light blue scrubs. "I really am quite excited to be working with you on this development. I think our collaboration will be beneficial to so many parties."

Seokga freezes, then flinches. Her voice is so—professional. Eager, but only in a hungry, scientific way, stilted by the jondaemal she still uses. It hurts more than any weapon ever could. *Fuck.* Anything—even the old man passing gas at his crochet club— would be better than this detached clinical-ness. Like this thread between them is nothing more than a cold, dead scientific phenomenon meant to be studied, not something so pure and magical and *alive.*

"Red thread manifestations are so rare that we would be foolish not to, well, investigate it entirely. A, well, research collaboration could benefit so many in the magical communities . . . If we record our findings, it could be instrumental in the understanding of Threaded soulmates. There are so few books about it, you see, unless they're kept away in Okhwang's Heavenly Library, which I've always wanted to learn more about, by the way . . ."

Her words fade to a dull roar, for Seokga's mind is being crushed with waves of deep, bitter hurt. He sees what this is. For him, it is his best friend, his lover, reincarnated. For her, it is an experiment. *Research.*

For him, it's love.

It's as if he is being ripped apart, but somehow, Seokga still manages to stand. If he stays here, he knows he will break down entirely and there will be nothing left of him but bones and dust. And then what will she think of him? Kisa will be frightened away before he can collect himself. "I'm sorry," he hears himself saying, his voice thankfully cool and collected rather than the shaking mess he is inside, "I have to go."

Kisa hesitates. "Oh," she says, looking uncertain. "Okay."

He opens his mouth to say something else, anything else, but he knows if he uses his voice again it'll be a jagged cry. Hurriedly, heart breaking in his chest, Seokga turns on his heel and leaves.

The red thread stretches longer and longer with each step he takes.

CHAPTER SEVEN

KISA

Kisa's coffee has long gone cold by the time she returns to the sick bay. She keeps her head down to hide her disappointment from Hajun. *I've stepped in it,* Kisa thinks bitterly, trying not to look at the red thread. That's the problem with her, isn't it? She gets so enthusiastic, so very lost in her own whirring mind, that she forgets to slow down. Kisa feels her throat tighten in shame as she brushes off a curious Hajun and slips into the bathroom for a few moments of privacy.

Seokga was quite clearly, obviously, visibly upset. Of course. *Why did I say it like that?* Kisa curses herself, pumping some of the sweet-scented foam soap into her hands and scrubbing them underneath a jet of warm water. Technically, such sanitization is unnecessary when one is already in the underworld, but old habits quite literally die hard. *A research collaboration? Working with him on this development?*

It's true, of course, that she's jubilant to be experiencing something like this—the gap in the literature is astounding; if she can manage to write something, that could be *invaluable*—but she should have eased into it. Kisa has frightened him off.

The right thing to do would have been to tell the god she was looking forward to getting to know him. That's almost certainly what a normal woman would have done, right after finding themselves thrilled—*exhilarated,* even—to be Threaded to a *god* . . . and, at that, one as—as handsome, as powerful, as Seokga. There would have been no flustered ramblings about research or libraries or awkward stammers to fill an equally awkward silence. She'd just been so excited . . .

"Kisa?" Hajun asks, gently knocking on the door as she dries her hands. "Are you okay?"

No. No, she's not. She's a bloody mess. Taking a few deep breaths, she reknots her hair and slips back out into the clinic.

"Oh, no," Hajun says, staring down at her with those wide, heavily lashed eyes she so often envies. It's not uncommon that a deep sadness churns in their depths, but right now, only a tender concern shines through. "You blew it, didn't you?" His tone isn't accusatory at all (it's empathetic, really), but Kisa still winces.

"Was it that obvious that I would?" Her shame grows. Why, she thinks bitterly, can't she be *normal*?

Her friend's eyes soften even further. "I think anyone would blow it. I mean, the fact that you didn't scream and run away is already impressive. You saw me. I threw a *paperweight* at him."

She can't hold back a small smile as she steps behind the counter, riffling through a few charts. In her absence, Hajun has logged treating a few guests for seasickness. There will be more in the coming hours.

"Besides," Hajun continues, leaning on the other side, "if you really are soulmates, he'll forgive you for whatever you said." His pink lips curve into a hesitant smile as he props his chin on a hand. "And I promise he'll come to love that freaky brain of yours . . ."

"Hajun." Kisa almost laughs.

"I'll never understand how you keep so much *stuff* in it."

Slowly, with Hajun's light, kind teasing, Kisa's mood begins to rise. By the time the clinic is flooded with gwisin (who, despite being dead, are still capable of vomiting from seasickness), Kisa has managed to lose herself in her tasks, pushing her disastrous meeting with Seokga from her mind.

It's what she's always done, burying her emotions in work. It's what made her such a brilliant shaman, why the SH Magical Maternity Unit had a mortality rate lower than .02 percent. Gods, how Kisa misses being a shaman. Samsin Halmoni's patronage, and gifted powers, ended the moment she died. The goddess has no use for dead shamans.

The loss of it, that power, was debilitating at first. Like learning to walk again with only one leg. Kisa has learned to stumble and hop, but there is a dry, empty well within her where her shamanic magic used to gather and grow.

Up to her elbows in seasick gwisin and determinedly compartmentalizing her emotions into little boxes on a shelf, Kisa hardly notices the woman who practically sashays into the med bay, grinning with teeth stained blue with blood. It's only when Hajun, having walked over to the woman with a correct amount of trepidation, politely inquires how he can help her that Kisa snaps to attention and hurries out of the small patient room (where a man is dry-heaving into a bucket) and into the clinic's foyer.

"What, uh, um, happened to you?" Hajun eloquently asks through a terrified smile that still somehow manages to be sweet and concerned.

Kisa narrows her eyes. "Who did you try to eat?" she inquires sternly, having already noted the woman's small white canines and the distinctly unhinged look in her eyes. Gumiho. It's a problem on board: Unruly gumiho crew members (placed on the *Flatliner* as punishment for murder) will try to steal souls through their usual method of kissing. They'll soon realize it's impossible: Everyone on here *is* a soul. After realizing that, they'll shift into their fox forms and try to directly eat their victim.

But the woman isn't dressed in uniform. She's wearing a vintage black peacoat, curly black hair chopped into a distinctly French bob, feet slipped into Jimmy Choos. An Unruly gumiho—but not a crew member? Warily, Kisa watches as the guest smiles.

"Some old banker," she says, wincing, a hand fluttering to her stomach. "He got away. You might want to expect a patient with a big bite mark sometime soon. I don't feel all that great now, unfortunately. Do you have any Tums?"

Hajun backs away. "Please don't eat me," he whispers.

The woman tilts her head, looking at him. "You're too pretty to eat," she says and—to Kisa's shock—Hajun *blushes* before hurrying over to one of the seasick patients.

"You can't eat people on board," Kisa says, folding her arms. "Not only is it not allowed, but—as you're experiencing—it's very uncomfortable. You've basically imbibed a part of somebody's raw essence... Which is fascinating, really, but beside the point..." Walking past the gumiho, Kisa rummages through one of the medicine cabinets, and shakes a few green pills into the woman's hand. "Flesh doesn't really exist here. We're all souls, pure energy under the illusion of physical form because we're *used* to existing in bodies. But it's really not the same as it is in the world of the living. If you absorb a portion of someone else's soul, symptoms will include—"

"Stomach cramps," says the woman after swallowing the pills. "Dizziness. A powerful urge to gargle dish detergent." She shudders.

"And cold sweats. Those will start soon, but the pills will expel the foreign essence." Kisa sighs, grabbing a clipboard. "Name?"

"Nam Somi," the woman says with a self-satisfied smile.

The name doesn't mean anything to Kisa. "You're a guest?"

"Yes," Somi says, pouting sarcastically. "I worked *so hard* in my life. It's actually pretty difficult being a serial killer."

Frighteningly enough, Kisa doesn't think that Somi is joking. She stares at the gumiho, who meets her eyes—and curiously, seems to falter for a moment.

"Do I . . . know you?"

"I'm afraid not," Kisa replies blandly. "Now, if you don't mind me asking . . ."

"I know what you're thinking," the gumiho says slyly as her face clears from whatever confusion had clouded it a moment before. "That I don't deserve to be a guest on board. That's where having illicit affairs with jeoseung saja come in handy." She sniffs. Although the two women are similar in height, Somi's heels boost her at least five inches above Kisa. "I *guess* I'll stop trying to eat people. Only if this will happen every time, though. It's worse than the Jitters and Cravings I used to get."

Jitters. Cravings. Kisa arches a brow. Gumiho hypersensitivity to soul-absorption and liver-imbibing is rare, but so are Unruly gumiho. Many of the nine-tailed foxes steer clear from eating men at all, a modern taboo. "If you do this again, it'll be the same result," Kisa confirms, unamused, finishing her log. "I'll also have to report this to the on-board haetae." Officer Shin Korain is head of the ship's security unit, and asks that any wrongdoing be reported to him immediately.

Somi shrugs. "He knows. I did it in front of him." She wipes her mouth. "I told him I slipped and fell. My teeth just happened to puncture the banker. I think he believed me. I'm just banned from Deck 6 now, which is a shame. The greenhouse is so pretty. Thanks for the pills."

Hajun joins Kisa's side again as Somi struts out.

"That one is going to be trouble," he says, but he's smiling a little bit.

Kisa's lips are a thin line. "Yes," she replies. "I think so."

CHAPTER EIGHT

SEOKGA

As Seokga stumbles into the suite he will be sharing with Hwanin, his brother leaps to his feet from where he was sitting on one of the plush armchairs.

The suite is just as lavish as any mortal hotel, with two bedrooms joined by a sitting area facing a large window displaying the Seocheongang River outside. It's the biggest suite—the King Suite. Only the best for Okhwang's emperor. Art that Yeomra would probably insist is "interpretive" but is really just ugly splashes of paint hangs proudly on the walls above the black-carpeted floor that Hwanin currently treads on as he makes his way over to Seokga. A fire crackles merrily in its hearth—too merrily. Seokga wishes to violently extinguish it. He just might.

"Seokga," Hwanin says as Seokga leans heavily against the doorframe, "I'm going to assume from your expression that you're either nauseatingly happy or very seasick." He hesitates. "Did you find her?"

On trembling legs, Seokga manages to carry himself to another armchair, sinking into the soft fabric and running a shaking hand down his face. "I found her," he confirms in a whisper.

Hwanin's brows furrow together. "This is not the happiness I've expected for years," he says. "You look ill. What happened?"

Throat dry, Seokga tells him, detailing everything from the flying paperweight to the café. Hwanin watches him, face growing more and more somber. "I knew not to expect Hani," he whispers, throat dry. "I've been telling myself not to for years. But I still . . ."

"Expected her," his brother finishes, eyes kind. But the trickster god's mood is already turning.

"This never would have happened," he pants, hurt suddenly replaced by hot anger, "if you hadn't made that bargain in the first place. Did you have fun?" He launches out of the chair, glowering down at the emperor. "Watching it all unfold? Watching me fall in love with the woman I was meant to hunt down? They say I have Father's cruel streak, Hwanin, but yours—yours is *unparalleled*."

Hwanin's eyes flash. "Do not compare me to Father."

Mireuk. The original creator god. Hwanin and Seokga's father, who went mad and shaped the worlds' sufferings. As Mireuk had spiraled further and further into evil, Hwanin and Seokga were given no choice but to imprison him, far within Jeoseung, beneath the river on which the SRC *Flatliner* cruises.

"You did this," Seokga sneers, undeterred. "You—"

"I made that bargain for you," Hwanin interrupts, voice deceptively calm. "To reinstate you as a god. And later, I *modified* it for you, to save your life. All for you! How was I meant to know you would fall in love with her?"

"No," snaps Seokga, breathing hard. "Stop lying. You know as well as I do that you did it to betray me the way I betrayed you—"

It is an old argument between them. One that constantly interrupts a newer friendship.

"*Enough*," Hwanin retorts, a vein on his temple pulsing as he stands. "If you want to play this game, allow me a turn. Hani would never have died if you did not attempt a coup, if you did not get yourself exiled. If she had stayed away from meddling in your business. If you were a better detective and unmasked Eodum quicker. If she hadn't drained her fox bead. If, if, if. There were so many variables in her death, brother. So many moving pieces and yet, in your anger, you only blame me. But who orchestrated her reincarnation?" Hwanin shakes his head, mouth a thin line. "So she is not what you expected or wanted, deep down. Fine. She is not going to be Hani, Seokga. She is going to be Kisa. I know that logically you are aware of this. So do not set unrealistic expectations for the girl. She doesn't *know you*. There is an imbalance, don't you think? You want something from her that she's not ready to give." His face gentles as Seokga flinches, hard wall of fury beginning to crumble. "Time, brother. Give her time. Humor her curiosity. Don't push her away until you *really* know her. And let her get to know you."

Tired. Seokga is so utterly tired as he stands there, shoulders slumped. The exhaustion weighing down his bones is ancient and lumbering. "I miss her," he whispers. "I miss Hani." He stares at the red thread, aching with the worst type of loss. *The Ship of Theseus,* Seokga thinks. *Is it still the same ship? Is she still the same woman I loved?*

"I know."

"I would burn down the entire world just to see her again."

"Unfortunately, I know you mean that literally." Hwanin sighs. "Look, brother—I'll call Dr. Jang over for an emergency session. But I know you, Seokga, and I know that you've likely decided to dramatically mope for the foreseeable future regardless of any professional intervention. So we're going out tonight."

Seokga swallows the pink pill that he must, every day, take at precisely seven o'clock. An anti-depressant, prescribed to him by Dr. Jang. Although he's not sure it's been doing much. He is practically drowning in misery.

"Are you ready?" Hwanin asks, hovering by the suite's door.

He gives his brother a withering look.

"It will be fun," the emperor says with forced cheer.

"I highly doubt that," Seokga replies coldly, but still follows Hwanin into the hall, where Dr. Jang waits. The therapist has gotten dolled up for the occasion, swapping out her Hawaiian shirt for an extremely frumpy dress with a rubber-duck print that Seokga dearly wants to laugh at. Hwanin's elbow digs into his ribs before he can snicker.

"Shall we?" Hwanin asks, offering his arm to Dr. Jang. The elderly woman smiles, excitement rolling off her in waves. Seokga ends up walking behind the pair as they take the glittering, diamond-crusted spiraling stairs down one flight to Deck 6, joined by a handful of other guests, all buzzing with excitement.

The last time Seokga was on a ship had been an unfortunate journey with a handful of pirates, all of whom were Unruly dokkaebi, and all of which he'd had to kill. That ship had been small, cramped, and dirty—certainly not large enough, nor sturdy enough, to hold a *greenhouse*.

It's a massive building of neat white beams and polished glass, which displays a sea of rich greens and vibrancy beyond.

"Emperor Hwanin," says the cruise director—a woman named Soo-min (in accordance with her golden name tag) whom Seokga had already decided to dislike based on nothing but his grumpy nature and inherent distrust of smiling people—"and Prince Seokga. Welcome to tonight's garden party." She stares for a moment at Dr. Jang, at the ridiculous dress. "Um . . . Is she with you?"

"Clearly," snaps Seokga, suddenly protective of Dr. Jang as her face falls. Now that his awe at the SRC *Flatliner* has mellowed, part of him writhes uncomfortably about how he spoke to her that morning. "She is."

"Right," says Soo-min, still staring at the dress. "Well, please enjoy your time tonight."

"It's rude to stare," Seokga whispers as he passes her.

The cruise director jumps. He smiles.

"*Boo,*" he all but cackles before following his companions into the greenhouse. It is even larger on the inside. Seokga's ears fill with the gentle murmur of a large, man-made stone pond, in which lily pads float atop earth-hued water. It is a veritable forest in here, humidity-slick cobblestones clicking underneath the heels of a small gathering. Various exotic plants stretch up toward the roof far, far above: high ferns, arching lemon trees, even palm trees which tower over clusters of vibrant flowers. Seokga can almost believe they're on land, in a rather large garden. The only indication of their true location is the glass walls, which must jut out of the ship. The red river swims below.

Waiters carry platters of hors d'oeuvres through the winding paths. None of them are Kisa. The red thread stretches far beyond the greenhouse—she's likely still working in the ship's clinic. Not knowing whether he's disappointed or relieved, Seokga takes a flute of champagne, downs it, grimaces in disgust (coffee is the only drink besides water he more than tolerates) and then places it back on the tray as a live band—hidden somewhere in the foliage—begins to play soft classical music.

Dr. Jang is chatting away with an elderly couple who seem to be fawning over her dress and laughing as she contorts her voice to a surprisingly good imitation of a popular daytime show host. Staring at the rubber ducks, Seokga hopes that terrible fashion sense isn't an incurable disease of the old. He is, after all, ancient. Hwanin attempts, futilely, to engage Seokga in conversation with a few other guests—all of whom mumble their excuses as he turns his penetrating green gaze onto them.

"Seokga," Hwanin says, "you're scaring them away. Stop it."

But Seokga doesn't hear him. No, Seokga is staring over Hwanin's shoulder, feeling his blood steadily begin to boil as he catches sight of something—some*one*—whom he has dearly wanted to throttle for some time now.

It was Hani's last wish that Nam Somi go free. If it were up to Seokga, he would have hung Somi's pelt in his palace long, long ago. Thirty-three years ago, to be exact.

She looks different now. The years have hardened her. He realizes, with growing disgust, that her clothes mirror what Hani would once wear. Perfect, polished, fashionable in the nineties but perhaps a bit outdated now, out of place amongst the more modern wear of the party. The way she flirts, laughs . . . Somi is mimicking Hani. Mimicking her former friend, her mentor, the most notorious gumiho to ever exist.

His stomach rolls.

But oh, how Somi pales in contrast to Hani. This air of cheer and confidence is so calculated. So plastic and fake. For years, Somi terrorized country after country, eating her way through their supply of men—almost as if following in the Scarlet Fox's footsteps. But some paws are too small to fill the prints left by the Scarlet Fox.

She's a cheap knockoff.

Seokga feels a bitter regret that he was not the one to end her life or put her on this ship.

But now that she's dead . . .

A wicked smile curves Seokga's lips. It's the same curve that graced them moments before he unleashed a horde of Gamang-nara monsters into Okhwang. The same crooked grin that Hwanin stared at as Seokga rode a roaring Unruly jangsan beom into the throne room, the massive tiger-shifter launching for the throne.

Now that she's dead, he can *really* begin to torment her.

How Seokga adores loopholes.

"Excuse me," says Seokga and, with that same nasty smile, makes his way toward Somi. The gumiho's eyes widen as she looks up, clocks the six-foot-three trickster god shouldering his way toward her.

And, *there*. She freezes, a deer in the headlights, prey cowering before predator. He can practically smell her terror, rolling off her in waves as those big brown eyes widen even further. Somi tries to smile but oh, how clearly Seokga sees right through her act. She's just as much of a coward as she ever was. That nervous, trembling café worker isn't too far beneath the surface. A bumbling teenager in a woman's skin.

"Hello, Somi," Seokga sneers, shoving aside her conversation partners.

She attempts bravado. It's laughable. "Seokga," she greets, drawing her shoulders back. He has the feeling his name is supposed to drip with disdain, but all he hears is trepidation. Good.

"I hope your death was painful and bloody," he drawls.

Somi swallows and he feels a surge of triumph when she flinches. If he had to guess, some truth hit home. He doesn't care. Perhaps a better man would stop now. But Seokga has never been a better man. He has only ever been a wicked, wicked god.

"And I hope," Seokga whispers, cocking his head, "it's nothing compared to this."

In one swift *snap*, Seokga has transformed his cane into the long silver sword he has carried for thousands of years. Partygoers shriek, and Seokga snorts in disgust. He's never really understood how Jeoseung works—hasn't really bothered to understand it, at any rate—but he knows one thing.

Even if he can't kill those who are already dead, he can *hurt* them.

"Seokga!" That's his therapist, rushing toward them as fast as her aging body allows, rubber-duck dress flapping. "Seokga, please, you *cannot* bring out your sword during a garden party, you cannot *stab* somebody—"

"WHAT ARE YOU DOING?" *That's* his brother, howling his heavenly emperor head off in outrage. The music grinds to a halt.

Somi's eyes are wide. Seokga's blood is boiling, hotter and hotter. All of the frustrations, the *heartbreak,* of the past day has reached its tipping point. He knows what Dr. Jang will say. He's projecting his own self-hatred onto Somi who, admittedly, played a rather small part in the Dark Days. He's letting his grip on his anger problems slip, he's giving in to the darker parts of his nature, he's subconsciously imitating the rage his father showed when his sickness began. He's attempting to compensate for his complete lack of a sense of control by being entirely in control of someone else's pain.

Oh, well.

He grins in a way that has the frozen gumiho paling . . .

"Seokga?"

The trickster god freezes. Slowly, so slowly, he turns his head over his shoulder.

Kisa stands behind him, breathing hard, curls in a state of flustered disarray. Her bright eyes dart from him to the sword to Somi and back. The woman's face is slack with shock—and disappointment. Between them, the red thread *tightens* and once again, for a moment, glows scarlet. Seokga's next thought is not his own.

—would—hurt—she didn't mean—eat the banker—is that why—

The shock of it is enough for Seokga to drop the sword. It clatters to the ground and he is vaguely aware of Somi hissing something at him, of Dr. Jang taking one of his shoulders, of Hwanin leaping into a furious lecture . . . But none of that matters. Amidst the chaos, Seokga and Kisa stare at each other, fate glowing between them.

He can hear her thoughts.

He can *hear Kisa's thoughts.*

And judging by the growing roundness of her eyes, she can hear his, too.

CHAPTER NINE

KISA

IT WAS PURE ANXIETY and desperation that brought Kisa to the greenhouse party. She had been pacing back and forth in the sick bay, much to the dismay of Hajun, who was attempting to nap on one of the cots before the next flood of seasick patients arrived. It always grew worse after dinner. But in the current lull, with nothing to distract her from what Seokga must think of her, Kisa was drowning in an itching embarrassment and a visceral need to redeem herself.

"Just *go to him,*" Hajun moaned into his crinkly pillow. "The more you wallow, the more I worry about you, and the more I worry about you, the more my head hurts..."

She hesitated, chewing on her nail—a nervous habit that she couldn't seem to break. "I don't know what to say."

He rolled onto his back, fixing his dark eyes on her. "Just say 'sorry'..."

Kisa shook her head.

"...for speaking with your gigantic brain and not your heart..." Hajun sat up as Kisa threw a pen at him. He laughed, eyes crinkling at the corners. But he wasn't laughing at her. No, Hajun was always laughing *with* her. It was one of the things she loved about him.

"You really think I should go?" Kisa twisted a curl nervously. "You'll be okay here without me? You'll remember to use the buckets and—"

Hajun wrinkled his nose. "It's kind of common sense to use a bucket if somebody's throwing up, Kisa," he ribbed.

"Right . . ."

After a few moments more of hesitation, Kisa had nodded and hurried out of the med bay, following the thread up to Deck 6. She had barely managed to slip by Soo-min, who was staffing the greenhouse doors. The interior was at least, according to her guesstimations, the size of an indoor soccer field.

She had found Seokga with his sword pointed at a frightened Nam Somi's throat. Not quite the scene she had been hoping to stumble into. In her mind, Kisa would have plucked a flute of champagne from one of the servants, winding through the sweet plants and milling guests with a soft, apologetic smile until she found him.

I'm so sorry for my callous insensitivity, she would have said, polite enough that she wouldn't appear desperate, but empathetic enough that she wouldn't appear *too* polite. He would have forgiven her, and they could start over. Instead, she's watching him drop the sword, the sword that had been pointed at Somi's *throat,* and she is hearing . . .

She is hearing his voice in her head.

She is—could it be that she is hearing his *thoughts?*

—Kisa—Kisa—Kisa—

Kisa stares up at him, slowly beginning to register that they are experiencing a sort of . . . cerebration transference. At least, she reasons, that is the only way she is able to explain the thoughts that are most decidedly not hers echoing through her mind in short, clipped fragments:

—*Kisa—here—thoughts—she—hear—too—*

His thoughts are like serpents, she thinks, sleek and strong and *fast*. Kisa slowly moves her gaze down to the thread, the thread that must act as the wire carrying their messages from mind to mind. What possible material could it be composed of? She is completely fascinated, and it is only with extreme effort that she manages to refocus on the events around her.

During some point in time, a silver-haired man has restrained Seokga, while an older woman in an interesting rubber-duck dress fills the air with a lecture on anger management. Kisa stares at the man with silver hair and realizes—with a surge of excitement—that his description, down to his regal, traditional hanbok of dark blue—perfectly matches that of Okhwang's emperor Hwanin.

"*What*," the emperor is demanding, "did I *tell* you about *murdering innocents?*"

—*not innocent—killed—Scarlet—how could—forget—*

Chaos erupts as Kisa watches, utterly unsure of what to do. Somi is shouting something, finger pointed at Seokga, and the other guests in the greenhouse are watching in shocked fascination. Kisa stumbles as Soo-min, having run over in a panic, shoves her aside.

"What is going on here!" the cruise director cries, Officer Shin Korain hot on her heels. The young haetae's eyes are wide, but he hovers back, as if unsure whether inserting himself into a fight between two gods, a gumiho, and an elderly rubber-duck-loving woman is a good idea. "Stop it!" screams Soo-min. "All of you!"

"Hey, Kisa," Korain pants, propping his hands on his hips. A lock of black hair falls into his golden eyes.

"Hello, Korain," she greets distractedly. The two are familiar with each other as only long-suffering workers on the SRC *Flatliner* can be—there's always a shared sense of pained solidarity as well as a bitter irony at their less-than-ideal situation. Although Hajun is really Kisa's only friend, Korain has always been kind in passing, and she half-wishes he had also been assigned to the sick bay instead of the security staff. They rarely see each other except for the brief moments when they pass in the halls or when there's a staff meeting. But he's unfailingly nice, which is more than she can say for crew members like Soo-min, who watches her like a hawk twenty-four seven.

"Crazy turn-around day, huh?"

"Yes," she says faintly, watching Seokga's eyes bulge as Hwanin squeezes him into a headlock. "Yes, you could definitely say that."

Seokga wrestles out of Hwanin's grip, eyes flashing in victory, and as his brother attempts to again tackle him, the god—in a flash of emerald mist—shape-shifts into a small black raven and flaps upward toward the glass ceiling. Hwanin crashes to the ground, cursing, as the raven plummets in a nosedive toward Somi. The gumiho screams, frantically trying to swat the god-turned-bird away as it pulls her hair with its beak. She falls into a patch of flowers, and the raven makes a distinctly pleased noise that could very well be a chuckle.

"YOU'RE RUINING THE PARTY!" Soo-min wails, wringing her hands. Her already shrill, snooty voice amplified at such a volume hurts Kisa's ears. "STOP IT! ALL OF YOU!"

Somi launches back to her feet and—getting in a lucky hit—sends Seokga-the-bird hurtling toward a server. He shifts into his usual form at the last second, and the server falls, flutes of champagne crashing with her.

Kisa winces as the glasses shatter and tries to rush toward the fallen girl, only to be yanked back by Korain. "You don't want to get into that mess," he warns. "That's my job, and I'm at least paid to do it." All crew members get a small monthly stipend of coins to spend in the ship's cafés and other shops.

"I suppose you have a point there," Kisa murmurs, but he doesn't reply. Korain's eyes are on the server, who's shoved Seokga off. As the girl winces in clear pain, Korain seems to find the courage to wade into the chaos.

He's stopped, abruptly, by the heavenly emperor.

"This is a family matter," Hwanin snaps, and Kisa watches as Korain's face darkens. "Do not involve yourself," the emperor adds in warning, turning to his brother, who is untangling himself from the pale server who is currently glaring daggers at the gods.

"That gumiho has been *banned* from the greenhouse," Korain snarls back. "She shouldn't even be up here. I think I have jurisdiction over *that*—"

Hwanin gives him a look so withering that Kisa can finally see the family resemblance between him and his brother.

Seokga brushes crushed glass off his suit and fixes his hair moments before Somi—yelling something unintelligible—launches herself toward him. Thus ensues *another* fight, one in which the two circle each other, utter hatred on both their faces.

Kisa frowns, watching the pair. Clearly, they know and loathe each other. But how?

"I don't care if it's a family matter," Korain snaps, attempting to shove past Hwanin. The emperor doesn't budge. "You're disrupting the party, you're abusing the cutlery—" Indeed, Somi has swiped a fork from a nearby server and is trying to stab Seokga with it. Kisa can't stop her mouth from dropping open in growing alarm. Really. Forks are *not* meant to be used as weapons. "—and if you don't get control of them, our reincarnations will be set back by years! We'll be held liable for this—"

The words send a flare of acute anger through Kisa as the haetae reminds her of what, exactly, is at stake. Korain is completely right. Yeomra will hold the *crew* responsible for this utter fiasco. Well, she thinks firmly, if Korain can't get past the glaring emperor, *she* can. Korain is distracted and won't pull her back this time.

Determinedly, Kisa marches toward Seokga, inserts herself between him and Somi (narrowly dodging the fork), and stretches her arms out between them. "Stop this!" she demands.

Somi pants, narrowing her eyes at Kisa, a ball of energy. "If you don't move out of my way, I'll—"

"You'll what?" Seokga snarls. "Betray her again? Sell her out to an insane demon?"

Bewilderment replaces indignation. Kisa falters, glancing back at Seokga's snarling face before returning to Somi, who blinks rapidly. Brain aching, she shakes her head.

"I only met her this morning," Kisa says—rather stupidly, she thinks a moment later as she realizes what Seokga is implying. She stares at Somi, who's still stricken. Did they know each other? In her past life, as an ATM-stealing woman? Is Seokga referencing Eodum, the demon who instigated the 1992 Dark Days? How very, extremely interesting . . .

"Look at her eyes," Seokga spits to Somi, yanking Kisa out of her musings. A hush has fallen over the greenhouse. "They're the same, aren't they?"

To Kisa's bewilderment, Somi is the one who is trembling as she meets Kisa's curious, wine-brown stare. "Hwanin's tits," Somi whispers, and takes a step backward. The same expression from this morning in the sick bay—confusion and disbelieving recognition—flashes across her face again. She suddenly looks very young and very uncertain. "H-Hani?"

Kisa blinks. *Hani*. Yes—*that* was the name of the gumiho, the one that still makes headlines in *Godly Gossip*. THE LONELY GOD CON-

TINUES SEARCH FOR KIM HANI! and SEOKGA CONCUSSES HANI-IMPOSTER: YOU CAN'T OUT-TRICK THE TRICKSTER!

At the name, there's a sudden influx of thought fragments from Seokga.

—Hani—miss her—gone—forever—different—Kisa—

Kisa swallows hard. Whoever Hani was, she knows she's not . . . her. Not anymore. Kisa has her own answer to the Ship of Theseus problem, and it means that Seokga will forever be wishing that Kisa is somebody she'll never be.

Before she can taste the bitterness of confused disappointment, Somi is clapping a hand to her mouth. "Oh my gods," she whispers. "Hani, unnie? Is it really you?"

Feeling totally at a loss, Kisa shifts from foot to foot. "Er," she says stiffly, "I was born in 1995. I think you're older than me." It's the only thing she can think of to say, correcting Somi's incorrect usage of *unnie*. The gumiho looks to be either in her late twenties or early thirties, but could very well be even older thanks to gumiho immortality.

"Right," whispers Somi, still staring. "Right . . ."

"Seokga!" That's the elderly woman in the rubber-duck dress. "What did I tell you! The next time you—"

"The next time I feel like attacking somebody, close my eyes and count to ten," the god drawls, eyes never leaving Somi and Kisa. "It didn't work, Dr. Jang."

"You didn't even *try*."

Emperor Hwanin's voice joins in the bedlam, but Kisa doesn't notice. She's watching Somi as the gumiho slowly backs away, eyes shining with . . . tears?

"Wait," Kisa whispers, dozens of questions brimming on her tongue. But the other woman doesn't listen. A moment later, she's slipping away, weaving through the aghast guests and disappearing.

"... embarrassment," Hwanin is hissing, and Kisa blinks, turning around to focus on the new conversation. "I don't even know how to *handle* you right now." The emperor barely spares Kisa a glance, concentrating all of his fury onto Seokga, who looks relatively unbothered.

"It was karmic," is what the trickster replies. "You resent me delivering karmic justice? It's a divine duty that I happen to take very seriously."

"No," Hwanin hisses in an undertone, "I resent that you did it *in public*—"

"Oh, please, you love attention. Remember those *Godly Gossip* exclusives you used to do about our tragic, broken relationship?" Seokga's green eyes dart to Kisa, and something almost like a small, mischievous grin curves his lips.

Kisa doesn't smile back, eyes flickering to the shattered glass on the floor, the crushed flowers, the mess of black feathers and curly black hair where raven-Seokga had attacked Somi. The server Seokga knocked over—a tired-eyed young woman with long, dark hair—is already on her hands and knees, collecting the shards. Nearby, Korain is futilely attempting to fix the flowers with Soomin, the cruise director uncharacteristically sacrificing her impeccably ironed skirt to kneel on the mulch next to the haetae.

Heavy-hearted, Kisa joins the girl, crouching down to help collect the glittering shards, fingers becoming damp with spilled champagne.

"Thanks," the girl whispers over the steady beratements from Hwanin directed toward Seokga, and occasionally joined in by the woman named Dr. Jang.

"Are you all right?" Kisa asks, glancing up at her. "I work in the sick bay. If you need anything for bruises or . . ."

She shakes her head. "I'm fine. Just upset. The CEO will hear about this." A soft sigh. "I'm so tired of working down here. But all my points for good behavior will be docked because of tonight. Yeomra will see my name on the list of greenhouse workers."

Kisa is acutely aware of Seokga's gaze on her back. "We can submit our own report..." HR in Jeoseung and especially on the SRC *Flatliner* is laughable at best, but it's better to try than to not.

"No." A bitter laugh. "Hwanin and Seokga are gods. We can't exactly go around blaming them." With a sad smile, the server shakes her head as they collect the rest of the glass, setting the piles back on the metal tray. "Thanks, anyway. I'm Chaeyeon. Lim Chaeyeon."

"Yoo Kisa," she replies, and the two share quick, half-hearted smiles as they drag themselves back to their feet.

"I can't even look at you," Hwanin is finishing, glaring at Seokga. "I can't even—" The emperor pinches the bridge of his nose. "I'm leaving," he says. "Please do not follow me. If you do, I may resort to physical violence and give you the punch in the face that you so *dearly* deserve."

Seokga's smirk is thin and razor-sharp. "Oh, no. I'm so very threatened, brother."

Hwanin glowers in disgust for one final moment before turning on his heel, making his way to the exit. Kisa watches as Dr. Jang shakes her head.

"I'm extremely disappointed in you, Seokga," she whispers. "As we have discussed before, trying to stab people is *not* part of your recovery plan. I expect to have a discussion with you tomorrow morning." Kisa watches as, with a final disappointed sigh, the doctor trails after Hwanin, Chaeyeon following close behind, carefully balancing the tray of shattered, glittering glass.

The crowd remains frozen as Seokga stands there, eyes glittering with unrepentant amusement. Kisa shakes her head, staring at him from where she stands amongst the feathers. He turns to her, and the apology that Kisa had crafted on the way here dissipates into ash.

"You think that was funny?" she whispers. Seokga freezes in a way he hadn't even when his brother threatened to punch him. His expression is suddenly uncertain.

—did—for her—why does—glare—me—

"No." Kisa shakes her head. "No. You didn't do this for *me*. Whatever Nam Somi did to me in a past life, I don't remember it. I don't remember her. I don't remember you." She tries to ignore how he flinches, and pushes onward. "It wouldn't have made a difference to me if you had left her alone. You did this for yourself. But you're not the one who will have to pay."

The crowd holds their breath as she steps toward him. Going head-to-head with a god is never advised: Kisa cannot count the number of myths, of tales that advise against doing exactly this . . . But she doesn't quite care, even though all the stories are true.

"This—this was inconceivably thoughtless." The red thread quivers as, in a fit of rising anger, Kisa props one hand on her hip and points the other at Seokga's pointed nose. "All of the crew has been waiting for reincarnation for a very long time. But the CEO will blame tonight's workers for this *fiasco*. Do you understand the gravity of that?"

She watches as his throat bobs. Once, twice. His eyes cross slightly to watch her finger with growing concern as she jabs it. Around them, the frozen crowd slowly begins to disperse, murmuring amongst themselves. Somewhere hidden, the live band tremulously begins to play again.

"What would you like from me?" Seokga quietly asks, and the worst part is that he doesn't even seem to know. His words are hesitant, softened by the informal and that odd, uncertain hint of familiarity she first noticed in the café. Unfortunately, the temptation to draw her hand back, form it into a fist, and then send it crashing into his perfect nose is interfering with Kisa's capability for rational thought. She understands perfectly how Emperor Hwanin must feel. "Whatever it is, I'll do it," the god adds.

She has an itemized list prepared. "One, please do not attack people on this ship! Two—which I'll put in as a clause in case you *do* attack somebody: Clean up after yourself, and don't barrel into workers holding a tray of glasses in the first place. Three, inform the CEO that the workers here tonight had nothing to do with your—your—" She struggles to find the word before finally selecting: " *shenanigans.*"

Seokga's eyes crinkle at the corners. Kisa steadfastly ignores how that small change transforms his face from hard to surprisingly gentle in just one moment. "Is that all?" the trickster asks, sounding amused.

"Yes—I mean no." Kisa can't help herself. Her eyes fasten on the sword that Seokga has reclaimed from the ground, on the strangely luminous silver metal. "Four, tell me . . . Is it true that godly weapons are crafted by moon-harvested silver and forged in bulgae fire?" The pantheon is notoriously close-lipped about their relics. Entire fields are devoted to dissecting the few artifacts shamans have been able to get their hands on, attempting to discover what ore the blades are composed of.

The god gapes at her.

Kisa frowns impatiently. "Well?" She jabs at his nose again—and accidentally hits the tip.

Somebody in the crowd gasps sharply as if expecting Kisa to be struck down then and there. But nothing happens, save for the odd expression that crosses Seokga's face. He looks, somehow, both mortally offended and incredibly pleased.

"Dokkaebi fire," he says a moment later, expression fading into something like... hesitantly fond confusion. "Bulgae fire is too unpredictable. The Okhwang weapon-smiths use dokkaebi fire. As for the rest..." Seokga hesitates before crouching down and beginning to pick up the feathers.

After a moment, Kisa joins him.

CHAPTER TEN

SEOKGA

"It has to be some sort of conduit that allows for cerebration transference," muses Kisa, hands cupped around her late-night coffee, knees drawn up to her chest as she sits across from Seokga in the Creature Café—which is now a twenty-four/seven chain, practically a dream come true. The café is empty save for them, and the weary worker behind the counter. "It's exciting, isn't it? Although, I think if it was constant, we'd both go positively mad. The thoughts seem to be transferring at random. I wonder what function it serves. And you're hearing mine in Korean?"

"Yes," Seokga confirms, which sparks a lengthy musing on cerebration transference translation from English to Korean. Kisa has been vocally pondering the red thread, this new development of hearing each other's thoughts, for the past fifteen minutes they've been in the café. Seokga, grudgingly taking Hwanin's advice, has simply let Kisa talk. And in this time, he's learned that Yoo Kisa is frighteningly intelligent, with a mind that works at least twice as fast as his own. Her thoughts, which he hears in short clips, are spat into his brain so rapidly that he can hardly make sense of them. They're like frantic scribbles, marking the ridges of his mind in smudged ink.

The greenhouse "fiasco," as she put it, is less than an hour behind them, but Kisa seems to have warmed back up to him already. One other thing he has learned: Yoo Kisa is quick to forgive.

"Intimacy," Seokga suggests, taking a long drag of his iced coffee and savoring its coldness. His body feels uncomfortably warm underneath Kisa's gaze. Hani's eyes.

Kisa blinks, cheeks tinting blue. "I, er—what?"

"Its function," he explains, unexpectedly finding some amusement in the way Kisa is blushing. So different from how Hani would have reacted—a coy smile, a sweetly sarcastic joke—but it's . . . it's endearing. "Hearing each other's thoughts. It lends a sense of intimacy, don't you think?" He can't help but smile a bit wickedly and take at least a little delight in how Kisa squirms, still blushing. "The red thread connects soulmates," Seokga continues explaining as Kisa buries her nose in her cup. "Maybe they're strangers at first. But what better way to know somebody *intimately* than to hear their thoughts?"

—wish I could—stop blushing—intimacy—intimacy—my cheeks are blue—ugly—

"Your cheeks aren't ugly when they're blue," Seokga says with a small frown that masks a smile. It's the first time her thoughts have been anything other than swiftly calculated jumbles, and it sends a little fissure of hope through him. She's not as clinical, as emotionless, as he'd thought. It occurs to him, for the first time, that Kisa is just as nervous as he is. Already, their second meeting in this coffee shop is going much better than their first one only this afternoon.

Even if she still views him as an exciting research project, perhaps they can still become . . . friends. Seokga will take as much of her as he can, or as little as he's allowed. After thirty-three years of searching, he's finally found her.

But she's dead, he remembers, and something tightens deep in his stomach.

No. He won't think about that right now.

Kisa is peeking up at him over her mug. "Thank you," she mumbles. "That's very nice of you, actually." A hand rises self-consciously to her indigo-stained cheeks before she hastily looks away.

He shrugs, even though he's preening like a peacock inside. "Yes," he replies, tracing the lid of his coffee cup. "I'm very nice." It is important to him that she knows this. So important that Seokga risks sounding like a bumbling fool. Which he does. He grits his teeth and takes a long, long sip of his drink.

Kisa's left eyebrow raises, nearly touching that little heart right above. "Hundreds of history books and tonight's events might suggest otherwise," she retorts. "You're notorious for being, well, a bit of an unpleasant person."

"I'm very nice," he amends, "to the people I like."

"And to the people you don't?" Kisa looks like she might—just might—be hiding a smile. "Do you usually shape-shift into crows and attack them?"

"I usually prefer to shift into a panther and maul them," he deadpans. "But the greenhouse was too small for that." A moment later, he regrets it. Hani might have understood his dark humor, but Kisa . . .

Kisa stares at him and Seokga clamps his mouth shut, feeling embarrassed in a way that a god most certainly should not feel. Seokga, the great trickster, the prince of Okhwang, feels *awkward.* It is a terrible emotion and he wishes immediately to pull it out of his skin, then set it on fire.

But then something peculiar happens. Kisa's eyes scrunch in the corners and a strained, quiet laugh escapes her. Seokga freezes.

Her hand flies to her mouth, but it's too late. Triumph has welled inside of him, and Seokga can't help but smirk as Kisa covers her face in her hands.

"That's horrible," she whispers, sounding mortified, "and I should not be laughing. I don't know why I am, really."

—I can tell—he means it—too—a panther—

Seokga settles back in his chair, his smirk transforming into a slow grin spreading across his face. "Aside from being very nice, I'm also terribly funny. Perhaps you'd like to take that into account," he says with an indolent wave toward the Red Thread of Fate. "I'm told I have many other pleasing traits, too. I can gather and organize them into a list, if you'd like." It seems to be the sort of thing that Yoo Kisa might appreciate.

"Humility clearly isn't one of them," Kisa replies before her eyes widen and she hastily raises her mug to her lips, cleverly hiding her face, which Seokga has seen is burning blue.

—cannot believe—I said that—it's like I—know him already—shouldn't feel comfortable—

A startled burst of laughter erupts from Seokga's lips. The weary barista behind the counter practically gapes at the trickster god as he laughs, one hand on his stomach. That statement was so *Hani*.

"Please don't smite me," Kisa murmurs into her cup, but she's smiling again.

"Smiting people takes too much energy."

—"smiting"—that reminds me—need to ask—can't not ask—

"Speaking of smiting," she begins, and he's coming to recognize that thread of eager curiosity in her voice as an insatiable thirst for knowledge, "do you recall the exact number of Unrulies you killed during your penance on Iseung? There's so much speculation—"

"I lost count around thirty thousand." Seokga folds his arms and tries his best to look Very Cool and extremely worthy of the red thread currently shaking (like it's laughing at him) around their pinky fingers.

Her brows furrow. "I thought your penance was only twenty thousand?"

Shit.

Seokga now finds himself desiring a speedy exit where he can suffer through humiliation properly in peace. He shrugs, a bit awkwardly, and finishes off his coffee. Kisa is quiet, face thoughtful as she traces words in the table's wood. There's still a hint of a smile on her face, a wry one this time.

"I'll see you tomorrow?" Seokga asks as he stands, not wanting to push her, or come off as a creepy, obsessed stalker even though—admittedly—that's how he feels.

Kisa hesitates. "You're going to contact the CEO, right?"

"Yes." A twist of guilt. "I will. I swear on Hwanung. I'll do it right now—" He takes out his phone, and with difficulty (he is exceptionally bad at typing on touch screens) sends the god a quick message.

She stands, too. "Then, um, if you wanted..." Kisa hesitates, averting her eyes to the thread between them. "At night, on Decks 9 and 10, if you look at the river, you can see ineo swimming along the boat. Well," she amends, "dead ineo. Ineo gwisin. But I like to go up at night, to watch. If you wanted to come with me, I wouldn't mind."

Seokga feels his brows raise. Ineo, mermaids, are notoriously rare in the world above, having been hunted by sailors for their scales. It makes sense that there would be an abundance here... But it's not the prospect of seeing them that has him fighting back a grin. Kisa wants to spend more time with him. "I'd love that," he says honestly, and when her eyes light up, he nearly falls to his knees.

Deck 10 is the highest point on the ship, an expansive sundeck stacked right above Deck 9's pools. As he leans over the metal rail with Kisa, a night wind lashes at his face, carrying the bittersweet smell of the Seocheongang River, which flows with a vengeance. The river is currently bordered by dark, massive mountains—the natural lands of the underworld that Yeomra has not yet developed. Strange sounds echo from those mountains, and once in a while, there will be the sound of beating wings far up above. Seokga is not worried. Whatever demons lurk in this realm, they know better than to provoke Yeomra's wrath, lest their lands be plagued with office buildings and then polluted with the thick yet invisible smog of corporate workers' miseries.

Kisa's curls are whipping in the air, and she's smiling—smiling so widely, and so happily that Seokga's heart stumbles—as she points to something in the water below. "There!" she cries, and—to Seokga's pure joy—tugs on his sleeve. Suddenly, the jondaemal doesn't seem so cold. Not as she nearly hops up and down, loose curls bouncing in excitement. "Do you see her?"

—always wanted—learn—about them—nearly extinct—conservation efforts not nearly—

He doesn't bother to look at the water. He's looking at her, at the way she becomes a bundle of excitement when she's learning something new.

—I hope he—realizes—how wonderful—this is—

Kisa, glancing his way, frowns slightly. Her nose scrunches. "Seokga," she says breathlessly, "you have to *look*—she's marvelous—" Her gaze catches on something over his shoulder, and her face briefly flashes with pity before she turns back to the river. Seokga barely notices, so urgent are her demands for him to lean over the rail and stare down into the currents.

The corner of his mouth twitching, he humors her request and stares into the scarlet depths below where an ineo keeps pace with the SRC *Flatliner*. She's long and lean, dark tail lashing through the air as she dives and surfaces. Her long, inky hair is crusted with barnacles. As if sensing their stares, she glances up at them for a split second with a pale face and glittering black eyes. Thin lips stretch to reveal pike's teeth before she dives back into the water.

Seokga tightens his grip on his cane, feeling strangely wary. That smile was, if he is being quite honest and lets go of his massive ego, quite terrifying.

Kisa's mouth is agape. "They've never looked at me before," she breathes. "That was—"

"—disgusting," Seokga offers. Back when ineo on Iseung were common, they weren't nearly as terrifying. The waters of the underworld must do something to them.

"—*magical*," Kisa finishes, glaring at him.

"She was severely lacking in dental hygiene," Seokga mutters. Kisa rolls her eyes—and he freezes. *That*—that, too, is so completely Hani, down to the exact fluttering of the lashes. It nearly kills him. *Perhaps,* he thinks, heartbeat accelerating, *perhaps the ship isn't a completely different ship.*

Kisa pushes off the rail, shooting him a curious look—and he knows she heard that.

His throat dries out.

"I didn't ask you that question to torture you," Kisa says hesitantly, as they step into the stairwell, feet melting into the velvet carpet. "I really didn't mean—I wasn't think—" She cuts off a moment later, stumbling back into him, gasping so sharply that Seokga grabs her, spins her around, and frantically checks her small body for any signs of injury, any—any—

It happens so quickly that Seokga does not have time to realize that it is a hilt of a dagger—a scarlet dagger—before she is gripping his hand in hers and dragging the tip of the blade downward to her chest.

Hani guides the dagger they both hold through her heart.

"Hani," he whispers, feeling sick, before he can stop himself. "Hani—"

Kisa flinches, but he barely notices, for he's finally examined her face. It's so pale, and her eyes are brimming with tears and panic. "Seokga," she says in a wavering voice, "Seokga, I-I'm fine, but he's—*he's*—"

Slow, cold realization trickles through the god. Heart sinking in his chest, Seokga gently moves Kisa aside, not knowing whether he really wants to look, knowing that this will change *everything* . . .

On the stairs below them, Emperor Hwanin's body is crumpled face down. His expensive hanbok is soaked through with blood, rich, thick, warm blood that permeates the stairwell with its horrible smell. There's a keening sound, a low wailing, and Seokga does not realize it is coming from his own mouth as he rushes to his brother, flips him over . . .

And turns away, retching, tears sliding down his cheeks.

Hwanin's heart has been torn out of his chest.

His brother is dead.

CHAPTER ELEVEN

SEOKGA

His brother, with whom he laughed and fought. His brother in blood and also once in arms, before the favoritism from their father and Seokga's jealousy, before the coup. Hwanin, who Seokga had looked up to, who he had *idolized* in the very early years of his life. Seokga walked because Hwanin could, and if Hwanin could, that meant he could, too. Seokga learned his favorite curse words from his older brother, during the hours spent giggling together behind their father's throne. It was Hwanin who taught Seokga how to pet the wild bulgae, the dogs of stardust and sunlight. *You have to let them sniff you first,* the older boy had whispered encouragingly. *Go on, reach out your hand.*

His brother, who loved him even through the years of bitter envy, who still reached out a hand to the one that bit him, over and over.

"Why?" Seokga had snapped one night when Hwanin had ventured into his room at Cheonha Palace. It was right after Seokga had shaved off Hwanin's eyebrows, hoping that if his brother looked hilarious enough, their father's attentions might shift to him. Yet it was still before Hwanin somehow turned shaved eyebrows into a trend around Okhwang. He knew his brother was hurt and angry, but still he stood in the doorway, hands clenched uncertainly around a tray of food from the kitchens. Fluffy white rice and sokkoritang. Seokga had missed dinner in favor of curling up on his bed, ridden with a humiliating mixture of shame, anger, self-hatred, and above all a terrible jealousy. "*Why* do you keep *forgiving* me?" His voice was hard with rage yet weak with bitter resentment that could not find a strong enough flaw in Hwanin to cling to.

The crown prince seemed to attempt a sage expression. Without eyebrows, it did not work. Actually, it looked rather disturbing and would haunt Seokga's nightmares in the years to come. "Because you're my brother," he replied softly. "If we do not have each other, Seokga, who do we have?"

Seokga knows the answer now.

Nobody. They have *nobody*.

"I'm sorry, Hwanin," Seokga weeps. "I'm so sorry—"

Something in the air shifts. Some hidden force that spirals and curls around the small landing, brushing against the walls and bringing with it the indescribable scent of *change*.

A moment later, the heavens sing and a naked baby plops into Seokga's arms.

The baby has dark blue eyes flecked with stars, a tuft of black hair not yet dyed silver, and a gurgling, self-satisfied smile as he stares up at Seokga.

Seokga's wailing abruptly stops.

He stares down at the baby.

The baby stares back.

"Oh, for *fuck's sake*," the trickster swears. "You have got to be kidding me."

"*Grrmurgrrmur*," babbles the baby toothlessly, shifting in Seokga's arms to better grab his own tiny foot and stare at it in amazed delight. "*Brrrbrrrmmbrrrm!*"

Fucking deity reincarnation. Seokga blinks away his tears and sighs in extreme annoyance.

"Seokga—" He turns to see Kisa, who's still staring at Hwanin's body, eyes filled with tears. Seokga glares at the corpse as the baby's chubby hand swats at his cheek.

"Here," he says, passing the baby into Kisa's arms. Her mouth falls open, but she handles the baby expertly as Seokga—ignoring the ensuing twinge of pain in his right leg—drops down to crouch near Hwanin's body.

"You *idiot*," he snaps, all hints of grief forgotten. "You just had to get yourself killed, didn't you? You just *had* to land me with babysitting duty for the next eternity? I hate you. I hate you *so much*."

The baby makes inane baby noises as Kisa, nestling him close, gasps softly. Turning back to her, Seokga watches as her expression of horror shifts into hungry curiosity, to sharp realization, and, finally, something almost like delight. It vanishes a moment later as she, looking somewhat guilty, reverts to sadness.

Under any other circumstance, Seokga would be laughing.

"Godly reincarnation," she whispers, as if reciting from a textbook. "Only an eoduksini can truly kill a god. If a god is murdered by any other means, or has aged enough that they require a new body, their soul will find its way to jeolmeojineunsaemmul, the spring of eternal youth. The god will be reincarnated into its baby form . . ."

". . . and return to where they were last," Seokga mutters, quite embarrassed to have put on such a show only to be reminded that he'll never truly be rid of his brother. The feeling in his chest is certainly not relief, he tells himself sternly. Not at all. "You're currently holding baby Hwanin, Kisa."

Baby Hwanin burps and delightedly claps his tiny hands.

"Why would anyone kill him?" Kisa whispers as Seokga crouches over his brother's corpse, examining the messy cavity where his heart should be. She's soothing the little boy, bouncing him on one hip with such expertise that Seokga suspiciously—jealously—wonders if she's *had* a child. Baby Hwanin, the colicky thing, snuggles closer to her chest and yawns gigantically.

"*Mmmmahhhhh*," sighs the baby, who is his brother but not really, having lost all of his memories and the tiny intellect he had to start with.

"Hwanin had the unique capability to annoy many people," Seokga mutters. It has been years since he was a detective of any kind, but even now, he can feel himself slipping back into the role. His annoyance at Hwanin is fading, replaced by a cold, simmering anger.

Somebody on this ship murdered his brother, and shoved him into the role of babysitter.

Seokga is *not happy*. At all.

"They moved him," he says, standing with help from his cane. "Somebody moved him here so that I would find him. There's no sign of any struggle, and the floor is relatively clean. There should be significantly more blood around him than there is." Seokga stares at the gore, the ruined flesh. Hwanin was powerful and physically strong. It would take a beast to put him down. "Without a coroner or a forensic pathologist"—Seokga thinks of Lee Dok-hyun with a familiar guilty pang—"I can't place the exact time of death—"

"—but it's quite obvious that it was between approximately seven-thirty and eight forty-five," Kisa finishes, eyes narrowing thoughtfully, checking a thin silver watch on her wrist. "After he left the greenhouse party, and sometime before now. That's a window of over an hour..."

"...on an extremely large boat, with an extremely large number of guests." Seokga sneers. "But that doesn't matter. I have a rather solid suspicion of who did this." With one last look at his brother's body, he continues down the stairs.

"Wait—" Kisa pants. "You're not going to just leave him there, are you? Shouldn't we do something? A-a funeral? A... *something?*"

—his brother—shouldn't just—his body—all that blood—

"You're holding him," he returns through clenched teeth. "Hwanin is fine. He's a baby, but fine. Him as an infant might actually be a nice fucking change. No more of that holier-than-thou act for once, since he can't *talk*. And his body will disintegrate in a few minutes. Probably into fucking glitter," he mutters.

"*Gnggblahberp,*" sings the infant (tauntingly, Seokga thinks).

"Be quiet," snaps Seokga.

Baby Hwanin sticks out his tongue and blows a happy raspberry.

"I really feel like you're not taking this as seriously as you should," Kisa pushes. "Somebody murdered the emperor of the gods. That's—that's the worst thing you could possibly do. It's sacrilege."

"I've tried it myself more than once." Seokga reaches Deck 8's landing, shoves open the door, and strides through. "A delightful pastime. I had a natural predilection for it."

Kisa makes a small choking sound. He is forty percent sure it is another hidden, smothered sign of amusement. The other sixty percent of him is certain she's actually horrified. Perhaps he's one hundred percent sure she's feeling a combination of the two.

"His chest was ripped open by claws," Seokga continues, leaning heavily on his cane as he increases his pace. "I've seen enough wounds made by fucking Unrulies to tell. Claws lack the precision of a knife. The edges were too jagged. And what creature has claws?"

—*nine-tailed—foxes—*

"You think Nam Somi did this." Kisa hurries to catch up with him, holding baby Hwanin tight. "The gumiho."

—*so quick—to accuse her—*

"Who else would fucking do it?" he snarls, and when she cringes away, he also winces. He shouldn't have snapped like that. He needs to get himself under control. Now.

"No," Kisa says firmly, apparently having heard his thoughts. "No, it's all right. Your brother was just, er, turned into a baby. Murdered. But—what motive?"

"Nam Somi is a murderer," he grits out. "I know of her terrible deeds . . ." Somi is the only gumiho in existence to have figured out a quicker way to steal souls, the only gumiho to have become a mass murderer in so short a time during the Dark Days.

"I'm not saying that isn't true," Kisa admits, and Seokga's mind is flooded with her rapid musings, so fast that he can barely track them. Luckily, those rapid fragments are collected and neatly arranged into coherence for her next sentence. "She stopped by the sick bay earlier today and quite literally admitted to being a serial killer, but her bone to pick seemed to be with, well, *you*. And . . . historically, assassinations of leaders tend to have some political aim. Lincoln. Doumer. Rabin. Even as far back as Rimush of Akkad. That's something we really do need to consider."

Seokga has no idea who any of those people are. To be frank, he doesn't quite care.

Kisa follows him as he stomps past the greenhouse, where the party has hesitantly begun again. Officer Korain is by the window, watching the trickster god with folded arms and a furious expression. Kisa gives him a nervous wave. "Seokga, I really do think we should tell security. We need to check the security cameras, find out where the murder took place—and by who—before we jump to any conclusions."

"And let it get back to the pantheon that Hwanin was murdered on a ship that, coincidentally, *I* was on? No." Seokga sharply turns into the corridor of suites. "Once news of Hwanin's death breaks, his son, Hwanung, will officially ascend to the throne as interim emperor until his father reaches maturity. Hwanung doesn't like me and will probably throw me from Okhwang again. I'd be the number one suspect amongst the pantheon. So we absolutely *cannot* tell them until we've found the perpetrator." He strides up to a door.

"Is that Somi's room?" hisses Kisa. "Seokga—"

"No," he replies, "but I plan on knocking each door down until I find her." He pulls his hand back, fully prepared to make a ruckus until the gumiho shows herself.

"No need," a familiar voice snorts. "I'm right behind you."

CHAPTER TWELVE

KISA

Nam Somi looks bored as she glances between Kisa, Seokga, and the babbling Hwanin. "Well," she says, "I see that you two got really busy, really quickly." She takes a step closer to Kisa, staring at the baby. "Aw, *cute*. He has your nose," she says to Seokga, "and her smile."

Kisa swallows hard. Despite her adamance the fox lacks a motive, she has to admit that there is a chance that Somi killed Hwanin. She steps back, hugging the child protectively as Seokga joins her side.

"I didn't kill him," Somi says a moment later underneath the trickster's death glare. The intensity of it frightens Kisa—she's not seen him look at *her* that way before, and never wants to. "But okay, I've been following you two since you came up on Deck 10, where I was..." Somi winces. "Where I was, um... Where I was."

"And we're just supposed to take your word for it?" hisses Seokga, and with a snap, his cane transforms into a sword. "I think not."

"Seokga, no. I think I saw her," Kisa quickly cuts in, remembering what had caught her gaze over Seokga's shoulder. A huddled woman on a sun lounger, crying. "Where exactly on the deck were you?" she asks the other woman.

"On a pool chair," Somi mutters. "One in the corner of the deck."

"And what were you doing?" she tests.

"Sitting."

Kisa waits.

Somi sighs. "I was crying," she admits. "Like this." Glaring at Seokga, she sits on the ground, draws her knees up to her chin, lowers her head, and starts to sniffle. Everything, down to the shaking shoulders, is accurate.

Kisa turns to Seokga, who looks distinctly unamused. "She's telling the truth," she informs him as Hwanin sleepily claws at her shirt. "I saw a woman behind you, covered in shadow. She matches the figure. But why follow us?" She turns to Somi suspiciously.

The gumiho rises to her feet with as much dignity as one can after pretending to cry on the floor to avoid being a murder suspect. Kisa carefully watches her face for flaring nostrils, lip biting, blinking, or nervous perspiration. It's well-documented, after all, that even the best liars have tells—as subtle as they may be. She watches as Somi looks at her and notes how her face crumples for a moment. (Grief? Guilt? A combination of the two, mixed with something else, like love gone sour?)

"I went up to Deck 10 after the greenhouse to be alone," she explains. Kisa mentally catalogues her voice—steady but with a wavering edge that seems more due to emotion than anything else. "I don't like it when people see me cry. When you came up, I followed because I wanted a chance to talk to you—alone," Somi adds, glaring at Seokga. "I knew you in your past life, which I'm sure you've figured out by now. We were . . . We worked in . . . You were my . . . That's not the point. I'm not sure how much you remember, but there are some things that I wanted to say, um, sorry for." Her eyes grow glassy. "Obviously, I didn't get a chance because of the *dead body* that *I did not murder*. Also..." Somi crosses her arms. "I don't recommend that you dive into this murder investigation with Seokga. For one, he's a shitty detective. Last time, he never even suspected me—or Hyun-tae—before the Dark Days began."

"Who?" asks Kisa, frowning—was Hyun-tae the name of the eoduksini's host body? Its anonymity has been preserved for years. How was Nam Somi involved in the Dark Days?—but Somi plows on.

"For another, the last time you got involved with him on a case, you got yourself killed."

"I'm ... already dead."

"And, by the way..." Somi clears her throat, ignoring Kisa's matter-of-fact statement. Perhaps if she says it enough, it won't bother her anymore. "It couldn't have been me anyway. I don't have claws," she says very quietly. "Not long enough to murder anyone." Eyes averted, she holds up her hands. *Snikt.* Kisa's heart falls as the dark stubs, the ragged edges, protrude from between the gumiho's knuckles as if somebody had taken a blade and...

A long silence follows.

Seokga slowly sets down his sword and reverts it into a cane. When Kisa looks at him, his face is emotionless, but his thoughts are almost resignedly pitying.

—*looks—painful—not—to dig out—heart—can't—be—suspect—how did she—die—shouldn't have said—in greenhouse—still—hate her*—

Kisa takes a careful step toward the gumiho, after gently depositing Hwanin into a reluctant Seokga's arms. To her exasperation, he does not look thrilled, and holds Hwanin at an arm's length. "Can I see?" she asks softly. "I'm a doctor," she reminds Somi as she hesitates. After another long moment, Somi gives Kisa her hands. The gumiho's face is full of shame. "How did this happen?"

Somi shakes her head. "I don't want to talk about it."

Kisa can respect that. "Okay," she murmurs and bends closer to the ruined claws. Gumiho anatomy. She rummages around in the shelves of her mind before finding the information she needs, tucked away under her first semester at NSUMD.

> Gumiho claws differ slightly from the claws of a regular fox in length and sharpness. However, like the typical *Vulpes vulpes,* gumiho claws are keratinized modifications of the epidermis and will take, in the case of traumatic breakage or removal, an extended amount of time to grow back. For gumiho with broken claws, a practicing physician may administer a smoothing salve that will round jagged edges and decrease the chances of accidental harm befalling the gumiho from their own appendages. There is not much else to be done but wait for the claws to heal themselves ...

Somi's hands tremble as Kisa looks up at her. "There's a salve I can make," she offers, releasing her hands. "It'll round out the edges so you don't hurt yourself."

"What's the point? We're all dead here." The claws disappear, and Somi shakes her head as Kisa attempts to explain that yes, they're dead, but she's carried wounds into the afterlife and it really is imperative to treat them for the benefit of the soul's health. "I'm going to help you find whoever killed Hwanin," Somi interrupts. "Like I said, Seokga is a *really* bad detective. And—" She glances up at Kisa's eyes, glances away. "It's the least I can do."

"Absolutely not," sneers Seokga, but Kisa turns to him with a sharp frown, wishing the trickster god could see—as she does—how extraordinarily beneficial this could be. Somi is, after all, a former serial killer. What better consult to have on the case? She watches in satisfaction as the god pauses, takes a good look at her pointed expression, and sighs. "Fine," he grinds out, nostrils flaring. "But one wrong move, Somi, and I'll—" He cuts himself off as Kisa's eyes narrow even further in warning.

Satisfied with his silence, she turns back to Somi. Kisa isn't entirely sure what Somi did to her in her past life, but from what she's been able to decipher, there was friendship—and then a betrayal that somehow played into the Dark Days.

When she'd been a child at the academy, Kisa had harbored a morbid fascination with the Dark Days of 1992, spending hours in the haunted library poring over articles and the heavy novels that had been written since while the resident gwisin read over her shoulder.

Gods, what Kisa would give to be a library ghost.

Not much was known by the general public about what, exactly, had happened. Seokga was notorious for refusing interviews left and right. All that's known is Seokga and his gumiho companion defeated an eoduksini. Nam Somi isn't mentioned anywhere. Perhaps Somi expects Kisa to despise her. Seokga certainly does. Yet the emotion of betrayal is so very intricately tied to memory... And when Kisa reaches for Somi in the neatly organized filing cabinets of her mind, there is nothing. A notable absence of anything and everything. Trying to hate her feels like trying to hold the wind—a faint, cool flickering of nothing at all.

Kisa doesn't know Somi save for what she's seen today, aboard the SRC *Flatliner.* She's not at all sure what Hani would say, but Kisa *isn't* Hani—a fact that she suspects Seokga is becoming increasingly disappointed in.

A funny feeling sinks her stomach, but she ignores it as she smiles at the gumiho.

"Thank you," she says, and Somi swallows hard before nodding back.

One diaper change later (the now-empty med bay luckily has a supply), Kisa is more than ready to follow Seokga's rather sneaky plan of slipping into the security den on Deck 2 and going through the tapes (murder mysteries have the potential to be rather fun when you're already dead and can't be murdered again). "Shall we go?" she begins to ask, but in a burst of sound, the clinic doors slam open and the CEO of Jeoseung strides in. His coal-black eyes burn with fury as he looks from Seokga to Hwanin to Kisa.

The CEO is ruthless. Notorious. Kisa has never met him before, but she's heard horror stories from other employees. He's a business titan in Jeoseung, an accomplishment that only comes second to the fact he's the god of death itself.

She stumbles backward in terror, clutching Hwanin close to her chest as Seokga steps protectively in front of her and Somi . . . looks utterly unimpressed. Sweat trickles down Kisa's neck as Yeomra hurls something at Seokga.

A light blue gift bag. Kisa peeks around nervously as Seokga pulls out a set of baby clothes in disdain as Yeomra folds his arms. Kisa forces herself to calm down, to neatly pack away her panic and shove the box into a dark corner. He's not here to toss her into the seven hells. Kisa is a rule-abiding citizen, no matter how much money she stole from ATMs in her past life.

"What the fuck, Seokga?" the CEO finally snaps. "I literally can't believe this. First you text me about whatever you did in the greenhouse, and now"—he points one pale finger to Hwanin, who squirms happily in Kisa's arms—"you've managed to get our holy, heavenly emperor turned back into a baby on *my* ten-deck, state-of-the-art ship." He pulls out a sleek black Samsung. "Yeah, I'm sure the pantheon will love to hear about your colossal fuckup.

How long do you think it will take your nephew to hurl you back down to Iseung? My bet's on five minutes—"

Somi is picking up the baby clothes, tilting the tiny garments left and right. "These are cute," she tells Kisa, ignoring the quarreling gods. But Kisa cannot tear her attention away.

In a flash, Seokga has tossed aside the baby clothes, launched forward, and wrestled the phone out of Yeomra's hand. He slams it to the ground, crushes it under his foot. In a voice that reminds Kisa of a wolf's snarl, he says, "If you were going to call them, you would have already. Why are you here, *cadaver*? Let me guess. Word gets out about this, and it's bad for business. Your investors, the rest of the pantheon, will pull out. Nobody wants to associate with the realm that the emperor was killed in."

Somi is trying to fit a tiny gray hat with cat ears onto Hwanin's head. Kisa suppresses a shudder—cats have always made her sneeze uncontrollably. "Aww, look at his ickle wickle smile," she croons as Kisa turns back to continue watching the two gods with growing wariness. The trickster god versus the death god. It's riveting, but she doesn't like how Yeomra's eyes are glowing like coals.

"Who killed him?" Seokga demands in a low voice. "You know it wasn't me. If you've seen that Hwanin is now"—Kisa meets his eyes as he looks over his shoulder, nodding toward the giggling baby—"very small, surely you saw who killed him. Hmm?" Shivers roll down Kisa's spine. The trickster, she's noticed, speaks to everyone but her in a tone cold enough to grow icicles. "Or is it another case of, 'I don't know'? Like how you somehow completely fucking *missed* an eoduksini slipping into a jeoseung saja skin thirty-three years ago?"

Yeomra grimaces, shoving Seokga off him. Kisa has an inkling that Seokga has let himself be shoved. He's much taller than the death god. Despite his slender build, Seokga has broader shoulders, muscled arms, legs she suspects are just as toned under his pants, and a palpable aura of violence. Not that she endorses violence, but... Kisa's mouth dries out and she immediately flushes in embarrassment as she realizes her gaze has drifted down to Seokga's bum. She's studied anatomy for years, and she has to admit that the god's posterior really is spectacularly formed.

Stop staring at his bum, she tells herself. *Stop it. There are important things going on and besides, you've only just met him.*

"Heh," Yeomra is saying. "Heh. Well. Funny you should bring that up."

"Hwanin's *tits,* Yeomra," Seokga snaps, and then grimaces. "I mean—"

"Can't use that one anymore," Somi snickers, tickling Hwanin's tummy. He squeals and kicks his feet.

Yeomra sighs, glancing at Hwanin. Kisa takes a step back protectively, and the CEO rolls his eyes. "Okay, fine. Yes. I was distracted. Usually, I can see every concerning event that happens in my realm—the eoduksini thing was a *fluke,* Seokga—but I was distracted. With a very beautiful demon, I might add."

"Funny," sneers Seokga, and it's truly jarring how he's been so very kind to Kisa tonight and so incredibly rude to everyone else. "That was your excuse last time."

—fucking—inept—can't do—one job—want—slap him—

Kisa winces at Seokga's barrage of heated thoughts, like furiously snapping vipers.

"She's very demanding." He rubs the back of his neck. "This looks bad. For me, specifically. Twice now, something like this has happened under my eye. So, uh, here's the deal."

"Oh, goody," the trickster god drawls. "Another fucking bargain. That's how it always starts, doesn't it?"

The other deity ignores him. "Cover this up. I mean—" Yeomra shrivels underneath Seokga's gaze. Kisa feels a thrum of awe at the sheer power Seokga holds in one withering glare. Do all the gods fear him? "Find the murderer. Quickly, before the cruise ends. Don't let any staff know."

Surely she's misheard him. "Why?" demands Kisa, somehow finding her voice for the sheer foolishness of it all. "Aren't they—we—to report to you?"

Yeomra's eyes don't even dart her way, but she still shivers, suddenly regretting her outburst as he scowls. "Because," he says, like she's a very unintelligent child (and it rankles—Kisa can take many insults, but insults against her intellect cut deep), "usual protocol doesn't apply to this. The emperor was murdered. Do you think they'll call me when there's an emergency button to contact Okhwang directly? Fucking stipulations," he adds. "I didn't want that button. But Hwanin insisted.

"Once you've got the murderer, let me know and I'll descend very dramatically, like this was the plan all along, and deliver divine justice. In the meantime, I'll keep quiet." It's only then that Yeomra actually seems to look at Kisa for the first time since storming into her sick bay. He does a double take, something strange flashing over his face. He seems to be staring in growing confusion at her eyes. "You work here?"

Kisa grits her teeth. "I have for the past seven years," she informs her employer, resisting the urge to stalk over and stomp on his foot like an immature child.

The death god tilts his head, considering her. He looks at Seokga, and then back at her.

"Is this—" He gestures to her eyes.

"Yes," Seokga grits out.

"Shit." Yeomra falters. "I didn't know. I would have called you."

The trickster god makes a noise halfway between a scoff and a snarl.

"Look, Seokga." Yeomra is rubbing the back of his head a little ruefully. "I'll, ah, toss in something nice for her. A show of good faith." Kisa watches intently as he turns back to the scowling god. "Solve this and she'll be released from her duty on this ship. I'll write her name down on the reincarnation queue."

Kisa gasps softly as her heart begins to pound. *Reincarnation queue.* She's waited nearly a decade for those two words and hearing them has sent her into a state of jubilant shock. Lost in a daze of excitement and hope, she doesn't see how Seokga stiffens, knuckles suddenly shining around the hilt of his cane.

"And Hajun's name?" Kisa blurts before she can stop herself.

The look that Yeomra gives her is ripe with disbelief. "What?"

She forces herself to look him in the eye and refuses to retreat. "My friend," she says quietly. "If we solve this mystery, I'd like for his name to be written down, as well."

Yeomra's upper lip curls into a sneer. "Are you seriously trying to *negotiate?*"

"I, erm—yes," she manages to push out with absolute finality. "Yes, I am."

For a long moment, the CEO stares at her. Stubbornly, Kisa stares back. She can go long bouts without blinking, and refuses to yield until Yeomra's eyes twitch.

Finally, the death god scowls. "Fine," he relents. His gaze shifts back to Seokga. "But if you fail, I will absolutely be speed-dialing Hwanung and trying to place all the blame on you. Capisce? Great." Yeomra backs toward the door, smiling nervously. "Use your mind-reading powers. I'm sure the mystery will be solved in no time."

Kisa exhales in relief. Of course. Seokga, being the trickster deity, has an array of sneaky powers including teleportation, illusion-crafting, shape-shifting, and reading the minds of creatures. She's always wondered what it would be like to have a patron other than Samsin Halmoni—not that, of course, she didn't love her goddess and the healing powers that had come with her patronage when she was alive. But watching the Seokga shamans had always been so very fun. They seemed to have an affinity for shifting into birds and, well, shitting on the Hwanin shamans' heads.

But as her eyes slide to Seokga's wincing expression, her relief turns to anxiety. "Seokga?" she urges quietly. "You *can* read minds, can't you?"

"I've been having some trouble with that," he mutters.

Yeomra freezes near the doors. "I'm sorry. What?"

Seokga sneers, but not at Kisa. "I have been—according to the wise Dr. Jang—extremely stressed." His mouth twists. "It's affected that power. I can't reach it. Stop gaping, Yeomra. You look like a dying fish."

Kisa watches as the death deity's mouth drops open before he abruptly shuts it. "I am going to leave before I have a mental breakdown," he says slowly. "When I come back, at the end of the cruise, you'd better have found the murderer. Mind-reading powers or no. And keep our esteemed heavenly emperor safe, please. I would, but I'm probably even worse with infants than you are. A demon might eat him." In a burst of black smoke, Yeomra is gone.

The doors suddenly swing open, and Hajun stands in his place, waving the smoke away from his face. Kisa winces as her friend's eyes shoot straight to the baby before his head whips to Seokga.

"I—who—how—when?" Hajun gasps. "Kisa? The baby? Did you—"

"Congratulations," Seokga snarks in a biting tone. "You're a godfather."

For the love of the gods . . . Hajun looks as if he might faint.

"No, I did not birth him in the time since you last saw me," Kisa replies firmly, setting Hwanin down on a nearby cot and wrangling the squirming baby into the tiny shirt and pants. Hwanin, it seems, does not want to wear any clothing besides his cat hat and diaper. Finally successful, she turns to a bewildered Hajun, excited to tell him the news. They might be free of the *Flatliner* sooner than either of them ever thought possible. "How do you feel about helping us catch a killer?"

CHAPTER THIRTEEN

SEOKGA

"Make him stop this ridiculous babbling," Seokga hisses as the four of them—one god, one shaman, one gumiho, and one supposed K-pop idol whose hair rivals Seokga's own (fucking idols, they've basically replaced the pantheon, stealing their worshippers)—creep through the SRC *Flatliner*'s shadowy second level, where the security room is tucked away at the end of the corridor's corner. At this time of night, Kisa has promised that Officer Shin Korain will be on Deck 8's bridge with the watch, ensuring the currents remain stable and no demons swoop in to attack while the captain is asleep. Korain is, apparently, the most capable security officer on board. The others aren't even haetae, but bored souls who were dropped down into the security den because they were extremely bad at cleaning staterooms. "This is a stealth mission."

"*Eeeegreeek!*" Baby Hwanin gurgles in Kisa's arms.

Seokga cannot wait for him to regain both his adult body and memories so he can *deck* him. How—how does an all-powerful emperor get himself killed? Save for one, his natural powers were even more impressive than Seokga's own: control over the heavens (Hwanin had liked to ruin Seokga's good mood by turning a stormy sky sunny), the generation of a heavenly light that he insisted on using for dramatic entrances, the ability to fly, and—most bewilderingly—the capability to shape-shift into either a cloud or a star. And like all gods, Hwanin had also been able to teleport.

But Hwanin's *true* power had come from the throne on which he sat. The throne in Cheonha Palace gifted Hwanin with abilities that no other god shared, and influence over the other deities to an unholy extent. The catch, of course, was that Hwanin had to be sitting on, or at least near, the throne to do things such as cross into other gods' jurisdictions (like reincarnating Hani the first time around), play with time, grant immortality, astral project ... The list goes on and on and *on*.

The security room's iron door looms into view as they round the corner, its one small square window giving nothing away. The lighting on Deck 2 is nothing like the warm, expansive glow above: It's hard and roughly contours anybody unlucky enough to be below. Glancing behind him at his companions, Seokga initiates a series of silent, quick signals using his hands. He does it very skillfully, he thinks, and the quick, capable motions from his days of Unruly-hunting are sure to impress Kisa.

She nods with a wise expression as if she knows exactly what he means, but a moment later her thoughts betray her.

—*why—hands flapping—like—pigeons—*

The red thread, winding past Hajun, shakes like it's fucking giggling. At Seokga's offended, but amused, expression, Kisa flushes blue.

"Here," Somi whispers at the back of their line. "I'll create a distraction. When they run out, you can run in."

Seokga narrows his eyes. The gumiho has come a long way from the timid girl she once was ... and despite everything she's claimed, he still doesn't trust her.

Somi crooks a finger at Hajun. "I'll need to borrow you," she whispers.

The boy's eyes widen. "Me?" he whispers, cheeks flushing a light blue that seems equally pleased and scared.

"Yes, you." Somi grabs his shirt, bunches it in her fingers. "Unless you're too *frightened?*"

"I, um, I, um . . ." Hajun straightens, staring down at a smiling Somi. "I'm not frightened at all."

Seokga, sensing that it will be best for him and Kisa to keep out of the way, steps back around the corner and gently tugs Kisa with him. His heart flutters as he touches her, and as she stands with her back to him, nearly against him. Seokga hears her breathing hitch, and a moment later she's turning around so she faces him directly. Seokga's stomach sinks as he realizes she's gone a bit pale.

Does she not want him to touch her? He won't, if that's the case, but it hurts all the same.

"It's . . ." she murmurs as around the corner, Somi whispers something to Hajun. "It's not . . . that. I just prefer not to have people directly behind me, if I can help it. An odd quirk, I suppose." He would look away in embarrassment, but she's worrying her lower lip and he's fixated.

The unmistakable sound of a door crashing open hits him in full force. There are a few gruff cries of startlement, and then Somi's voice, slurring slightly. "Oh, sorryyyyy," she sings. "I thought this was our rooooom!" And there's another unmistakable sound: this one of a sloppy kiss.

Kisa's eyes widen, and her mouth drops open. Seokga can't hold back a snicker of his own as Kisa begins to giggle. Hwanin grins up at the trickster as he laughs, and Seokga reluctantly gives the baby something that's not quite a scowl. His brother is delighted, grabbing his own foot and shaking it excitedly as Seokga rolls his eyes. Kisa's smile grows as she adjusts her grip on him. She really is so natural with him, and Seokga once again wonders how.

"Oh," Hajun says hoarsely, sounding incredibly dazed and therefore entirely drunk as well. "Oh, wow... That was... I've never... Um..."

"I've always wanted to dooo it in public," comes Somi's response, and Kisa loses it. Seokga can hardly breathe as she covers her mouth with her hand and laughs, eyes pinching in the corners from the effort of smothering the soft, gentle peals. And he can tell, even with Kisa's hand muffling the sparkling chimes, that her laugh is *Hani's* laugh, as much as her eye roll was. "Do you mind if weee take your chair? Pleeeaaase?"

"No! Get out!" A struggle ensues, and less than thirty seconds later, footsteps are pounding out of the security office and down the hall, echoing through the mostly empty corridor.

"Let's go," whispers Seokga (although part of him would like to stay in the hallway and listen to Kisa laugh forever) and together, they slip into the now-abandoned room, shut the door, and lock it. The large room is plain except for the fact that it's filled with dozens of monitors, footage from dozens of locations on the SRC *Flatliner* feeding onto the screens.

Seokga stares in bafflement at the many keyboards spanning the long, neat white desks. The most that he has ever managed to do with technology includes, one, operating a cellphone (nowadays, they don't have enough buttons: Seokga's fingers keep slipping on the ever-growing screens) and, two, having once used New Sinsi's nineties technology with passable proficiency (but those days are long gone, and keyboards are not supposed to be this *flat*). Where are the wires? Where are the bulky consoles and fuzzy screens? In the thirty-three years since Seokga has left the New Sinsi haetae precinct behind, technology has morphed into something he has no clue how to operate.

Aware that Kisa is hovering expectantly beside him, Seokga attempts to conceal his complete bewilderment with an expression of absolute capability and sharp intelligence. Hopefully she believes it, and he can manage to figure out how to play back all monitors to previous footage without fumbling too badly.

"I heard that," she half-laughs. His cheeks flame as Kisa slides into one of the rolling chairs and flexes her fingers, having sat Hwanin down carefully on her lap. "I think I can do it. Would you watch the door?"

"I suppose," Seokga grumps, wishing he'd been able to impress Kisa by hacking the mainframe, or whatever the fuck it's called. Reluctantly, and with a profound sense of defeat, he turns to face the door.

Her fingers dance over the keyboard before she clicks something with the mouse and swears under her breath. "The security system is asking for a password," she says over her shoulder. "Unfortunately, I've no idea what it might be."

There's still no sign of Somi or Hajun, nor the security workers, but Seokga isn't fooled. They don't have much time. What, he thinks, would a dick like Yeomra choose as his security system password? "Try Y-e-o-m-r-a," he says. "Or d-e-a-t-h." Yeomra is not high enough in Seokga's esteem for him to believe the death god is capable of imaginative passwords.

"It didn't work."

Seokga grimaces.

"Isn't there any way you can ask him?"

Personally, Seokga would like to avoid interacting with the god in any way he can, but under Kisa's pointed look, he reluctantly tugs his phone out of his pocket.

"Seokga," Kisa whispers impatiently a moment later, bouncing a leg nervously. "What has he said?"

"I'm still typing," he mutters back.

He can practically *hear* her wince, and Seokga turns to glare at her before he can stop himself. She surprises him by glaring right back, cheeks blue with flustered panic.

"Please just hurry up," she hisses, eyes darting nervously to the door.

"I am going as fast as I can," he grits out.

> **Seokga:** whats the pissweee

> **Seokga:** I wasn;t don e sending that

Then, with painstaking slowness:

> **Seokga:** What is the passwoord for securty systm?

> **Seokga:** answer no w

A moment later, his phone vibrates and he nearly drops it on the ground.

"Ultimatevacationcruiseship2235," Seokga reads before shoving the damned thing into his pocket. Kisa nods and—quicker than he would ever have thought possible—enters the password. "Playback button," she muses, staring intently up at the monitor. "Playback button . . . here." There's a quick click, and then the screens are shifting, the strolling people on them moving backward. A second later, there's a sharp knock on the door.

"It's us," Hajun calls, sounding breathless.

Reluctantly, Seokga lets them in. Somi is grinning.

"We led them on a wild chase," she says. Her usually immaculate bob is mussed and her eyes are bright. "They're somewhere on the upper decks, convinced we're hiding around any corner.

Isn't that right, *honey*?" She bats her eyelids at the idol, who blushes blue and grins while ruefully rubbing the back of his neck.

"Nicely done," Seokga grudgingly admits.

"I learned from the best." Somi glances over to Kisa, smile falling when she doesn't look back and share the grin. Instead, Kisa is staring up at the screens,

"We ran all over the ship," Hajun pants, laughter in his voice. "I mean, *all of it*. We found a karaoke bar—I didn't even know we had one here."

"And a candy store," Somi adds, and elbows Hajun conspiratorially. The boy snorts as he reaches into the pocket of his scrubs and pulls out a handful of wrapped sweets. The white-on-red font reads KOPIKO.

"Here," Hajun says, and tosses them to Seokga. "She says you'll like them."

He closes his fist around the candies in disdain. "Doubtful." Seokga loathes mortal sweets. He prepares to toss them in the garbage.

"It's coffee-flavored," Hajun tells him with a knowing smile before walking over to stand behind Kisa with a casual, gentle hand on her shoulder before she noticeably tenses and he, with a distinctly apologetic cringe, hurriedly stands off to the side.

Seokga pockets the candy and also moves toward Kisa. The monitors are quickly playing footage in reverse, so quickly that Seokga nearly misses it—but Kisa's sharp eyes catch the flare of white on the upper-left screen. She quickly pauses the others, rewinds, and presses a few buttons that seem to make the footage play normally, at a neutral speed.

Hwanin, in all his towering adult annoying-ness, paces in a corridor with his phone held to his ear. His lips are moving silently, perhaps almost angrily. Seokga leans forward, reminding himself not to stand directly behind Kisa and positioning himself next to her instead.

"I know where this is," she says slowly. "It's part of the I-95 on Deck 0."

"Part of?" Seokga asks carefully.

"Due to its massive length, the rest of the corridor isn't on-camera. He's near the center." Kisa is so focused that her words are absent-minded and perfectly factual. Seokga wishes he had time to admire how her brows pucker and her lips purse when she focuses, but unfortunately, his brother is about to be murdered onscreen.

For a brief, bitter moment, he wonders if he even *wants* to solve this mystery. If solving it means letting go of Kisa so soon, perhaps it's not even worth it. Perhaps he'd *rather* have Hwanung lose his shit and possibly strip him of his godliness once more if it means keeping Kisa close . . .

But Kisa isn't a butterfly that he can keep trapped in a jar for his own amusement. He tries to remind himself of that. A part of him is disgusted that he's even considered sabotaging this bargain. For a moment he wishes that deceit wasn't so very ingrained in his nature, that he didn't have thoughts like these. Dr. Jang has *tried* to weed it out of him, but it's as much part of his nature as his DNA. It composes him.

And as much as he may deny it, Seokga is deeply *furious* at whomever hurt his brother. Nobody is allowed to do that—except him. Never mind that he's been fucking saddled with a drooling baby with chubby cheeks and a button nose. Somebody hurt his older brother. And that somebody wasn't him.

Somebody has killed a god.

And that somebody must be punished.

Seokga leans in farther, watching the tight set of his brother's mouth, the way he drags a hand down his face—the same way that Seokga does when he's tired and irritated. "He's speaking to Hwanung," he realizes. His brother and his nephew often fight. Every month, Seokga will wake up in his own palace to angry shouting literally shaking the heavens and causing him to tumble out of his bed and bonk his head on the hard floor. The indignity of it. And in the hours before both Hwanin and Hwanung exploded, Hwanin's facial expressions would be much like this. Tense, with a certain air of *Why did I have a son, again?*

Baby Hwanin gurgles sleepily, as if in agreement.

"They're arguing," Kisa muses analytically. "Hwanin is agitated. His attention is fully focused on whatever's being said on the call. What was their relationship like?"

"Hwanung is a little shit," Seokga answers, rolling his eyes in great disgust. "Although he did for a while, he now refuses to accept that his occupation is the god of laws and kept promises." In other words, he's the divine equivalent of an angsty teenager. It is baffling to him how the delinquent can possibly have been the founder of the original Sinsi on Mount Taebaek, or the *mayor* of New Sinsi when he can barely remember to do his laundry. "He wants to be the god of sex, drugs, and rock and roll." The only time Hwanung seems to act as a law god is, conveniently, when he is trailing Seokga and attempting to catch him red-handed in wrongdoing. Gone are the days of Hwanung copying his father down to wearing beautiful hanboks even to the simplest occasions. The god now prefers—to both his father's and uncle's dismay—faded T-shirts advertising mortal bands that do little but scream into their microphones.

It's horrific.

Hajun looks surprised. "Can gods change their occupations?" he asks.

"No," snort Seokga and Kisa at the same time. There's an exception, of course, but not just anybody can become heavenly emperor.

Even if they try very hard by, say, instigating a coup.

Kisa hesitates, and as the footage continues to show Hwanin angrily speaking into the phone, she picks up a notebook lying on the table. Seokga watches as she grabs a pen and flips to an empty page, writing down *Hwanung* in smudged, scrawling letters, followed by an almost frantic question mark, the dot nearly puncturing through the paper. Briefly, he remembers Hani's looping font as she scribbled notes on his couch, puzzling over Suk Aeri's frustratingly obscure clue from their Daegeumsan excursion. Kisa's writing, he notes with twists of guilt and disappointment in his gut, is messier. As if her hand is trying, futilely, to keep up with the whitewater river of her mind.

"Interesting," muses Somi, jerking his attention away from Kisa's scrawl. "Do you think the crown prince did it?"

Seokga frowns—but his gaze is immediately drawn back to the screen. Hwanin has pocketed his phone into the folds of his hanbok with a black scowl and is taking a deep breath. Seokga holds one of his own as he watches his brother's gaze slide to somewhere down the corridor . . . and as his eyes flare wide, blue and panicked and dotted with stars.

So rarely has Seokga seen Hwanin panic.

On the monitor, his brother stretches his arms out wide. The time reads 8:32 P.M.

Oh, no. Seokga well knows what follows from such a dramatic pose and curses his brother as a moment later a brilliant, bright white light engulfs the screen. Seokga winces, shying away and wondering why, exactly, Hwanin decided to protect himself against whatever was approaching with a harmless display of light.

Panic, he seethes. Hwanin, the idiot, *panicked.* And in a knee-jerk reflex, he'd released his flashy divine light rather than reaching for one of his more *useful* powers.

What had made a godly emperor like Hwanin panic?

"H-holy *shit,*" breathes Hajun. The light slowly recedes, and there's . . . nothing.

Nobody on the floor. No signs of a struggle. No heavily breathing murderer, splattered with blood.

Just . . . nothing.

The camera flashes white and black before going entirely black.

"As a former mass murderer, if you killed a rather tall man with divine powers," Kisa says to Somi, "and you didn't want to be seen lugging his body around a ship, how would you go about that? Hypothetically, of course," she adds with a hasty glance at a seething Seokga. "It's all *hypothetical.*"

The five of them are on the humid I-95 in the belly of the ship, having exhausted their eyes searching for any clues they might have missed on the monitors. Even after sifting through the other recordings, no new footage of Hwanin has surfaced. But he'd had to have been dragged through the ship, below the dozens of other security cameras. It doesn't make sense.

Nothing about this makes sense.

Somi seems to be smothering a yawn. The gumiho is leaning wearily against Hajun's side. He looks equally wary and shyly pleased. Somi looks as if she views him as a convenient doorpost upon which she can lounge. "I would chop him into little pieces and then put him in my pocket," she replies.

"For fuck's sake," snarls Seokga, in no mood for games. "Answer the question."

Kisa begins to pace. The harsh lighting makes her frown stand out on her small, heart-shaped face and highlights a subtle smattering of freckles across her scrunched nose.

"It's getting late," Hajun says with a frown, arm twitching as if he wants to wrap it around Somi protectively, but doesn't quite have the courage yet. "We're all tired."

Chest tightening, Seokga slams his cane down on the ground. The resounding thud echoes throughout the hall. "We're not done." They won't be until the murderer is found. Preferably by dawn.

"Hajun's right," Kisa quietly argues a moment later. "Hwanin needs to go to bed. And, I think, so do you. We won't solve anything if we're exhausted."

Seokga spares a glance at his tiny brother. He's nestled against Kisa, face pressed into the crook of her neck, asleep and whimpering softly. A flicker of guilt stabs through him. *Oh, brother,* he thinks, suddenly stooped with fatigue. *It's always one thing after another for us.*

"We'll reconvene in the morning," Kisa is saying, rubbing a circle on the baby's back. "Tomorrow, we'll split up. Look for witnesses, return to the stairwell. Figure out a motive. Get some alibis. Hajun and I have shifts in the med bay—you can meet us there." She hesitates. "Until we're sure Hwanin was the only target, we need to be careful. Somebody on board this ship is a murderer. They killed a god. Don't let your guard down, not even for a moment. They can't kill *us,* but you . . ." She glances at Seokga, who grits his teeth. "You have a lot to lose."

"I hope the murderer comes after me," he half-snarls. "It would save us a lot of time and investigation."

Somi laughs at that, walking past them down the I-95. "With your rotten luck," she calls over her shoulder, "I'm sure they won't be striking again tonight. Good night," she adds in a kinder, more hesitant—maybe even shy—tone to Kisa. A few moments later, after a quiet farewell between himself and Kisa, Hajun leaves, as well. Soon, it's just the three of them in the abandoned corridor beneath the mammoth ship.

"You have a way with children," Seokga says carefully as he and Kisa hesitate there, the red thread swirling between them, his baby brother snoring on her shoulder.

Again, there's that wondering. There's so much he doesn't know about Yoo Kisa.

Kisa's shy smile is small and almost sad. "When I was alive, my goddess was Samsin Halmoni. My father's side of the family have been her shamans for centuries. My mother wasn't involved in the Korean pantheon in any way. Although sometimes I wonder if other pantheons exist, if she was connected to the Anglo-Saxon one . . . Have you ever met Woden, perhaps? Or—"

"Samsin Halmoni?" Seokga grinds out. "Did you say *Samsin Halmoni*?"

Kisa blinks. "Yes." She's swaying slightly, soothingly rocking Hwanin. "Her patronage allowed me to heal mothers and deliver their children, as long as they were creatures." A funny expression crosses her face, and her voice becomes pinched. "Only creatures. I wished . . . I wished I could help humans, too. My mother, she, well, she died delivering me. There's a certain irony in that, don't you think?"

"I'm sorry," Seokga says quietly, anger at the goddess banking in the face of Kisa's hesitant vulnerability. He knows the pain of losing a mother well. Although Mago is alive, she has slumbered for near an eternity, lost to her sons.

Kisa gives a funny little shrug and clears her throat. "I became so sick of it—the work, I mean—but I sometimes miss it now. No, I miss my *life*. It's like this . . . sharp longing in my chest. An ache in me that won't go away." She smooths Hwanin's hair away from his sleeping face, a small frown crossing her own. "Although... I suppose it's abated, actually," she murmurs. "With everything that's happened, I suppose it's harder for me to wallow in my own self-pity..." Kisa trails off, lips twitching a bit wryly. Yet Seokga doesn't smile back.

For in her encroaching silence, his anger toward Samsin Halmoni has returned, crawling through his veins with a molten, deadly heat. He inhales thinly through his mouth, struggling to keep his composure so as not to frighten Kisa.

But *fuck*.

Samsin Halmoni, the old bat. It was *her*. She kept Kisa from him all these years, leaving him to find her only when it was too late, when she's dead. A murderous rage tints his vision red. Controlling his fury is now an exercise in futility.

—*looks*—*upset*—*why*—

"Seokga?"

He is going to march right up to Okhwang and give Samsin Halmoni a piece of his mind. He is going to send his shamans on a war against hers. He is going to *explode* as his blood pressure continues to rise and rise and *rise*...

Kisa's face swims into his blurry vision. "Let's get you to your room," she murmurs in concern, and he's acutely aware of how her free hand wraps around his arm, guiding him back up toward Deck 7 after he manages to mutter what suite he's staying in. Room 7345. Kisa makes a quick stop in the sick bay, stuffing some jars from the medicine cabinet into a bag which Seokga carries. He supposes he should carry his brother, but he's much too overwhelmed to tote around a baby. What if he *drops* him? Sure, Seokga has had dozens of children in his long lifetime, but the children aged so fast in comparison to himself that he usually forgot to pop down for a visit until they were at least twenty-five (or forty-seven, maybe even sixty-two).

Babies are foreign entities to him.

He doesn't think he likes them.

At all.

Back in the suite, Kisa sets Hwanin down on a stuffed settee in the adjoining room between the two brothers' suites. Seokga slumps into an armchair in exhaustion.

Kisa looks at him curiously over her shoulder, pausing from fussing over the child. "Something crinkled when you sat down."

"Oh," he mutters, hand drifting to the pocket of his dark pants. Seokga pulls out the candies that Hajun gave him and wrinkles his nose. "These."

She raises her brows. "Have you tried them?"

"Shan't," he says, rather mulishly. "I don't like sweets."

"You seem to like coffee," Kisa points out, sitting down before the fire and rummaging around in her tote bag. "Those will taste like your Americano."

Seokga sighs but unwraps the hard candy anyway. He gives it a tentative sniff while Kisa watches in amusement. Reluctantly, he places it in his mouth.

"See?" she asks with a satisfied expression as Seokga experiences a moment of complete and total euphoria when the taste of coffee explodes on his taste buds. "I told you . . ."

Seokga decides he needs to find the SRC *Flatliner*'s candy store immediately and raid it for more of this magical concoction. He finds himself calming down from his earlier exhaustion and rage as he plays with the wrapper. In its hearth, the fire pops and crackles, illuminating the stray strands of curly hair framing Kisa's face as she takes the jars out of her bag, glancing up at him across the length of the thread.

His tired puzzlement must show on his face. "He needs to eat soon," she explains and Seokga curses himself. Shit. Yes. He'd forgotten that babies have appetites and that, since Hwanin is now a baby, he needs to eat far more often than he did as a god. Kisa pulls out a mortar and pestle, adds the dried flower petals to the earthen bowl.

"Salsarikkot," Seokga says, recognizing the pale golden hue of the flowers. It's one of many flowers from Hallakkungi's flower garden. Its properties are nothing short of impressive: With salsarikkot, flesh can be regrown. It's the flower that reincarnated gods live off, one that aids their growth. Combined with bbyeosarikkot, a flower that brings bones back to life, infant gods will grow strong and healthy once more. The reincarnation flowers are precious, and he watches with interest as Kisa grinds them into a fine paste. "How do you know all of this?" Never has he met a mortal that knows so intimately the secrets of the gods.

Kisa gives him a slightly amused glance as she pours a vial of water into the bowl, thinning the paste to a shimmering liquid and placing the mortar on the edge of the fire where it heats while she stirs it counterclockwise. "Samsin Halmoni," she says, and he grinds his teeth together. "I don't suppose you'll tell me why you seem to hate her so much?"

"No," he says sulkily, not wanting to dwell on it. He finishes the first candy and starts on the next. "I'm sure you'll figure it out."

Hwanin gurgles and he turns his attention to his brother, who has captured one of his own feet in a tiny hand and is staring at it in shock.

Kisa pours the liquid into a small bottle from her bag. "I didn't know if we'd have the flowers," she murmurs, almost to herself. "But the sick bay is so *stocked* . . ."

"Ironic," mutters Seokga, wondering if he should remove the foot from Hwanin's mouth.

"It's only for Restorations," she says with a sigh, and hands the bottle to Seokga. "Not that it's not rewarding, but, well, you can't save anyone if they're already dead. Even these flowers won't change that. Restorations are really only cosmetic at this point. You have to hold him," Kisa says abruptly as Seokga stares in thinly veiled confusion at the bottle. "To feed him." She raises her brows impatiently. "Seokga, really."

—acts like—Hwanin—has rabies—or something—

"I'd rather not," says Seokga, and is immediately bombarded with more impatient thoughts from Kisa, the red thread quivering between them. "Fine," he groans, and with complete indignity, props Hwanin on his lap and administers the drink to him as Kisa watches. Hwanin sucks greedily and drools all over him. Disgusting. "Ew. Please take him back?"

"No." She looks distinctly amused.

Seokga assumes an expression of supreme distaste as Hwanin's drool taints his black cashmere sweater. Kisa sits back on her heels and looks as if she's watching a very entertaining show.

"You and him," she suddenly says as Hwanin makes disgusting little slurping noises. "I take it you weren't close."

Seokga sighs, staring down at the chubby blob in his arms. "We were, and then we weren't. And then we were . . . getting there. Until he went and got his heart ripped out of his chest."

"Yes," says Kisa, looking slightly queasy. "That was unfortunate." She hesitates. "I don't want to, well, exhaust you more than you already have been . . ."

He raises his eyes to hers and thinks that he would gladly be exhausted for her. Hells, he went to *Antarctica* for her and poked around the penguins and fat, snarling seals. Kisa blushes, and he knows the red thread carried that particular thought of his down to her.

"I just," she says, and then frowns. "You went to *Antarctica?*"

"Yes," he grumbles. "It was cold." Too cold, even for him. "There were penguins." *Would you name them, if you saw them?* he wants to ask, but refrains, and waves a languid hand. "Continue."

Kisa blinks, and then clears her throat. "I just want to revisit what I said about most leadership assassinations being political in nature."

Seokga fixes her with an exasperated look as Hwanin continues to drool all over him. "I know my reputation precedes me," he drawls, ignoring the small stinging in his chest, "but I promise you, if I wanted to kill him, I would arrange it so *I* didn't get stuck with babysitting duty. This is the very last thing I ever dreamed of doing."

"No . . ." She looks entirely unimpressed and even slightly annoyed. "I wasn't going to point a finger at you. I was just going to ask if there was any controversial legislation Hwanin had passed recently. That could give us some sort of starting point."

"Oh," says Seokga, attempting to appear nonchalant and not at all jubilant that Kisa trusts him to some small extent. "Well . . ." He thinks back. Most of Okhwang's recent laws are a direct result of *him*. There is, for example, that law forbidding certain gods from duping other gods into extremely elaborate pyramid schemes. Then there's that one prohibiting "pranks of a malicious nature, specifically theatrical re-enactments of coups, no matter how 'innocent' the intent." The latest decree explicitly forbids Seokga from shape-shifting into his brother and forcing the pantheon to arrange surprise parties for a certain trickster god. Unfortunate.

Some deities just don't know how to have fun.

Kisa is watching him suspiciously.

—*he is*—*most certainly*—*hiding*—*something*—

Seokga purses his lips and puts on a good show of thinking very hard. Those recent laws were controversial to *him,* but all the other deities had seemed unanimous in their opinion that they were necessary. "Not really," he says. "Many of the new laws pertain to very small things."

—he likely means—they pertain—to him—

He tries to look grievously offended at her train of thought, but Hwanin burps a moment later and Seokga sets down the bottle. As Kisa tilts her head, apparently lost in thought, Seokga lifts his brother so that the two are eye level. "What am I going to do with you?" he murmurs. "Really, brother. This is embarrassing. For you," he adds as Hwanin smiles a gummy smile and blinks innocently back at him. He rolls his eyes.

"I've never solved a mystery before," Kisa mumbles, almost to herself. "I'm not sure I'll be any good at this." She nibbles on her bottom lip, looking anxious. Seokga softens. He is beginning to get the sense that Kisa is harder on herself than she is on others.

"You're right. It's late," he says, setting Hwanin down to wipe his drool away with his sleeve (a great and terrible sacrifice).

"Right. Yes. Come to the sick bay in the morning," Kisa tells him as she rises and slings her bag back over her shoulder. The jars clatter within. "We can continue on then." She hesitates, and when she speaks again, her voice wavers slightly.

—feel like—owe him—some explanation—

"I've been on this ship since 2018. I was so tired when I died, and I'm tired now . . . All I want, really, is to rest. Just for a little bit."

His gaze pulls up to her, to her eyes glazed slightly with tears, to the haggard lines of her face. Throat suddenly dry and tight, Seokga swallows hard. The taste of coffee in his mouth suddenly turns to sour ash and a heavy mourning pulls at something deep within him. He'll have to let her go. And he will. Gods, he will. For her. For Hani, for the woman she became. For Kisa.

Once this mystery is solved, Kisa leaves. And who knows if he'll be able to find her again.

After thirty-three years, has he found her only to let her go?

Fate's cruel streak never fails to wound him.

His thoughts must seep into her mind, for Kisa blinks rapidly. "Good night," she whispers, and before Seokga can reach for her, she hurries away. The door clicks shut behind her.

Seokga stares at the fire and holds the child close to his chest.

CHAPTER FOURTEEN

KISA

Curled up in her bed in the tiny, windowless cabin she shares with a dozing Hajun, Kisa uses a weak flashlight to write in the notebook she filched from the security room. Her writing is a mess of scribbled words. There is, of course, the suspect list. But so far, only Hwanung's name is written in the blue ink.

She's not working on that right now. Instead, on a different page, Kisa is fervently writing in English: her first language, the one she spoke in England as a child, after her mother's death and her father's grief. He mourned her loss by staying in her London hometown until the memory of her had faded enough for him to return to his birthplace of New Sinsi with his daughter, but without feeling a crushing guilt. His new wife helped with that, too.

Kisa wonders if they miss her—or if her father has dulled her loss by spoiling the children he shares with her stepmother. If he's replaced her, just as he did her mother.

No matter how hard Kisa worked, no matter how much greatness she accomplished, her stepmother never spared her a passing glance. Kisa had wanted very badly to love her, tried to like her, and eventually settled for tolerating the hawk-nose woman. It wasn't that Eunjeong disliked her, exactly—only that she wasn't interested at all in her husband's daughter.

Kisa wonders, not for the first time, what was said at her funeral. Did her father cry? Did her half-sisters mourn the sibling that was always tucked away in an academy or hospital? In a morose sort of way, she wishes she could have been there to see.

She takes a shallow breath. She's gotten distracted.

In English, Kisa writes notes. Notes on the red thread, how it behaves. Observations regarding cerebration transference. The red thread, at times, even seems to have some form of consciousness. She details how it twisted into little hearts between herself and Seokga. How it will shake, sometimes, in what seems like it could be laughter.

Ink smudges her hands as she records the imbalance of emotion between them: how in love Seokga seems with her due to who she was in her past life, a woman she can't remember. Falteringly, she writes of her own attraction to Seokga, as small and hesitant as it is—before hastily scribbling it out. It's ridiculous. They've just met. Kisa went twenty-two years without forming any sort of romantic attachment. If she were to develop a . . . a *crush,* it surely wouldn't be so sudden. Yoo Kisa is *not* a spontaneous person, nor is she a character in one of her favorite romance books. No matter how badly she wishes to be at times.

Seokga is attractive, of course, and there's a . . . lingering sense of familiarity. One that she didn't feel at first, but just might now. He can make her laugh, something that not many—aside from Hajun—can do. It's the kind of familiarity that leads people to say, "It feels as if we've known each other forever, even though we just met" in one of those exhilarating, clinch cover novels. She winces as a pang strikes deep in her heart and rubs it absentmindedly.

And why do you think that familiarity is? a little voice asks sarcastically in her head.

Kisa ignores it. She is *not* going to get distracted. She is *not* going to develop a crush.

They have a bargain with Yeomra. Find the murderer, and she leaves this ship for good. She *lives* again. Kisa is so very sick of being dead.

After filling out all she's observed thus far, Kisa moves to a different page and dutifully writes down all the details they know regarding the heavenly emperor's death. This fevered writing is a remnant from her days at NSUMD—there, her frantic, stressed mind calmed itself only when she was plowing through her piles of assignments. She lists all the guests she saw leave after Hwanin when he left the party. After watching the recording the first time, they'd tracked Hwanin's steps through the ship. He'd gone straight down to the I-95 from the party, meaning that it's possible he was followed directly from the greenhouse disaster. Yet nobody else showed up on the cams as stalking him.

There was the therapist. Kisa writes down Dr. Jang's name thoughtfully, remembering the woman in the rubber-duck dress. Then, there was Lim Chaeyeon, carrying the tray of broken glass. Kisa chews on her pen as Hajun snores softly in his sleep and rolls onto his side.

"Don't touch my hair," her friend mumbles nonsensically in his sleep.

If Seokga had been the one attacked, perhaps she would consider Chaeyeon more seriously. But Hwanin himself, to her knowledge, hadn't done anything to anger the server. Would she seriously kill the emperor to infuriate his brother? Likely not. Still, it's worth investigating. Perhaps Chaeyeon is a creature, one with claws. The cruise director, Soo-min, had been there, too— and had been so upset at the night's turn of events, although she'd left later than Hwanin. Soo-min is also a samjokgu, with four claws on each of her dog form's three paws. Yet try as she might,

Kisa literally cannot imagine the easily ruffled cruise director somehow finding the courage to kill a god.

Growing frustrated, Kisa writes down another list: this time, of creatures with the ability to summon talon-like appendages. Gumiho. Yong. Inmyunjo (although there is no evidence of an Unruly inmyunjo *ever* existing). Samjokgu. Bulgae...

Haetae.

Pen moving to the list of greenhouse party suspects, Kisa hesitantly writes down Shin Korain's name, remembering the small altercation between the two men. Korain had tried to insert himself between Seokga and Somi, Hwanin had held him back. She'd seen resentment on the haetae's face. But is that enough of a motive for murder? No.

"Not in the practice room," grumbles Hajun. "No Yakult in the practice room...sticky..."

Unless Hwanung, who—to Kisa's knowledge—doesn't have claws, decided to take out his father by hiring somebody on the ship to dispose of him. After all, if Hwanin dies (or, more aptly, is reverted to baby form), Hwanung takes the throne for an extended period of time. Instead of being the god of laws, he'll spend years as heavenly emperor. Not quite "the god of sex, drugs, and rock and roll"—but it's close enough that she underlines his name once more and adds an exclamation mark.

Still, something doesn't feel *right*. Kisa is no Sherlock Holmes or Hercule Poirot, a fact that she's sharply reminded of when she stares despondently down at the mess in the notebook. Admitting that she is completely out of her depth is almost revolting to her, but the greatest scholars aren't afraid to admit that they *don't know*. And Kisa absolutely does not know.

All names should be investigated, of course, but she has the sinking feeling that she's not getting anywhere.

The feeling continues into the morning, as Kisa slips on her light-blue scrubs and tucks the small notebook into her bag with the pen. As she and Hajun wearily begin their shift in the sick bay, Kisa's mind continues to stumble over the mystery.

How has nobody showed up on the cameras, following Hwanin and then moving the body? Teleportation is something she jots down in her notebook, but the number of creatures with claws and the ability to move through the confines of space are low... practically nonexistent.

"Is Somi coming?" Hajun asks nervously as she writes.

Kisa glances up at him in amusement from where she stands behind the reception desk of the sick bay. "You know, I can't tell if you're terrified or excited to see her."

The idol grimaces, rubbing the nape of his neck. His ears have gone blue. "I'm actually not sure, either," he admits ruefully. "But I could say the same thing about you and Seokga."

Kisa jolts and drops her pen onto the tiled floor. Blushing furiously, she ducks out of sight to grab it. When she slowly straightens back to her feet, she sees that Hajun has snatched the notebook and is riffling through it. Mortification spreads through her as her friend squints down at a messy page.

"Kisa," he says, like he's trying very hard not to snicker, "I'm not as good at reading in English as I am in Korean, but... did you write 'he has a good arse' before scribbling it out?"

She closes her eyes and wishes that the ground would swallow her whole. "No," she says, with what she hopes is a stern finality. Unfortunately, her voice squeaks a bit at the end.

"Are you sure?"

"Positively certain." She opens her eyes and crosses her arms, ignoring Hajun's amused grin. "And if I had, hypothetically, written something about his... posterior... it wouldn't matter. We're getting off this ship, Hajun, and I-I refuse to be sidetracked by *bums.*" Besides, she has never been one for staring at men, and she's certain she's gone a bit insane. There's really no good reason why she should have been admiring Seokga's arse while he spoke with Yeomra, or as they walked down to the I-95 from the sick bay. It's ridiculous.

Hajun's smile fades as he slides the notebook back over to her. "It's okay to like him," he tells her slowly. "I mean ... I know you don't remember him, but you loved him in a past life. And it's pretty clear that he loved you. That must mean something, right?"

Kisa swallows hard, and when she speaks, her voice is tense—almost brittle, on the verge of breaking. "I'm not made of pine. I'm made of oak." She stares down at the battered notebook as her friend makes a small uncomprehending sound of complete confusion that grates on her nerves. Can't he understand? Can't anybody? Never has she felt so unheard, so—so *unseen*. "And I want to—to live again. I want to read my favorite book while it's storming outside, and feel the sun on my skin, and do all the things I was too busy to do this time around—"

"You felt something!" Hajun is staring at her, looking equal parts triumphant and concerned. "You've felt it already. You've felt something for him, and now you're scared. Kisa, you're pulling away because—what? You think you won't leave the *Flatliner* if you let yourself stare at his butt?"

"Yes," she snaps, finally giving up the act. "Yes, Hajun, that is precisely what I'm afraid of. How discerning of you."

"Oh, Kisa." Hajun is snorting, pressing a hand to his temple like he has a headache. He just might. Kisa certainly does. "I've never seen you like this before. So frazzled over somebody's posterior."

"It's a great bum," she whispers sadly, anger flickering and fading to a pathetic sort of longing. She massages the spot over her heart where it's lodged itself, panging in desolate despair.

"Please, Kisa, for my sanity ..." He drags that hand down his face, pulling on his eye and giving her a grotesquely woeful look. "Have some fun with him while you wait for reincarnation. You need it, and I think you'd like it—"

She shakes her head. "I don't know how," she interrupts in a mutter. It's the ugly truth.

"You don't need to know *how*." Hajun frowns in clear concern. "Fun isn't like medicine, where you need a giant textbook and time to study. You don't need to do anything but be in the moment."

"It doesn't matter." Kisa shakes her head stubbornly, avoiding Hajun's eye. "We have a deal with the CEO, and there's no point in getting distracted by—by anything." And she will *not* let herself get distracted by a certain green-eyed trickster god.

Her friend hesitates, like there's something more he wants to say, but evidently thinks better of it. For the next half hour, they wait for the others and lapse into their daily routine. Day 2 of the cruise means that there are virtually no patients, many having already been treated for seasickness.

This routine of cleaning the sick bay and checking medicine stock is only broken when Kisa's head jerks up from the shelf of medicine she's hunched over and—in a markedly improved mood—exclaims: "*Blueprints!*"

"Uh," says Hajun in bewilderment, "what?"

Kisa whirls to him, curls slipping from their band to flutter around her face. "I'll be right back," she says excitedly before dodging out the door and racing down the hallway and back down the stairs that will take her to the security room one deck below.

The door is ajar, and Kisa peeks inside, hastily drawing back when she sees Korain leaning against the table and wearily drinking a cup of hot coffee. Her hand floats to her scrub pockets, where the little notebook rests, Korain's name jotted down inside it. Keeping quiet, she leans back so she can watch the haetae as he takes another long sip of coffee.

He looks tired, she realizes. His mouth is bracketed with lines of exhaustion, and his white shirt is rumpled. Kisa narrows her eyes as Korain sets down the coffee and pulls a cellphone from his pocket. He types in a number, waits. "Hey," he finally says in a voice like gravel, hoarse from disuse. Whoever he's speaking to, he's speaking to in the informal. Kisa grimaces; she can't hear anything on the opposite end. "Yeah. I took care of it."

Took care of—what? Kisa hesitates before drawing closer. Although he's the only one in the room, Korain's voice lowers. "There'll be no trace—yeah. As we agreed."

She lurches back as he heads toward the door, and flattens herself around the corner. Korain's footsteps draw near, and Kisa strains to hear as he begins to speak in a whisper. "You promised you'd put in a good word . . . uh-huh. Great. Thanks. Bye."

His footsteps recede down the hall. Mind whirring with what she just heard, Kisa wastes no time slipping into the security room and—with slightly trembling fingers—filches what she needs from one of the unlocked file cabinets.

When she returns to the sick bay, a babbling Hwanin greets her from Seokga's arms. The god looks immensely displeased with the squirming bundle in his arms, but his green eyes soften when he catches sight of her. "Good morning," he says almost hesitantly.

—looks—beautiful—want—it hurts—

Kisa blinks, cheeks heating. *No. No. Stop.* No distractions. "Good morning," she manages, struggling to meet his stare. Seokga's gaze is like molten gold, warm and glittering. She swallows hard and holds up the snatched ship blueprints. "I, erm, I have some updates."

Seokga's face falls and a dart of regret shoots through her, but she hardens herself a moment later. Oak, not pine. Kisa, not Hani. It's not her that he wants anyway. She's doing them both a favor, really, by squashing this potential crush underfoot. Saving him from the inevitable disappointment, and her from a missed opportunity to escape this horrid ship.

It's for the best.

"Let's hear it," a new voice says from behind her, and Somi waltzes in, looking refreshed. She makes her way to stand beside Hajun, whose lips twitch into what's either a smile or a grimace. Kisa isn't sure.

She takes a deep breath and spreads the stolen blueprints over the counter before carefully flipping to the page in her notebook listing suspect names. Briefly, she explains why she chose those names, before turning to the blueprints. "I spent last night wondering how the murderer avoided the ship's security cameras to dump the body where Seokga would find it," she says. "I couldn't make sense of it. Teleportation was a possibility, but no creature with claws—to my knowledge—also possesses that capability. It's reserved for deities. I thought—perhaps—the camera avoidance was instead a mundane feat, achieved without magic. And the only way I thought that could happen was, well . . ." She hesitates, suddenly aware of how ridiculous this might sound. Seokga's eyes meet hers, and his gaze is somehow reassuring. "Hidden passageways," Kisa finishes, quickly looking away. "It sounds ludicrous but some ships have them, for the workers to move about more quickly. Like the I-95, but spanning across the boat. So I stole down to the security room to grab some blueprints, just to see if it might be a true possibility. Shin Korain was there."

Somi makes a thoughtful noise, tapping his scribbled name with a glossy nail. "He's a haetae."

"And he was at the party last night. He and Hwanin had a brief altercation while you and Seokga were . . ."

"Beating each other to a pulp," the gumiho concludes.

Seokga rolls his eyes. Hwanin giggles up at him.

"Right. Well—Korain took a phone call on his personal cell."

She hesitates, something niggling at her. Something that explains *why* a simple phone call is bothering her so much. "*None* of us have phones. None of the crew, I mean. Everybody we're allowed to contact is already on the ship."

"So how does Korain have a phone?" Hajun murmurs. "Who was he talking to?"

Kisa quickly explains the conversation. "I couldn't hear who was on the other end. But he was so furtive about it, that I found it of interest. Last night, I had thought . . ." She huffs in weary frustration. "We have so little to go on, so few clues, and I know that hypotheses need some sort of solid observational foundation at the very least—but, well, I've never done this before and couldn't think—I thought maybe—or if it's too soon and it's better to go in blind, I—"

"Kisa," Seokga says kindly, "it's all right. Tell us your idea."

Her nervous rambling trails off, and a small kernel of reassurance glows within her as she looks at Seokga's expectant expression. Kisa doesn't quite feel like examining *why*. "What if Hwanung *hired* somebody to go after Hwanin? From what you've told us, he could have a motive. With Hwanin a baby, Hwanung gets the throne and a break from being the god of laws. He might have hired somebody on the ship to kill him without having it trace back. The claws tell us that Hwanung enlisted a creature. But he didn't come onto the boat himself. He distracted his father with a phone call, giving the murderer the element of surprise."

The trickster god is silent, considering. "It's a good idea," he says slowly. "It's a *very* good idea," he adds with a wicked grin. "If I'd thought of that myself back in the day . . ."

Exasperated—and before she can stop herself—Kisa gives him a *that's not funny and you know it* look.

He smirks, and she grimaces, wondering—not for the first time—at how *natural* it feels to speak with him. *Squash this immedi-*

ately, Kisa chides herself, and is rewarded (or punished, really) by the bemused expression forming on the trickster's face.

"Erm— We need to focus on Korain," she manages to say, her gaze breaking away from Seokga. "Someone should come with me to subtly obtain an alibi and confirm it with the security footage."

"I'll go," Somi offers at the same time Seokga does.

The two glower at each other.

"We're Threaded," Seokga sneers.

"I was her best friend," Somi snaps.

"Until you betrayed her," the god hisses, and evidently lands a punch on his opponent as Somi shies away.

Exchanging a tired glance with Hajun, Kisa shakes her head in a mixture of reluctant flattery, exasperation, and deep exhaustion. Somewhere in the mix, there's also an itching curiosity that Kisa ignores for the moment. "It really doesn't matter who comes with me," she interrupts, although part of her secretly wants to choose Somi, putting as much distance between herself and Seokga— with his reassuring smiles and sparkling eyes—as possible. "But there's more to do." She stares down at the blueprints, the mammoth ship sketched out in concise white lines. Her finger taps Deck 10 before moving to the etched stairwell where the body was found. "This stairwell doesn't have a camera," she murmurs, reminding them of their discovery the night before. "If it connects to a passageway..." There's no indication, however, of any on the blueprint. Her heart falls.

"It can always be checked in person," Seokga offers, shifting Hwanin in his arms uncomfortably. Kisa sighs and gently repositions the baby emperor in his brother's tense grip.

"You're not supposed to hold children like you're scared they're going to bite you. He doesn't even have *teeth* yet, Seokga." Honestly, it's hilarious how frightened Seokga seems to be of the tiny god. It *should* help Kisa in her squashing endeavor, but unfortunately seems to be having the opposite sort of effect. Drat.

"*Greeeeeh!*" agrees Hwanin, wide blue eyes shining with mirth.

Seokga's mouth twitches in what she hopes is amusement. "So we'll take Korain?" he asks, but a moment later, Somi is breezing toward Kisa, looping her arm around hers, and dragging her out of the sick bay.

"*We'll* take Korain," Somi calls over her shoulder. "You two boys can snoop around the stairwell. Ta!"

When it's just the two of them, it's as if Somi's mask begins to fray. Kisa watches with quiet interest as the loud, confident gumiho draws into herself and occasionally peers at her with wide brown eyes riddled with guilt. It's as if Somi suddenly becomes very young and uncertain. As they descend the stairwell leading down to Deck 2, Somi abruptly grabs Kisa's narrow wrist, bringing her to a halt.

Warily, Kisa waits for the words that seem to be stumbling around inside the gumiho's mouth. "You really don't remember anything?" she finally whispers, holding tight.

"No," she replies softly, twisting her wrist from Somi's grip. "All I know is this life, the one I lived as Yoo Kisa." Memories make a person. It's in the literature on nature versus nurture, in the question of the Ship of Theseus.

In Kisa's opinion, it is *not* the same ship.

It is physically *incapable* of being the same ship.

The two ships are separate. And if the sailors are upset about that, perhaps they should reduce their bloody expectations for the new ship. Ships made of oak are just as nice as ships made of pine—and it can even be argued that oaken ships are more durable than easily rotted pine ships. Plus, oaken ships would *never* steal from an ATM—

Kisa wants to throw her hands exasperatedly up in the air. What she would give, truly, for her mind to be quiet sometimes. *What does it matter?* she chides herself. *It doesn't. Stop it.*

There *must* be a way to stop a crush from taking root within her, some sort of—of concoction to make the inconvenient thing shrivel and die.

"I remember nothing from Hani's life," Kisa continues to the gumiho, an ache beginning to pulse in her right temple as she tries, very hard, not to ruminate on her dilemma.

Something almost like relief crosses Somi's face before it's replaced by sadness. "I'm assuming you know some already."

Kisa can't keep a wry little smile from turning the corner of her mouth slightly upward. "From what you and Seokga have quarreled about, I know, at the very least, that we were friends. That my name was Hani, and you betrayed her—me—somehow during the Dark Days."

Somi gnaws on her bottom lip. "I'd say that's mostly true . . ." But she doesn't follow as Kisa makes her way down a few more steps. "I could tell you, if you want to know. About you and me. About you and Seokga."

As Somi's offer floats through the air, Kisa's fingers twitch imperceptibly at her sides, as if she might grab it. For some unknowable reason, she thinks of Seokga's green eyes and how they might light up if she remembered . . . If the two ships didn't have to be so separate after all . . .

Slowly, Kisa turns. "You can tell me about you and Han—*me*," she says with difficulty, "but I'd rather not hear about myself and Seokga." It fills her with an anxious dread to think of what Seokga might expect from her if she learns about their past.

What *she* might . . . feel for him.

And a tiny part of Kisa has decided if, at some point—for whatever reasons she cannot fathom now—she does want to hear their story (for purely scientific purposes, of course, nothing more), she wants to hear it from *Seokga*.

If the gumiho is confused by Kisa's refusal to learn more about her Threaded partner, she doesn't show it. It is something that Kisa is beginning to appreciate about Somi. Despite being a former mass-murdering Unruly gumiho (Kisa is still, admittedly, wrapping her mind around how the petite woman with a French bob and manicured hands can possibly be a serial killer), Somi is, well, polite. To a degree.

She's polite to Kisa, at least, she amends. She tried to take a large chomp out of a guest, after all.

As the two women slip toward the security room, Somi begins to tell a story in a low voice. It's a story about two gumiho who worked together in a café. Somi and Hani. The portrait that Somi paints of the older gumiho is vibrant. A woman full of life and mischief, an older sister, in many ways, to the younger Somi.

As they carefully trail Korain out of the security room and toward the upper decks, Somi tells Kisa in a whisper of how Hani killed two NSU men and brought her the livers. How Somi began to spiral, suffering from the Jitters, feeling unwell in both mind and body. How scared she was.

They're careful to blend into the morning crowds on board as they follow the haetae, hoping he's heading to a café or somewhere equally casual, where Somi can—in her words—charm an alibi out of him. Cautious not to be spotted, or to lose him, Kisa keeps her eyes on the officer's retreating back as Somi continues.

Hyun-tae was the name of the possessed jeoseung saja. As Somi speaks of him, there's a sense of real grief—the first time she met him, in the café, he was fully himself and maybe even smitten with her. The next day, Eodum—the eoduksini—had slipped into his body. What follows is a saga of manipulation, in which Somi seems like a pawn... Although Somi never puts it in those terms. Instead, the gumiho's voice is heavy with regret as the Dark Days begin, and her killing spree starts. Kisa gets the sense that Somi isn't very upset about the murders themselves, but rather her decision to side against Hani.

"You let me go," Somi whispers, shamefaced, as they trail Korain up a winding staircase, a dozen or so feet behind and hidden by throngs of breakfast-hungry guests. "I ran from you, and you let me. I would have lost that fight," she adds with a bitter smile. "You were the Scarlet Fox—"

Kisa chokes on her own spit. "*What?*"

"You have the same eyes, you know," whispers Somi. "The same eyes as Hani. I always thought they were so pretty..."

It was enough of a shock hearing that she had been an *Unruly* gumiho.

Hearing that in her past life, rule-abiding Yoo Kisa had been, like Somi, an infamous and centuries-old *serial killer*—a terrifying urban legend that she shivered to as a child—is enough to turn her legs into jelly. The two ships are most certainly not the same. At this rate, Kisa is not a ship at all. She's a perfectly respectable *airplane*.

They learned about the Scarlet Fox in the shaman academy, and then later in NSUMD. Her upperclassmen's anatomy class's autopsy portion focused heavily on Unruly murders, and diagrams of the Scarlet Fox's victims had been pulled from the archives.

She had been brutal.

Kisa... had been *brutal*.

Her vision swims. Somi grimaces, grabbing Kisa by the shoulder before she can fall. "I see I left out that particular subplot," the gumiho mumbles as Kisa has an existential crisis right there on the spiraling staircase, underneath the ship's ginormous chandelier. In the grand scheme of things, it's a rather lovely place to have a midlife crisis. Or an afterlife crisis, in Kisa's case. "But, Ha—Kisa, I . . . I shouldn't have been so angry at you, all those years ago. You gave me the greatest gift of all."

Gods.

Kisa is an enabler of serial killers.

Extremely woozy, Kisa staggers up the remaining stairs to Deck 7, where Korain is turning in to a corridor of suites.

"You introduced me to my true nature," Somi is saying, hand sliding down Kisa's back and rubbing soothing circles. "You told me it was okay for me to be who I really am . . ."

The hand on her back is too much. Kisa lurches away, *hating* the feel of it and despising how her neck erupts into a sweat. She pretends not to see Somi's brief expression of hurt, turning away from it. *It's not personal,* Kisa wants to say, but that's not the truth, is it? Her inability to allow anybody behind her, for anybody to touch her back, is deeply—*deeply*—personal.

She sincerely regrets ever letting Somi tell her their story. It is, succinctly put, all shades of incredibly bollocksed up. ". . . and thanks to you, I came into my power," the gumiho continues, faltering only slightly. "I reached my—my potential. When I heard you'd died in the warehouse, I mourned you. I'd come back to New Sinsi, to . . . to apologize"—her voice breaks on the word—"but you weren't there. I looked everywhere. Seoul, Itaewon, Jeju. Geoje." Somi's eyes are glassy. "Aeri, a yojeong on Daegeumsan, told me you were gone. You burnt out your fox bead saving Korea. No—saving the whole mortal realm. Eodum's motive had been to turn Iseung into the Dark World."

The more Kisa hears about her past life, the more she's convinced that she's having auditory hallucinations. "Gamangnara," she manages to rasp, leaning against the wall, unable to go farther—even to follow Korain. "The locked realm." Locked, by

Hwanin and the rest of the pantheon after Seokga's infamous (and, if Kisa is being honest, pathetic) attempt at a coup. "How could Iseung be turned into Gamangnara?"

Somi hesitates, guilt flashing across her face, but Kisa's sharp mind is already whirring and piecing together an explanation. She's read about Gamangnara, of course—in its heyday, the realm was nothing short of notorious, a breeding ground for Unrulies, a cesspool of chaos and evil. After Seokga's coup, it was shut down, creatures thrown from it. Some, like the eoduksini, were dispatched to Jeoseung. But once, Gamangnara was alive, teeming with Unrulies . . . And even before that, if Somi is to be believed, it might have been a place just like Iseung. Until the demons of darkness came.

"Oh," croaks Kisa as comprehension settles in. "*Oh*."

The world doesn't know just how *narrowly* it dodged a bullet with the Dark Days. Even now, hearing it herself, Kisa has to take deep breaths to calm herself.

Gamangnara is always a point of debate in the creature communities. The politics surrounding it are as intricate as a spider's web. Some believe that it should be unlocked (no matter how *impossible* that is), and that all Unruly creatures should be clustered there, leaving the mortal realms alone. Others are perfectly content with its being locked, arguing that giving Unrulies a realm of their own is a *terrible* idea—the wars they could wage, the power they could exert. Besides, the dark magic of Gamangnara is steeped with ancient evil. The Mad God, Mireuk, is said to have once loved the realm before his imprisonment. And anything the Mad God loves, one must be wary of.

"Kisa?" Somi asks.

"I'll be fine in just a moment," she manages to gasp out, peeling herself off the wall and swiping a film of cold sweat from her forehead. "Where has Korain gone?"

The abrupt refocus on the haetae is, Kisa knows, a coping mechanism—the same one that prompts her to dive into piles of work rather than to sit with her own emotions. Even so, they've delayed for too long, and have lost sight of Korain. Somi winces, and with a silent agreement to speak more later, the two women hurry off down the hallway.

"Does he have a room up here?" Somi asks as they pass Room 7340. The door is agape, a housekeeping cart sitting a few feet away, piled high with towels.

"He shouldn't," Kisa replies warily. All staff sleep on Deck 1, in the small windowless cabins like the one she shares with Hajun. Looking ahead, Kisa's eyes widen, and she hastily tugs Somi down so they crouch behind the cart together, side by side. Korain is leaving a suite just up ahead—and he's not alone. Heart in her throat, Kisa counts down the doors and when she reaches the door he's just exited, her blood grows cold. Room 7346.

The room that connects to Room 7345, Seokga's room. Which means that Room 7346 is—

"Why is he leaving Hwanin's room?" Kisa hisses, and although her knees are beginning to ache from sustaining an uncomfortable crouch, she hunches even lower and peers around the cart. Korain isn't alone. A young woman with long, inky black hair is with him.

Lim Chaeyeon. The serving girl from the greenhouse party.

"My," Somi whispers. "This suddenly got very interesting."

CHAPTER FIFTEEN

SEOKGA

S EOKGA IS LOATH TO ADMIT that Hajun looks vaguely familiar, and that Seokga *might* know precisely what popular boy band he's from and even like a few of their songs. Perhaps even have attempted some of their complex choreographies himself (and failed spectacularly). This is because Seokga has decided on one of his many whims to dislike Hajun, a decision that is reinforced only when Hajun mentions that he and Kisa *share a cabin*.

A *cabin*.

His fury only grows when Hajun proves to be hard to hate. The boy is disgustingly *nice*. He offers to hold Hwanin for him, and—unlike Seokga—doesn't hold the baby like he's a mangy cat carrying rabies. Before heading to Deck 10's stairwell, Hajun even buys Seokga a large iced coffee from Deck 8's bustling Creature Café.

"For morale," the boy offers over the chatter with a kind smile that makes Seokga grimace. He dearly wishes he could be as revolted as he'd *like* to be by this kindness, but the truth is that after the hideousness of the past day, he is not capable of his usual spectacular rancor.

"Thank you," mutters the trickster god reluctantly, and sucks a long drag of coffee with one cream, one sugar, into his mouth.

Hajun smiles, orders an iced matcha for himself, and Seokga watches in a growing bad mood as he makes easy small talk with the cashier before paying in Jeoseung coins—black coins with Yeomra's grinning, winking face on them. Somehow, Hajun manages to hold a dozing Hwanin in one hand and his small drink in the other.

The second morning of the SRC *Flatliner* is just as packed as the first. Shoes clatter against the polished corridors as excited guests rush to the many attractions of the day, cheerful despite their state of being very, very dead. Surprisingly, though, there are few gwisin who bear the scars of their deaths, even when they're young (which means, Seokga concludes, their endings had to be vicious and nasty). Hajun catches him staring at a grinning young boy, no more than ten, who is carrying a large stuffed teddy bear—presumably won from the noisy casino and arcade a deck below.

"He's a repeat guest," Hajun explains in a quiet tone. "The kid isn't ready to reincarnate just yet, so the CEO's let him stay on for another cruise or two. Kisa fixed him up with some Restoration when he got here. You'd never even know he was in a crash. It helps him, being here and looking whole. In time, he'll be able to move on."

Seokga glances sideways at Hajun. The idol has no signs of injury, either, though if what Seokga remembers from the papers about ST4RL1GHT's beloved maknae, Kim Hajun . . . Seokga's gaze drops to Hajun's wrists.

"She fixed me up, too," Hajun says, and Seokga feels a peculiar jolt of shame at his subtle scrutiny being not so subtle, after all. The idol smiles, though, as if recalling something pleasant rather than awful as they walk through the cruise's throngs. "Kisa is wonderful. I was scared as shit when I got here, but she's helped me in so many ways." He shrugs, adjusting his grip on Hwanin. "I think if I'd met her while we were alive, maybe our stories would have turned out differently. Maybe they wouldn't have ended so soon. She's a good friend."

Seokga takes a small sip of coffee to settle his stomach. "Kisa said," he manages after a moment, "that she fell off a roof..."

Hajun's smile slips. "Is that all she told you?" he asks quietly.

A cold shiver of foreboding slithers down Seokga's spine, and he grips his cane tight. "It is," he manages. Hajun's eyes are sad. "Why?" snaps Seokga, fear like a vise around his heart. He can't mean...

The idol hesitates as they reach the chaos of Deck 9. No longer indoors, the deck is open-air, covered in a mess of glittering pools and spiraling waterslides. A live band plays festive music in the corner, and the air smells of a strange mix of Seocheongang River and lemonade. Guests splash in the pools, leaping into their depths or flying through the air from the slides. With an expression of supreme distaste, Seokga sidesteps a throng of giggling women who eye him with more than a little interest. Below, the Seocheongang River churns and flows, blood red as the ship cuts through it.

"Kisa and I might have more in common than you think," Hajun finally says, heading toward one of the stairwells connecting it to Deck 10—the stairwell where Seokga found his brother's corpse. It will be gone by now, unable to remain present in a world where the baby form also exists.

"She told you this?" He's struggling to accept this. He won't. He can't. Seokga will not accept that Kisa felt so alone, so...

"She didn't have to," Hajun replies as he pulls the stairwell's door open, stepping aside for a cluster of swimsuit-clad men with thinning hair to waddle out. "Some wounds are deeper than skin. And—" He shakes his head, looking slightly guilty as he speculates on his friend. "I don't know, it's just... hardly anybody just falls from a skyscraper. Why was she up on the roof to begin with? She's not a reckless person. She always thinks things through." As the final Speedo jauntily struts out the door, Hajun and Seokga slip inside. The former turns as they enter, blocking the god for a moment as his normally kind hazel eyes narrow. "I'm telling you this so you're gentle with her," he warns, a fiercely protective light in his eyes. "She's apprehensive about you already, but still, there's the red thread. Anything can happen. I don't want her to find the courage to dive in only to get hurt in the end. Okay?" He sounds almost terrified for Kisa, and Seokga closes his eyes, steadying himself.

"I think," he hears himself saying, "that you should warn her to be gentle with *me*."

The other man laughs, and he hears Hwanin yawn, waking from his nap. "You're both so scared of each other. For the record . . ." As Seokga opens his eyes, he sees Hajun offering him a small smile and gestures to the red thread tied to his left pinky, the knot like a floral ring around the small finger. It's invisible to anybody but Seokga and Kisa, but she must have told him about it. "I don't know much about mythology, but I know that's there for a reason."

"Right," mutters Seokga, uncomfortable with the amount of kindness Hajun has shown him. He hates nice people, but still adds another rough and awkward "Thank you" before gulping down some more coffee and attempting—in vain—to find a hidden passageway for what feels like hours, but can only be fifteen minutes before a wrinkled hand clamps around his shoulder.

Stiffening, Seokga whirls away from the wall he's been knocking on (hidden passageways, he hopes, would at least throw him a bone and *sound* hollow) . . . and makes eye contact with a very grumpy-looking Jang Heejin. She's no longer wearing the rubber-duck dress, and Seokga finds himself muttering "thank the heavens for small mercies" aloud. A few steps above, Hajun freezes, holding baby Hwanin with an uncertain expression.

Luckily, Dr. Jang doesn't seem to see the infant. Behind a giant pair of flamingo-pink sunglasses, he gets the sense that she's glaring at him, stare boring through the inner depths of his soul. "Seokga," the elderly therapist chides. "You're avoiding me."

"Uh," says Seokga, attempting to convey a message to Hajun with only his eyes. *Go. Run.* If Dr. Jang catches a glimpse of the baby with eyes suspiciously similar to Hwanin's, the gig is most decidedly up. The therapist will—as she's sworn to do—contact Okhwang in case of emergencies pertaining to Seokga, and this would undoubtedly count as an emergency. Hajun, to his credit, picks up the hidden plea and hurries away with Hwanin. Ignoring the annoying stab of anxiety at having his brother out of his sight, Seokga attempts a casual smile that does not at all seem to fool the good doctor. "I forgot about our scheduled session," he says. That much is true. That Dr. Jang had demanded a session in the morning after the disaster in the greenhouse had been completely forgotten by him.

Dr. Jang sighs, pushing up her sunglasses. "Well, let's go, then," she grumps, and—with one hand on the wall—makes her way back down the stairs. Seokga notes that she's being extremely cautious with her movements, feeling the wall or railing before she takes each step, and feels a spasm of guilt. Dr. Jang is an old woman, and running about the ship looking for him couldn't have been good for her bones—which she, on the way down to Jeoseung, complained of being incredibly arthritic. Seokga's guilt fades as he sits in the plush armchair across from hers in her cabin and watches as she pulls out a notebook. He wonders if he should mention she's still wearing her sunglasses, but decides against it. They match her neon Hawaiian shirt in a way that's most amusing.

"So," says Dr. Jang Heejin.

"So," echoes Seokga, crossing one leg over the other, determined to look as casual as possible. Nothing to see here. No murders, no baby-older-brothers.

"The greenhouse mess," prompts Dr. Jang, and Seokga almost snorts. With everything going on, his little tussle with Somi last night is the *least* of his concerns. "You were upset."

With a beleaguered sigh, Seokga allows Dr. Jang to guide him through an exploration of his *feelings*. Feelings are so inconvenient. At times like these, Seokga wishes he didn't have any. As Dr. Jang sagely suggests that the revulsion he felt at seeing Somi mimicking Hani stemmed from an unconscious attraction to a creature so *like* his lost love, Seokga abandons all politeness and begins to take great pleasure in causing the therapist unnecessary difficulty—as he used to do in the days before she somehow managed to *bond* with him. He refutes it emphatically and then, with a thin smile that tells the psychologist he knows precisely what he's doing, answers each prompt-slash-question with a roundabout reply that can make absolutely no sense to anybody. He speaks in riddles, takes long breaks to slurp (loudly) on his coffee, bothers Dr. Jang about what deity her patron is (one answer she's repeatedly refused to give him, although he's sure it's Hwanin), and goads her when she deflects. He grabs a Kopiko from his pocket and noisily crinkles the wrapper, even pretending that the small coffee candy is too big for him to talk around. But Dr. Jang is an admirable opponent, and Seokga grimaces when he realizes that *he's* the one growing tired.

It doesn't help that Hwanin cried the whole night, or that when he finally did manage to fall asleep, he was awoken by a strange *dragging* noise in the corridor. Yet when Seokga had slammed open the door, nothing had been there. It's possible his exhausted mind gifted him some auditory hallucinations.

"Seokga," Dr. Jang says, setting down her pen—she hasn't taken many notes throughout the session, he notes with some satisfaction. "I've been treating you for long enough that I've picked up on your tells. When you deflect, like you're doing now, it's to hide a deep anxiety, anger, fear... or all of the above. So." The old woman leans forward, hands lacing together. "I want to talk about Kisa. We spoke a little about her yesterday, during our emergency session, but I regret that we didn't have the opportunity to delve deeper—especially considering the events in the greenhouse." She hesitates. "You are, I assume, still adjusting to having found her— and the stark differences between herself and Hani."

Seokga bites down hard on his candy. "We went over this yesterday," he grinds out around the loud crunching.

Dr. Jang leans back in her chair, presumably studying him behind those ridiculous sunglasses. And she does what Seokga hates most—she waits. Silently.

Oh, how Seokga hates the silence. His crunching becomes unbearably noisy. It makes him feel awkward, and Seokga is *never* awkward (except in cases where Kisa is concerned, apparently). Four minutes and twenty seconds go by (the longest he's ever lasted is ten minutes) before he snaps out: "Fine. I knew not to expect Hani, but..." He clenches his jaw. "I think I did. And it's disorienting. One moment, she laughs or rolls her eyes like Hani, but the next... The next moment, she's somebody I don't even know."

His therapist's face—or what he can make of it, at least— softens. "I have a question for you, Seokga," she says kindly. "And I want to preface it by saying that I know it might stir up some complex feelings."

Seokga's entire body stiffens. He's had enough *complex feelings* for a lifetime. "I decline," he replies flatly, and that really should be the end of it, but of course it isn't.

Jang, the tyrant, is unruffled. "Have you given any thought, perhaps, as to why the red thread connected you and Kisa? Not you and Hani?"

His brows furrow before he can stop them. "It connected us because she was Hani," Seokga answers immediately, the words springing to his mouth like a knee-jerk reflex. "And Hani was my... She was..." *Everything.* Throat tightening, Seokga cuts off and attempts to compose himself.

"Hmm," Dr. Jang says, and above those ridiculous glasses, a thin eyebrow arches.

"I suppose you have an alternate theory," Seokga drawls coldly, rather wishing Jang's *hmm* wasn't so laden with skepticism. It makes him feel quite violent.

"I do, yes." She exhales, lacing her hands together. "I'd like you to consider, Seokga, that it is *you and Kisa* that fate has chosen to vouch for. That even if you'd never met Hani—stop making that face, please, and listen—that you still would have, *somehow,* met Kisa. Your Threaded. That you met her in her past life was just a coincidence—"

The grinding of his back molars is beginning to give him a headache. "A *coincidence?*" he demands in a voice that armies have fled from but the elderly therapist seems to find amusing.

"And what a wonderful coincidence, too." She reaches forward and pats Seokga's knee as if he's a small child and not a notorious god. He gapes at the sheer audacity. "But your expectations are holding you back from knowing Kisa for who *she* is."

It can't possibly be healthy for his mouth to be this dry. A long silence stretches out between Seokga and Jang in which the trickster god experiences a complete nervous breakdown while expertly hiding beneath a façade of bored indifference.

"Seokga," Jang says when the silence has stretched out to five minutes. "Are you all right?"

"No," he tries to say with a certain cold pointedness, but it comes out as an undignified wheeze instead, his mask finally cracking.

"It's only a theory..."

But what if it's not? What if his time with Hani meant *nothing*? His stomach roils and he thinks he might be sick. *It isn't true,* he tells himself. Hani is—*was?*—the love of his life. It didn't mean *nothing.* It couldn't. Even if Dr. Jang's idea is true, what he shared with Hani was special and achingly real, red thread or no. And Kisa...

She was Hani, once.

"I *want* to know her—it's just that I'm not sure if she wants to know *me*," he rasps, and then grimaces at the admission of his insecurity. Seokga wishes, for a moment, that he could tell Dr. Jang of Yeomra's bargain... Of how Kisa will be reincarnated if they succeed in catching the murderer, how her face lit up like a fucking firefly's ass when the bastard god offered that (knowing *exactly* what he was doing—godsdamned Yeomra).

Dr. Jang nods. "You've struggled with rejection your whole life," she says, rather fucking bluntly in Seokga's opinion. Suddenly, he greatly desires to hurl himself off the cruise and leave himself at the mercy of the ineo. "Your father, especially—"

He stiffens even further, if such a thing is even possible. "I don't want to talk about Mireuk. You've tortured me enough for the day as it is." He's practically begging for a reprieve.

His therapist only tilts her head. "It's imperative that we talk about Mireuk, Seokga. His favoritism of Hwanin has affected you deeply, even now. I see a connection between your issues with your father and this situation with Kisa."

It's nothing Seokga hasn't heard before, but each time Jang offers up this conspiracy of hers on a golden platter, he wants to smack it right out of her hands. In Dr. Jang's opinion, the imbalance of respect his father showed to Hwanin and Seokga has ingrained within him an unconscious sense of "worthlessness," which the trickster attempts to compensate for through things like bloody coups. It also, apparently, accounts for Seokga's long history of women, but rather short list of partners he has truly loved (Hani being the only one on that particular list). He is terrified of rejection, of being loved only for that love to shift to something—somebody—else.

Even before Mireuk went mad, he was a less-than-stellar father... To Seokga, at least. Mireuk didn't hate him (at least at that point), but it was Hwanin that he really took under his wing, it was *Hwanin* that Mireuk showered in praise and affection while Seokga watched from the shadows, jealousy festering in his heart. As the second-born, Seokga was largely ignored. As the first-born, and crown prince to the throne, Hwanin was showered in anything and everything he could ever possibly want.

It was during Okhwang's annual talent show that Seokga and Mireuk's relationship really began to fester. Seokga was, by godly standards, only a teenager at the time: hungry for his father's approval and appreciation, hungry for a modicum of the affection shown to his oh-so-perfect brother. For Seokga's talent, he declared, he would challenge Mireuk to a flower-growing contest— a random, and largely useless, talent that Seokga inherited from his earth-goddess mother, Mago. As the crowd tittered, Mireuk reluctantly agreed.

The young trickster god had believed he'd succeed. He had been practicing, and had purposefully chosen this challenge as an acknowledgment to Mago—who loved him fiercely, even though he was only the second son. Confident he would win, young Seokga grinned at his mother, who grinned back.

But, as the competition commenced, his father quickly overtook Seokga's progress. The impending humiliation beginning to flush his cheeks, he had glanced out into the audience, and Mago's disappointed face had struck him like a slap. So Seokga did what has always been in his nature to do: He cheated. With one of the many sleights of hand he is so skilled at, Seokga ruined Mireuk's flowers and unjustly won the contest.

His father was not fooled.

Never until then had Seokga seen the emperor so enraged. It was then, over something as simple as a flower-growing contest, that the beginnings of Mireuk's madness began. Even now, there is a part of Seokga that whispers it's all his fault—his father's slipping grip on sanity, and what came close after. The creation god began to weave sufferings into existence, sending them down to torment the mortal world. The years that followed were heavy with grief and horror. Mireuk tortured Seokga every chance he got. The god's pride and fragile ego had been dramatically (and even *nonsensically*) wounded over the talent show's result, and he took a sadistic pleasure in cutting Seokga down whenever the chance arose. Okhwang became a place of terror, and Seokga began slipping off to Gamangnara to hide in the shadows and chaos.

As Seokga and Hwanin both came into early adulthood, they imprisoned their father beneath the Seocheongang River they now cruise on, having been left no choice. Mireuk had become the Mad God. Hwanin took the throne, and Mago—stricken with grief and regret, exhausted by the years and "all these testosterone-fueled battles"—went to sleep. She'd not awoken since.

Seokga has been determinedly trying not to think about how, leagues and leagues beneath the SRC *Flatliner,* his father lies trapped.

Until now, he's been doing a rather decent job of it.

Dr. Jang is still speaking, but Seokga isn't paying attention. Every day of his life, he regrets the flower-growing contest. A part of him—as disgusting as it is—still longs for his father to see him and love him as he once did Hwanin.

Fucking daddy issues.

"How much would you give to earn his pride?" the therapist asks, jerking Seokga out of his reverie. Jaw tense, he narrows his eyes at the therapist. *This* is a new question.

The truth is, honestly, that he would give any of his bodily organs to go back in time and prevent himself from cheating at the flower contest. But Seokga will never, ever admit that. It's a dangerous line of questioning, and Dr. Jang knows that. If Seokga displays any hint of ideating upon treason, she's instructed to report it to Okhwang immediately. "I don't want anything to do with him," Seokga answers stiffly.

"Good," says Dr. Jang, pushing up her sunglasses. "And you're still taking your medication?"

"At seven each evening," he mutters back.

And that's that.

CHAPTER SIXTEEN

KISA

"Did you get it?" Korain asks. Kisa and Somi exchange wide-eyed glances behind the housekeeping cart as Chaeyeon shrugs, flicking a strand of hair away from her face.

"Are you gonna *arrest* me if I didn't?" she asks with a wry smile.

Korain doesn't look amused. "This is serious, Chaeyeon. Did you find anything or no?"

A long sigh escapes Chaeyeon's lips, and she glances furtively around the empty hallway. As the vacuum starts up in one of the nearby rooms being cleaned, Kisa strains to hear what's being said over the dull roar. "It's basically barren in there. The bed is still made. I went through his suitcase, but it's all pretty standard. I did, however, find out that he's more of a briefs guy—"

Thoroughly bewildered by whatever this is, Kisa gapes as Chaeyeon pulls something out of her back pocket. Underwear. *Hwanin's* underwear.

"I also found something else . . ." Her voice is drowned out by the vacuum.

The briefs. Whatever possible reason—?

Next to her, Somi snorts, and then hastily presses a hand to her mouth and nose. Chewing nervously on her lip, Kisa wonders—

with increasing concern—what plot, exactly, is unfolding right beneath their eyes. Korain says something in reply, but with the vacuum cleaner roaring in the background, Kisa cannot make it out. Determination lowering her brows, Kisa rises slightly from her crouch and wraps her hands around the cold metal of the cart's handle.

"We need to move closer," she whispers to Somi.

If either Korain or Chaeyeon notice the housekeeping cart very gradually scooching closer to them, neither let on. When they're near enough to hear the next words, both women duck back down and exchange satisfied looks.

"—gets what he deserves," Korain is saying in a low, hard voice. "When you let the boss know that we took care of him, we get what *we* deserve."

Well. Kisa's hands are suddenly very sweaty around the cart's handle. This is, she thinks, exceptionally incriminating. Her anxiety mounts, and she does her best to package it up nice and neatly in a little box and shove it into a corner of her mind. This requires focus, after all. Unless the context in which she's taking this conversation is terribly wrong, it seems that Somi and Kisa have managed to find the murderers.

Yet, even as Somi nudges her giddily, Kisa forces her mind to slow down. It's not helpful to lose all rationality at the sight of a clue or two: even as damning a sight as this one. She still must think this through.

Eyeing the two, she writes down a list in her mind. Motives: Both were upset by Hwanin—or someone related to Hwanin—at the greenhouse party. Evidence: Chaeyeon vocally expressed her anger at Hwanin and Seokga:

"The CEO will hear about this. I'm so tired of working down here. But all my points for good behavior will be docked because of tonight. Yeomra will see my name on the list of greenhouse workers."

She left at the same time as Hwanin. She is currently standing outside of Hwanin's door, holding his underpants. In their conversation, they have mentioned a "boss"—somebody sent them to dispose of Hwanin?—who could possibly be Hwanung if her theory is at all correct.

Something still doesn't seem *right*.

"Did you hear that?" Somi whispers so quietly that Kisa can barely hear her. "Got 'what he deserved,' they 'took care of him'..."

Wait, Kisa mouths, intent on listening more. If they rush them now... Korain is an incredibly strong haetae—one who possibly tore the heavenly emperor's heart right out of his chest. Somi and Kisa are both immune to death, but there are other considerations that they cannot ignore. Korain might get away. So might Chaeyeon. And something about Chaeyeon is worrying her... Other than the fact she's holding Hwanin's underwear. An instinct low in her stomach tells her that now would be the wrong time to strike.

The haetae draws his phone out of his pocket. "I can call Boss right now—"

Chaeyeon stiffens, holds up a hand. Her eyes suddenly shrewd and unnervingly birdlike, she looks around the hallway. Her eyes land on the cart, and Kisa holds her breath, heart hammering rapidly against her ribs. Somi is silently snarling in anticipation, and summons her claws. The ravaged talons appear, and the gumiho's face goes pale—as if she forgot.

The girl's eyes finally move away from the cart. "Not now," she says. "Go somewhere more private." She rolls her shoulders, turning—and Kisa's stomach drops as she sees the faint outline of feathers on the girl's arms and neck, bare underneath her collared white shirt. As if they were sketched onto her skin with pencil, and are growing darker, more lifelike, by the second. Alarm blares through Kisa, and she frantically riffles through her memory to confirm that she is correct in her assumption that Chaeyeon is...

> The creatures' bodies, when in alarm or otherwise tense situations, will unconsciously begin the shift into their great and powerful animalistic form. Anatomically, it is impossible to say where the animalistic form is stored when the human form is in place, but it is generally assumed that the transformation process is a transformation of "inside-to-out" (Lee et al., 2004). When watching these individuals transform, it is fascinating to note how the feathers seem to push up from underneath the skin to commence the process—soon after, the human form will be entirely replaced by the body of a gigantic bird—or, in rare cases, yong—save for the face, which remains human...

Anxious sweat breaks out on the back of Kisa's neck as Chaeyeon hesitates, scanning the hallway one last time before finally turning and following after Korain, the feathers fading back into flesh. As the two disappear, Kisa whirls to Somi, whose face is unusually grim.

"The feathers," Somi says, and there's even a hint of fear in the Unruly gumiho's eyes. "That girl is an inmyunjo. And I've never, *never*, met an Unruly inmyunjo."

"It can't be her," Kisa says, staring down at her flat white. "Inmyunjo are the biggest proponents of peace and harmony..." Her head swims.

They attempted to relocate both Chaeyeon and Korain, but to no avail. Now, they wait for Hajun, Seokga, and Hwanin to join them in the bustling Creature Café as they sit in a corner, barely listening to the pleasant jazz music and hardly tasting their drinks.

"It's them," Somi says, stirring her boba thoughtfully. The straw is smudged with her red lipstick. "I can't explain it, either, but it has to be . . ."

Kisa shakes her head. Facts. They're what Kisa lives off, they're what she has always thrived on. She lives and breathes facts—cold, unshakable logic. Comfort can be taken in facts' unchanging rigidities, and facts tell her that inmyunjo are no more inclined to be Unruly than a mouse is inclined to attack a mountain cat. "I don't think it's Chaeyeon and Korain," she says as she pulls out her notebook, flipping to the *Suspects* page and nibbling on her pen. "It doesn't *fit*."

"What other context would you take the conversation in?"

She falters. "I don't know *what* context to take it in. The underwear . . ."

"No, that *was* strange." Somi sighs as she chews on a boba. She lets Kisa scribble away in silence for some time before asking abruptly, "Do you—do you still like romance books?"

Her pen falters at the startlingly random change in topic. Setting it down, Kisa blinks. "I, well, yes, I do," she admits slowly. "Did . . . Hani?" Could a serial killer enjoy something as wonderful as a sweeping love story? Surely not.

Right?

Across from her, Somi smiles a bit bashfully—a startling contrast to her usual confident grins—and reaches into her vintage black YSL purse. "I took a few things down with me," she says, and Kisa grimaces, reminded of the hell that is turn-around day. "This book was one of them." From the leather depths she withdraws a book that is in the worst possible condition a book can be in. Kisa, who kept her books meticulously uncreased and had heart palpitations whenever she accidentally cracked a spine, cannot help an offended gasp at the sheer mess the novel is in. Yellow pages that look like they've been drenched in water at some point or another, a cover that's half falling apart, and a distinct smell of mildew.

"*Great bloody hells,*" Kisa hisses, staring at Somi in ripe offense and wounded accusation. "Did you do this?"

Somi blinks, and then smirks, pushing the book over to her. "I preserved it as best as I could, actually. That was all you, unn—Kisa."

That is the worst thing anybody has ever told her. "Sacrilege," Kisa croaks, feeling rather faint, and delicately smooths out the cover as to better see the artwork and title.

Kidnapped by the Time-Traveling Highland Pirate-King, the font over the clinch cover reads in shiny English. A shirtless man stands on the lookout post of a pirate ship, one hand around the wooden pole as both his hair and bright red kilt stream in the wind. In his other arm is a buxom blond woman who seems to have swooned.

It looks delicious. The sort of *smutty* delicious that Kisa would hide in her dormitory from Yuna, reading only at night under her covers with a flashlight and a pounding heart. It's been so long since she held a book like this in her hands. Seven years. Her mouth practically waters.

"That was your—Hani's—favorite," Somi says with a hesitant smile. "I grabbed it from my room this morning, because I thought you might like to read it."

"Have you read it?" Kisa asks curiously, delicately flipping to page forty-five. The black letters are dark with water stains, but still perfectly legible. Kisa blushes as she reads a few *interesting* sentences in chapter fourteen. Oh, yes. This looks quite good indeed.

"What if I told you . . ." Somi suddenly giggles, before masking the almost girlish sound with a cough. "What if I told you I learned English just to read that book?"

"No," Kisa chokes out, caught between laughter and shock. "Did you really?"

"*Yes,*" Somi replies, grinning, and Kisa decides in that moment that she might even be glad she met Nam Somi—even if they met because Somi had tried to eat somebody. "I have a trunk full of them in my room if you want more. There's this one that I've read thirteen times..."

"What is *that*?" Neither woman had noticed Hajun as he silently crept to their table, but he's here now, holding a sleep-bleary Hwanin. He's staring at *Kidnapped by the Time-Traveling Highland Pirate-King* in horror.

"Er, nothing," Kisa blurts, stuffing the mass-market paperback in the deep pocket of her scrubs.

Somi grins at Hajun a bit devilishly. "A very, very dirty romance book."

Hajun goes blue. "Uh," he says eloquently, clearly fumbling for words. "Is this a book club? Could I join? I know how to read—"

"We know you can read, Hajun." Kisa quickly rises before he can embarrass himself further. The look he gives her says *thank you* and *oh my God, why did I say that*. "How's Hwanin?" she asks as she takes the baby.

"I just fed him, with the recipe you left me," Hajun replies, clearing his throat and glancing nervously at an amused-looking Somi.

"Oh, good," Kisa breathes, and then frowns. "Where's Seokga?" The red thread stretches out of the café, and the god that it connects her to is nowhere in sight. A hand flutters distractedly to her heart as she feels a small, insistent tug deep within it. "Weren't you two working together?"

Hajun takes the seat across from Somi. "He was pulled away by an old woman with huge sunglasses, actually."

"His therapist," Kisa realizes, smoothing Hwanin's hair away from his small face. "Did you find any passageways?" Chances are slim, she knows, with a lack thereof on the blueprints—but she still feels a prickling of hope.

"Um, unfortunately not... It was a great idea, though, Kisa. One of many more to come from your gigantic brain, I bet," he ribs. "Besides the, uh, book—what else did you guys find?"

Somi opens her mouth to explain, but a moment later, a very disgruntled-looking Seokga is stalking up to their table, slamming his cane down on the floor with each step as if he'd very much like to cleave the SRC *Flatliner* in two. Kisa's hand falls from her chest as the red thread shakes, and she resists the urge to flip to the page in her notes on the Threaded connection and observe how even the *string* seems afraid of Seokga's moods. But she resists, keeping the pages on the list of suspects and scrawling down what they've learned while Somi quickly relates it to the two men. Kisa peeks up at the seat across from her where Seokga sits, eyeing her flat white like he'd gladly guzzle the caffeine despite it not being iced as she's noticed he favors.

Don't do it, she tells herself. *Don't you dare do it. Squash instead.*

But then he's looking up at her, eyebrows furrowed in a way that tells her he's heard her thoughts, and the notorious, infamous god looks so—tired. So vulnerable. And she's remembering how he watched the mermaids with her, grinning as night air whipped his dark locks, entertaining her excited ramblings in a way that even Hajun sometimes grows tired of.

Well, drat.

This won't be *at all* conducive to her determined squashing.

Hesitantly, and with a sense of great defeat, Kisa pushes her cup toward him. His eyes widen in surprise. She tries, furiously, not to blush as she returns her attention to the notebook, but she's very aware of how he raises the mug to his lips and tentatively sips it.

—needed—this—fucking—therapy—daddy issues—Mireuk—damn it—want—Kisa—coffee—

His thoughts are a distressed jumble, and Kisa is suddenly overcome with the intense desire to smooth them out. Something happens then, in the Creature Café, in the midst of a murder investigation—something that is incredibly fascinating from a scholarly level, and amazing from a, well, Kisa level. The bond between the god and the gwisin begins to glow at Kisa's end—not scarlet, but a calm silver. Silver travels from her pinky to his, where it seems to seep into his skin . . . And a moment later, the lines on Seokga's forehead smooth.

What in the world . . . ? Kisa's lips part in confused wonder a moment before Somi concludes, with no lack of confident gusto, that she is 99.99 percent certain that Shin Korain and Lim Chaeyeon are the perpetrators they're looking for.

Shaking her head to clear it, Kisa rips—with a difficulty that surprises her—her gaze away from Seokga and focuses it on Somi. "We can't ignore that .01 percent," she informs them, absentmindedly stroking a dozing Hwanin's head. "Inmyunjo Unrulies . . ."

". . . are practically nonexistent," her god corrects. No, not *her* god—Seokga. Seokga. Kisa's cheeks flush. This is horrible. "It was my job, thanks to this one here"—Seokga gives his baby brother a withering glance that reluctantly softens a moment later when Hwanin toothlessly yawns—"to hunt down twenty thousand Unruly monsters. In all the ten thousand something I hunted, I never once came across an inmyunjo. Not even in Gamangnara."

"Ten thousand?" Kisa can't help but repeat with a wry smile before she can stop herself. "Not thirty thousand?"

Seokga grimaces and mutters something into her coffee. Kisa attempts to wipe the smile off her face and fails quite miserably.

"There are always exceptions," Somi rebukes, glaring at Seokga who returns her glower with animosity. "There are Unruly haetae. Why not inmyunjo?"

"Inmyunjo take the values of peace more seriously than any other creature. It's ingrained in their culture . . . And it's too easy," Seokga snaps. "And anything that's too easy is wrong." He glances at Kisa, and the weight of his stare is heavy and sad. "I learned that the hard way."

Her hands spasm in her lap and she squashes the urge to reach for him.

"We can't just ignore this, though," Hajun argues, drumming his fingers on the table.

"No," admits Kisa. "No, of course not. I'm only saying that we shouldn't view this case as fully closed yet. We have enough incriminating evidence to focus our attentions on them, but we can't close our minds off to other possibilities—although I struggle to come up with an explanation as to why they were snooping through Hwanin's room, or said the things they did . . ." It's hard to write with Hwanin in her lap, but Kisa manages. "Seokga, is there any way you might contact Hwanung without revealing what's happened? If he's the 'Boss' they spoke of, he might let something slip."

Seokga nods, then curses. "I should have grabbed Hwanin's phone," he hisses. "There might have been evidence on there. Texts, calls . . . Fuck. *Fuck!*"

"World's shittiest detective," Somi sings under her breath, and nudges Kisa with a smile that's rather smug. "Aren't you so happy to have *me*?"

A zip of green shoots down the red thread from Seokga to Kisa, and she is suddenly struck with an intense feeling of jealousy that is most decidedly not her own.

"Erm," she eloquently manages, hands itching to flip to the page on the red thread in her notebook. "Er . . ." Her mind whirls. First silver, then green. It can't be a fluke. Emotional transference? She has decided that yes, the red thread is some sort of conduit—a conduit through which thoughts—and now emotions—can be shared. Does this new development mean that the red thread is growing stronger?

The thread itself quivers, and Kisa gasps as it *twists* itself into scarlet letters—WOULDN'T YOU LIKE TO KNOW—but smooths itself out so quickly that by the time Kisa has kicked Seokga under the table in alarm it's a perfectly normal Red Thread of Fate. Figures.

Seokga frowns at her, reaching down under the table to rub his shin.

—*why*—*kick me*—

Perhaps she imagined it. Kisa clears her throat. "Can you get the phone now?" she manages to ask Seokga.

"It will have disintegrated with the body," the trickster seethes. "Blinked out of existence. But, yes, I can call Hwanung on my own. Although he'll undoubtedly be suspicious. The last time I called him, it was to read him an entire *Godly Gossip* article about how his fashion sense has diminished in recent years."

Hajun winces. "I think *Godly Gossip* is distributed down here, too," he says, and Kisa is quite sure that Somi is playing footsie with him underneath the table (judging by his half-pleased, half-frightened expression that so often pops out around her . . . and the suspicious thumps on the table's underside). "It's a magazine, right?"

"Hwanin's ti—I mean, *Hwanung's* tits." Seokga scowls. "It's down here, too? Is there no escape?"

"It actually reminds me of..." Alarm rises in Kisa when she sees Hajun's face fall as he trails off. The footsie abruptly stops, and Somi's eyes widen almost imperceptibly with concern.

"Did I kick you too hard?" the gumiho asks nervously, but Kisa knows it's not that.

"Hajun..." Kisa reaches across the table for her friend. His fingers are trembling slightly as they wrap around hers.

Every so often this will happen—her kind, sweet friend will be dragged down by his demons. In the weeks after Kim Hajun arrived, bits and pieces of his story trickled out. During the last years of his life, Hajun had been hounded by paparazzi. His name was everywhere in the tabloids, vicious rumors swirling after he met a girl he liked for lunch at a small ramyeon shop. That was all she was—a girl he really, really liked—but she happened to be in the public eye as well, and their innocent, hopeful meeting started off a chain reaction that ended, ultimately, in a torrent of malice surrounding both idols. Hajun's agency hadn't let him leave the complex in which he and the other members lived until the storm died down. But for Hajun, the storm had begun a long, long while ago.

When he'd arrived on the SRC *Flatliner,* Hajun's weight had been significantly lower than it should have been for a man of his age and height. During the Restoration process, Kisa had almost immediately diagnosed him with anorexia nervosa, specifically the binge-eating/purging subtype—not to be confused with bulimia. The demands of the idol life had taken an extreme toll on him after his debut with ST4RLIGHT. Hajun would eat meals that *seemed* nutritiously fulfilling, even excessively healthy—but would purge them from his body straight afterward with extreme and obsessive exercise paired, at times, with vomiting. His expertly styled hair had been so brittle, his skin so dry.

It broke her heart. Kim Hajun had been called the "golden light" of the K-pop industry. He was heralded as one of the happiest, kindest idols—videos of him laughing during fan-signings had at least half a million views on YouTube each—and when he died by his own hand, Kisa has no doubt that the same tabloids that tormented him published long, money-grabbing pieces mourning him. His agency, too, seems no better from what Hajun told her. SPOTLiGHT was the driving force behind Hajun's disorder: policing what he ate, how he dressed, scrutinizing his every smile, every word he spoke or sang. Parts of Hajun's audience were no better. One quiet night aboard the *Flatliner,* her friend whispered to her some of the comments he'd received—and they were awful, truly awful. She'd felt the slow crawl of horror as she realized that Hajun had memorized them so completely he could recite them, word for word.

It had been Hajun's hand and razor that cut through his veins, but Kisa feels a surge of anger at the world that put the blade in his hand in the first place. She squeezes Hajun's palm tight, holding his eyes with her own—which are suddenly swimming with tears. The love she has for Hajun is so very deep that his pain is her pain. He's the brother she never had, and she *hates* seeing him slip back into such a dark place.

"They're not here," Kisa tells him firmly. "They can't get to you here. *Godly Gossip* only focuses on the pantheon. Never mortal idols. You're safe here, Hajun. I promise."

A glistening tear slips down his face, and he hastily wipes it away, shrinking down in his chair in clear embarrassment and shame. Kisa feels her throat tighten. If Somi makes fun of him for crying, she'll . . . she'll . . . Well, really, Kisa has no idea what she'll do, but it won't be pleasant. At all.

But the gumiho surprises her. Somi abruptly stands from her seat and pushes her way to the front of the Creature Café's line. When she comes back a minute or two later, she's holding a large boba drink. She places it in front of Hajun, along with the fat straw. "Stab it through the plastic covering on top," Somi tells Hajun as she slides back into her seat. "Stab it *hard*, and then take a long drink."

Kisa slips her hand away from Hajun's grip as he stares at Somi in bemusement. "Why?"

"It helps," says Nam Somi with a tremor in her voice, and Kisa feels a surge of remorse—not for the first time—about how horrible her death must have been. "Stabbing it can be cathartic."

A little bit of light blinks back into Hajun's eyes as he unwraps the thick straw and—with a swift, almost violent motion—does what Somi says. It stabs through the thin plastic covering the cup, and Hajun *laughs* before he takes a sip of the drink, dark boba blurred within the slightly transparent pink straw.

Kisa feels a small surge of surprise, relief, pride. A few months ago, Hajun would never have touched the sugary drink despite the food in the underworld being pretty illusions with no caloric benefits (save for candies like Kopiko, smuggled from the world of the living above). Now, he takes a second sip, and then smiles a tiny, hesitant smile. "This is . . . really good," he whispers. "I love it, actually."

"It's winter melon with honey, boba, and grass jelly," Somi replies with a grin around her own straw. "Mine's jasmine milk tea with lychee, if you want to try it."

Kisa glances at Seokga, wondering if she is the only one feeling as if she is witnessing something unexpectedly profound and delicate. The god's face is surprisingly soft as he watches the two switch bobas. Somi tries Hajun's and laughs—an unexpectedly girlish sound, innocent and bright. When she met Somi for the first time in the sick bay, she never would have thought the gumiho's laugh would sound like that. Like tinkling bells.

"It's so sweet!" she half-gasps, spluttering. "I didn't expect it to be so sweet!"

Hajun's lips tilt upward. "Yeah," he murmurs, "me neither." But he isn't looking at the drink.

He's looking at Somi.

CHAPTER SEVENTEEN

SEOKGA

Seokga tries very hard to ignore the fact that Kisa is sitting next to him on his bed.

It is just a bed, he tells himself, clenching his phone hard enough that he worries he might break it. *It is just a bed. And you are a terrible pervert.*

Hwanin, perched on his other knee, gurgles.

From the way Kisa's cheeks go blue, he can tell that she's had the incredible misfortune of hearing some of that thought.

"I'm sorry," he manages, wishing—not for the first time today—to hurl himself off the ship and let the ineo take some chomps out of him. Seokga expects Kisa to stiffly stand up and move, but to his surprise, she stays where she is: perched at the edge, hair a mess of soft curls that fall to her waist as she fidgets with the hairband in her fingers.

He has discovered that he quite likes her hair: an untamed lion's mane, streaked with so many shades of brown . . . like coffee, Seokga realizes with a strange swelling of his heart. There are strands of mocha intermingled with warm macchiato. And her roots are somewhat lighter than the Irish coffee ends, reminding him almost of a frappé . . .

Seokga jerks back to himself as he realizes Kisa is saying . . . no, *thinking* something.

—*squash*—*just*—*squash*—*squash*—

It's not the first time he's heard this particular mantra. "Out of curiosity," prompts Seokga, "I was wondering if you could explain your fixation with *squashes*."

She blinks. Frantically. "It's a—just a—"

"Mmhmm," says Seokga. "Do you prefer acorn or butternut?"

"It's a *method*," Kisa finally settles on, sliding off the bed to stand on the floor (*ah,* he thinks, *there it is*), shifting her weight from foot to foot. "Of, well, staying focused. On the mystery. And not on, erm, other things."

He feels a slow, dangerous smile stretching his lips. "Am I distracting?"

"No . . ." Yet the pained grimace of annoyance and something *else* on her face is confirmation enough. He blinks. Is Kisa . . . *attracted* to him? Subtly, he shifts in his seat to better pose for her admiration.

Unfortunately, it doesn't seem as if she's taking any notice. His disappointment flares down the bond, a morose and humiliating shade of gray-blue.

Immediately, Kisa's eyes are shining as she tracks the color, and Seokga guesses that she's about to launch into a detailed explanation of the red thread's new ability to share their feelings down the bond. He's proven correct. "First cerebration transference," she says excitedly, past awkwardness forgotten, "and now emotional transference! It's a brilliant discovery—"

He dearly wishes to believe that Kisa is excited about feeling his tangled emotions down the bond, but he suspects she's more thrilled by the sheer discovery of it. As she excitedly speaks on, pacing the length of the room, Seokga stares at his cellphone, wondering what in the seven hells he's going to say to Hwanung and wishing that Yoo Kisa didn't possess the unique ability to make him feel like a science experiment.

Kisa's voice slowly dies, and Seokga feels a surge of guilt as he realizes she must know he wasn't listening. Stopping in front of him, her cheeks are azure, and when she mumbles an apology, he feels a surge of anger at himself. "Don't *ever* apologize for being excited about something," he tells her, and his voice comes out harder than he means it to.

—*need to stop—doing this—to him—*

Her eyes, her damn eyes, widen—and warm before she averts them to the ground. "No," she murmurs, "in this case, I really should. I forget, sometimes, how it must feel to be in your shoes."

His breath catches in his throat. Kisa looks back up at him, and her expression is pained. And damn it, Seokga can feel his heart cracking down the middle, the fissure spreading and spreading through the useless organ. He would do anything to kick off these *shoes*.

What rotten luck—to have the red thread manifest the same day Kisa died. The same day, if Hajun is to be believed, that Kisa gave up hope.

I'd like you to consider, Seokga, that it is you and Kisa that fate has chosen to vouch for. How, he thinks bitterly, could fate be so cruel? He's never done anything to upset Gameunjang Aegi, the pantheon's shy goddess of luck, fate, and fortune.

(Well, except for the time he secretly submitted an application to Okhwang's most popular dating show on her behalf and—through an expert work of deception on his part—got her to show up on set in a two-person cow costume. A bewildered Samsin Halmoni had been the rear. In a rare act of solidarity, Seokga and *Godly Gossip* had had a field day with that one.)

Now, both ends of the red thread glow a deep, dark blue. The colors seep through the thread and cross to the opposite side, both god and gwisin tasting each other's depthless sadness.

"It's not a walk in the park," Seokga manages to finally reply. "Or rather, it is—but a walk in the park while wearing a pair of shoes lined with pins and needles."

Kisa's eyes soften.

—has to be—the biggest understatement—

Seokga snorts despite himself. "Yes," he finds himself saying. "Yes, I'd say that's an understatement."

Her eyes widen. "Oh, no—did you hear—"

"I did."

Kisa stares at the thread in what seems like betrayal. And, so fast that he almost misses it, the thread seems to curl itself into small blue letters before innocently smoothing itself out.

"Did you see—?" she chokes out. "It did that in the café— I thought I imagined it . . ."

"It spelled 'HAHAHA,'" Seokga replies, narrowing his eyes at the bond. "I think."

"That is . . ." Kisa shakes her head. "I'm *really* quite certain this thing is alive, somehow." She reaches out with a finger as if to poke it, but her skin passes through it. She tries again, to no avail. Kisa raises her pinky to her face and stares at the knot with burning intensity.

"*What* are you trying to do?" Seokga asks with laughter in his voice despite himself. The thread returns to red from blue. "Goad it into speaking? I think that's stretching the bounds of what's possible."

"If anybody could do it, you could," she replies, nose crinkling in confused concentration. "Go on, try."

"What?"

"Try to make it admit to being a sentient creature." Kisa turns her hopeful eyes onto him. "*Please*," she adds, and he sighs, setting down the phone. It seems Hwanung will have to wait. Kisa has somehow mastered the art of puppy-dog eyes to the extent that Seokga will willingly behave like a fool for her.

He fixes his eyes on the thread, which seems to him to be putting special effort into looking like ordinary red string. "String," Seokga says with a very menacing, authoritative air, "reveal yourself!"

Nothing happens.

"It was a good effort," encourages Kisa. "Try again. Perhaps use some threats. You're historically very good at that."

He preens under her praise. How kind of her to notice. "Yes, I am." Seokga clears his throat and proceeds to tell the Red Thread of Fate, in great and gruesome detail, how he is perfectly capable of finding a pair of craft scissors and chopping it up into small, shredded pieces. If he's not mistaken, the thread shivers. Yet nothing else happens.

Except Kisa's laughter. Her shoulders are shaking and she's clapped a hand to her mouth. A grin pulls at the corner of Seokga's lips as Kisa shakes her head. In his lap, Hwanin begins to giggle, too, although it's clear that the baby has no idea why he's laughing.

"This is concerning," Kisa half-gasps. "Whenever you say the most horrible things, I *laugh*."

—*squash*—*squash*—

Whatever this *squashing* is, Seokga intends to put a quick stop to it. He shrugs, attempting to appear nonchalant and failing as the thread carries his bright golden triumph down to her. He glares at it before realizing that Kisa is looking at him with those godsdamn twinkling eyes of hers.

"I think it's time you use some of your threats on Hwanung."

Ah. Right. With a start, he yanks his phone out of his brother's gummy grip and makes a face of disgust as he wipes the saliva-ridden device on his pants. Kisa laughs then leans over to take the baby from him with a knowing smile, and a small part of Seokga feels as if he is on the precipice of finding something he once lost.

The phone rings once, then twice. Seokga grimaces as he stands by one of the suite's ginormous windows, staring down at the rushing river below. Kisa is off in the bathroom, changing Hwanin's diaper—and *that* actually sounds more appealing than making this fucking call. When Hwanung doesn't pick up, Seokga calls again. And again. The fifth time, his nephew finally answers.

"*What?*" Hwanung snaps. "Another *Godly Gossip* article you want to read to me?"

I wish, Seokga wants to say. Hajun and Somi are currently off infiltrating the security room *again* to pull Korain's and Chaeyeon's locations during the time slot of the murder. Even if that checks out, it doesn't mean that Hwanung isn't somehow involved in this. Kisa is right—he has a motive. "You finally picked up," he says smoothly instead, and he can practically hear Hwanung's eyes roll.

"It's not like you left me much of a choice," Hwanung says sourly. "I was trying to play CookieRun, and I can't do that with your calls popping up all over the place. What do you want, *Uncle?*" He spits the word out like it's something dirty.

Seokga has planned what to say in order to probe some sort of indication of knowledge from Hwanung, and thanks to his trickster nature, he's rather certain he can pull it off. "Hwanin wants to know if you'd like anything from the—"

"WRAHHHH!"

His eyes flare in alarm as Hwanin releases an unearthly yowl from the bathroom.

"If you'd like anything from the gift shop," Seokga finishes, quickly moving away from the closed door of the suite's restroom.

"And why doesn't my father call me himself?"

"*ERRRRGREEEEEEE!*"

"He's . . . occupied," Seokga manages. "I heard about the fight that you two had last night," he adds, the lie flowing easily from his notoriously silver tongue. "Would it really be so surprising if he doesn't want to talk to you?"

Hwanung is silent for a moment. Seokga listens intently to that silence, and dearly misses his mind-reading ability. It wouldn't work on Hwanung anyway, of course: Gods aren't technically *creatures*, but if he had it, he could easily pry the secrets from Chaeyeon's and Korain's minds. Yet his head pounds with a dull ache: For the better part of the morning, he attempted to reach for that power, but it's as if it's blocked by something. Stress, most likely. Hells know that Seokga is *stressed.*

"You were listening?" Hwanung finally demands, voice considerably more strained. When Seokga replies in the affirmative, his nephew is silent again before hissing, "Eavesdropping *snake.*"

Better a serpent than a traitorous rat. "Having a nice time ruling Okhwang?" Seokga asks, abruptly changing the subject to disorient the other god.

"Jealous?" A dry snort.

"The argument greatly affected your father." Seokga picks a stray lint off his black turtleneck. "I wouldn't be surprised if you're sitting smug on the throne right now."

On the other end of the line, Hwanung pauses. "What do you mean?" he asks carefully.

"He cries rather a lot," the trickster muses, "and naps constantly. Would you happen to know anything about that?"

A longer silence this time. Seokga licks his lips, cocks his head, and goes in for the kill.

"You could say that he's unrecognizable. What did you do to him?"

"It's what he deserves," Hwanung finally replies in a voice cold enough to freeze ice. *The little shit.* Seokga hopes he's truly involved in this, if only to finally give the insufferable asshole the punch in the face he dearly needs.

"And what is it that you think you deserve?" Seokga's reply is quick, viper-like in its speed—but still casual, with a hidden layer of sharpness. It's easy enough to guess what their altercation was over. "A new godly affinity? Still hung up on 'sex, drugs, and rock and roll'? Or are you desiring something a little... different? Something bigger?"

"Well," snaps Hwanung, "I'm sitting on the throne, right now—and he's not. I *have* something different, and I like it. Maybe"—and here, his tone becomes white-hot with resentment—"I don't plan to give it up anytime soon. Enjoy your cruise. Goodbye, Uncle."

The younger god hangs up.

The audacity of youth these days.

Seokga stares down at his phone in offended disbelief as Kisa joins his side, Hwanin in her arms. When he glances at her, he's surprised to see that her light blue scrubs are splattered with soapy water and that Hwanin (scowling) looks freshly cleaned.

"So?" she asks, seemingly ignoring how the baby glowers up at her like he wants to throw her to the wolves.

"Hwanung is involved," Seokga mutters. Kisa peers up at him, brows pulling together.

"You're certain? Did you record the call like I showed you? With the app?"

"Probably," says Seokga (who honestly isn't sure—how in the hells the app works is lost on him), and grudgingly takes Hwanin so Kisa can poke around on the infernal device. A moment later, the conversation plays from the phone, and she listens intently before playing it one more time and grabbing her notebook from her pocket and scrawling down a half-page of notes. When she finally comes up for air, she looks troubled.

"It certainly doesn't sound good," she admits, and he sees that she's transcribed the entire conversation onto the page.

"I'll text Yeomra," says Seokga, eager to rid himself of his drooling brother. He attempts to trade baby for phone, but Kisa shakes her head, stopping him.

"Wait," she says. "I want to listen one more time."

She's so careful, so meticulous. Seokga watches her, admiring the way her nose wrinkles in concentration. He can't help but remember how he and Hani had dived right into their investigation, throwing caution to the wind, ready for a whirlwind adventure. A pang of sadness strikes at his heart, but there's a pang of something *else,* too.

A wanting.

Kisa scrubs at her face, stopping the recording as Hwanung says "cruise." Her thoughts bound into Seokga's head, but at such a speed that he can hardly follow them. They're like race cars, bending into hairpin turns at a breakneck speed. Finally, she hands him the phone and takes Hwanung. "Send the recording to the CEO while we wait for Hajun and Somi."

"How do I send the recording?" Seokga asks blankly, and what follows is another baby/phone swap where Kisa sends the recording and Hwanin sneezes on his brother's shoulder. When he has his phone again, Seokga reads what Yeomra has sent back with high brows and a vast amount of irritation.

Yeomra: Maybe I'm cynical, but this isn't enough evidence for me to descend in all my fury and accuse the crown prince of

> murdering his own father. Context is everything, and you were being deliberately subtle . . . It's good, but I need more.
>
> **Yeomra:** Was Hwanung even *on* the ship? I would have known if he took a trip down into my realm.

Kisa sighs, reading the text over his shoulder. "Explain that we think he sent two lackeys," she says, and it's even harder than usual for Seokga to tap his fingers across the screen. If they're right, he loses Kisa. With painstaking slowness, he types out a typo-riddled explanation, and waits for Yeomra's reply.

> **Yeomra:** Seven hells, Seokga. Learn to text. Please. I can't read whatever the fuck it is you tried to send over.

When Kisa giggles (sounding as if she'd attempted very hard not to), still leaning over his shoulder, Seokga thinks he might have a heart palpitation. Her hair smells like cinnamon and soap and it tickles his nose. His fingers tremble slightly as he types out a new explanation, and he hopes his bumbling, nervous thoughts aren't finding their way into Kisa's head. How inept he must seem in comparison to her. Seokga is halfway certain that Yoo Kisa is some sort of genius.

"You are awful at texting," she informs him a moment later.

—*actually the worst—I've ever—seen—*

"I heard that," he mutters and presses SEND on his second attempt.

Yeomra: Slightly better. And I mean SLIGHTLY.

Yeomra: When you have solid proof of the "lackeys," send it over to me. Until then, I'm not counting this case as closed.

Yeomra: P.S. Seokga . . . This cruise ends in five days. So hurry up, or your new reputation is ruined and the girl doesn't reincarnate.

Kisa's breath catches. Angrily, Seokga punches the tiny little letters on the screen into what he feels is an elegant way of defending his—of defending Kisa.

Seokga: fucko ff leave her OUT of ti his!!

With gusto and some pride at his improving texting skills, Seokga shuts off his phone and rams it back into his pocket. A hesitant light yellow color blooms on Kisa's end of the thread, and when it reaches him, Seokga is surprised to feel such warm gratitude from her.

"Your spelling is still atrocious," she says quickly, looking embarrassed.

Seokga smirks.

"While we wait for Hajun and Somi," Kisa adds a long moment later, almost shyly, "perhaps we can take Hwanin to the sundeck? Babies need air, you know, even if the air here isn't exactly . . . well, *fresh* . . ."

Seokga hesitates. Jeoseung's ungodly blazing red sun will be out, and even as an adult, Hwanin's skin was abnormally sensitive to heat. "I don't want him to get a heat rash," Seokga explains after a moment, feeling a strange surge of protectiveness toward the child.

Kisa smiles. "That can be easily prevented," she reassures him, and ten minutes later, they're in one of the SRC *Flatliner*'s many shops, browsing for a tiny pair of sunglasses and a tiny sunbonnet for the former heavenly emperor.

"This one," Kisa suggests, holding up a bright pink atrocity with little flowers all over it. Seokga gags.

"It's too *cheerful*," he snaps before he can stop himself, and winces. But Kisa—to his pleasant surprise—laughs softly.

"You like fashion," she guesses, returning the hat to its shelf and picking out another, this one a dark green that Seokga immediately likes. "You always look . . . You're always in style. Don't you ever wear T-shirts?"

"I would rather die." He's holding Hwanin uncomfortably in his arms, and he could swear the infant snorts at his dramatic words.

The dokkaebi at the boutique's counter snickers before Seokga glares at her and she turns her attention back to the glossy magazine she's flipping through. It's an issue of fucking *Godly Gossip*. The headline reads, HUNKY HWANUNG FOLLOWS IN HIS FATHER'S FOOTSTEPS! READ MORE ABOUT THE INTERIM EMPEROR HERE! Hwanung is winking on the cover in a way that makes the trickster god want to set the page on fire. Perhaps he will.

Seokga clenches his jaw and refuses the urge. With difficulty.

Dr. Jang should be proud.

"Even this one?" Kisa asks, holding up a horrible tie-dye. His face wrinkles in disgust before he can stop it.

"Hwanung's *tits*—" On the atrociously blotty fabric, big bubble letters read: LET'S GET SHIP-FACED!

"Yoo Kisa!" Seokga's back stiffens as a pair of high heels click against the small boutique's tiled floors. A woman who looks vaguely familiar stalks past the rows of swimsuits and merchandise before coming to a fuming stop before Kisa and Seokga. Her eyes are narrowed, and her lipsticked mouth is pressed into a tight line. LEE SOO-MIN, her golden name tag reads.

The dokkaebi at the counter makes an *ooooh* sound, eyes lifting from *Godly Gossip* before hastily averting them back down as the woman directs her glower to *her*.

Hands on her neatly pressed skirt, Soo-min narrows her eyes at Kisa, who's quickly shoving away the shirt. "And why aren't you in the sick bay? Why are you bothering this guest?"

Kisa flushes and opens her mouth to reply, but Seokga gets there first. "She isn't bothering me," he snaps with withering coldness, and Soo-min's head whips to him.

"You!" she hisses, hands balling into fists at her sides. She stomps a heeled foot on the glossy tiled floor. "You *ruined* the greenhouse soiree! You trampled the flowers; you broke the glass—"

Seokga stares down his nose at her, unimpressed. The woman huffs and puffs for a long moment before clumsily regaining her composure. "Kisa," she warns, attention turning back to her, "if you continue to shirk your duties in the sick bay, I will be forced to notify the CEO. You have five seconds to leave."

"Yes, fine," Kisa mutters, looking rather peeved. But there's no way that either of them can explain that the CEO is allowing her to shirk her duties without explaining the little fact of Hwanin's murder. She looks to Seokga, who feels rather frustrated at being thwarted of a mid-morning spent lounging on the sundeck with Kisa, before hastily leaving the little boutique, the red thread growing longer and longer with each step she takes away from him.

"I'll thank you not to consort with the ship's workers," snips Soo-min. "The girl should know better: It's in direct violation of Rule 5 of the SRC *Flatliner*'s handbook."

Seokga's right hand, which is not holding Hwanin, tightens on the hilt of his cane. "I'll thank *you*," he sneers, "to stay out of my business."

The woman's face is growing blue with anger. "As cruise director, everything that happens on this ship is *my* business—"

His smile is small and sharp. Dagger-like. If Soo-min knows what is good for her, she will run away. Very fast. "Mere sniveling mortals have no business meddling in the affairs of their gods. I will spend as much time with Kisa as I please, and if you choose to interfere, I'll make your job as cruise director more of a living hell than it already (and literally) is. Now, if you'll excuse me"—Seokga takes a menacing step closer to her, letting her hesitate in his shadow, allowing his eyes to darken and fill with ice—"I have a bonnet to buy."

CHAPTER EIGHTEEN

SEOKGA

Seokga is not sure which he hates more: Adult Hwanin or Baby Hwanin. Both are exceptionally annoying, but only one wails so loudly that Seokga fears his ears might fall off. Sitting on a sun chair on Deck 10, Hwanin in his lap, Seokga closes his eyes and wishes for the end. He has tried everything to cease his brother's relentless crying, but the child seems determined to make his every moment miserable by *screaming his head off* . . .

Often, Mireuk had told Seokga that *he* had been the most difficult out of the two to raise. With Hwanin shrieking loud enough to scare away some of the sundeck's guests, Seokga feels entirely inclined to vehemently disagree. Hwanin is a nightmare. A raging nightmare shaped into the form of a tiny person.

"Please be quiet," he begs his brother.

Hwanin's response is to glare at him.

Seokga glares back and—to his complete and utter shock—Hwanin grins and abruptly cuts off his wailing.

A shadow suddenly falls over his face, and he protectively scoops Hwanin closer to him. Although the mustachioed man leaning over him looks generally harmless with his salt-and-pepper hair and bespectacled eyes, it would be a lie to say that every moment spent on this damn ship isn't taking a toll on the trickster god. For motives still relatively unknown, his brother was murdered. Seokga has absolutely no desire to be reverted to baby form, and is well aware that he could be next—hence why, before he slept, he transformed his cane into a sword and slept with it in one hand while waking every ten minutes to ensure he—and the baby—were unharmed. Seokga is running on fumes and caffeine at this point: Apart from waking every ten minutes, Hwanin also apparently took a great delight in screeching his lungs out during random points in the nighttime.

An effective torture method. Seokga took copious notes.

So, needless to say, Seokga is inherently suspicious of this man, even as he takes in the white suit and its shoulder stripes, indicative of the ship's captain. A gold name tag indeed reads, CAPTAIN LEE.

"Is there something in particular you want?" Seokga snaps, very rudely.

The captain shakes his head, crouching down to look at Hwanin. "Always a shame when there are babies on board," he murmurs, reaching out a finger to poke Hwanin's nose. Seokga grits his teeth and moves Hwanin away. He didn't give the man permission to touch him, and contemplates slapping his hand away. But Captain Lee seems to have gotten the point, folding his hands behind his back. "How did it happen?"

"How did *what* happen?" Exhausted, and wishing Kisa were here, Seokga doesn't even attempt to be polite.

Captain Lee's bushy brows rise. "You died together, I assume?"

With a start, Seokga realizes that Captain Lee doesn't recognize him. He smiles slowly, and most unpleasantly. "Yes."

"How?"

Will this man not leave? "A gigantic volcano exploded," Seokga says nastily. "On us."

Hwanin blows a raspberry, either amused by the lie or more probably amused by the man's mustache, which he swipes at.

"A shame," the captain says again then sighs. "To die so young... I'm very sorry." As Seokga continues to smile unpleasantly, Captain Lee's cheeks tinge pink and he rubs his mustache awkwardly.

Pink?

"You're alive," Seokga realizes, surprised. He'd assumed the captain was just as dead as his guests. And—from what he's observed—Captain Lee is very human. What sort of living mortal accepts a job navigating a ship in the underworld? Why in hells did Yeomra employ him?

Captain Lee's expression turns guilty and he suddenly looks hesitant, possibly fearing Seokga's jealousy. "Well, yes," he admits, and is quick to add, "I'll be dead eventually, though. Just like you two." He tries to tap Hwanin's nose again. Seokga fixes him with an icy stare, and he gives up.

"What are you doing down here?" he demands, still rather shocked. "Yeomra doesn't employ the living."

"Ah. The CEO." Captain Lee sighs. "He heard about my former ship, the *Seoul Carnival*. Apparently he views it as the SRC *Flatliner*'s competition, although they're in completely different realms— literally and figuratively. He, uh, offered me a deal I couldn't refuse."

Seokga is quite an accomplished blackmailer, and thus immediately recognizes what Yeomra likely did—sending a jeoseung saja after the captain with some mellow bribery (*How'd you like to skip the seven hells in the afterlife?*) and reverting to other tactics (kidnapping) when the mortal man refused/expressed disbelief in the Korean underworld. To his great disgust, he feels a twinge of respect for Yeomra. It was nicely done. Very nice. He's taking notes. "Ah," says Seokga. Captain Lee appears to be sweating nervously.

"It's not so bad. I get Seollal off. Sometimes my birthday, too."

He glances around anxiously, as if worrying that Yeomra might be listening in. It's not exactly unlikely. "Well, I hope that you've been enjoying the cruise together." He rises. "Just off for a quick stretch of the legs myself. Navigating these waters can be a tiring business... If you and your son are ever interested in watching how this ship is piloted, the bridge is on Deck 8, just past the spa. We'd be happy to have you."

Seokga only relaxes when the captain has walked off. He's cradling Hwanin protectively and, in that moment, realizes his brother has stopped crying and is instead staring up at him with those ridiculous, star-studded eyes.

"What do you want?" Seokga mutters in annoyance, but finds himself delicately adjusting his tiny bonnet and slipping sunglasses. Jeoseung's sun is disgustingly hot on the sundeck, and he checks Hwanin's exposed arms and toes to make sure they're not burned. He relaxes slightly when he sees that they're fine. "You look ridiculous, brother," he informs Hwanin. "You should see your hat. Absolutely atrocious. A disgrace to the pantheon."

There's an ache in his chest when the baby stares cluelessly up at him. Although he'll eventually regain his memories, his stomach knots with the knowledge that this child knows nothing of Seokga's ancient betrayal, or the years of resentment festering between them. For a moment, he longs for the adult Hwanin. He misses *fighting* with him. They would never again be brothers that casually hugged and laughed, but they'd developed a new kind of brotherhood—one built on insults. For thirty-three brief years, it had almost been glorious. But only now does Seokga realize that.

And one can't exactly insult a baby or blame a baby for machinating a series of events that led to Hani's death. Some of his bitterness begins to unwind, and Kisa's question—about the Ship of Theseus—comes back to him. Is this the same Hwanin? Will he ever be the same Hwanin again, even when his memories come back?

Perhaps this could be a clean slate for both of them.

Hesitantly, Seokga smiles down at the baby. It could be magnificent, a terrific story of redemption wherein he raises Hwanin like his own, and Hwanin—when he regains his memory—is entirely indebted to him... Perhaps Hwanin might even offer to share his throne...

Seokga's smile abruptly drops as Hwanin sticks out his tongue and begins to float up into the air.

CHAPTER NINETEEN

KISA

GUILT THRUMS THROUGH Kisa's blood as she enters the sick bay to see little Kun-woo waiting expectantly by the reception desk. The ten-year-old's head barely reaches its top. He's holding a teddy bear, and hugs it tight as Kisa approaches.

"Dr. Yoo," Kun-woo sniffles, and she sees that there's a trickle of blue blood spilling from somewhere underneath his messy mop of hair. "I'm bleeding again. Can you help me, please?"

That's the problem with Restorations, Kisa thinks grimly as she ushers Kun-woo to a patient room and seats him on the cot before hurriedly pulling on her latex gloves and gently beginning her work. Depending on the level of emotional trauma that patient experiences, the healing Restorations might come undone if the gwisin is distressed enough. And Kun-woo, who died in a horrific seven-car pileup, is often distressed. For the eight weeks—and eight cruises—he's stayed on the SRC *Flatliner,* Kisa has had to Restore him six times.

A familiar sadness tightens her throat. Although Kun-woo is well past the age of being one of her small, newborn patients in the Magical Maternity Unit, an old guilt churns in Kisa's stomach. If only the powers that Samsin Halmoni granted her had extended to human mothers, human babies. If only she had been able to save *more,* help *more* . . .

Like her own mother. But even the interventions of Samsin Halmoni's shamans on her father's side hadn't been enough to save her.

Kisa's hands tremble, and with a pinch of her lips, she forces her mind to go blank, fixating intently on the minute work of weaving flesh back together. Repairing the stitches takes almost an hour, and when she finally sends a groggy Kun-woo off to buy a bowl of miyeok-guk from one of the ship's restaurants (doctor's orders), she's exhausted and angry at herself. Kun-woo hadn't been waiting long, he'd said, but if Soo-min hadn't gotten to her, who knows how the little boy would have fared. All of his stitches might have unraveled, leaving him a bloody mess, and dragging him back down into despair. She curses herself for having gotten too distracted with Seokga.

She's never had to balance friendship and work before—she never had anybody more than an acquaintance to juggle with her hospital responsibilities. Kisa vows to become better at it. As she exits the bathroom, hands scrubbed and smelling of lemon soap, the sight of Hajun and Somi greets her. They're leaning against the counter, waiting for her.

"Hey." Hajun's eyes flick to her furrowed brow. He's still drinking his boba. "Is everything okay?"

"Kun-woo," she explains, in a tired way of explanation.

Pity crosses the idol's face. "The last Restoration came undone again?"

"It had just started to." Kisa rubs her face wearily. "He's doing well, though. A bit woozy from the sedative, but he'll bounce back within the hour. I sent him to get some soup. Did you find where Chaeyeon and Korain were around the time of the murder?"

"About that," says Somi, and then pauses. "Where's the baby?" she asks, frowning.

"Right here." The red thread gives a little tug around her finger, and Kisa looks up to see Seokga stalking through the doorway, Hwanin on his hip. To her surprise, the child is wearing the bonnet that she loved and Seokga so vehemently hated—along with a tiny pair of sunglasses. Seokga looks frazzled, and Hwanin looks suspiciously smug. Seokga's verdant gaze snaps to hers and softens. "Kisa," the trickster says, "is it normal for babies to float ten feet up into the air?"

As if to demonstrate, Hwanin grins and begins to rise out of his brother's arm. Seokga snatches him back down by his chubby foot, looking extremely panicked.

"He's flying already?" she asks, eyes widening. "Oh, that's—that's *incredible!*"

The trickster looks extraordinarily unhappy.

"Books on infant gods are so scarce, with such limited information, even for Samsin Halmoni's shamans," she explains, attempting not to gush, but failing spectacularly. She's practically quivering with excitement. "It's possible that Okhwang's Heavenly Library has numerous volumes, but, well, nobody but the pantheon is permitted clearance. So it's been widely *assumed* that powers don't emerge until early childhood, perhaps three or four, but Hwanin doesn't seem—by my estimations, of course—more than a year old at the very most. With demigods, powers don't appear until six or seven, and I've never seen a child this young *flying* . . . I wonder if it's altered his density, at all, or his gravitational center—"

She cuts off abruptly as a flash of intense violet, much more vibrant than the deep, royal shade of embarrassment from earlier, shoots down the thread. It's hot and sharp, as if hundreds of little needles are prickling at her skin. Panic—Seokga's panic and worry. His face is so . . . pale.

"Kisa," he says in a voice that she suspects is barely controlled, "that's all very fascinating. But is it *normal*? Or is there something wrong with him?" Again, that panic.

Right. Kisa presses her lips together. She's gotten carried away again. "Infant gods do have their powers, just not the same control over them as their adult selves. He'll be all right, Seokga." She wonders why the god seems to know less about infant deities than she does, but it's apparent that Seokga doesn't like children very much. She wouldn't be surprised if he actively avoids them at all costs.

Relief smooths out his face, followed by an expression of supreme annoyance as Hwanin's tiny hand smacks his mouth. Kisa watches in amusement as Seokga's eyes meet hers, silently begging for help.

You're on your own, she thinks, hoping the thread carries her thoughts to him.

By the way his green eyes narrow to slits, she knows it has.

—*Kisa—please—he is—insufferable*—

She ignores it. Brotherly bonding is important, after all. Hwanin needs to have a secure attachment to somebody, and since she'll be reincarnated soon (if this all goes well, mystery and squashing both), it's best to leave Hwanin where he is in Seokga's arm. Something in Kisa's chest twists, and she winces as light blue streaks from her side of the thread to Seokga's. The god falters, staring back at her. His thoughts are a jumbled mess.

—*why—sad—Kisa—Hani—want—wish—hope*—

Clearing her throat, Kisa turns back to Hajun, who's watching her in worry—close enough to understand her tells. "So?" she asks before her friend can say anything. "Where were they around eight-thirty last night?"

Hajun hesitates, setting down his boba and glancing at Somi.

"Chaeyeon left the greenhouse at the same time as Hwanin," the gumiho says, lacing her hands together and meeting Kisa's eye, as if delivering a formal report. "Hwanin made his way to the I-95, and for a short while, Chaeyeon wasn't too far behind him."

Kisa holds her breath. "She was following him?"

Hajun shakes his head ever so slightly and gestures for Kisa to keep listening.

"But while Hwanin continued on to Deck 0, Chaeyeon stopped on Deck 2, where she disposed of the broken glass in the garbage compactor. Afterward, she continued on to Deck 1, where she entered a cabin and stayed for the duration of the night. Meanwhile, Korain left the greenhouse around eight-fifteen P.M. ...."

"With Lee Soo-min," adds Hajun, and Kisa chews on her bottom lip.

"And where did he go?"

"The cameras track Korain heading up to Deck 8, to the bridge for the night watch."

Her heart is sinking in her chest. "And he stays there?"

"Until midnight, when he swaps out with another man," Somi confirms.

"But that's well past the time of the murder..." Exhaling in disappointment and growing confusion, Kisa draws out her notebook and flips through the pages. "Are we sure—are we *certain* that's the correct footage? Why was Chaeyeon going through Hwanin's room? Who's their 'Boss' if not Hwanung?" She hands the transcript from Seokga's phone call to Hajun and watches anxiously as he reads, Somi looking over his shoulder.

The gumiho's brows rise. "I would say that's some solid evidence," she says. "But as to your question about why the two were rummaging around in Hwanin's room..." Kisa watches as Somi glances to Seokga warily. "He's not going to like this. At all."

"Try me," the trickster grits out, snatching Hwanin back down from the air like the child is an errant balloon.

Somi hesitates, looking surprisingly nervous, before she licks her lips and smooths down her expensive-looking silk blouse. She's carrying her usual black purse, and with hesitant fingers, reaches into it and delicately retrieves a glossy, light pink Samsung. After pulling up a screen, she hands it to Kisa, whose mouth drops as she stares down at the blog post.

THE INTIMATE SCOOP ON HOTTIE HWANIN'S INTIMATES! the text reads in swirly pink letters, followed by:

> We at *Godly Gossip* have received *intimate* info on the gorgeous HOTTIE HWANIN! Readers beware: Some *steamy scoops* lie ahead!
>
> One question that has plagued pantheon fans for centuries is if the gorgeous emperor prefers boxers or briefs... And thanks to an anonymous source, we now have our answer! Underneath those majestic hanboks, the divine royal loins are most often clothed in (drumroll, please) *briefs*!
>
> (Specifically, Calvin Klein 1996 Micro Hip Briefs in white, size M. "They're the only underwear he has," our source tells us, although they're quick to add that he has one pair of pajama pants of the silken variety.)
>
> An ages-old mystery is now solved! Now, the only thing left to wonder is: What does SEXY SEOKGA prefer? Something tells us here at *Godly Gossip* that he leans toward boxer briefs (specifically of the Lacoste variety, size M, colors black or dark green)... but the tantalizing trickster always has a surprise or two up his sleeve! Place your bets now, because we are confident this is another question we'll receive an answer to soon!

"It will be in the physical issue tomorrow," Somi says, backing away from Seokga as he snatches the phone from Kisa and stares aghast at the text. She's certain that her own expression is just as horrified. "Their 'Boss' must be someone at *Godly Gossip*. Perhaps the editor in chief offered to put in a good word with Yeomra if they got them this information."

"If I ever find out who their editor is," snarls Seokga, "I will wreak havoc on their lives. I will set fire to their home and office. I will slowly and painfully rip them into tiny little pieces and—"

Somi smirks. "Wait. You don't know who runs *Godly Gossip*?"

Seokga looks as if he's just bit into a sour lemon. "*Obviously.*"

The gumiho's shoulders are shaking with silent laughter. Seokga is glaring at her suspiciously. "Who—"

"This explains the underwear," Kisa mutters in growing defeat, reaching back for her notebook and slowly crossing *Chaeyeon* and *Korain* off the list. Her chest aches with disappointment. For a moment, she'd felt so close to victory, to reincarnation.

"Hey, Kisa?" Hajun whispers. "Are you okay?"

She feels the weight of his worried stare and attempts to collect herself. A mystery like this one does not take only a day and a half to solve, she reminds herself. And just because Chaeyeon and Korain weren't involved in the murder doesn't mean that Hwanung hasn't sent a different assassin. The only question is *who*?

The god's thoughts are irate.

—*meddling*—Godly Gossip—*fucking*—*underwear*—*my*—*boxers*—*next*—*fucking*—*hells*—

"Hold the baby," Seokga tells Kisa, practically thrusting Hwanin upon her, before turning on his heel and storming out of the sick bay. The doors anxiously swing back and forth for a good few moments after his violent departure.

Kisa nervously glances down at Hwanin's head. If *Godly Gossip* has informants here, the risks of Hwanin's murder being outed have soared astronomically. "Well... At least we now know that we'll need to keep well away from Korain and Chaeyeon."

Somi grimaces. "It's a little too late for that," she says, a bit wryly. "Where do you think Seokga has gone? He's on the hunt for a certain haetae and inmyunjo. I almost feel bad for them."

A very uncharacteristic curse word slips from Kisa's mouth and she shoves Hwanin into Hajun's arms as if they're playing a game of hot potato. "Hold him!" she cries before racing after Seokga, following the red thread with a pounding heart.

"*Seokga!*" Kisa half-shouts, finally on Seokga's fast-moving heels. Her chase has brought her to Deck 4, a bustling level brimming with restaurants and shops. It's the deck that most resembles a shopping mall, down to the throngs of people. She accidentally steps on dozens of toes as she fights to reach the god, and when she does—desperate not to lose sight of him again—grabs his free hand in hers. Her heart stumbles (in surprise, she tells herself, pure surprise) as he whirls on her. The red thread swirls through the air at the motion, and so focused is Kisa on the way Seokga's thumb brushes over her skin that she forgets, completely and absolutely, to squash.

Or perhaps she decides not to.

As his flashing eyes scan her face, Seokga seems to relax... and he doesn't let go of her hand. His fingers, despite their delicate appearance, have calluses. Years spent hunting down Unrulies, Kisa supposes, will do that.

"Kisa," he says, and his voice is hoarser than usual. "Don't try to stop me."

"What are you even planning on *doing*?" she retorts, suddenly annoyed as she props her free hand on her hip. "We really do have bigger problems than the world knowing about your brother's underwear preferences... And it's *because* we now know they work for *Godly Gossip* that we need to keep away from those two! If they find out..." Nervously, Kisa glances around the bustling deck before lowering her voice. "If they find out about the *you-know-what*, there could be serious consequences. Imagine if it was broadcast all over the tabloids! The CEO would be furious."

Seokga eloquently suggests, in detail, what the CEO can do to himself instead.

"I can tell you right now that's not anatomically possible," Kisa replies primly. Taking advantage of the fact that his hand is still secure in hers, she gives him a good yank. "Come on. We're leaving before you find Korain or Chaeyeon and cause trouble."

Reluctantly, the god allows Kisa to drag him up to the eighth deck. When he looks in interest toward the corridor leading to the bridge, where Korain might be, Kisa grips his hand tighter in warning.

"Don't you dare," she warns as she hears his thoughts, which detail how very much he wants to tackle the haetae to the floor.

Seokga scowls.

Besides, the bridge isn't their destination—*this* is. Kisa pushes gently on the spa's glass doors to enter, stepping into the elegant, aromatic waiting room. Seokga's cane clicks against the cool marble floor as they walk underneath a miniature version of the fifth deck's gigantic chandelier and breathe in some blend of essential oils with hints of coconut and vanilla.

The woman behind the desk looks up as Kisa and Seokga venture forward. "How can I help you? Two for the wet spas?" She reaches underneath the desk and retrieves two small towels.

"Er—" With a start, Kisa realizes that she didn't think this through much at all.

All she wanted was a place to calm Seokga's ire, to talk some sense into him before he sabotaged their mission. She'd forgotten, momentarily, that Korean spas are significantly different than western spas. Whereas in a London spa, one might be given a fluffy robe, Korean spas tend to supply only a teeny tiny towel that eventually must come off in the wet spas.

Underneath Seokga's curious stare, Kisa feels her cheeks burn. "Oh, erm, uh . . . Could we do the dry spa instead, please?" The dry spas are communal, coed, and, most important, *clothed.*

Clothing is rather important.

Especially on Seokga. For her own sake, he must keep his clothing well and fully *on.*

"Sure," says the woman, and replaces the towels with two neat shirts and bottoms resembling soft gray pajamas, along with two small towels and keys. "Lockers are right around the corner," she adds, before turning her gaze back to the computer. Kisa scoops up the clothing, while Seokga grabs the towels and keys. There's a bemused sort of amusement radiating down the bond as they walk past the reception desk, down a small corridor leading to two changing rooms—one for women and one for men.

"Well," says Seokga as he gives her a key and she hands him the clothing, "this is unexpected."

"You need to calm down. I thought this might help, that's all." Her cheeks are burning again. "We're just doing the dry spa. I'll meet you out here in a moment." Ducking quickly into the female changing room, Kisa shakes her head to clear it as she slips out of her shoes and replaces her scrubs with the spa-wear. She sets them neatly down in the wooden locker, uses the key, and takes a moment to *breathe.*

It is, she thinks, really not a good sign that the thought of seeing Seokga naked has gotten her so frazzled. With complete concentration, Kisa stops herself from thinking about his bum. Instead, she attempts to gather those thoughts and dump them unceremoniously into the very back of her filing-cabinet mind. Unfortunately, a few flutter out through the drawer's crack.

Kisa closes her eyes and counts to ten. Then twenty. Then fifty-four. Then sixty-seven.

Sufficiently cooled down (and rather hoping the red thread kept those thoughts of hers private), Kisa meets Seokga back in the corridor, the stone floor cold on her feet. It's odd, seeing him out of his dark, designer garments... Almost like seeing him naked. Her face feels like it's on fire.

Stop that.

Kisa mentally recites boring textbook passages as she leads him farther into the spa. The marble floor gives way to warmer wood, and the ceiling expands, making room for the varying levels and the wooden staircases leading to them. In this first large communal area, small pools of water, decoratively lined with potted plants, burble softly. A white formation, rather like a very large onion made of white stone, sits near one of these small pools. Kisa makes a beeline to it, followed by Seokga. The wet areas will be deeper into the spa: This is just a simple sauna, and as Kisa steps into it, she's happy to see that it's empty, save for them.

Her feet sink into the salt piled on the floor as she makes her way to a wooden bench. Seokga takes the one opposite her, leaning his head against the slightly sweating wall. *It's certainly warm in here,* Kisa thinks, focusing on not looking at the strong, exposed column of Seokga's neck. She gathers her curls into a high bun, letting her own neck breathe.

For a while, both god and gwisin are silent. Seokga's eyes have fluttered shut, and his previously tense shoulders have loosened.

When he does speak, Kisa nearly jumps out of her skin (for reasons thoroughly unknown to her, she was watching a small bead of sweat roll down his neck onto his collarbone). "This is . . . nice," the god says, opening his eyes as Kisa averts her own. "Thank you."

She smiles, fanning herself. It's really so hot in here. "Are you perhaps feeling less murderous?"

A crooked, almost sleepy, smirk. "Maybe."

"Then I've done well." Kisa pulls her knees up to her chest and lifts her hand, examining the red thread tied around her left pinky. Her eyes narrow as it quivers—as if giggling—and curls itself into little hearts. "It's doing it again!"

"Hmm?" The god's gaze is heavy-lidded.

"The thread . . ." Kisa sighs in exasperation as it smooths itself back out and swirls innocently through the air. WHO, ME? it spells. She glares at it. That *cannot* be a hallucination. Can it? "Never mind."

Seokga blinks a few times. "Why didn't you want to do the wet spas?" he asks, and Kisa's entire face flames.

"Erm . . . the wet spas . . ." She fumbles for words, but her embarrassment turns to frustration as she sees a tiny sliver of a smirk curling his lips. "Oh, really! You know, don't you?"

"I do," he snickers, and she glares at him. "I just wanted to see you squirm."

"You're honestly terrible," she mutters, and unexpectedly, there's a burst of yellow from his end of the thread to hers. His happiness is bright and pleased. Kisa arches her brows at him, and Seokga grimaces. He glares at the thread.

"I don't know why that happened."

—*happy*—*teasing*—*me*—*like*—*friends*—

Kisa quirks a brow, and it's Seokga's turn to blush. This immortal trickster—*blushing*. Kisa bites back a smile, watching Seokga swat at the insubstantial thread almost playfully. Unable to suppress her amusement, she snorts, before her hands fly to her nose in embarrassment.

Seokga gapes at her. "Was that *you*?"

"No," she insists, attempting to withhold another undignified sound. "There's a pig somewhere in the spa... Lends to the experience, you know..." A surprising pleasure fills her as the trickster dissolves into laughter.

"Hwanung's tits," he wheezes, wiping at the corners of his eyes, where a silver lining has formed. "I thought you laughed like her, but that... That was wholly unique..."

She feels her smile waver. *I thought you laughed like her.* As she tries to shove aside some inexplicable feeling of inadequacy, Kisa is thoroughly betrayed by the Red Thread of Fate as it carries a glow of green from her side to Seokga's. Her envy. She watches as it melts into Seokga's finger, as his laughter dies, and she fights against a swell of embarrassment as he looks, in concern, to her.

—shouldn't have—compared—Hani—Kisa—she—looks so—upset—fuck—Jang said—theory—

"It's all right," Kisa manages to say, staring down at the salt floor. "To be expected, really." She hates this feeling of envy and wishes it could feel as ridiculous as it sounds—jealous of herself in a past life. But Kisa knows what conclusion she draws from the Ship of Theseus question. And despite this new feeling of friendly familiarity around Seokga, she's *not* Hani, not a mass-murdering gumiho that steals from ATMs. If Seokga fell in love with someone like that, what must he think of her now? In nature versus nurture, nurture has won. She knows he must be disappointed.

It shouldn't even matter. It doesn't.

"Kisa," Seokga says—awkwardly. The godly prince is *awkward* before her. It warms something in her to see him fumble for words that come so coldly and quickly when he speaks to others. "I am sorry. I didn't mean..."

"It's fine," she replies quickly, too quickly. Seokga's expression becomes almost wretched before it quickly smooths out. "Really. I understand. I'm not her. You looked for her for so long, and I'm not... her." With slightly trembling fingers, she scrapes back a loose strand of hair. "I suppose I'm sorry for that, too."

She hadn't meant to say it, and she almost wishes she hadn't.

His eyes flare in alarm. "*Don't* apologize—"

She hates this conversation. Despises it. Despises herself for her envy, for having been watching his neck, having been *thinking* about his *bum* earlier. Time to move on—and quickly. "We should strategize," she cuts in. "Now that we know Korain and Chaeyeon are, well, not innocent exactly—but not guilty of the murder, either... There's so much to do."

Seokga's jaw twitches in a way that tells her he's not done with the previous conversation, but runs a hand down his face. "Fuck," the god mutters.

"The cameras didn't pick up any witnesses on the I-95, or near the stairwell, but perhaps someone heard something. If there's a way that we can subtly poke around... Seokga?" The god is slumped against the wall, and for the first time, Kisa notices the dark circles under his eyes. "Are you..."

"I'm exhausted," he rasps. "Hwanin kept me up all night with his crying. I had no idea how to make it stop. I kept thinking the murderer had snuck in. I've barely slept. I don't know how I'll survive tonight, much less five more days of this." She watches in growing concern as he thumps his head softly against the wall. "I'm tired, Kisa," he says. "I'm so tired."

Dark gray crawls down the thread, and Kisa nearly bows over when she feels his exhaustion. So similar, in so many ways, to her own. Perhaps that's what possesses her to make the offer, or perhaps it's the way he looks so rumpled—and so young, not at all like a powerful god—in the spa pajamas...

It is a terrible idea, she tells herself. *A really truly and terrible idea. Don't you dare offer. It is not at all going to assist in the squashing. Why are you opening your mouth? Don't say it—*

"I could help," she hesitantly murmurs. "With... Hwanin. At night."

Seokga stares at her. Honestly. Where has her self-control gone? Down the gutter, that's where.

Kisa clamps her mouth shut, yet feels no guilt—even as her logical self groans in frustration and buries her head in her hands.

The god is still gaping.

Perhaps it's necessary to explain why she's offering in a purely factual way (although she is quite certain now that her reasoning is not motivated by her beloved facts, nor logic). Quickly, she rushes out, "I was one of Samsin Halmoni's shamans, remember? I was a doctor in the MMU—the Magical Maternity Unit. I can help you with Hwanin at nighttime... Show you what to do, how to tell what he needs..."

His face twists at the mention of her goddess, and once again she wonders what he could possibly have against her. But then his face clears, and his eyebrows shoot up. "You do realize," he says slowly, "that would require you to stay..."

"Overnight. Yes." Soo-min will have her head if she finds out, but Kisa—rule-abiding, authority-fearing Kisa—doesn't care. It's decidedly uncharacteristic, and she decides not to linger too long on *why*. Perhaps that's what Hajun meant when he so valiantly attempted to explain "fun" to her. Perhaps fun is harmless. Fun is fine. As a temporary stop on the way to the DAR, of course. "If it helps you get some rest, especially in the middle of this investigation, I really don't mind."

Seokga's throat bobs. "Yes," he blurts, before a rush of purple embarrassment shoots down the bond. "I mean," he says a moment later, more slowly (as if trying very hard to sound dignified), "that it would... help. Yes. It would help."

Kisa flattens her lips to keep them from spreading into a thoroughly unnecessary smile. "Can I ask you something?"

"Anything," says Seokga, who looks as if he's fighting off a smile, too.

"I still haven't figured out why you hate Samsin Halmoni," she admits. "My goddess." As she expected it would, his face darkens at the name. "Why, Seokga?"

"Why?" he half-snarls, taking her aback. "Because the entire pantheon knew I was looking for you, Kisa. Running myself ragged scouring the earth for a man or woman with your eyes. Angular and wine-brown, with those lashes... Hani's eyes. And Samsin Halmoni clearly knew—and didn't tell me. All this time, you were within my reach. But I didn't get to you before you..."

"Died," she offers helpfully.

Seokga flinches. "Yes."

Kisa tries not to think about that night, but the hairs on the back of her neck still rise up, and she can't stop herself from twisting around. But it's only the wooden wall.

—*Hajun*—*said*—*more in common*—*than*—

"That night," Seokga says carefully, "when you fell..."

"I don't want to go into any more detail about it," Kisa replies automatically, and when her mind threatens to go there, to the moment before she fell when it all suddenly seemed so terrifying and hopeless, she yanks it back. "Samsin Halmoni is a kind goddess," she says. "Perhaps she didn't know."

"She knew," the trickster spits, and Kisa can't help but wonder if that's the case. She'd only met Samsin Halmoni a few times, but each time, the goddess had commented on her eyes. *Such a pretty color,* she'd crooned—and now Kisa feels a sharp sting of betrayal at the memory, and a stab of pity for Seokga. All those years spent trying to find her, for nothing.

Why? Some petty grudge?

"Samsin Halmoni despises me," Seokga continues. "She always has. She's one of the deities who never forgave me for the coup, and who never want to see me happy. When I return to Okhwang..." He trails off. "I don't know if she'll even be punished. Without Hwanin, I'm..."

—*alone*—

Kisa's throat tightens. Seokga shakes his head, averting his eyes. "Tell me something, Kisa," he says suddenly, desperately. "What did you want?"

She blinks, taken aback. "What?"

"What did you want, in life?"

Oh. Kisa nibbles on her bottom lip. It's a private question, but she feels strangely comfortable answering. "I wanted a lot," she replies honestly. "And I got most of it." Acclaim, accolades, a world of knowledge stored safely in her mind...

"Was there anything you didn't? Get, I mean?" Seokga's face is strangely vulnerable as he returns his gaze to hers. It makes him look young, Kisa thinks. Much younger than his immortal years.

"There was... there was one thing, actually." She kicks a bare foot over the salt floor, suddenly self-conscious. "A dream of mine, I suppose, although an impossible one." Kisa hesitates, a part of her rather frightened that Seokga will find her dream *lacking,* somehow.

"Tell me," he murmurs.

Kisa swallows hard, nervous. She's never shared this with anyone before. Her secret dream, what she would fantasize about as she lay in bed, staring up at her ceiling. "Okhwang's library," she whispers, and she knows that it means something now that she's told him this secret. That something might... change. She supposes she should be terrified, but strangely, she's not.

Seokga's brows raise, but there's no amusement on his fine features as she'd so feared. Bolstered by his lack of disdain, Kisa pushes forward. "The Heavenly Library is—to shamans—something like the Library of Alexandria. Its halls are filled with hidden knowledge, the secrets to... *everything.* I know that nobody but the gods are ever allowed inside its halls, but that's never stopped me from wanting it..." Kisa trails off, worrying she's lost him. But Seokga is studying her with an intent expression, truly *listening* to her in a way her family, or her acquaintances at NSUMD, never did. She could talk about the Heavenly Library for hours, and if Seokga doesn't stop her soon, she just might. "I used to dream about it. The books it must have. How beautiful it must be in there..."

"I've been in the Heavenly Library," Seokga says, and Kisa leans forward, itching to know more. "It's dusty and cold." The words are spoken with such nonchalance that Kisa nearly falls off her bench. "Quite eerie, actually. The librarians quit some centuries ago, and finding a book in that mess is *impossible.*"

"Say you're lying, please," Kisa manages to choke out.

"Sadly, I'm not." He smirks.

How can the great library of Okhwang possibly be dusty, cold, and *messy*? How can the pantheon possibly take such a wonderful thing for granted? "No," she says. "Absolutely not. I simply won't believe it."

"There are bats in the Heavenly Library," Seokga continues, and she *knows* he's goading her, but she falls for it anyway. "Bats and moths..."

"That is *sacrilege.*" Even worse than the tattered condition of the romance book Somi gave her, which is currently in her spa locker and begging to be read. Kisa balls up her fists. "It should be polished and grand and—and use the Dewey decimal system! Those books are treasures, they're *priceless,* they hold the secrets to the universe and *everything* in between—"

"You're lovely when you're angry," Seokga interrupts, and his surprise shoots down the red thread, as if he hadn't meant to say that at all. Kisa's cheeks flush and her heart gives a peculiar little flutter.

If he had found her sooner... Before the red thread, before she died... What could they have been?

"Thank you," she mumbles, blushing.

Seokga smiles, looking rather pleased with himself. He's very sweaty by now, Kisa notes, his golden-beige skin shining with perspiration. The heat of the sauna is the only reason her mouth dries out as Seokga tugs at the thin fabric of his shirt, which is now damp. "I'm beginning to think that you actually brought me in here to punish me," he half-pants, half-accuses.

"Oh, yes," Kisa says, staring fixedly at his collarbone. "I thought you might sweat out the anger. Is it working?"

"A little too well." He stands, tugging off his shirt. Kisa's eyes nearly bulge out of their sockets as she stares at his chest, the firm pecs and deeply cut muscles of his torso, the sharp V just below his hips. Little beads of sweat glimmer on his skin, and she suddenly feels the thoroughly *insane* desire to lick them off. Where—where on *Iseung* did that come from?

She's *still* staring at his chest. What is wrong with her?

Get yourself together. Kisa bites down hard on her bottom lip, fumbling for some way to squash these absurd desires. Desperately, she shuffles through the filing cabinet of her mind for the fourteenth chapter of *Complete Anatomies of Iseung's Species,* remembering the old tome being as painfully boring as watching paint dry—

> His Scottish brogue trailed heat, like whips of fire, over Elsie's bare skin. "God," Finlay was rasping as she arched toward him, aching desperately to completely

and utterly succumb to him. "Ye canna know how long I've been wanting this, lass. Waiting for this."

She bit back a moan as his calloused hands curved around her arse and as his rough stubble grazed the inside of her thigh. "Please," Elsie whimpered, hardly caring how brazenly wanton she sounded. "I need you."

Finlay's dark green eyes raised to meet hers. A devil-may-care smile curved that sinful mouth. "Aye?" the captain of the *Jolly Scotsman* asked huskily. "How badly? Will ye show me, love?"

A sharp gasp flew from Elsie's lips as Finlay's own finally met her where she ached. The sensational glide of his tongue, the carnal noises—

Kisa jerks backward as if she can escape her own thoughts, and chokes hard enough that tears rise to her eyes. That—that was *certainly* not chapter fourteen of *Complete Anatomies of Iseung's Species*. No, that was chapter fourteen of a *different* book, yes, a *very* different book—the excerpt of *Kidnapped by the Time-Traveling Highland Pirate-King* that Kisa had peeked at just this morning.

She is vaguely aware of Seokga's alarm as she gasps, finally drawing in a huge breath of air. Certain that her face is an obscene shade of blue, Kisa buries it in her hands, staring at the darkness provided by her trembling fingers.

Her first coherent thought: *Well. That was rather embarrassing.*
The second: *Captain Finlay has the same color eyes as Seokga.*
The third: *I wonder what it would be like to—*
No. Squash. *Squash.*
Now Kisa is certain her face is midnight blue. Wonderful.
—*what*—*the*—*fuck*—
"Kisa," Seokga is saying, "are you . . ."

"Yes," she croaks. "I'm quite well, thank you."

"Right," she hears the god say slowly, as if savoring this bewildering—yet apparently amusing—moment. Horrible. He is simply horrible. "Only that... I heard some very interesting things down the bond."

It's not enough to be dead. Kisa wishes to be entirely obliterated into nothingness. Hands falling to her lap, she stares at Seokga in complete and utter horror. The god looks extremely baffled, adequately concerned, and yet also incredibly entertained—all at once.

She can't blame him.

Oh, yes, Kisa has entirely lost it.

"I," she attempts to say with a haughty dignity she does not at the moment possess, "have absolutely no idea what you mean."

He's smiling now, just a bit. Perhaps he's even trying not to, in order to spare her feelings, but he's really failing quite spectacularly. "What's this about 'the sensational glide of his tongue'?"

Bollocks. "Er." Kisa cannot think of anything else to say. She fears she looks like a cow chewing its cud as her mouth works speechlessly.

Seokga tilts his head. "Right. Well. I'm going to the wet spas to... cool off. Maybe you should come with me." A deliberate sideways smirk that somehow manages to both incense her and befuddle her senses.

"Um," Kisa manages to blurt, face burning. "We have a mystery to solve, we should get back—"

Seokga grins over his shoulder as he leaves the sauna. "We won't be long," he tells her.

Kisa is frozen to her seat.

The trickster winks at her. *Winks.* Kisa unfortunately feels as if she might take a note from Elsie and swoon. "I'll be in one of the private baths."

As he disappears, she sits there, in the sauna, debating with herself for almost five minutes. She shouldn't. She really *shouldn't*. There's no reason for her to. She should instead scurry back to her cabin and wallow in her humiliation.

Yet she told him—about her dream. Never before has she told anybody... And Seokga listened. He'd teased her, yes, but with... affection. And she'd enjoyed it.

Her hand absentmindedly comes to rest above her chest, where a deep ache, a longing, has lodged itself since Seokga left the sauna.

Perhaps this whole *squashing* experiment is a mistake.

Yes, a-a scientific misstep. Perhaps there's something else to discover instead. She's experiencing the *Red Thread of Fate,* after all. Squashing is not at all helpful to understanding such a rare phenomenon, the very act of squashing is not at all conducive to—to what she'd originally set out to do. Researching the red thread in *all* of its effects. No, the squashing is holding her back. Making her recite *smut* down their bond, *smut*—

Have some fun with him while you wait for reincarnation. You need it, and I think you'd like it—"

It's for science, Kisa tells herself as she exits the sauna and follows the thread to Seokga. *For science.*

Every single part of her knows she's lying to herself.

CHAPTER TWENTY

SEOKGA

The cold water of the secluded cavern bath is bliss on Seokga's too-hot skin. The private room, by some magic of Yeomra's—or, possibly, the spa's interior designer—perfectly resembles a small cave. This spa is certainly more impressive than any mortal one would be.

Stalactites hang from the dark ceiling, and the waters themselves could easily be an underground pool with the way the rocky ground slopes to create both a shallow end and a deep end. The illusion is only ruined by the room's gray door, which Kisa *could* come through, but he knows she won't. Seven hells. People who met only two days ago don't swim naked together—even if there's the history of a past life between them.

He tips his head back in the water, floating somewhere in the pool's middle. The sauna had become too much for him. Seokga doesn't do well with heat. He despises summer and just barely tolerates the spring. Seokga only likes the cold, and his body revolts when subjected to too much warmth. He is a cold thing, a statue of ice, a frigid god who shrivels in the sunlight.

Except when he's standing with her. With Hani.

I swear on Hwanung, the god of laws and kept promises, that the sun will shine on us both once again.

Seokga lets himself drift underwater, letting his naked skin soak in the water's frigidity. When he breaks back through the surface, shaking his head like a dog, there's a small hitch of someone's breath.

Blinking back droplets of water hanging from his eyelashes, Seokga's blurry vision clears to reveal Kisa, who hovers hesitantly near the door. Her eyes are on his crumpled stack of clothes.

Shock jolts through him. Seokga hadn't thought she would come. He'd only been teasing earlier, convinced that Kisa would rather perish than swim with him... But she's *here*. Something flutters in his chest, and Seokga is reminded—as he always is around Kisa—that he actually has a heart. She's surprised him.

Yoo Kisa can be *spontaneous*.

Perhaps she does need to... cool off, as he put it. He can't deny that it pleases him, although he's still completely bewildered about what, exactly, had been going through her mind at the spa. *The sensational glide of his tongue,* indeed. (The thought has inspired some of his own. Yes, Seokga can be *quite* skilled with his tongue when he wants to be.)

"Er," she whispers, tucking a curl behind her ear, "hi."

"Hi," he rasps, treading water. *Hi.* When has he ever, in his immortal life, said *hi*? It's disgraceful. Humiliating. Absurd.

And yet he will be all of those things for her.

Kisa shifts nervously on her feet, looking as if she doesn't know what she's doing there.

—*I really—should squash—what—am—I—should—leave—*

"You don't need to come in," Seokga tells her gently, wanting more than anything to put her at ease, wanting her to stay.

"I know." But she hesitates, and his eyes are fixed on the wildness of her curls, no doubt due to the sauna's humidity. Kisa's forehead is shiny with sweat as she shifts her weight from one foot to the other. "Is it cool?"

"Mm," Seokga says noncommittally before smiling wickedly and sweeping his arm to send icy water arcing toward Kisa. She splutters as it drenches her, and in the very bottom of his vision, Seokga is half-certain that the shaking red thread is spelling out HAHAHAHA again.

"That's—freezing—" Kisa gasps, but she's laughing.

"It's nice," Seokga promises, and he watches as Kisa hesitates, looking to the small sign on the cavern's wall, reading PLEASE NO FABRIC IN WATER. There's a moment of deep contemplation from her, and Seokga is captivated by how she tilts her head and scratches at her cheek. Finally, she takes a deep breath and says, "Turn around."

Seokga practically spins away. He's never been gladder to meet somebody who follows the rules so strictly. Is she coming in? His heart is thumping like he's a smitten teenage boy. There's the soft rustling of clothing falling to the ground, and then a faint splashing. The waters of the cavern are cloudy with what Seokga knows must be buckets of minerals, salts, and whatever gives the water an almost clean, soap-like fragrance. Neither will be able to see any part of the other that's below the surface, but his blood still stirs knowing that Kisa is nude like him beneath the cold water. "Okay," Kisa says softly, and Seokga turns around. If he's suddenly trembling, it's only due to the cold.

—can't believe—I'm—doing this—what has—gotten into me—

She's leaning against the bath's rocky wall a healthy distance away from him, the waters reaching her neck. Her eyes flutter shut. "You're right," she murmurs reluctantly. "It is nice."

—what am I doing—what am I doing—what—am—doing—

Seokga's eyes snag on the exposed slope of her neck and his

knees weaken. He quickly looks away, pasting a casual grin on his face (rather than a lovestruck expression) and trying not to think about how his lips might feel on her neck, if she would writhe under his gentle kisses.

Kisa's eyes open and she rolls her eyes. "You look precisely like the cat that caught the canary," she informs him.

He attempts again to smooth his face into something more... subtle. Kisa snorts and pushes off the wall to tread water. "You're so obvious," she murmurs.

"What?"

"Nothing." Kisa's eyes twinkle. Her hair is a beautiful cloud of brown in the water as she drifts closer and then ebbs away a moment later, reminding him of a gentle tide.

Those twinkling eyes. "What were you thinking about?" he asks quietly, arching a brow and pretending his pounding heart does *not* feel like it's going to break free of his ribs and fall out of his chest. "In the dry spa?"

Here, Seokga hopes that a grand romantic confession will follow. That she will admit to being utterly infatuated with him, and full of wonderings regarding the skill of his tongue. Then he will say he would be happy to show her, and she will fall in love with him, and they'll—

Kisa grimaces. "Sometimes," she mumbles, "when I... Sometimes, I recite book passages in my head. The thread"—a ferocious glare toward her pinky, at the red knot—"decided to let you listen in, I suppose. Really, it has the worst sense of humor..."

"Ah," says Seokga, indescribably disappointed. Then he frowns. "What sorts of books are you *reading*, Kisa?"

"...Good ones," she replies after a long pause, very blue. "Very... good ones. About many... things. Different sorts of... things."

He smirks. "I can see that. Or, rather, *hear* that." But his response is a moment late, for he's faltered. A flash of vibrant memory has smeared itself across his mind: a cluttered bookshelf in a New Sinsi apartment. A grinning gumiho offering to let him borrow one of the absurd titles. Something about a pirate. Or was it a Scotsman? Or both?

Perhaps Kisa would know. A passion for raunchy books, it seems, has carried over from one life to the next. Warmth spreads in his chest and yellow happiness flows down the bond. Before Kisa can shoot him a puzzled look, Seokga tips his own head back and stares at the stalactites. His soft joy falters. The last time he was in a cave, he was imprisoning his father. He would bet anything that Mireuk is staring up at stalactites now, too. Has been for thousands of lifetimes, underneath Bound God's Pass on this very river. This cruise is the closest Seokga has been to his father in lifetimes.

"What are *you* thinking about?" Kisa asks quietly.

His heart practically stops in his chest.

The trickster is so thoroughly shocked that Kisa has just used banmal, the informal (inwardly, he is screaming in victory and pumping a fist in the air), that he entirely fails to realize what she's actually *said* until she repeats herself. In banmal. *Banmal.*

"Seokga," she prompts again.

"Uh," says Seokga, physically unable to use any semblance of eloquent language at the moment. His heart has begun to beat again, so violently that he wonders if he could possibly be going into cardiac arrest. "Um."

Kisa's concern spirals down their bond.

—because—used—banmal?—should I—not?—thought—because—we're—naked—after—all—

"No," Seokga gasps out, struggling to tread water without resembling a dying fish. "Please use banmal. *Please.*"

So much for her "squashing." He attempts to withhold a shout of triumph.

"None of... this"—a vague gesture at the thread, her slender arm lifting from the water and causing Seokga's mouth to dry out rather pathetically—"means that we can't be—friends. Would you, I mean, can we do that? Just friends?"

Friends. His heart shatters and mends itself all at once. "Just friends," he repeats, voice little more than a croak.

"I'd like that. To be your friend." Her smile is like a shy crescent moon barely peeking out of the clouds. "Now will you tell me what you were thinking? The way you were staring up at the stalactites made me curious."

Compose yourself, Seokga tells himself, although he's becoming certain that he is in the middle of a heart attack. "The red thread is keeping my secrets now, is it?" he croaks, his attempt to sound suave and nonchalant failing miserably.

Kisa shrugs and smirks. "Apparently."

"I was just... I was remembering my father." Seokga straightens in the water and shakes his head, spraying drops all over Kisa—a quick way to change the topic.

A knowing glint in her eyes tells Seokga that Kisa knows precisely what he's doing, but she humors him all the same. She tips her head back and, with gusto, jerks it up again and shakes water from her long, waterlogged curls. Hands raising to protect himself from the onslaught, Seokga finds himself chuckling.

"Fine," he begrudgingly admits, "you and your mane have won." He despises losing, but with Kisa, he doesn't mind.

She smirks, but a moment later, she shivers. When she raises an arm from the water once more, he sees that delicate bumps have raised all over her skin.

Again, it's as if he's a gentleman from the sixteenth century or something. Seokga can think of no other reason the sight of a single bare arm and a neck should have such an effect on him. "I think I need to get out," she says through chattering teeth, staring up at him. When did they get so close? "How you can stay in this water for so long, I've no idea. Don't you have *any* goosebumps?"

"I have plenty." Seokga makes his way to the shallow end, where he stands and walks until the waters only reach his lower back. "They're on my back," he says, though of course that's not the reason he's focusing on flexing his back's muscles with tremendous concentration. Seokga is quite pleased to feel the water sluicing down him (it will lend a certain effect to the whole view, he thinks) and even more pleased to feel Kisa's gaze on him. The goosebumps multiply as he feels her look, and as her gaze seems to drift lower.

"Erm," Kisa breathes, and then coughs. "Right. Yes. You've proven me wrong... Well done."

—*can't stop*—*looking*—*he's*—*per*—

A peculiar emotion travels down the red thread. It almost feels like...

There's a loud and abrupt splash.

Seokga turns to see that Kisa has dunked herself entirely underneath the cold water.

CHAPTER TWENTY-ONE

SEOKGA

IT'S GENIUS, REALLY.

Seokga applauds himself as he shape-shifts into the adult version of his brother and combs through his newly long, silver hair in the bedroom's mirror. Hwanin's punchably perfect face looks back at him, entirely alive and noticeably not-murdered.

Kisa sits behind him on Hwanin's bed, pursing her lips as she holds his now-baby brother. Her hair is still damp from their swim. "You'll need to change into one of his hanboks," she tells him, and banmal has never sounded so beautiful. "I'm not sure Hwanin would ever wear all black like you do. Will you need your cane?"

"Not in this body," Seokga says, leaning his beloved cane against the wall, already missing the feel of the silver imoogi hilt in his hand. "If I were only casting an illusion to appear as Hwanin, I would. But with shape-shifting, my body *becomes* another's." He strides to Hwanin's suitcase, perched on the room's ornate wooden table, and rummages through it before finding a vacuum-stored blue hanbok. Seokga *might* again flex his back muscles just a bit as he tugs off his dark sweater, since his showcase in the pool was such a spectacular triumph. If Kisa wants to look, which he dearly hopes she shall, he wants her to be suitably impressed.

And then Seokga remembers that he's baring his *brother's* back. Fucking hells.

He grimaces. "Don't look," he mutters over his shoulder. If anyone can one-up him, it would be his brother.

"I won't," she replies, sounding amused, but he believes her. "Why not cast an illusion? It seems like it would be easier." Seokga had spent ten long minutes fixing minute details on Hwanin's face, and wincing as bone and skin shifted.

"How much do you know about illusion work?" he asks, shedding his pants, as well.

"Not much," Kisa admits, sounding curious. "The Seokga shamans I knew—*your* shamans—went flinging them around like confetti. Illusions of rabid animals, frightening monsters... Those were the popular sort."

—they were—terrifying—

"That's mere child's play." He can't repress a snort of disdain. "They have only a modicum of my powers. My shamans are able to create illusions but can't access the well of power I can. When I work with illusions, I make them not only look real, but *feel* real. If I were to create the illusion of a rabid animal, I could also create the feeling of its hot breath, the exact experience of teeth sinking into flesh. Whoever's unlucky enough to be attacked would *believe* they were being ripped to shreds—their brains would process it as real. Although the animal is not, technically, real, their pain would be. It's a delicate process," he adds proudly, "and requires extensive training and control." As he smooths out the dark blue fabric of the hanbok he's just donned, he worries that he's frightened Kisa off. But when he turns, he sees that she's open-mouthed and bright-eyed, staring at him like he's hung the moon.

It's intoxicating. Seokga feels quite drunk.

"I don't suppose," Kisa says, "that you could cast an illusion for me right now?"

His lips twitch mischievously and Kisa blinks in surprise.

—so strange—Hwanin would—never smile like that—so wicked—but kind—at once—

"What would you like?" he asks, and feels like a complete bumbling fool as she grins at him. Seeing Kisa so excited is his drug of choice.

"The rabid animal!"

"Absolutely not," says Seokga.

"For research purposes—"

"No." This time, those pleading eyes will not work on him.

"Fine." She huffs, looking incredibly peeved. "I *suppose* a rain cloud will do."

"A rain cloud?" Seokga asks, delighting in how she blushes.

"I just—I love when it storms."

For some reason, that small admission—this tiny detail about her—is so precious to him that for a moment, he can barely breathe.

"I do, too," he whispers and then is promptly and absolutely humiliated when affection courses down the thread from his end to hers—a blazing hot pink color. The red thread loops itself into one big heart, and he glowers at it, half-fearful of Kisa's reaction.

Just friends. Just friends.

But she's smiling. "If that's not sentient, I'm a manatee," she says, laughing, and before the red thread can attempt once more to make a fool out of him, Seokga shakes back the sleeves of his hanbok and begins the illusion. For Kisa, he'll conjure more than a rain cloud. He'll weave an entire storm.

Drawing from the well of divine power deep within him, Seokga begins to weave strands of thought together. In his mind, he pictures a tumultuous gray sky, heavy and ripe with cold rain.

The bottom swell of a cloud, almost navy blue, dark and delightfully ominous. The air would smell fresh, heavy with hints of the coming ozone, rich with the ground's damp, expectant soil.

Kisa's delight fills him as the bedroom darkens, the ceiling overtaken by a blanket of swirling storm clouds. Her hair... Seokga longs to see it flutter in a cold, rain-tinted breeze, and so it does. "Brilliant," she whispers as he brings forth a crack of lightning that illuminates her upturned face in a burst of white. The thunder is next, a contralto rumbling that grows to a crescendo just as fat raindrops burst from the clouds, freezing cold, splattering to the bedroom floor below and forming glistening puddles.

She laughs, and it is (as always) the most gorgeous sound Seokga has ever heard. Kisa jumps from the bed and twirls around in the rain, Hwanin's giggles mingling with her delight as she spins him around. With eyes misty from the rain (just the rain, nothing else at all), Seokga watches with trembling pride as they grin up at his creation and find it beautiful.

As Hwanin, Seokga mills about the ship, doing his best to look Absolutely Authentically Hwanin-y. He has interpreted this as smiling at passersby (the horror), maintaining an indulgent expression of humble superiority at all times (quite hard, he's used to an expression of plain derision), and stopping various times to spit his own hair out of his mouth (not what Hwanin usually did, but what Seokga must do as a necessity—it's so *long*).

Kisa with Hwanin, Hajun, and Somi all trail him from various points as he makes his rounds. The hope is that his presence will draw out the murderer, fool them into thinking that Hwanin somehow survived that fatal night (sans heart), et cetera. It's a long shot, but it's the best any of them have got. It also can't hurt to keep up appearances, reassure the world that Hwanin is most definitely alive and well.

Seokga-as-Hwanin makes his way into Deck 7's casino, which is alive with the flashing lights of game machines and heavy with the sound of rolling dice. He fully desires to cheat guests out of their money, but Hwanin would never make his way toward the roulette tables in the back. Instead, Hwanin would politely order something from the glossy mahogany bar, which is what Seokga does. Comfortable with the knowledge that three (or four, if real-Hwanin is counted) pairs of eyes are subtly watching for any hint of the murderer, Seokga tries to enjoy his rum and Coke. It's disgustingly sweet, but he makes himself drink it while waiting. The casino, in its chaotic semidarkness and loud noise, would be an opportune place for the perpetrator to grab a closer look at the Not-Dead god. There aren't many other drinkers at this time of day, but he notices in his peripheral vision that the woman sitting a few seats away from him seems to be admiring his hair. Typical. Seokga cuts his gaze toward her, and his mood immediately sours when he sees that it's Soo-min. The hypocrisy.

"Aren't you *working?*" he bites out before he can stop himself, still rather peeved at her earlier interruption. But his voice is Hwanin's voice, and the usual smooth tone sounds extremely odd with Seokga's rough demand. Grimacing, he clears his throat. "I mean, hello."

Soo-min chokes on her drink, still gaping at him.

Seokga sighs. Hwanin would reach over and pound her back, so he does.

"Thank you, Your Majesty," she gasps out, rubbing her throat.

Your Majesty. Instead of imitating Hwanin's pleasant nod, Seokga finds himself abruptly turning back to his own drink. Once, all he'd wanted was his older brother out of the way. Before Hwanung, Seokga was next in line for the throne. Even when his nephew was born, Seokga had a grand plan to take both of them out at once and steal the title for himself. So many of his life's greatest longings and sufferings are because of two little words—*Your Majesty.*

Years ago, perhaps Seokga would have reveled in being acknowledged as emperor, even in Hwanin's form. Now he feels strangely dissatisfied. There's something, some*one,* he wants instead, a bright-eyed woman with wild curls and a sharp mind who surprises him at every turn, whether it be with her fierce intellect or by dancing in the rain and joining him in cold waters.

Dr. Jang would call this *positive growth.* Seokga isn't sure how *positive* it is, if the one thing he desires chooses to leave him—abandon him—once more. He hopes that, after Kisa is gone, he won't again spiral into villainy... But who's to say, really, what path he'll turn to. This time, when she's gone, she's gone.

And all of this, these thirty-three years of searching, were for nothing.

He drains the rest of his drink, and signals for another despite its general disgustingness.

"May I ask how you're enjoying your cruise so far?" asks Soo-min.

"Fine. Yes. Good," mumbles the trickster god, suddenly extraordinarily depressed. He doesn't notice that Soo-min has swapped her seat out for the one closest to him until she's placing a hand on his shoulder. Seokga stiffens.

"If there's anything I can do for you, sir, to make this cruise more enjoyable, say the word." Soo-min smiles pleasantly. "I'm in charge of guest entertainment. Maybe you'd be interested in another greenhouse soiree? We can keep your brother away this time."

He shakes off her touch. "My brother is *fantastic* and would likely be an even better emperor than me," he replies shortly, hoping the woman will leave. She doesn't. Instead, Soo-min is staring at him. Again. Seokga clenches his jaw in irritation as she runs her eyes across his face, no doubt struck with the inane attraction Hwanin somehow managed to procure from almost every living woman. The cruise director looks almost *hungry*.

"I'm sorry for asking, but I'm curious. You look so . . ." Soo-min tilts her head, licks her lips. "Healthy. Youthful. Whole. How did you do it?"

"Pardon?" Seokga grits out.

"Your skincare routine," Soo-min quickly clarifies. "How do you do it?"

The woman listens in annoying rapture as Seokga grudgingly formulates some bizarre ten-step skincare routine that he's quite certain Hwanin never did. It involves various creams, ice cubes, and—mostly for Seokga's own amusement—a specific procedure involving a raw, peeled potato and a ballpoint pen. When he's finally concluded his bullshit skincare speech, Seokga manages to make an excuse and slink off, determined to lure the murderer *away* from the hungry-eyed cruise director.

Yet to his vast disappointment, the perpetrator seems to be steadfastly ignoring Hwanin's regal parade about the ship—even when he returns to the exact spot on the I-95 where Hwanin was murdered. Only once does somebody yank him into a secluded corner, and that person is a frustrated-looking Yoo Kisa.

He's rather excited by this turn of events, but Kisa makes no move to tug him into a fervent embrace (pity).

Instead, she sighs and shakes her head. "This isn't working. We need to try something else."

The rest of the day is spent futilely investigating a mystery that doesn't seem to want to be solved. Seokga shape-shifts into the SRC *Flatliner*'s most common sort of guest (an elderly, sagging man who formerly worked in a bank or a business or some other boring establishment) and pokes around for hidden witnesses, stealthily and subtly probing other guests for any indication they observed any part of the murder.

"Well," one woman slurs through sips of a frozen lemonade that is clearly spiked with some sort of alcohol, "last night I heard a big splash."

"That might be because we're on a cruise ship," grits out Seokga, wanting to rid himself of his old, sagging stomach as soon as possible.

The woman rolls her eyes. "I mean, who knows?" She sucks coquettishly on her straw, eyes unfocused. "Maybe somebody fell overboard. Wouldn't that be so sad?"

"Not what I'm looking for," Seokga grumbles, and leaves before the woman can annoy him further. Convinced he won't be getting anywhere useful, Seokga waddles (the indignity) into the candy store on Deck 6 and emerges with a giant bag of Kopiko.

Aside from the candy and it being a humiliating experience for his vanity, Seokga gains nothing from the expedition. At the urging of Somi (who can fuck off) and Kisa (who wields the art of puppy-dog eyes against him), he'll be diving back in tomorrow. But for now . . .

In his suite, Seokga hides his underwear as a precaution, extremely conscious of the fact that the SRC *Flatliner* hosts not one, but two, *Godly Gossip* spies—and a murderer. Some fucking vacation this has turned out to be. He's *glad* to take his anti-depressant at seven.

In the hallway, Kisa knocks on his door—a knock that has his heart thundering in his chest. Before opening the door, he smooths down his hair and makes sure the underwear he stuffed under the bed isn't visible. Is it wrong to play house in the middle of a murder investigation? Undoubtedly so. But Seokga simply gives no shits.

She's radiant in the softly glowing hallway, and when she slips inside, she brings with her an intoxicating scent of cinnamon, and—who knew Seokga could find the smell of lemon antiseptic so alluring? "Hi," she greets in a whisper as he closes the door. She's wearing her usual scrubs, but has a tote bag with pink pajama pants peeking out of the top. "Where's Hwanin?"

He gestures to the bed. Hwanin dozes in the middle, a tiny chubby blob surrounded by a white sea. As if sensing Kisa's attention, the baby opens his mouth and lets out a scream. Seokga grimaces as the night begins.

It comes to him, between being shown how to soothe the child and crush Hallakkungi's flowers for his drink, that Kisa is preparing him—for when she's gone and he's left alone with this wailing demon. The realization has him clenching his jaw and attempting to force the grief and regret down before the thread reveals it to Kisa.

When Hwanin is finally asleep (in *Seokga's* bed, he might add), they slump in the room's overstuffed armchairs, both exhausted but not yet ready to sleep themselves. After Seokga's performance as Hwanin tonight, the murderer might return for a second try. As Seokga scrubs his eyes wearily, Kisa draws her notebook out of the bag, and begins to write.

"What are you writing?" he whispers, voice hoarse even to his own ears. She pauses guiltily. Exhausted and slightly intoxicated by the sight of Kisa in her pink pajama pants and wrinkled gift-shop I LIKE BIG BOATS AND I CANNOT LIE shirt, Seokga can't help a wicked grin. "Love poems, perhaps? Or something more . . . explicit?"

It's like a reward when her face goes blue. "I—you—the—*no!*" she splutters. Embarrassment shoots down the thread, a humiliated purple.

"My eyes have been known to be described as 'evergreen' and

'verdant,'" he tells her helpfully. "You could also mention my impressive height once or twice. And perhaps my beautiful, chiseled jawline or my excellently shaped—"

"If you *must* know," Kisa interrupts, blushing fiercely to his great delight, "I'm, um, writing down some observations. About the bond."

And he's back to feeling rather like a laboratory rat.

Her alarm skits down the thread—she must have heard his thoughts. It's becoming inconvenient, this connection. Seokga wishes he could wallow in peace.

—*need to—explain—*

"It's not like that for me," she says quickly, and her hands are nervously twisting together as she speaks. "Not—I'm not using you as a lab rat . . . Although being compared to one isn't always an insult, some are quite intelligent—although that's often a result of conditioning . . ." Kisa abruptly clamps her mouth shut, grimaces, takes a deep breath, and starts again. "When I was a student, when I chose my research projects, I chose things that I was . . . or could be . . . passionate about."

Some of his dejection slowly begins to chip away.

"Not," she hastily adds, "that I'm caught in any, well, throes of passion around you . . ."

He smirks. The fire crackles merrily in its hearth.

". . . and I'm not trying to say that you should take it as a compliment because I *hate* when people say that—it's always either for plagiarism or some backhanded insult, or used by creepy men who stare at your chest—but . . ."

"But I should take it as a compliment," Seokga finishes, unable to stop his lips from curling upward in a teasing smile. And then he frowned. "Who stared at your chest?" he demands, unable to keep the violence from his voice.

"That's not the point." Kisa looks and sounds positively frazzled. "And, well—for you, you shouldn't take it as an *insult*, exactly," she mumbles.

"Can I read some of it?" Seokga's eyes narrow on the journal. He's suddenly intrigued.

Kisa appears horrified. The red thread shakes in possible laughter. It's an effort for Seokga not to join in.

"If you don't let me read at least some," he pushes, unable to help himself, "I'll assume you're writing that poetry . . ."

"Oh, fine," she huffs, flushing. "Here. Take it." She holds it out, but when Seokga gives it a tug, she doesn't let go. Kisa's eyes widen. *I—forgot—that I wrote—about—* "Just ignore . . . Just please ignore what's been scribbled out."

Raising his brows, he manages to steal the notebook from her. And, contrary to her plea, he does not ignore what's been scribbled out. "Your handwriting is atrocious. This is English?"

"Yes," is the sullen reply. "Can you read it?"

"Passably." Personally, Seokga *hates* English. It's an awful, inconsistent, mutable language to learn. But learned it he had, just in case Hani's reincarnation lived on the other side of the globe . . . He has also learned Spanish, French, Italian, Thai, Chinese, Hebrew, and Swahili. He had just started on Arabic and Hindi when he was forced into this vacation.

"Maybe you should give it back." Kisa suddenly looks extremely anxious. "Actually, yes—I think you should . . ."

Too late. His eyes have already latched onto something very, very *intriguing*. A scribble. And underneath that scribble . . .

"Interesting," says Seokga, a grin stretching his lips.

Kisa's hands fly to her mouth. "*Ignore* the scribbles!"

"I've always thought my 'arse' was my best feature, too—"

She practically launches herself over to his chair, leaping over the low coffee table, and snatches the notebook back. She's breathing heavily as she glares down at him, and Seokga's heart is hammering at how she's half on the chair, one knee between his legs, a hand gripping one of the armrests...

He blinks lazily up at her. Her hair falls like a curtain around them. Before he can stop himself, Seokga reaches up and tugs one of the beautiful brown curls with a finger. To Seokga's extreme satisfaction, Kisa's eyes widen, and her lips part.

His gaze snags on those lips, on their perfect cupid's bow, their luscious color that reminds him of crushed berries. He gives her every chance to pull away as he slowly moves his hand to her lips, brushing the plump bottom one with his thumb.

Kisa's eyes darken.

Heat curls low in Seokga's stomach as her tongue peeks out to tantalizingly swipe against his finger. A moment later, Kisa goes completely blue in clear mortification.

—no idea—why I did that—oh—my gods—

Kisa's shakily backing away, cheeks flushed, eyes bright. In her hands is the notebook. "Just friends," she whispers, almost to herself.

"*Mmgmumph,*" he manages, his brain a jumbled mess.

Eloquent.

Kisa is staring accusatorily at the thread. "It's up to something," she says. "I just know it. It's making me feel..."

WHO, ME? writes the thread before smoothing itself back out.

She points at it, eyes wide in alarm. "Did you *see* that?"

He's choosing to ignore the question of the thread's sentience in favor of a more pressing issue. "Actually," Seokga says, shaking his head in a poor attempt to clear it, "you might be intrigued to know—scientifically, of course—that the thread can't *make* you feel anything." Even on his own face, his smile feels smug. More of a sharp, satisfied smirk than anything. "To my knowledge, the sharing of thoughts, of emotions... None of that manipulates your *own* thoughts and emotions. You can write that down in your notebook," he adds graciously, waving an indulgent hand.

—*could it—be—true—not—the—thread?—*

Kisa narrows her eyes at him, but a moment later, furiously scribbles something down.

—*what—could—that—mean?—*

A few minutes later, Seokga arches a brow. "You never finished your sentence."

"What sentence?" The way the words are forced out from in between her teeth tells Seokga that she knows precisely what sentence he's referring to. Still, he humors her.

"What did you feel?" he asks, internally delighted.

Kisa glares at him. "A nice, platonic *friendship*."

"I'm curious," replies Seokga with a hope unlike any he's ever felt before, "does a platonic friend admire their friend's 'arse'?"

She scowls, but Seokga can tell that underneath, she's trying not to smile. "I'm going to bed," she snaps.

"I'm not sure that's a good idea," Seokga calls, arching a brow. "If the murderer comes tonight, the first place they'll check is Hwanin's room..."

Kisa hesitates.

"Unless you'd like to take your chances, you're better off staying in here." Seokga does his best to look extremely pleasant and gestures to his bed, where Hwanin dozes. He's not afraid to admit that he very much would like Kisa to stay with him tonight.

Unfortunately, it appears that she's fully aware of his ploy. "There's a settee in the connecting sitting room," Kisa informs him, lips twitching. "Good night, Seokga."

He makes a disappointed sort of grunt in response, earning a laugh.

Unable to sleep for the next few hours, certain the murderer will return, Seokga gets up to stretch his legs and grabs a spare blanket from the foot of his bed. In the sitting room, Kisa is curled up on the settee, a tattered book held close to her chest.

Curious, Seokga eyes the cover. His breath hitches in his throat at the sight of the Highlander pirate and his swooning woman. That book looks *familiar*. For the second time that day, his mind drifts back to that bookshelf in Hani's tiny apartment, how she hoarded romance books like a squirrel hoards nuts. Ah, yes, this is it—the book about the Scotsman who is also a pirate who is *also* a time-traveler. Bewildering.

And this must also be the book blessed with the "sensational glide" of somebody's tongue. Seokga shakes his head, trying not to laugh. Trying not to overthink it.

He fails.

The Ship of Theseus question is always on his mind. And this falling-apart book makes a little fissure of hope jolt through his heart.

He doesn't like or agree with Jang's (rather depressing) theory, but perhaps... perhaps he can formulate his own, one that says the red thread connected him to Kisa because of what they once shared, and what they might again. Perhaps it was Hani he needed first, Hani with her history in espionage to sneak past his defenses and pick the lock on the cage around his heart. To show him he could love, and be loved in return. To show him he was deserving of it.

And perhaps it's Kisa he needs now, Kisa with her healing hands and gentle nature. There must be some intrinsic part of her soul that calls to him, no matter the time—whether it's the bustling nineties or thirty-three years later. No matter the place—whether it's New Sinsi or a rather monstrous underworld cruise ship. No matter the body her spirit rests within—whether she's a deadly gumiho as seductive as the night itself, or a genius doctor with a mane of coffee-colored curls and the shyest, sweetest smile. Oh, Seokga thinks, he could fall in love with her forever, in all her forms. She's not Hani. She's Kisa. And he is beginning to adore her.

Ardently.

Kisa doesn't stir as Seokga drapes the blanket over her, admiring how the moonlight seeping in through the window illuminates the soft curves of her face, the small part of her lips. The way her brows furrow and unfurrow even in her sleep, as if she's solving complicated equations in her dreams.

"Good night, Kisa," he whispers.

When he finally gets to bed, his smile reluctantly grows as his little brother drowsily rolls toward him.

Kisa's hair resembles an angry porcupine in the mornings.

"Good morning," says Seokga, who has spent the last fifteen minutes meticulously arranging his own hair into artful messiness, brushing his teeth, and ensuring that he looks overall attractive (sans shirt, he might add) before hopping back into bed with the sleeping baby and excitedly awaiting Kisa.

She blinks at him as she stands in his doorway. "You're right," she says sleepily. "Hwanin *does* cry more than the average baby." The pair of them were up through the night, constantly awoken by the child and the general anxiety of being on a cruise ship whereupon a murderer is sneaking about. To his disappointment, Kisa is not staring at his pectorals as he sits in bed. Instead, she's staring at . . . his lips?

He attempts to subtly pucker them. The lip balm he applied must be paying off.

"You've got some toothpaste on the corner there," she tells him with a wry little smile that would bring him to his knees if he were standing up.

Hwanung's tits. Seokga grimaces, hastily wiping it away—and freezes when there's a sharp rapping on the door.

"Seokga?" a familiar voice calls. "I need to speak with you."

Dr. Jang. Seokga launches himself out of bed, and then abruptly stills, glancing toward Hwanin—but his brother slumbers quietly on, no hint of the yowling tomcat in sight. "Shit," Seokga whispers. "Shit, shit, shit." Dr. Jang *cannot* see that his brother has turned into a baby. "Kisa—"

But Kisa is one step ahead of him, hurrying to gather Hwanin in her arms and then practically sprinting out of the bedroom, across the sitting area, and into Hwanin's room. The door shuts, and then locks. Seokga takes a deep breath before walking to the sitting room's door and opening it to a smiling Dr. Jang.

If only Seokga had a camera to commemorate each and every one of Dr. Jang's outfits on vacation. If he'd thought (or *hoped*) that nothing could top the rubber-duck dress, he was severely mistaken. The elderly woman stands before him clutching a humongous floral tote bag and clad in her bright pink sunglasses, a glaringly yellow bonnet riddled with daisies, along with a matching set of Hawaiian print shorts and shirt topped only in vibrancy by giant green plastic clogs riddled with holes. "Good morning, Seokga."

A noise halfway between a wheeze and a *hello* escapes his mouth. He clamps it shut. Dr. Jang smiles. "May I come in?"

"Sure," he manages to gasp out.

Dr. Jang walks primly past him, and after a moment's hesitation takes a seat on one of the armchairs. After shutting the door, Seokga grudgingly takes the one across from her, praying that Kisa keeps Hwanin silent and hidden.

"Where's your brother?" Dr. Jang asks. "I haven't seen much of him recently."

"He ate a bad clam."

"Ah." She smiles, pushes up her sunglasses. "Well, I wanted to check in with you about Yoo Kisa. I glimpsed the two of you yesterday, checking in to the spa. It seems like you two are getting closer—and I imagine some more complicated emotions are coming with that."

Seokga's heart lurches before he remembers that Hwanin hadn't been under their care while they'd been at the spa. "I," he replies, before remembering that Kisa is just next door and can possibly hear every word.

Dr. Jang waits as he runs through various replies in his head.

"We're friends," he finally settles on.

"Friends," repeats Dr. Jang, and her usually clinical voice has a hint of grandmotherly pity in it. For a moment, she reminds him painfully of Chief Shim Him-chan, who passed on years ago. It was Chief Shim's paternal meddling that led Hani to him, and Seokga misses the old man dearly. "It must be a rough adjustment, going from soulmates to simple friends."

"No," he replies sharply, a knee-jerk reflex to her scrutinizing stare and speculating words. "No. I'm glad to have her. As a friend." In fact, he'd been rather jubilant about it until his therapist's *pity*. Now he feels extremely pathetic.

Jang waits.

"She's not Hani," Seokga continues once the silence has become nearly painful. His voice sounds distant even to his own ears as he remembers the grinning, cheerful gumiho whose cluttered room was stuffed with outrageously smutty romance books and who drove like a madman. "And I've ... I've accepted that. She doesn't remember me. I will take whatever she will give me, even if they're just crumbs from her table."

"It's hard to feel satiated on crumbs."

"I know," he snaps, before taking a thin breath through his

nose. "But I'd rather have them than nothing at all. And she's—" Seokga glances to Hwanin's adjoining door. "She's . . . incredible. Smart and kind and—and beautiful." He smiles despite himself. "I like spending time with her, even if it's just as friends." It's an unusually vulnerable admission for him, but he *wants* Kisa to hear.

Dr. Jang sighs quietly, so quietly that he barely hears the sad exhale. Seokga narrows his eyes at her. "What?" he demands.

"I've noticed a pattern," the psychologist replies, "and I feel it's important that I share it with you."

He attempts to keep his face impassive as she begins. "You love fully and completely, only to have it returned in less than half."

It cuts him in half, that statement. Right down to the bone.

"You loved your father. You still do."

"Doubtful," Seokga sneers.

"You do," Dr. Jang continues, unperturbed. "You love him. I think that you would still do anything for him."

Grief gives way to an appalled affront. "I most certainly would *not*," he retorts. "He's a madman. We locked him away for a *reason*." Brows lowering, he glares down at Dr. Jang, who doesn't seem to notice, or feel, the wrath of his glower. "Where are you going with this?" She knows, as he well does, that any hint of traitorous intent must be reported to Okhwang. Immediately.

Her lips purse. "I am not sure if you've noticed, Seokga, but I have not been taking my usual notes during this session. I'm coming to you as somebody who has come to care about you very deeply and is concerned. This conversation will remain between us. You have my word."

"Are you aware," demands Seokga in a low voice, "that you're violating several of Hwanin's rules—"

"I don't care," Dr. Jang says firmly. "The subjects that you need to talk about most regard your feelings for Mireuk, and I'm certain that I will not be adequately able to help you if I don't create some sort of safe environment for it. I want to help you. Is that so hard to believe?"

Yes, thinks Seokga, but he lets Dr. Jang continue.

"For you, I fear it probably is. Any help you've received in your life has been double-bladed. Hani, who agreed to help you find the eoduksini with the purpose of sabotaging your hunt for the Scarlet Fox . . ."

"I'm well over that," he snaps, balling his hands into fists.

". . . Hwanin, who allowed you to become a god once more only if you killed the woman you loved . . ."

Seokga bites down on his tongue. He'll never be truly over *that* one, but Hwanin is currently a sleeping baby without the capacity to hurt anybody.

". . . the Gamangnara monsters you led to Okhwang. They abandoned you the moment things turned sour. And, of course, there's your father."

"I don't have one of those," grits out Seokga, who is being purposefully obtuse. "I was born from old household items, like dokkaebi. I was a steak knife, I think."

The doctor piously ignores him. "It all circles back to Mireuk. Did you ever get closure?"

"Shutting him up in a prison after he invented murder, rape, plagues, floods, serial killers, orphanages, et cetera, *was* closure."

"Was it?" Dr. Jang shakes her head. "Do you mean to say that a part of you doesn't still long for his approval? Doesn't wonder about what would happen if you earned it?"

Seokga hesitates.

Yes, he wonders about the crazy old man all the time. He wonders if Mireuk regrets any of his crimes, if the meager amounts of food and water the prison provides are enough to keep him alive, but in a desiccated form incapable of exerting any power. If the magic-restricting skeletal shackles will continue to work for the coming millennia. His dreams are filled with memories of Mireuk choosing Hwanin, each and every time. The following waking hours are spent trying not to be like his father, although he inherited his curmudgeonly streak. When Seokga is feeling especially depressed, he plays morose songs and wonders what his life would be like if Mireuk hadn't gone mad and had loved his second son as much as his first.

After his own fall from the heavenly kingdom, Seokga fantasized about journeying to Jeoseung and staging what would be an impressive prison break filled with his own fantastic heroics. His father would be waiting for him, and would smile when Seokga—drenched in sweat and splattered with the blood of his enemies—freed him. His handsome face, so like Seokga's own, would glow with pride as he spread his shackled arms in greeting. "My son," Mireuk would say. "You are very impressive and I am so extremely proud of you. I now vastly prefer you over your brother and forgive you for locking me up in here in the first place. Let's go exact our bloody revenge, and stop for some soju on the way." Then he'd take Seokga's hand in his, and they'd have some lovely father-son bonding time while sieging Okhwang.

Sometimes, when Seokga is feeling especially evil (an ingrained tendency for trickster gods), he revisits that little fantasy. But he's gotten better at jerking himself out of it and imagining harmless pranks instead—like gluing Hwanin's ass to the throne or starting up a grand pyramid scheme to cheat other gods out of their money. The latter was how he spent most of the 2000s. The former is how he spent the last half of the nineties.

Dr. Jang is waiting expectantly.

"No," says Seokga.

"I don't believe you," Dr. Jang says, not unkindly.

"And why's that?"

A rueful shake of her yellow-bonneted head. "You, specifically, would amaze and baffle Freud. It's as if your unconscious id rules where your ego should—in consciousness. And the id lacks a certain ethical code that the ego does... All of this is undoubtedly due to your nature as a trickster god. I want you to feel comfortable with me, Seokga. You can tell me the truth, whatever that truth may be. I'm here to help you." Her voice is warm and earnest, reminding him almost of his mother, Mago.

But the back of his neck is itching fiercely, and Seokga shifts uncomfortably in his chair. Although the therapist's tone is kind, he automatically shirks away from her words. Nobody *truly* wants to hear the trickster god admit that he's not as *reformed* as the world believes. All the other members of the pantheon are so high and mighty—deities of harmless, fun things, like babies or doors, rainfall or fortune. They fear him, the god of deceit. He doesn't fit. He never has.

He never will.

Seokga already has the distinct feeling that he's on thin ice, what with Hwanin being murdered and all—and one misstep will send him plummeting into the cold waters, drowning in loneliness and a familiar bitter hatred.

"I barely think about my father at all," Seokga lies in a hard voice.

"I see," replies his therapist, and he has the feeling that behind those ridiculous glasses, she really does see more than he ever intended to reveal in the first place.

CHAPTER TWENTY-TWO

KISA

Kisa snatches Hwanin down by his foot as he rises into the air in his sleep. She does so without missing a word of the muffled conversation beyond the bedroom door. It's wrong of her to eavesdrop—she knows that, *of course* she knows that. It's an invasion of privacy, a terrible thing to do, listening in on something like this . . . But the voices carry, and something about the conversation has struck her as odd.

Not the part where Seokga called her beautiful, although it's constantly playing on a repeat in her head. *Beautiful. Beautiful. He thinks I'm beautiful.* Kisa knows she's pretty, in a factual sort of way, but that's never stopped her from overanalyzing the slightly uneven curl pattern of her hair, or the way her eyes are constantly rimmed with some form of exhaustion. To hear what Seokga truly thinks of her has her heart fluttering in an odd and spastic rhythm that would, if she were alive, worry her.

Just friends, she reminds herself, but cannot deny that a small, secret part of her is entirely relieved that she no longer must keep up the tiring pretense of squashing. Friends, after all, are allowed to . . . to *feel* things that not-friends mustn't.

Hearing him call her beautiful . . . It has sent warmth blossoming in her chest and her cheeks, but it's certainly not the part of the conversation she marked as odd.

Perhaps it's the way the therapist has initiated this conversation as "off the record." Perhaps it's the focus on the Mad God, the subtle prodding toward... *something*. A manipulation. She gnaws on her bottom lip and presses her ear back to the door.

By the time Dr. Jang leaves, Kisa has the beginnings of a tension headache. As Seokga, with a look of exhausted relief, opens Hwanin's bedroom door, Kisa wastes no time.

"What sort of creature is Dr. Jang?"

She watches as he blinks once, then twice. "A shaman."

"Whose patronage?"

"Hwanin's, I suspect."

"You don't know?" Could it be Hwanung?

Orange crests down the thread, and Kisa stiffens when she feels Seokga's irritation as he eyes her. "Dr. Jang is not on the list of suspects," he tells her in a voice lacking some of its usual warmth—enough for Kisa to balk momentarily underneath his gaze. "She's not a claw-carrying creature."

She takes a small breath. "I wasn't trying to imply that she's who we're looking for," Kisa says, although they both know it's a lie. "It just crossed my mind. She seemed unusually interested in the Mad God, and broke more than one code of conduct—"

Seokga's shoulders stiffen. "The Mad God is my father, whether I like it or not. Is it so unusual to discuss one's father in therapy? Dr. Jang has been treating me for thirty-three years. If she had some resentment against Hwanin, or me, she had ample time to strike. We're not looking into her. That's *final*, Kisa."

There is, she thinks, a strange edge of desperation in Seokga's voice that she cannot help but latch onto out of concern and curiosity. As his chest rises and falls unevenly, Kisa wonders at his clear attachment to the therapist—his inability to even entertain the thought of her as a suspect. How alone has he been these past three decades? Surely he's made other friends since Hani's death.

But can he speak to them as openly as he speaks to Dr. Jang? Mago, his mother, has been asleep for thousands of years. His relationship with Hwanin—pre-murder—seemed precarious at best. And then there's his father. Evil and imprisoned. With nobody else to turn to, the trickster god is *dependent* on Dr. Jang.

Kisa wonders if such a dependency is really as harmless as Seokga believes. Thirty-three years *is* a long time for a con, after all, but something about their session has left a bad taste in Kisa's mouth. As has Seokga's tone. "Don't speak to me like that," she snaps, prickling, and the god looks momentarily taken aback.

"Like what?"

"Like I'm—like I'm a position *lower* than you in this investigation." Kisa narrows her eyes at him over the top of Hwanin's head. "If I want to look into Dr. Jang, I will. I've just as much riding on this mystery as you do, and I won't miss my chance for reincarnation because *you* decided something was 'final.' We barely have any other leads to go on at the moment anyway—"

Seokga rakes a hand through his hair. He's still shirtless, and Kisa concentrates exceptionally hard on staring at his face rather than his cut muscles. His jaw works for a moment. "I didn't mean to make you feel like that," he says in a slow, controlled voice, "and I'm sorry. But I don't think it's a worthy expense of our time and energy to look into Dr. Jang. I once made the mistake of suspecting Dok-hyun—someone who was only trying to help me—and I got him killed. I won't do that to her. Can you understand that?"

"I can . . . if you can understand why I need to check all possible boxes. We can split up," Kisa adds, although there's an ever-growing gnaw of disappointment in her stomach. "You don't need to come with me, or involve yourself at all in this."

"I won't." Seokga's jaw clenches.

"Okay, then." She averts her eyes, and there's a beat of silence so awkward that she longs for the easy banter of last night—the teasing about love poems and bums that are looking rather good in his pair of cotton pajama pants. Anxiety bubbles up in her, and before she can push it down, it all spills out in a humiliating rush.

"I'm not—I'm not hoping that she's the murderer. I hope she's *not*. I never . . . I never got help when I really truly needed it, and if I had, I might not be—well, dead. And I'm so sorry, Seokga, I know I shouldn't have listened in on your conversation, but for what it's worth . . . For what it's worth, I like spending time with you, too. I, erm, when you called me . . . I felt . . . I also think you're beauti . . . Never mind. Oh, gods. Uh—do you want to get breakfast?"

All of this is said so very fast that when Kisa finally comes up for a big gulp of air, her head is spinning. What is *happening* to her? Kisa has always rambled when she's nervous, but this is on another level entirely. She has been reduced from a creature of pure logic and fact to a bumbling bee in front of her purely platonic *friend.*

Kisa wants to close her eyes before she can see what will undoubtedly be a look of dismayed confusion from Seokga, but when she forces herself to look up, she sees that there's a small—almost affectionate—smile on the god's lips. And his eyes are warm again.

—Hani—also rambled—when—she was—nervous—

For once, the fond comparison doesn't cause any sense of envy. Only a strange sort of relief.

"I'd like breakfast," Seokga murmurs.

To avoid the *Godly Gossip* spies, Seokga shape-shifts into a dark-eyed man as they eat breakfast in one of the ship's many restaurants, shifting back into his regular form as he joins her in the sick bay. It's restock day. Kisa opens the packages piled on the counter and sorts the medicine into its proper cabinets. Hajun soon joins them, bringing startling news.

"You won't believe this," he says as he helps Kisa rummage through the boxes. "For all Soo-min's HR talk about *improper relationships* . . . "

Kisa arches a brow. "Who did you see her with?"

A mischievous glint blooms in his soft eyes. "The *captain.*"

"Captain Lee?" she asks in disbelief as her mouth drops open. "The SRC *Flatliner*'s rulebook *explicitly* states that crew members cannot date co-workers, never mind dating outside of their levels. Captain Lee is well above Soo-min. And he's . . ." *Alive,* she wants to say, but finds herself falling silent after glancing at her—the—god. "Never mind."

"An interesting tidbit," says Seokga, who is holding on to a floating Hwanin's foot like a child might hold the string of a balloon. "I find that interesting tidbits like these are very good for blackmail. The next time she tries to send you away from me—"

"Good morning!" a voice trills, and in waltzes Somi, bearing a cardboard drink carrier filled with two boba drinks and two coffees. There's also a book tucked under her arm. Kisa watches with a small smile as Hajun blushes upon being given one of the bobas, and helps herself to the flat white that must be hers. Seokga grudgingly takes the iced Americano, but sniffs it first, as if it might be poisoned.

"Here," Somi says, handing her the book. Kisa glances down to the title. *Banging the Vampire Billionaire* is printed in sparkling red letters. The man on the cover is (as always) shirtless, a black cape billowing behind him. He's sinking his teeth into a woman's neck while she smiles up at him. "I figured you already finished the book I gave you yesterday."

"I did," Kisa admits, taking the book and running a finger down its small, cracked spine. Elsie and Finlay's adventures had been quite... entertaining. The duo had found themselves in many perilous positions—treasure-hunting in the fifteenth century, facing English soldiers during the Jacobite Rising of 1745, roller-skating in the fluorescent eighties—and *other* sorts of positions, besides. Hajun is looking on curiously, and Seokga seems to be glaring at the vampire in a very competitive way.

"Did you like it?" Somi bounces on her feet. It's disorienting, how quickly the gumiho switches from a deadly, sophisticated killer with no small amount of sass to an excited woman with bright eyes and blue-tinged cheeks.

"*Very much,*" Kisa admits, and Somi snickers.

"This is the one I read thirteen times." She grins conspiratorially.

Hajun takes the book from Kisa and flips through it curiously while Kisa's face flames. She watches as her friend's eyes widen then hastily snatches it back.

"And here's one for you, Hajun," Somi half-purrs, drawing another small paperback out of her black purse. "If you were serious yesterday about wanting to join the book club, here's your official invitation."

Laughter bubbles up in Kisa's throat as Hajun is bequeathed a copy of *Kissed by the Mafia Cowboy.*

"I'm honored," Hajun says solemnly, "to join such a prestigious book club."

"As you should be." Somi winks. "Tell me what you think of chapter twenty."

Kisa hugs *Banging the Vampire Billionaire* to her chest and turns to Seokga with a smile. Seokga is still glaring at the shirtless cover model. "Do you want a book, Seokga?" she asks, trying not to laugh—and trying not to recall her accidental recitation of smut in the spa.

"I did bring one for him," Somi admits, and the look of horror on Seokga's face is incomparable. It only grows as Somi hands a book to Kisa, who snorts at the cover and title before passing it on to Seokga. He leans his cane against the sick bay counter to take it, holding it disdainfully between two fingers, as if afraid to catch germs.

Married to the Sexy Space Pirate.

—where is she—getting—all of these—what the fuck—

Kisa fixes Seokga with a warning look when it seems like he's about to hurl the novel across the room. Grimacing, he passes it back to her. She places both of their books with gentle reverence in her tote bag behind the counter for later reading. When she emerges, Seokga has turned on Somi.

"You're awfully cheerful," the trickster god mutters in disgust, "for an investigator with no leads."

"No leads, you say?" Somi asks, blinking faux-innocent eyes. "I beg to differ. Last night, I decided to take matters into my own little paws. I went back to the I-95 and poked around some more. And then somebody came."

Kisa's heart has begun to pound in her chest and she nervously sips at her coffee. "Who?"

"Don't keep me in suspense," Seokga snaps with all the sharpness of a honed blade.

"I ducked into a janitorial closet. It was a woman. I couldn't see her, but I heard her voice. She was speaking on the phone to somebody, and she *explicitly* said: 'They don't know it was me who killed your father. They're chasing their tails like dogs.'"

Kisa nearly chokes on her flat white. If this is true, it explains why nobody fell for their Hwanin-bait yesterday—the murderer must have known it was really Seokga underneath the silver hair and starry eyes. "You're certain?" she rasps. This is *confirmation* that Hwanung is involved. Her head aches with excitement and nerves. "Please, Somi, tell me that you managed to record that. If we send it to Yeomra, it will be the solid evidence he needs..."

Somi hesitates, nibbling on her thumbnail. "The bad news is—"

"Great," mutters Seokga acerbically.

"—that I... didn't record it." She winces, averting her eyes. Blue stains her cheeks and she suddenly reminds Kisa of a young, uncertain, and anxious girl instead of a notorious Unruly. It's as if she's constantly catching glimpses of the Somi that Hani might have known so many years ago, as if Somi's confidence and swagger are more of an act than anything else and this is the *real* Somi. "I'm sorry."

Kisa's heart falls. Hajun places a gentle hand on her shoulder, and she fights the urge to shrug it off like a petulant child. *It's fine,* she tells herself. *We have more leads than we did an hour ago. It will be fine.*

"And she knew I was there," Somi continues, seemingly gathering herself. "I was about to see who she was, to jump out at her, but when I tried the handle, it was locked. 'Meddlesome fox,' she said, and managed to hurry off before I broke out. I went to the security room right after to pull footage, but Korain—and Chaeyeon—were gathered in there." She glances warily in Seokga's direction. "Apparently they've had no luck solving your boxers-or-briefs mystery. They'll be attempting to solve it with renewed vigor today. From what I heard, they've managed to get a key to your room."

"Fucking hells," Seokga groans. Irritation glows orange down the thread. As worry swamps Kisa's mind and she nervously turns to him, he shakes his head. "I hid everything related to this"—he looks at his brother, and Kisa knows she's not imagining the flash of affection that crosses the god's face before being replaced by an annoyance that looks distinctly fake to her—"little demon before we left. And although I hid my boxers..."

"*Aha!*" Somi exclaims before receiving a death glare from the god.

"... I left one pair out where they might be easily found. The sooner those two pathetic, nosy slugs leave the room, the better. I don't want to risk them finding something else—like the box of diapers."

Kisa is strangely touched. "A noble sacrifice," she tells him sagely.

His cheeks are tinged pink. "Yes, well, I have elaborate plans to burn *Godly Gossip* to the ground within the month." But Seokga's smiling as he looks at her, and Kisa can't help her own face from heating, too.

"Arson really is a terrible crime," she informs him, pressing the backs of her hands to her blue-stained cheeks.

"Only if you get caught." His expression is positively devil-may-care.

Kisa shakes her head in a mixture of exasperation and a strange, growing fondness. And if the red thread truly can't influence attraction or emotion, as Seokga suggested... Well. She might find herself in a great deal of trouble soon enough. Yet staring up at his glittering eyes and crooked smile, Kisa finds herself thinking not of reincarnation but of the way he has a small dimple that she never noticed before. "Seokga—" *Did Hani care about getting caught?* The thought is almost intrusive, and her amusement falters. And there it is—that wondering if she'll ever be who Seokga wants her to be. Yet a rule-abiding shaman can't suddenly transform into a lawless gumiho.

"As cute as this moment is..." Somi clears her throat. "We have a murder to solve."

Right. *Right.* Kisa shakes herself out of her reverie. She's been getting distracted far too often these days. "Did you recognize the woman's voice at all? Were there any indications of age?"

"High and snooty."

"That's half of the female guests on this ship," Hajun says, sighing.

Somi looks affronted.

"Um, not you, though," he adds quickly.

Her smile is bright and sharp, her little fangs piercing her lips. "Good," she purrs.

Glancing between them—the blush on Hajun's cheeks, the twinkle in Somi's eyes—Kisa feels a strange twist of jealousy. Whatever the two of them have, it's completely . . . *new*. No expectations from a past life hanging over their heads, no muddled history stemming back to the Dark Days. Blinking rapidly, she takes a deep breath—but the thread has already carried her green envy down its length toward the trickster god.

—why—jealous?—might—understand—

Kisa clears her throat, avoiding Seokga's eye. "Here's what I think we should do," she says, clutching her coffee close to her chest and savoring its warmth. "When we get the chance, we obviously need to access the security room again. Now that we know we're looking for a woman, we can concentrate on locating one heading to the I-95 both last night and the night of the murder. We should update Yeomra as well, tell him we're close." She hesitates, nibbling on her bottom lip. Dr. Jang's voice isn't precisely high and snooty, but her inexplicable hunch still remains. At some point today, she'll slip off for a quick investigation—just to ensure it's not her—and return. There can't be any harm in that.

"It's a plan," says Hajun, and he sounds excited. "We're almost there. I can feel it."

Something begins to wither in her chest at the words, and Kisa mentally curses herself. What is *wrong* with her? Reincarnation is just within reach. So why does she find herself staring at the red thread, feeling as if she's about to suffer some great loss? A moment ago, her heart was falling at the lack of solid evidence from Somi. Now, it's breaking at the knowledge that the mystery is almost over.

Her blue sadness crests down the string, and she jerks away her gaze before Seokga's eyes meet hers.

—she'll—leave—wants to—why is she—sad?—is—there hope—

"We are," Kisa agrees quietly, and the words taste like ash on her tongue. She fights the urge to gag on them, and as Seokga moves closer to her in concern, Kisa acts on a base instinct—some primal remnant of fight or flight—and flees the sick bay.

Like a panicked animal, she shoves through the swinging doors, breaths coming in shallow bursts. Dimly, she hears Seokga shout her name in clear worry, but she's already running. As her feet pound on the corridor's hard floor, her eyes blur with hot tears.

Gods, she is so *confused*—and confusion has never been an emotion that she handles well. Clear comprehension has become, through years of study and discipline, Kisa's resting state, as easy as breathing. To be plunged into total incomprehension is like drowning. She cannot breathe like this.

Her muscles burn as she sprints, sweat trickling down the nape of her neck. Kisa barely feels the annoyed glares from the throngs of guests she pushes past on the stairs, doesn't hear the cries of *watch it!* and *hey!* All she hears is the dull pounding of blood in her head, and her own panicked thoughts. Kisa doesn't even realize where she's going until she bursts onto Deck 10, legs turned into absolute jelly, hardly able to breathe as she staggers to the sundeck's rail and leans over it so her tear-blurred eyes can take in the roaring, red Seocheongang below. Even from the highest point on the SRC *Flatliner,* a mist of the river's cold water sprays her face.

Before she can stop herself, Kisa is falling back on an old, terrible habit. She's swinging a leg over the rail, hands clutching the cold iron and feet slotting in between the lower bars as she swings over her other leg. Her hair whips wildly through the air as she perches on Deck 10's safety railing, hundreds of feet in the air, a deadly drop before her.

But she's already dead, isn't she?

And Seokga—he's so *alive*. So utterly and painfully alive, with his sharp smiles and glittering eyes. The way he tilts his head back when he laughs. The way his eyes soften when he looks at her, like she is someone more than precious to him, more than the anxiously frazzled ghost she sees herself as.

The way his blood runs red.

A god and a gwisin.

It is an impossible thing.

Isn't it?

A bitter laugh swells up in her tight throat, along with a painful ache in her chest as she stares down at the water through her tears. At the hospital, when it all became too much, sitting on the skyscraper's roof had been a way to, by facing imminent death, regain control of her spiraling thoughts. Perhaps it was also a way to punish herself—for not being as *capable* of withstanding the long hours and stress as she should have been. Now, Kisa doesn't know what will happen if she falls into the river, but she won't die. That ship has long since sailed. A tear trickles down her cheek, and Kisa furiously scrubs it away—only for more to follow.

She's so lost in her misery that, when the hand touches her back, her entire body seizes up painfully in surprise and terror. A scream rings out from her throat before she can stop it—and she's only saved from toppling off the ship by the same hand that closes around her arm and drags her back over the rail. Panting, shaking, and trembling, Kisa stares into a pair of outrageously pink sunglasses.

"I didn't mean to startle you," Dr. Jang says quietly. "But in my experience, sitting on a rail like that rarely signifies a peaceful mind. I wanted to ask you if you were all right. You're Kisa, aren't you?"

"I-I am," Kisa whispers, barely audible even to herself. She's shaking so fiercely that she's afraid she might collapse. When Dr. Jang gently guides her to sit on one of the deck's many reclining white plastic chairs, Kisa is too weak to refuse. She tries to sit on her hands to stop them from shaking as Dr. Jang sits on the edge of the chair next to her. She wishes she had sunscreen as sweat trickles down her temples and her skin burns underneath Jeoseung's hellish sky.

"Kisa," she says kindly, "I want you to breathe deeply in through your nose for a count of four, hold your breath for a count of seven, and exhale for a count of eight. Can you do that for me, dear?"

She latches onto the clear, logical instruction like it's a life buoy. Inhale for four. Hold for seven. Exhale for eight. Kisa obediently follows the doctor's rules, and gradually, her heart rate begins to steady. Her body still trembles, but the terrible panic is receding. Somewhere in between her counting, Dr. Jang ordered her a glass of ice water from a passing cruise attendant. Kisa gratefully wraps her fingers around the cold cup and drinks greedily.

"Thank you," she whispers, wiping her mouth with the back of her hand. "I'm sorry . . ."

"There's no need to thank me. Or apologize."

In her frayed state of mind, Kisa wasn't apologizing for the last ten minutes, but for suspecting Dr. Jang to be the murderer. Seokga is right—Jang is a shaman and has no claws. She doesn't fit the requisites. Kisa stares regretfully down at her now-empty glass.

All those nights spent taunting death above the hospital, and not one person—not her fellow doctors, not any nurses or assistants—came to help her. It means something to her that Dr. Jang is acting like she *cares*. It's . . . nice.

"It's none of my business, but can I ask what sent you running to the rail like a demon of the hells was on your heels?"

Kisa manages a small smile. "You can certainly ask, but I might not tell you."

Dr. Jang laughs. It's a nice, warmly quiet sound, like the crinkling of tissue paper during the holidays. "Fair enough. Fair enough."

Jeoseung's flaming red sun beats down on Kisa's face as she looks toward the rail, to the underworld beyond. Somewhere within the dark, mountainous peaks, there's a chilling cry. Despite the heat, she shivers and turns back to the therapist, who seems to be watching her through the dark shades. "I ran because I . . . don't know what I want anymore. And I suppose I'm terrified of wanting something I can never have."

"You're talking about Seokga," Dr. Jang guesses, voice kind. Kisa hesitates but nods. "Ah. It can be so complicated, can't it?"

"Friendships shouldn't be complicated. They're supposed to be—easy. Like Hajun and I—"

"I'm not talking about friendship, Kisa."

"Oh." She swallows nervously. "I see." Friends who are *purely* platonic probably do not feel faint with desire at the sight of each other's muscled backs. Her cheeks heat as Kisa remembers how she'd had to dunk underwater to collect herself and douse the heat blooming in places that it should *not* bloom with a just-friend. She's still astounded that she joined Seokga in the wet spa. It is not like her to do such impulsive, almost risqué, things—but he brings out another side of her that she didn't know even existed. Like the sun, coaxing a flower to bloom.

"Do you?" Dr. Jang's voice is so gentle and warm that it reminds her almost of the Samsin Halmoni she thought she knew—before Seokga told her of the goddess's betrayal. She feels herself relaxing as Jang smiles. "Let me ask you this, Kisa. Have you ever been in love before?"

"No," whispers Kisa.

"Why? Is it because you never met the right person?"

She pauses, thinking. Kisa supposes that there have been a few boys she might have allowed herself to love—if she'd had the time. But her first love has always been work. And work is a jealous lover, not allowing others to get too close. "I was busy."

"By coincidence or on purpose?" When Kisa frowns, slightly insulted, Dr. Jang holds her hands up in supplication. "I'm sorry if I overstepped. I'm just suggesting that work has been your defense mechanism in the face of affection—but now, having met Seokga, your defense mechanism isn't working anymore. But let me tell you something about defense mechanisms, Kisa. They won't work when we're not feeling threatened. Something to think about." She rises to her feet, drawing her floral tote bag up with her. There's a slight *thunk* as something falls from it, but Kisa barely notices, mulling over Jang's words. "It was nice to meet you, Kisa."

"Yes," replies Kisa distractedly, "you, too."

It's only when the therapist has left that Kisa sees what she accidentally dropped: a bottle of lotion. Kisa grabs it and stands, looking around for the yellow-bonnet-wearing woman, but there's no sign of her. The bottle is slick in her hand, and Kisa examines the label, wondering if it's some SPF she might borrow as she sweats under the sun.

Dermatrick's Anti-Aging Collagen Cream with Pulverized Licorice Root & SPF 50.

Just a little might do the trick, and she can return the bottle to Dr. Jang the next time she sees her. Brows furrowing, Kisa pops

THE GOD AND THE GWISIN

open the cap, and squeezes a dollop onto her hand. The scent of the lotion hits her in the back of her throat and she chokes, slamming the cap shut and staring down in horror at the little white blob as the powerful stench makes her feel ill. With hands that are once again shaking, Kisa slips the lotion into her pocket and scrubs the rest of the cream onto the leg of her pants.

It's a common enough scent for lotions, Kisa tells herself, even though the stench of it is—to her—wholly unique in that it's the worst fragrance on earth. *No need to feel ill over it.*

But she still hurries down to her cabin and changes into a clean set of scrubs, leaving the bottle on a shelf. Kisa stares at it, swallowing hard.

Dr. Jang has given her a lot to think about.

CHAPTER TWENTY-THREE

SEOKGA

"K*ISA!*" Seokga shouts as she tears out of the sick bay—and is only stopped from running after her by Hajun's gentle, but firm, grip on his shoulder.

"She needs some time alone," Hajun says, expression somehow remaining mild even after Seokga shakes him off. "And your brother is . . . uh"—he gestures helplessly above him—"up."

Clenching his jaw, Seokga realizes that Hwanin has floated completely up to the ceiling, where he's now gurgling happily down at the three wincing adults. Fuck. He is worse than a balloon, if such a thing is possible. Seokga hates those colorful things.

"You *let go* of him?" Somi accuses, and Seokga ignores her, staring up at his brother and wondering how in the hells he's going to get him *down*. Hwanin grins toothlessly at him, looking extremely proud of himself.

Seokga does not smile back. "Hwanin," he snaps, "get back down here. Now."

His efforts are rewarded with a taunting raspberry as Hwanin does a slow somersault midair. Frustrated, Seokga grabs a nearby stool, shoving aside the box of medicine perched on it. He steps onto the seat and snatches Hwanin by the ankle—a half-second before the stool wobbles and tilts beneath him. Pure terror seizes him, and as Seokga falls, he cradles his brother to his chest and turns midair, so his back takes the brunt of the impact. His teeth jar from it and the breath is knocked out of him but he doesn't care. Seokga sits up, heart pounding, frantically scouring Hwanin for any sign of injury, fingers quivering with fright as he combs through the soft, fine hairs atop his brother's head—terrified he'll find blood, or a bump . . .

"He's okay." Hajun is crouched over the two of them, but he's not looking at Hwanin. He's watching Seokga, eyes warm. "Seokga, he's okay. He's *okay*."

Relief has Seokga's body sagging. He lifts Hwanin into the air, so he and the baby are eye level. "You are a terrible pest," he tells the child, but his heart isn't in it. "A true menace."

Every time Hwanin comes close to being hurt, Seokga feels like he's being flayed alive. Those dark blue, star-flecked eyes crinkle as Seokga—possessed by some inane impulse—kisses the top of his head. Ridiculous. Really, Seokga doesn't know what's come over him.

Somi makes an *awww* sound, and he cuts a murderous glance over to her until she stops.

She averts her eyes, and there's the Somi he remembers. Her bravado is so easily disassembled. As Hajun grabs a box of medical supplies and says something about restocking the bathroom, Seokga climbs to his feet and looks at Somi.

"You're trying to be like her," he says once Hajun has disappeared, "aren't you?"

There's no question as to who "her" is. Somi's eyes flash with a rapid blur of emotions: first surprise, then indignation and guilt, followed by other emotions he has no interest in trying to discern.

"The clothes," Seokga sneers, "the personality. The *books*. I knew it from the moment I saw you. You're trying so hard and failing so terrifically to be the woman you helped kill."

Somi flinches. She's a child playing dress-up, Seokga thinks in derision, and he can't take it anymore. He's tried, for Kisa's sake, not to act like he did in the greenhouse. But he's always only one step away from losing control, and his fear of Hwanin being hurt demolished whatever was left of his self-restraint. "Stop that," she hisses, but her voice is ragged.

Seokga looks down his nose at her. "Stop what?" he drawls, voice freezing enough to encase a desert in ice.

The gumiho balls her hands into fists. "Stop acting like I didn't lose her, too." Somi uses the sleeve of her sweater—an oversized cream turtleneck just like the ones Hani wore in the nineties—to wipe away a stray tear. "I d-did something horrible. I'm not going to say that I didn't know better, because I did. I just lost control. I hadn't gotten my Jitters and Cravings under rein yet. You can h-hate me for it all you want, Seokga, but you'll never hate me as much as I hate myself. As for this?" Somi tugs at the hem of her sweater, her face twisting into a self-loathing expression. "She wouldn't have wanted her clothes to go to waste, or be tossed into the garbage—"

The world grinds to a halt. Seokga's blood goes dangerously cold as he stares at Somi. "Are you . . ." he breathes, gripping his cane so tightly in his free hand that his knuckles pop. "Are you actually wearing *Hani's* clothing?" He's noted the resemblance before, but he never thought . . .

Somi slowly releases her fingers from the fabric, which Seokga is now staring at in a new light. The cream-colored wool might have once sat atop Hani's skin. It would have smelled like her shampoo, the citrus and vanilla scent of her, mixed with that unique smell of smoke, like a crackling fire. Hani was always burning so brightly.

"Answer me," Seokga hisses, barely able to breathe. He never knew what became of Hani's tiny apartment after she died. He honestly had no idea how those affairs were handled on Iseung.

"Yes," Somi finally whispers. "It's hers. The bag, too. The books."

"I," snarls Seokga, "am going to *kill* you." Never mind the fact that Nam Somi is already dead. He will find a way to destroy her very essence, shred her into nothingness—just as soon as he puts Hwanin down somewhere safe. "I am going to *kill you*—"

"She *gave it to me!*" Somi half-screams as Seokga transforms his cane into a sword. He freezes. Panting hard, Somi hugs her waist with her own arms. "All of it," she whispers. "Hani gave me all of it. It was in her will. I snuck back into New Sinsi to tell her I was sorry . . . and got the will instead. The apartment, the clothes, the jewelry, the weapons, and the novels . . . Hani had left it all to me."

"Bullshit," Seokga snaps, but he's faltered. Part of him isn't too sure. "You were just her co-worker, a younger gumiho she took pity on—"

She bristles. "I was her *best friend* until you came along. We'd both fucked each other over by the end, but we were *friends*. And who else would she have left it to?" Somi fires back, squeezing her middle tight. "And . . . And she wrote that will before I went and r-ruined everything."

He is frozen, a statue that cannot take his eyes off that sweater. Hani's sweater.

"We all have different ways of grieving," Somi mutters, staring at the ground. "I wear her clothes, I . . . act like her, sometimes . . . because I *miss* her. For a long time, it was the closest I could get to being with her again." Defensive, Somi raises her head. "I don't expect you to understand, but I don't care. It's none of your business."

Seokga's lips are pressed so tightly together that he's certain they're bloodless. His mouth is full of words that he *could* say—

horrible, terrible words—but something in him won't let them emerge. Perhaps it's the memory of Hani, using her last words to beg him to spare Somi's life.

Somi hesitates, too. "Does it even matter if I have the sweater or not?" she whispers. "You found *her*. Kisa."

It matters, he wants to retort, but his lips don't let him utter those words, either.

The gumiho watches him warily. "Don't tell me that you don't *like* her as much as you liked Hani," she snaps, suddenly drawing herself up. "She's incredible. She's smart and kind and she deserves somebody who won't constantly compare her to who she was in her past life!"

He bristles. Anytime he's done that, he's felt like a complete asshole afterward. What does it matter if Kisa prefers coffee to hot chocolate? It doesn't. It *doesn't*.

"She doesn't owe you anything," Somi adds ferociously. The protectiveness in her voice reminds Seokga briefly of the way Hani had constantly looked after the younger gumiho. "If she doesn't like you, then you leave her alone and let her have the space she needs."

Seokga's amazed to find that his lips are twitching as Somi continues. "And the *last* thing you need to be doing is expecting her to stick around for you when the cruise is over. She deserves to make her own decisions about *her* life—"

"I agree," cuts in Seokga, suddenly feeling lighter as the last of his rage begins to dissipate.

She falters. "What?"

"I agree," Seokga repeats smoothly, snapping his sword back into a cane. "With everything you said."

Somi blinks. "Oh." She nods, once, then twice, twisting the hem of Hani's sweater. "Okay. Well, good. Because Kisa is going to be my best friend again, even if she doesn't know it yet."

Seokga smirks. "No."

Her mouth falls open. "Excuse me?"

Seokga smiles at Somi, but it's not a nasty smile. It's not exactly a kind one, either—it might never be. But it's something almost like a sort of grudging solidarity.

She's the only one who remembers Hani like he does.

And although they were on different sides, Seokga and Somi both made it through the Dark Days. Only they know what truly happened.

But the Dark Days are over. They're on the same side now.

And they need to work together. For Kisa.

"She's going to be mine."

"No," snaps Somi, suddenly looking very competitive. "No, no, she's—"

"—already *my* best friend," Hajun finishes, strolling back into the sick bay's lobby, the box of medical supplies now empty in his hands. He grins sheepishly as he sets the cardboard back on the counter. "Sorry. You guys are pretty loud."

Somi winces and looks completely mortified. "You heard all of that?" she whispers.

Hajun shrugs in a mild sort of way. The way that seems to say, *I did, but it doesn't make any difference to me.* "Look, I think it's wonderful that you both like Kisa so much," he says, leaning against the counter. "But all of this is going to overwhelm her."

"All of what?" Somi asks innocently.

The idol gives her an amused look. "If the two of you are going to fight over Kisa," he says, "don't do it in front of her. And definitely don't tell her you're wearing designer clothing from her past life when she's not allowed to wear anything but these itchy scrubs."

Seokga's mouth tightens.

"I would never fight anybody," Somi tells Hajun, who snorts in disbelief and then looks slightly terrified. "Are your scrubs really that itchy?" the gumiho asks. "Because I could help get them off your skin..."

"Enough," Seokga cuts in before Hajun can turn an even more alarming shade of blue. "We have better things to focus on."

"The offer's always there," Somi whispers, winking at Hajun.

The idol looks as if he might faint.

It almost makes Seokga miss the Somi who couldn't look at a man without blushing, but a part of him is pleased to know that Hani made an impact on her. On Somi. That Hani is still continuing to shape the world and its inhabitants, in some way or another... Even if it's through another dirty-talking gumiho wreaking chaos in the (under)world.

Hani, he thinks grudgingly, would be proud.

"Feel free to take me up on it," Somi adds to Hajun.

Thoroughly exasperated and slightly nauseated, Seokga turns on his heel and makes for the security room. After a brief moment, the idol and the gumiho follow.

A few minutes later, Seokga is waiting with Hajun around the corner when Somi returns from scoping out the security room to determine whether it's clear for them to enter. Her solemn face cuts through his worrying like a knife. He has the distinct impression that he does not want to know—for the sake of his sanity—but he asks anyway. "What happened?"

"The monitors," Somi replies, voice quiet. "They've been destroyed. All of them."

As they enter the destroyed security room, it's fucking déjà vu. Seokga can't help but remember when Hani—in a desperate attempt to protect Somi—stole cameras, monitors, and entire *bod-*

ies from the gumiho's crime scene. If he had access to the tools he'd had then, Seokga would order they scan for fingerprints or hairs, sending them for DNA testing. But he doesn't have those luxuries—what he has instead is a crying infant in his arms, a declawed gumiho, and a former K-pop idol with ridiculously nice hair.

"They know we're on to them," Seokga seethes, glaring at Somi. "If you had been stealthier last night—"

"I *was* stealthy!" Under his glower, Somi shrinks back into Hani's sweater, as if she's seeking comfort from it.

"—perhaps she wouldn't have noticed you hiding in the janitorial closet and wouldn't have destroyed the monitors," he finishes in a snarl.

Somi bares her teeth back but doesn't seem to have any scathing retort. She knows that he's right.

Broken screens and shattered glass litter the floor. File cabinets are completely upended, papers sprawling in a sea of crumpled white. It looks like a wild, rabid animal tore through. Seokga's mood only worsens when he crouches next to a ruined chair. The faux-leather backing is spilling Styrofoam, leaking out from huge tears. He narrows his eyes at the rips, and—letting Somi's bitter retort and his brother's wailing fade into the background—uses two of his fingers to measure one's width.

Interesting. The claw marks on Hwanin's body had been too messy to thoroughly examine, obscured by the cavity in his brother's chest. But here, on the chair, there's an opportunity to get a closer look.

"What is it?" Hajun asks, peering over Seokga.

"These marks are too big to belong to a gumiho," Seokga replies slowly. "They were made by claws, yes—four of them. But these aren't the claws of foxes. They're far larger." Eyes narrowing, he passes Hwanin to Hajun. "The perpetrator isn't a gumiho."

Standing abruptly, Seokga strides to one of the overturned file cabinets. "But the claws," he says, bending down to rummage through the papers, "the number rules out a yong, who would have three. It also rules out an inmyunjo, who has three, and a haetae, who would have five. That leaves a samjokgu, a bulgae, or a jangsan beom."

Somi sucks in a sharp breath. Seokga ignores her. Most gumiho have negative reactions to the mention of a samjokgu, whose powers exceed theirs by far and are known to goad the foxes into fights simply to torture and then kill them (despite such practices having been decreed Very Illegal some time ago). Perhaps it was an Unruly samjokgu that killed Somi.

"But bulgae . . ." Seokga pauses as he thinks of the cheerful, tail-wagging canines who work at the behest of Dalnim and Haemosu. "Those dogs aren't shifters. Whoever we're looking for has a human form, as well. And I haven't seen a jangsan beom in centuries."

The tiger-shifters are exceedingly rare, on the brink of extinction just like their mundane *Panthera tigris* counterparts. Their dwindling numbers are possibly due to their meager lifespans. Unlike creatures such as the immortal gumiho, jangsan beom live around one to two hundred years on average—rather short for such a powerful creature. The last one he saw was the one he rode during the Okhwang coup. It had been a supremely annoying monster, using its voice mimicry to imitate Seokga's own voice and deliver faux orders such as *Spin around and touch your nose!* at the least opportune moments for its own amusement. Only the consequences of that coup had been as embarrassing as the sight of his army following some ridiculous choreography.

In hindsight, it's really no surprise that his siege ended on such a pathetic note.

There had been other jangsan beom in that realm, Seokga remembers, but only a few.

"Statistically speaking, we're probably looking for a samjokgu. On each of their three paws, they have four claws—and know how to use them."

"It's not impossible that it's a jangsan beom," Somi says quietly. Seokga doesn't even spare her a glance as he continues to riffle through the papers. "I . . . think I saw one, once."

"Unlikely," Seokga dismisses. The gumiho is clearly frightened of Unruly samjokgu, but there's no point in pretending that it's more likely that a jangsan beom did this. Living in scared denial doesn't solve cases.

Somi falls into seething silence.

"Based on what you heard, we're looking for a female samjokgu shifter, likely no younger than thirty." It's the "snooty" tone that gives her away: In Seokga's experience, it takes a while to perfect such an impressionable tenor. Twenty-somethings can *try*, of course, but hints of their not-so-recent teenage whines always slip out eventually. "But we can also check the passenger lists for a female jangsan beom, as well," he adds grudgingly as Somi continues to glare at him. It'll be easy enough to do. The papers crammed into this particular cabinet are physical lists of passengers, hundreds of pages full of names and other personal details printed onto the thin white paper. Now that their suspect list has been so narrowed down, they can easily use these sheets to find the perp . . .

"Wait." Hajun's voice is sharp enough that Seokga looks up, brows raised. "A female samjokgu over thirty . . . A snooty voice . . ."

"Are you going to add anything worthwhile or repeat what I just said?" he demands irritably, turning back to his hunt.

"But I *know* someone who fits the profile," the idol replies, voice tight. "It's—"

"What the *fuck* is going on in here?" a new voice roars, and Seokga could *throttle* Officer Shin Korain as the haetae rushes in, taking in his destroyed room with furious eyes. A tense moment of silence passes as Korain absorbs the destroyed monitors, the ripped chairs, and the waterfall of files flowing from the upturned cabinets.

"Officer," Somi tries sweetly, batting her eyes in a way she must have learned from Hani, "I promise, this isn't what it looks like—"

The attempt at charm fails miserably. Korain's face contorts into a vicious sneer as he stares at Somi. "You. And *you*." He's seen Seokga. "Everybody—" He glimpses Hwanin, and his face turns even more blue than before. "Come with me."

It's a broom closet.

A large one, yes, but they're being held in a *broom closet.* Seokga does not know if his dignity will ever recover. Korain sits on an upside-down bucket in front of them, arms crossed. What makes matters worse is that this should be an easy escape for Seokga— create an illusion of himself sitting compliantly on the floor, shift into an ant, and scurry away—but he cannot leave Hwanin, and is wary of leaving Somi and Hajun alone in front of a *Godly Gossip* informant with direct access to the next morning's headline.

"The baby's mine," Somi declares loudly and unnecessarily. Seokga has already seen Korain peer suspiciously at Hwanin's remarkable eyes. The haetae is smart. And right now, that makes him dangerous. "I am . . . a mother."

Seven fucking hells. Seokga refuses the urge to bury his head in his hands. "You're not helping," he grumbles.

"Be quiet," snaps Korain. He's waiting for somebody.

Seokga hopes it's not another deity.

Hajun stiffens. "Don't talk to her like that," the idol retorts, and his usually soft voice is harder than Seokga has ever heard. Somi is sitting on the floor next to him, and he wraps an arm protectively around her shoulders. The gumiho looks amused. It is, agrees Seokga, rather funny. A serial killer being protected by a happy-go-lucky boy-band star.

"My knight in shining armor," murmurs Somi, but her cheeks are blue.

"Where's Kisa?" Korain glares at Hajun. "Aren't the two of you usually attached at the hip?"

"She's not involved in this," Hajun replies quickly. Too quickly. Korain frowns.

Seokga watches in disgust as Hajun snaps his mouth shut. As the god of trickery, he is both horrified and embarrassed by Hajun's lack of deceitful capabilities.

A moment later, the closet door opens, a sliver of light creeping in along with the black-haired serving girl Seokga knocked over. Chaeyeon.

For a moment, Seokga is so relieved that it's not a member of the pantheon that he fails to realize how bad this might be.

He is trapped in a broom closet.

With *Godly Gossip* informants.

Chaeyeon gapes at Somi, then Hajun, then Hwanin—who's sitting happily in Hajun's lap—before her eyes narrow viciously at Seokga. Korain stands and whispers in her ear, undoubtedly recapping the events that led them into the broom closet.

Right. Seokga's grown bored with this. For the sake of conserving his energy (he's barely slept a wink since boarding this foul ship), he was humoring this insane procedure—but enough is enough. It's time, he decides, for some magic.

Seokga stands, attempting to look dignified even as his head bumps the ceiling. "You're going to let us go," he says, "and you're not going to tell anybody what you saw." Green tendrils of mist swirl out from his hands, hooking around Korain's and Chaeyeon's limbs. *You're going to let us go. You're going to forget what you saw. You're going to let us go. You're going to forget what you saw.*

He's only able to compel the sinful. Those who are truly good are unable to be swayed by his compulsions. Judging by their side gigs as *Godly Gossip* spies, Seokga figures that this will be easy enough. Most everyone has a little bit of wickedness inside of them . . . It's so rare to meet anybody truly "innocent."

But his magic doesn't take hold.

Korain and Chaeyeon exchange unimpressed glances.

"Wait," mutters Seokga. "This time it should work." He grits his teeth together, concentrating all of his will on the duo, but . . . nothing. Panting, Seokga stares at them. "Do you mean to tell me you're *good* people?" he demands. Unbelievable. First his mind-reading ability leaves him, and now *this*—

"I died saving orphans from a fire," deadpans Korain.

Chaeyeon snorts. "Liar." Turning her attention back to Seokga, she says, "You're in Jeoseung. Powers like that are reserved for the realm of the living. Down here, the dead can do whatever they want—unrestricted by alive things like you." She tilts her head. "But we might consider doing what you ask. For a price. *Godly Gossip* wants . . ."

"I wear boxer briefs," he snaps. "Happy?"

"Not yet." Chaeyeon holds out her hand, and Korain places his Samsung into it. The phone that *Godly Gossip* must have smuggled its informants. Holding Seokga's stare, she opens up the recording app, and presses RECORD. "We want a tell-all, exclusive *Godly Gossip* interview in exchange for our silence regarding . . . whatever it is you're up to. One full hour of your time, and mandatory, honest answers to every question we ask."

Hwanung's tits. "I'd rather pull out my own tongue."

Korain smirks. "You don't have much of a choice."

The bastard's right.

Seokga has no power in this situation, no bargaining leverage. This is the deal they're offering, so it's the deal he's been forced to take. Seokga grinds his molars together.

A long, long moment passes with torturous slowness.

How he wishes he could smite them down.

"Fine," he finally hisses. "But *no* questions regarding the baby, or the security room, or my brother . . . who, for the record, is perfectly fine. He's watching television in his room and there is absolutely nothing wrong with him." And, he adds silently, "honesty" means nothing to a trickster god. He'll answer the questions in whatever way he damn pleases.

"That *baby* could be our biggest scoop," Chaeyeon argues, pointing at Hwanin. "We'll ask about it if we want to."

Seokga sees red. "Ask about the baby and I'll tear you limb from limb. You might not be able to die again, but you can feel pain—plenty of it."

The girl pales.

"Whatever." Korain shrugs, but there's a malicious gleam in his eyes. "Let's just start. There are plenty of other questions to ask."

"Right." Chayeon clears her throat. "We at *Godly Gossip* would like to thank you for sitting down with us today—"

"Fuck off," Seokga snarls, glaring at the blinking red button of the recording app shoved in his face. "You and I both know why we're here. Go on, ask. Before I lose my patience."

"Fine. First question: Do you wear a toupee?"

CHAPTER TWENTY-FOUR

KISA

THEY MIGHT HAVE, Kisa thinks as she stares at the god who's just walked into the Creature Café, a teeny, *tiny* problem.

Or perhaps it's not a problem at all. Perhaps this is *good*. Yes, perhaps it's a *good* thing that Hwanung, son/probable-murderer of Hwanin, is ordering an iced tea on the SRC *Flatliner* and smiling flirtatiously at the flustered barista. His hair is purple rather than long and dyed silver, and he doesn't wear the traditional robes like his father, but the resemblance is plain as day. This is Hwanung.

Hwanung, who is wearing a faded Elvis T-shirt and a ridiculous number of earrings.

Hwanung, who is one of their primary murder suspects.

With a trembling hand, Kisa sets down her pen, which she's been using to scribble new theories that coat her in a cold, damp sweat and send chills down her spine. Theories that suggest that this entire plot has gone on for much longer than anybody has suspected.

Perhaps Hwanung is meeting his accomplice for their next crime. Are they going to murder Seokga? The thought petrifies her, but Kisa forces herself to remain seated, carefully watching as the god pays and wanders out the door, sipping indolently. After a terrified pep talk to herself, Kisa follows him through the ship, careful to remain a healthy distance behind him as he reaches Deck 7 and wanders down the hall of suites, seemingly counting the door numbers until he reaches Room 7346. His father's room.

Kisa holds her breath. Hwanung pulls a keycard from his pocket and slips inside as Kisa watches avidly from around the corner, counting down the seconds until the god emerges, face carefully blank.

What could he possibly have wanted with Hwanin's suite?

A moment later, a door across the hall opens, and Dr. Jang slips out. The heavy door swings shut behind her, but doesn't click. Kisa's entire body stiffens as she watches the therapist slowly walk over to Hwanung and place a wrinkled hand on his shoulder.

Kisa notes that Hwanung tenses but doesn't look surprised to see Dr. Jang. If anything, he looks *relieved* by the sight of her—not even fazed by the hot pink sunglasses. Her mind whirls as she mentally scrabbles around for puzzle pieces to fit together. Could it really be that Dr. Jang is his lackey? Her hand drifts to her pockets, where her theories are scribbled down. If it's true . . .

"Hwanung," Dr. Jang says kindly. "I got your call. Have you had any luck so far?"

"Heejin." Hwanung shifts from foot to foot. "I can't find him. Do you know where he might be?"

Kisa frowns. There's a familiarity between them, but not the sort she'd expect from two accomplices. Remembering Seokga's lack of knowledge regarding Jang's god or goddess, Kisa wonders if she's one of Hwanung's shamans. No—she can't be. The protocol for meeting one's patron deity is to bow at a ninety-degree angle, and Dr. Jang offered only a more casual bow when Hwanung turned. Chewing anxiously on her lip, Kisa waits for Jang's response.

"Seokga informed me that your father ate a bad clam recently. He might be in the sick bay." Dr. Jang smiles sympathetically. "How are things in Okhwang? I hope it's not any trouble that's bringing you here to look for Emperor Hwanin."

Something flashes in Hwanung's eyes, but Kisa is too far away to guess what it might be. "They're—different," he replies. It's interesting, she thinks, that his tone isn't as cold—or as hard—as it was on his damning phone call with Seokga. He sounds... regretful? Tired? The god sips at his iced tea. "And how is my *uncle?*" There's a sneer that accompanies those words, and it brings forth a prickling of offended anger from Kisa.

"Seokga is doing well." Dr. Jang pushes up her sunglasses. "This vacation has been good for him."

Hwanung's face is still twisted in distaste. "And do you know where *he* is?"

Sweat slides down the nape of Kisa's neck as she waits for Dr. Jang's reply. The old woman is silent, as if considering something... and Kisa receives the terrible impression that somehow, she knows exactly where Seokga is. *Don't tell him,* she pleads. *You can't tell him.*

Dr. Jang finally clears her throat and offers Hwanung a friendly smile. "Around this time of day, Seokga is usually swimming on Deck 9." Sweet relief cools Kisa's anxiety—only slightly. The old shaman lied... for Seokga. Surely Dr. Jang knows that Seokga would rather die than swim in the cruise ship's main pool, where guests shoot out of water slides and more often than not land atop another swimmer.

"I'll be heading up there, then. It was nice to see you, Heejin."

Hwanung pauses awkwardly, a hand toying with his lip piercing. It glimmers in the hallway light. "Thanks for last time, by the way."

Her smile is grandmotherly. "Did things ever work out with that girl?"

A wince comes from the young god. "No. But the couple's sessions helped for a little while until she—" Hwanung breaks off, shaking his head. Metal glints, and Kisa sees that he has small silver piercings in his ears. "I don't want to bother you."

"Please, Hwanung," Dr. Jang says with a laugh, wrinkled face dimpling. It occurs to Kisa that she's deeply fond of him in an almost familial way. "I don't mind. I'll walk with you to Deck 9, and you can tell me everything. I won't even charge a session fee."

As the pair leaves, Kisa shakes her head. Hwanung isn't acting like a murderer revisiting the scene of his crime. If anything, he's acting like a confused teenage boy searching for his father. It could be a convincing act, of course, but as their backs recede down the hallway, Kisa doesn't find herself following them.

Instead, she's studying the door of Dr. Jang's room—the door that's been left slightly agape. Dread pools low in her stomach. The red thread flutters, perhaps in concern.

But the therapist's door has been left open, and Kisa has a notebook in her pocket filled with theories that she needs to either put to rest or confirm. She can dart in, then back out, before hurrying to warn Seokga of his nephew's presence on the boat. Besides . . . Kisa's hand flutters to the pocket of her scrubs, where she put the bottle of lotion before leaving her room.

She should return it. She can't stand the smell of it.

Determinedly, she slips down the corridor and into Dr. Jang's room. Her heart pounds fiercely in her chest as she takes in the small suite, the queen-sized bed and adjoining bathroom. There's a bright yellow suitcase resting on one of the suite's cushy chairs, spilling assortments of random, vibrant clothes. Kisa spots another rubber-deck patterned set buried somewhere underneath Hawaiian shirts and wide-rimmed hats.

In the bathroom, she finds Dr. Jang's tote bag and neatly slips the disgusting lotion back into it. When Kisa sneezes, her heart nearly stops—but Dr. Jang isn't here, she reminds herself, even as her palms begin to sweat. It's fine. It's all perfectly *fine*.

Leaving the bathroom, she feels another sneeze building up in her nasal passage and practically bursts a blood vessel as she tries to force it down, but it erupts with a vengeance. Eyes watering, she looks desperately around for a tissue . . . and sneezes again.

Gods, it's like the time Yuna brought home a stray cat to their dormitory. Kisa hadn't been able to stay inside for more than a minute without sneezing or hacking her lungs out.

Feeling too sick to linger much longer, Kisa stumbles to the desk, determined to at least find *something* of potential worth, something to make the journey into this room worth it. Through blurry vision, she spots a well-worn leather-bound notebook sitting on the corner. Before she can think better of it, Kisa swipes the notebook from the desk and hurries from the room, in desperate need of a tissue.

CHAPTER TWENTY-FIVE

SEOKGA

I<small>T'S ONLY AFTER</small> a series of humiliating questions that veer either on the raunchy or depressingly dark side (and after a stern warning from Korain that he won't be as merciful the next time they damage any property) that they are finally permitted to leave the closet.

Fucking *Godly Gossip*.

"I think I know more about you than I ever wanted to," Somi groans as they enter the sick bay, having finally made their escape from Deck 2. She looks vaguely nauseous as she disappears into the small bathroom, and there's the unamusing sound of retching—which Seokga can tell is entirely manufactured for Somi's own perverse amusement.

How he regrets not ending her during the Dark Days. He crunches down on his coffee candy with violence. Shards of sugar scrape against his teeth.

Hajun looks vaguely sick as well, but for another reason. Ever since he was interrupted in the security room, he's been nervously jittering his right leg and working his mouth as if physically attempting to rein in whatever it is he has to say. As Somi reemerges, it practically bursts out of him.

"*Soo-min!*" Hajun pants, and Seokga snatches Hwanin from him lest he drop the child in his excitement. "Soo-min matches the profile perfectly. She's a samjokgu, she died in her early thirties, and she has the snootiest voice I've ever heard..."

Seokga's brows rise up to his hairline. "Soo-min is a samjokgu?" This is news to him.

He nods, eyes wide. Seokga absorbs this. "She did seem unusually interested in Hwanin's skin yesterday," he says slowly. "She asked how it was so . . . *whole*."

Perhaps Seokga should have been paying more attention instead of wallowing in a pit of despair. However, when Seokga wallows, it's very hard to pull himself out of it and remember that other people do, unfortunately, exist. Even on a good day, he does not care very much about anybody else. Aside, obviously, from the woman who has always been his one exception.

Somi snorts in derision. "How did you miss that? *Really—*"

His phone vibrates, and Seokga sends Somi a withering glare before reaching into his pocket and checking his texts. A moment later, his heart stops cold.

Yeomra: Hwanung just teleported onto the ship.

Yeomra: I'm assuming you'll get on this immediately.

What in the seven hells?

Seokga gapes at the screen before shoving it back into his pocket and staring down at Hwanin. Why is Hwanung on the ship? He's nearly certain that the young god is somehow involved in his father's death, and his sudden appearance doesn't bode well—at all. Seokga's blood heats as he's suddenly overcome with a burning urgency to hide his brother, to protect him. He stares down at the little bundle in his arms, wondering when something so small became so precious. "Hajun, Somi," Seokga says, voice sharp, "hide the child."

Somi's eyes are wide as Seokga passes Hwanin to her, and he's relieved to see that the gumiho is gentle with him. Hwanin begins to cry as he leaves his brother's arms, and the sound goes straight to Seokga's chest—but he's already rushing from the sick bay. He's not entirely sure what he's planning on doing. Where is Kisa? He needs her. He needs her desperately.

It's almost as if Gameunjang, goddess of luck, has finally thrown him a bone as he rounds the corner only to collide with a smaller body. Seokga rushes to steady Kisa, who's breathing hard, cheeks flushed blue and curls in a rumpled disarray. Yellow happiness tinged with relief glows down the red thread, but her thoughts quickly dampen his joy.

—*Hwanung*—*with Jang*—*going*—*Deck 9*—*swim*—*lie*—*Seokga*—

"Your nephew," she pants. Seokga's hands are still placed on her shoulders, and he feels that she's trembling. "He's heading to—"

"To Deck 9," he finishes, and she nods breathlessly. Grimly, Seokga lets his hands drop from her narrow shoulders. "Let's go."

"I suppose the... cerebration transference... can be useful," Kisa puffs as they hurry up the stairs. Seokga's right leg burns, but he grips his cane harder, ignoring it. "I can barely... speak..."

Concern flares through him as she wheezes. How quickly did she run to the sick bay? "Elevator," he grits out, knuckles white on his cane as they burst onto Deck 4 and practically sprint to the nearest elevator, pushing past throngs of guests who mill about the restaurants and shops with glazed, dreamy expressions. For them, this cruise must be a dream, but for him, it's a fucking nightmare. Seokga pounds on the little white UP button, and when the elevator door finally opens, he hurls himself into it and closes the door before anyone other than Kisa can enter. The elevator might stop at every floor, and taking the stairs would be faster—but Seokga isn't sure his leg can handle running up the stairs from Deck 3 to Deck 9. That had been the original plan, but one flight up, he'd acknowledged defeat to the monstrous stairways. And Kisa looks as if she'll pass out if she's made to run any more anyway.

Seokga would very much like to rip out the sound system as cheerful Muzak begins to play. In the mirrored ceiling of the elevator, he and Kisa are so incredibly frazzled and sweaty that the vain trickster god does something he normally would never dream of, and looks away from the mirror.

He's relieved to hear that Kisa's breathing has begun to steady. The elevator stops on Deck 5, and Seokga impatiently jabs his cane against the CLOSE DOOR button before any of the other guests can board.

"*Hey!*" one of them shouts, a sunburnt man wearing the tie-dyed shirt he'd found so horrendous. The door closes on his outraged face.

"You're going to break the elevator if you keep doing that," Kisa warns, but Seokga ignores her, pounding the button again as they reach the sixth floor while simultaneously hitting DECK 9 with a growing determination. "Seokga, really, *stop* pressing the buttons! It's not going to get us there quicker, and besides, Hwanung might not even be who we're—"

"Even technology bends to my will," he informs her smugly, moments before he accidentally pounds in the EMERGENCY STOP button about a dozen times rather than the DECK 9 one. Kisa stumbles into his back as the elevator, caught somewhere between Decks 6 and 7, abruptly jolts to a stop.

There's a moment of terrible silence.

—*he is—so smart—yet so—exhaustingly dumb—*

"Perhaps I spoke too soon," admits Seokga. Kisa makes a sound that reminds him of a growling kitten who is trying very hard to be ferocious, and shoves past him—presumably to remedy his mistake.

"*You—*"

Her voice is abruptly drowned out by the sudden screeching over the cruise ship's intercom. Seokga's ears fucking *shriek* in pain and he grimaces as his head pounds. Kisa jumps about a foot in the air—which would be comical if the noises now being broadcast all over the SRC *Flatliner* weren't so . . . alarming.

Sharp, masculine grunts blare over the speakers, followed by a feminine laughing.

Kisa's eyes are wide. "Oh, gods," she whispers, a hand rising to her mouth, "are they . . ."

Seokga is considering it, too, but that particular theory falls away as the man starts to scream. And scream. And scream. There's no way to block it out, no way to ignore the sheer agony in the voice—in Captain Lee's voice, Seokga realizes, recognizing something in the anguished cries that remind him of the mustachioed man.

"*Oh, gods!*" the captain screams. "*Please, stop! Stop! Help! Please!*"

"Shut up," the woman snaps, followed by a wet squelching that makes even Seokga's hardened insides turn. The living captain, apparently, won't be living for much longer.

"Soo-min?" Kisa's eyes are bright, shining with horror and unshed tears. "That's Soo-min's voice . . . Why is she hurting him?" Seokga hesitates, but his thoughts must flicker down the thread, for Kisa's eyes widen. "*Her?*" she gasps out. "She's . . . ? But I thought—"

"*HELP!*" wails the captain as Seokga pounds on the elevator buttons, desperate for it to start moving, so they might help Captain Lee.

"Oh, gods," cries Kisa, burying her face in her hands. "I think I . . . I think I might be sick."

"Pull out the heart," a new voice demands over the speakers. "Throw it into the river. His ghost won't return to the ship if the organ leaves. He'll end up in some obscure corner of Jeoseung."

Hwanung. Seokga sees red. He'd know that fucking voice anywhere. His knees nearly give out with fury.

Hwanin's body was missing its heart, too.

Somewhere far above the elevator, screams resound through the ship, horrified guests clutching their ears and shrieking as Captain Lee lets out a terrible cry.

"S-Seokga," Kisa whispers, but he barely hears her. His body has begun to vibrate as he begins the teleportation process, itching to rip his nephew's head from his body and throw *that* into the river. He'll still reincarnate as a baby in the same spot in which he died, but clearly the fucking rookie didn't know that when he murdered his father and tossed his heart overboard.

What did he think? That baby Hwanin would reappear somewhere deep in Jeoseung and forever be stranded from Okhwang? Foolish boy.

Seokga is about to step through time and space, to bend it to his will and take him directly to the bridge, where the murder must be happening . . . But something, a sharp tug on his pinky, stops him. The red thread is quivering in concern, yanking him toward Kisa as over the speakers, Captain Lee screams himself hoarse—and then abruptly falls silent. There's a crackle as the intercom shuts off.

"Kisa?"

She's slid down to the floor, hugging her knees against her chest. Kisa's face is so pale behind her curls, and Seokga staggers, momentarily swarmed with terror. He has seen fear before, on countless different faces, but this is . . . This is not mere fear. Her eyes are fixed on something he cannot see—a memory?—and her chest is rising and falling so unevenly that it cuts Seokga to the bone to see the choppiness of her shallow breaths. He can't—*fuck, he can't* leave her like this, stuck in an elevator. What sort of fucking soulmate would he be?

"Kisa?" he asks, grabbing her shoulders in his own fear, giving her a gentle shake. But it's as if she doesn't hear, or even see, him. "Kisa?"

The red thread shakes and shakes as Kisa remains lost to him. Seokga tries to fight off rising panic. His hands flutter uselessly around her—smoothing down her hair, cupping her chin, holding her shoulders, her hands. Seokga doesn't—he doesn't know what to do. Doesn't know how to send a calm, silver serenity down the bond as she once did for him. He's too panicked, too frightened. What's happened to her?

"Please," Seokga whispers. "Kisa, please—shit, shit, *shit*—" It's as if he's back in that warehouse, watching Hani's life drain from her eyes, unable to do anything... Unable to help...

Around Kisa's pinky, the red thread glows black... And when that color reaches his end of the thread, the terror he feels—Kisa's terror—is *endless,* as suffocating as drowning in a dark sea. He's nearly sick from the taste of it. Only when it fades is he able to move again.

The red thread tugs insistently on his finger and he glares at it through a sudden onslaught of pained tears. "*Help me,*" he begs. "Help me help her. Please—"

It hesitates before rising farther into the air, twisting itself into a shape composed of one unbreaking red line that twirls and turns to create an image, a threaded pictorial of a man holding a woman. Seokga doesn't hesitate as he sits on the elevator's floor, gently pulling Kisa to him and mimicking the position of the couple in the thread's suggestion. Her head rests limply on his chest. Seokga's own fingers spasm as he holds Kisa's. "Kisa," he murmurs into her ear. "Come back to me."

It could be seconds, or minutes, or hours until she surfaces—but surface she does, her breathing slowly steadying. Seokga could nearly weep with relief as she looks up at him, as she sees him.

"Seokga?" she whispers.

"I'm here," he assures her, voice catching in his throat.

Kisa smiles—a trembling rictus on her face that dies as quickly as it was born. "Don't leave me . . ."

"Never," the trickster swears, meaning it with every inch of his wicked soul.

"I wanted . . . to be a leaf," she whispers, clearly delirious as her eyelids flutter shut. "I wanted to be . . . a leaf . . . but I never meant to fall . . ." Her soft, nonsensical words trail off as her eyes shut.

A moment later, the elevator begins to move slowly upward once more.

Seokga stares up at the mirror above and wonders what in the seven hells just happened.

The body is a fucking mess, slumped on the navigation console in the ship's bridge, a bloody, heartless slab of unmoving flesh. Seokga stares at it in disgust and pity as Yeomra—having kept his word and descended "very dramatically" onto the ship an hour before like it "was the plan all along" to "deliver divine justice"—secures the skeletal chains around Soo-min. The bonds are unbreakable, forged in Yeomra's death magic, the bones sourced from corpses of long-dead prisoners who died within penitentiary walls. Only gods can remove the shackles, as long as they are not the one imprisoned within them.

It looks as if Captain Lee put up a fight. One of the bridge's long, horizontal windows has a crack down the middle. The navigation console's many levers are all—according to Yeomra—disarranged. Somewhere in the struggle, Captain Lee must have hit the ship's intercom. His impressive leather seat is on its side, and the wheels had still been slowly spinning as Seokga (after setting Kisa gently on his bed under the watchful eyes of Hajun and Somi) sprinted into the room. Bloodstains splatter the floor, although Soo-min's hands and clothing are almost impressively tidy. The captain himself is slumped over the console.

Soo-min's typically unruffled hair is a mess, her lipstick smudged around the gag stuffed in her mouth. "I didn't do it!" she had been wailing to anyone who had listened. "I didn't! I-I would never—he was—we were—I *didn't do this*!" Unfortunately for her, Soo-min's voice exactly matches the voice broadcast over the entire ship. Yeomra had stuffed the gag in her mouth with gusto when he caught her running to the I-95, presumably to hide in the midst of the chaos.

Hwanung, unsurprisingly, is nowhere in sight. The god fled directly after the murder—Seokga has spent the past hour making various lengthy calls to the other deities, recapping everything from Hwanin's murder to today's events. There's a watch out for him, and once Seokga wraps up this fucking nightmare, he'll hunt his nephew to the ends of the fucking realms.

He's also flatly refused to bring the baby to Okhwang. As Hwanin's closest living relative who's (a) not imprisoned in the depths of Jeoseung for crimes against humanity, (b) currently awake and has not been sleeping for thousands of years, and (c) not a proponent of patricide (at the moment), Seokga can claim legal guardianship of Hwanin—and claim it, he shall. For some absurd reason, the thought of the child being out of his sight sends anxiety shooting down his spine. By Seokga's side is the safest place for Hwanin to be.

He's told himself not to think of *whys*—but as Yeomra finishes up his phone call to one of the seven hells, the one where they've decided to relocate Soo-min—Seokga can't help but long for an explanation. Why kill Hwanin? Why kill Captain Lee? The two murders hardly even seem connected save for the murderers.

How were Soo-min and Hwanung involved? How did they know each other? How did they meet?

It doesn't matter, he tells himself. Soo-min is clearly set on playing the denial game, although her voice was blared across the entire ship and she matches their suspect's profile perfectly. Hwanung's number was found stored on her phone, although any texts and calls had been scrubbed. There were times in the New Sinsi haetae precinct when the officers had to let go of the *whys* and focus on the evidence they had. Chief Shim had hated it, but back then, Seokga had never given a damn. Now, he understands Chief Shim's lingering confusion. It gnaws on him like a leech.

"When this cruise ends," Yeomra says, pocketing his phone, "the girl and her friend can head toward the nearest DAR. They'll be given a fast pass to the front of the line." He grabs Soo-min's shoulder. The woman sobs around her gag, pleading incoherently. Both gods steadfastly ignore her. "The ship can't go anywhere until I find another fucking captain, and it was so much work getting the first—"

"You didn't think to kidnap a co-captain?" Seokga demands, but his heart isn't in it. The sooner the ship starts moving, the sooner he must say goodbye to Kisa. He'd be fine if the ship remained stagnant forever, floating upon the red waters with nowhere to go, nowhere else to be.

The death god's mouth opens . . . and closes. With a grimace, he seems to admit defeat. "I don't like it, but you have a point. It's what I get for short-staffing." Yeomra's dark glitter-dusted eyes narrow. "I'll find one quickly enough." He pauses before reaching out a hand to Seokga. "I'm not going to say that you did a great job, because you sure as *fuck* didn't. It was passable detective work at best. But still, thanks."

Seokga rolls his eyes, but shakes the death god's hand anyway. It's as cold as ice. With a sarcastic smile, Yeomra disappears in a flash of dark smoke that leaves Seokga choking. When the smoke clears, both the CEO and Soo-min are gone. Unfortunately, the captain's body still remains. "Fucking cadaver," Seokga hisses, realizing Yeomra left him to clean up.

"Give me the child," Samsin Halmoni shrilly demands as Seokga grits his teeth and shoves his way through the still-panicking throngs of guests. Various crew members are attempting to calm the masses, but the gwisin are apparently not able to grasp the concept that they are already *dead,* and therefore not about to be brutally murdered. The goddess of childbirth, mothers, babies, and general annoyances waddles next to him, her hands folded over her swollen stomach. She's just appeared, the only hint of her impending teleportation having been the faint scent of floral perfume and baby powder. "Our heavenly emperor will be safest in my hands. Do you even know how to care for a baby, young man?"

He inhales a sharp breath of anger, stopping mid-stride to glower at the goddess. Samsin Halmoni blinks innocently back at him, the portrait of a kind, warm mother. But he knows she has the heart of a snake. "Thirty-three years," Seokga breathes over the general bedlam and panic, jostled by frightened guests as he stands still. Anyone who knows Seokga would recognize the deadly calm before the storm, the way his features are almost terrifyingly blank save for the roiling hints of thunderous rage beneath that escape in flashes like white-hot lightning. "You knew who she was, *where* she was, and you never told me. Why is that, Samsin Halmoni?"

No sign of remorse, or surprise, dashes across her face. "Because you are your father's son, boy. And I believed that Yoo Kisa deserved better than Mireuk's spawn."

The words carve something out of him, as if they are a honed blade. If there was no ring of truth to them, Seokga would have ignored them, firing back one of the scathing retorts he is so known for. Yet they hit true. Desperately, he attempts to keep his mask up, but the other deity sees through the cracks. He *is* like Mireuk.

"There was also your little pyramid scheme prank." Samsin Halmoni's smile is unkind, and he reassesses his opponent. She has a marksman's instinct of where, and how hard, to strike. "So I'm only counting down the moments until you storm into Okhwang's throne room and order us all to bow to your will."

"I'm . . . reformed." Seokga frowns uncomprehendingly at her words, which seem both strangely expectant and defeated at once.

Samsin Halmoni hesitates, clearly not receiving the reaction she was looking for. "Hwanin is a baby," she tells him, and he manages to give her a scathing *yes I am very aware* sort of look. "Hwanung is—if you're to be believed—patricidal and running from his crimes. *You* are next in line for the throne. You—" Her mouth works as if she'd like to spit in his face, but she spits the next words instead. "You are the heavenly emperor."

It's as if the world stands still at those words, as if the chaos around him freezes as realization sinks deep into his body. In the stress of the last few hours, the farthest thing from his thoughts had been Okhwang. The SRC *Flatliner* had taken up his mind, down to the little crevices. He hadn't spared a thought to realize that . . . that he is the emperor of Okhwang.

"The *interim* heavenly emperor," Samsin Halmoni hastens to

add, but she's staring at him as if he's some sort of circus monkey who has utterly failed to perform. Instead of cackling madly like he might have some years ago, Seokga is silent. Power. So much of it at his fingertips, should he only leave the cruise ship to take his rightful place on the throne. This is what he's desired since childhood, this is what he staged a massive fucking coup for . . . So why isn't triumph welling up inside him? Why isn't he smirking at Samsin Halmoni and telling her to kneel before him? Seokga opens his mouth to at least attempt a victorious cackle, but all that comes out is a faint sort of wheeze. Samsin Halmoni gapes as the trickster god closes his eyes, feeling rather sick.

Kisa cannot go to Okhwang, not like this. She is a gwisin bound to the SRC *Flatliner,* and the farthest she can go from the ship is to the fucking DAR when the cruise ends. Even if they're able to locate Hwanung, he's not sure that Yeomra will revise his terms to allow Kisa some other victory. But she doesn't seem to want one anyway. She *wants* reincarnation.

Don't leave me, she'd pleaded with him, and he'd sworn not to. Not until after she leaves him. Again.

She's always leaving him. Part of Seokga wonders, bitterly, if he should be the first to vanish this time around. Before his heart can be shattered into millions of shriveled little pieces for a second time. He can self-medicate on his newfound power, his control over Okhwang, lounging in Cheonha Palace's phoenix throne and amusing himself by ordering the other gods around like puppets. He wouldn't have to think of her at all—

—but he would. How can he ever forget the exact color of her eyes, the gorgeous curls of her hair? The way she rambles when she's nervous or excited, that razor-sharp intellect?

Seokga would hate himself more than he already does for an eternity if he left before the short days they have left with each other come to a close.

He opens his eyes. Samsin Halmoni looks stricken with shock and something that *could* be regret if Seokga squinted (and possibly used a magnifying glass). "I have business to conclude here first," Seokga says, voice hollow. "I'll return to Okhwang when the cruise ends, within the week. Hwanin will stay with me. Until then, keep watch for Hwanung. Alert me immediately if he is found."

The goddess swallows hard and shakes her head. "I don't understand. You're not . . . I don't understand."

Seokga's glare is withering. "Kisa is here," he tells her, as if it should explain everything. And it does. Samsin Halmoni looks almost mortified as she jerks her head in a nod. He pivots on his heel to leave, but can't resist throwing one scathing glower over his shoulder. "You might have taken her away from me, but you took me away from *her,* too."

Unexpectedly, Samsin Halmoni's eyes fill with shame. "I . . ."

His lip curls. "Scurry back to Okhwang like the meddling insect you are," he snaps. "Don't come near this ship again." Seokga doesn't linger to unravel the guilt wracking Samsin Halmoni's face. He stalks away instead, knuckles white around his cane.

Dr. Jang is waiting outside of his suite when he rounds the corner. Seokga is in no mood for an hour spent unraveling his *feelings,* and his shoulders slump in relief when he sees that Jang isn't holding her leather-bound notebook. "Dr. Jang," he greets wearily.

"Seokga." Her voice is more solemn than he's ever heard it— even during the stilted conversations about his father. "I've heard about everything. I need to speak with you."

Will this day never end? All Seokga wants is to tend to Kisa and hold his brother, but he still allows Dr. Jang to lead him into her suite. She seems tired as she locks the door, although it's hard to tell with those ridiculous sunglasses. When Dr. Jang turns around, he sees that her mouth is bracketed with deeper lines than usual.

"It's my fault," she whispers. "I was walking with him, but he escaped my sight... He must have snuck away to the bridge..."

Alarmed, Seokga steps toward the old woman. "What do you mean?" he demands, thoroughly bewildered.

Dr. Jang sucks in a shallow breath. "I should start at the beginning. I... used to work with Hwanung, much in the way I work with you. Hwanin sent him to me a few years ago. Hwanung was having relationship trouble, and his father was concerned." Dr. Jang takes a deep breath. "He'd fallen in love with a married woman. They were having an affair and Hwanung was besotted."

Slow dread trickles down Seokga's spine. "What was the name of this woman?"

"I only met her once," she tells him hoarsely. "She looked so different then. Her name was Soo-min..."

Well, Seokga thinks grimly, it seems as though the *whys* have found him anyway. "Go on," he says, folding his arms as he processes, quickly, the damning fact against his nephew.

"Their relationship was rocky, but Hwanung was infatuated." She shakes her head. "Most of their tension came from Soo-min's fear that her husband would find out about the affair. He was a violent man. At the behest of your brother, I attempted to intervene through couple's therapy sessions and subtly show Hwanung all the reasons it was wrong to be with her. *Godly Gossip* was the least of my worries. But they stayed together—until her husband found out." Dr. Jang laces shaking fingers together. "By that time, my sessions with Hwanung and Soo-min were over. I didn't find out... until today, from Hwanung, that Soo-min had been murdered by her jealous spouse. Hwanung begged Hwanin to do for Soo-min what he did for Hani, but Hwanung refused. That was three years ago."

Seokga tenses. Three years ago was approximately when Hwanung and Hwanin's relationship started to deteriorate. "Hwanung knew if he were heavenly emperor, he'd be able to do what Hwanin refused," he says slowly, putting the pieces together. "He waited until the moment Hwanin was alone and vulnerable—on a Jeoseung cruise ship without any other gods near. He was working with Soo-min. In her samjokgu form, she killed Hwanin and they threw his heart into the river, hoping it would deposit the baby somewhere he would suffer. They miscalculated." He feels as if he's missing something. What harm could baby Hwanin ever do? But he plows on, eager to close the case. "To gloat, she moved the body to where I would find it. Maybe that was done impulsively. It led to problems for her after—when Soo-min found out we were investigating, she tried to keep me from Kisa, and she had to destroy the security room after Somi overheard her calling Hwanung."

But how did Soo-min avoid the security cameras while dragging the body? Perhaps it was Hwanung, teleporting his father's corpse to the unsupervised stairwell. Yes, that must be it. How did he appear on the ship without Yeomra noticing, as he did today? Seokga grimaces. Yeomra must have been busy with his demon lover *again*.

"But why did they kill the captain?" Dr. Jang pushes.

Seokga remembers Hajun's news. The affair. It explains the rest. "Soo-min was seeing him on the sly. Hwanung found out, and—in an attempt to prove her loyalty to the god, Soo-min helped him kill the captain." After all, why settle for a mortal man when one can have an emperor? Soo-min must have regretted her infidelity and backtracked in the only way she knew how: with murder. "Hwanung came to the ship today to take Soo-min to the reincarnation queue. He wasn't expecting to catch her with the captain. In the struggle, he hit the intercom button. After realizing they'd been broadcast across the entire ship, Soo-min fled—and Hwanung teleported away." So much for true love.

Dr. Jang shakes her head, unsteadily moving to her bed, where she perches on the edge like an uncertain bird. "Why didn't you tell me about Hwanin, Seokga? I could have helped you. I could have told you all of this."

"You would have been mandated to report it immediately to Okhwang," he explains in exhaustion, running a hand through his hair. "I couldn't risk the pantheon suspecting me. We all know my history. It's over now anyway. The case is closed."

"And how are you feeling?" she asks, to his great weariness. "How has the pantheon taken the news?"

Seokga's lips twist bitterly. "Samsin Halmoni called me 'Mireuk's spawn.'" It stings more than he'd like to admit.

Dr. Jang's lips thin. "Does it bother you," she asks, "how the rest of the pantheon uses your heritage as an insult? It must be frustrating, when everyone only remembers the Mad God rather than the father he could have been."

He shrugs, but his throat is tight. Dr. Jang sighs softly.

"I want us to speak candidly, Seokga, without worrying about word getting back to the pantheon about what you say in this room. You're the heavenly emperor now. Nothing can touch you if you don't want it to, dear." Dr. Jang smiles, fiddling with the hem of her Hawaiian shirt. "Besides, I seem to have misplaced my notebook. I couldn't take notes even if I wanted to. What would you do, Seokga, if you could give your father a second chance?"

Seokga suddenly feels dizzy. "He doesn't deserve a second chance."

"The same case could have been made for you," Dr. Jang replies gently. "And now, look. What extraordinary growth you've had, Seokga. Your dream has come true, and you could hardly care less. You've *changed*. Why shouldn't Mireuk have been given that opportunity?"

"My father was a tyrant."

"And not so long ago, you were a villain."

Seokga flinches. Is this the purpose of these hypotheticals, then? Some skewed attempt at self-reflection? His knuckles shine as he grips his cane's hilt. "Excuse me," Seokga gasps out as he makes for the door, suddenly feeling nauseous with an awful mixture of regret, confusion, anger, and longing. It's one thing to fear becoming like his father. It's an entirely different one to consider not what could have been, but what still could be. Dr. Jang is goading him and she knows it. As he fumbles with the lock and staggers from the room, Seokga wonders why in the seven hells Dr. Jang is paid so handsomely to torture him like this. It's a relief when he slams the door to his own suite shut, a relief when he glimpses Kisa sitting upright in his bed. As he enters, her eyes widen and one of her hands flutters to the space above her heart. Somi and Hajun hover nervously beside her, Somi clutching one of Hwanin's small feet as the baby hovers in the air. Kisa's eyes widen and she stretches out her other hand, reaching for him.

"Seokga?" she whispers. "What in the realms happened?"

He doesn't take his eyes off her. "Out," he says sharply to Hajun and Somi as he strides for Hwanin, knocking Somi aside to tug the baby down into his arms.

"Absolutely not," the gumiho snaps, but Hajun has already met Seokga's gaze with a small nod of understanding, and is hauling Somi to the door. Her aghast protests echo down the hallway as Hajun totes her away, the door closing sharply behind them.

Aware of Kisa's intently curious stare, Seokga attempts—with extreme effort—to control his thoughts, so as to not overwhelm her. Slowly, he settles down on the bed next to her, Hwanin cooing contentedly as he snuggles against his big brother's chest.

"Kisa," Seokga says quietly, scanning what he can see of her above the heavy blankets.

"I'm fine," she quickly replies, reaching over to offer Hwanin her finger. The baby stares at it, unimpressed, before reluctantly curling his hand around it and inspecting the digit rather begrudgingly. "I don't—want to talk about it right now. Later, I-I might. But just for a bit, I want to . . . rest. But I want—need—you to tell me what happened to the captain. To Soo-min."

His mouth flattens, but the red thread is carrying Kisa's exhaustion over to him in debilitating waves, and she looks so frail—so haggard, without the usual brightness in those magnificent eyes of her. Seokga won't argue with her.

Not right now, at least. She's not a worthy opponent like this.

With a small sigh, Seokga settles back against the headboard and, in low undertones, recounts the last couple of hours' events to Kisa, who absorbs the information with furrowed brows. When she twists her finger to escape Hwanin's death grasp (the little god now looks extremely disconcerted to be deprived of the toy he didn't even want in the first place) and raises her hand to her temple, Seokga wraps up his summary as quickly as possible and—before he can stop himself—is reaching for her wild mane of curls, smoothing them out of her face, tucking one strand behind a small ear. "Enough," he says, and she glances at him, hand falling from her head to her side. "We'll go over the specifics later."

She blinks slowly. "That might be a good idea," Kisa mumbles, and burrows back into the blankets, lying down once more and resting her head on one of the ridiculously overstuffed pillows. When her eyes flutter shut, Seokga takes it—reluctantly—as his cue to leave. But as he slides off the bed, a warm hand shoots out from beneath the covers and grabs his wrist.

—*don't want—him—to go—not—yet—not—ready—to—go—*

"Stay."

It's as if his entire world unravels with that one singular word. Golden joy courses down the Red Thread of Fate as Seokga slowly kicks off his shoes and sets Hwanin on his back on the bed next to

Kisa. The baby yawns gigantically, and Kisa makes a small, humming noise as Seokga stealthily—so as to not disturb them both—edges onto the bed and lies down underneath the covers. Bleary, wine-brown eyes peek at him over the dozing baby beneath the Red Thread of Fate.

"Do you dream?" Kisa whispers, and he nearly laughs in fond exasperation at the hungry curiosity in her voice and the scholarly gleam in her tired eyes.

Instead, though, he only smirks, turning on his side to better trace the lines of her face, the waves of her hair. "I do," he replies quietly. "All gods do."

"What . . . do you dream about?"

"You," he says hoarsely after a long moment.

"Me?" Kisa closes her eyes again. "Or Hani?"

—*wonder* . . . —*which* . . . —*wonder*—*which* . . . —

Her thoughts are slow, sluggish, weighed heavy by sleep. Seokga hesitates, but the trickster god decides to be painfully honest. Never let it be said that it cannot be done. "Both," he murmurs. "I had a terrible nightmare once, about you."

"*Mmph?*" She sounds rather indignant, although it's hard to tell with her face now buried halfway into her pillow.

"You were an old man," he admits, closing his own eyes, a wave of exhaustion suddenly crashing over his head and sending him plummeting down into a deep, dark sea. Hwanin is sighing in his sleep, and Seokga gently tugs his small brother closer to him. "An . . . old man who terrorized his crochet group."

"I don't . . . crochet . . ." Kisa mumbles. "I . . . *knit* . . ."

"Same thing," he whispers, and the last thing he feels before drifting off to sleep is Kisa, kicking him half-heartedly beneath the covers and laughing sleepily into her pillow.

CHAPTER TWENTY-SIX

KISA

ONE PERFECTLY rejuvenating nap later, Kisa tips the shot glass of soju into her mouth with a small smile, relishing the sweet grape flavor that masks the edge of the alcohol astoundingly well. Deck 10 of the SRC *Flatliner* is empty save for the four of them—plus a babbling, floating baby Hwanin—with most guests hiding in their rooms as the clock strikes eleven, still traumatized from the day's events. The sundeck at night is strung with fairy lights, illuminating the rushing waters of the river below, where the SRC *Flatliner* is firmly anchored.

Somi is giggling as she drinks straight from the source, cheeks flushed as she passes the green glass to Hajun, who Kisa can tell is already on the verge of drunk. Her friend is lying on the pool chair next to Somi, eyes glimmering as he seems to trace the contours of her moonlit face with them. "Would you be my Valentine?" he whispers, despite it being not at all close to the day of love. Kisa bites her lip, smile faltering while she watches as Somi bursts out laughing, the gumiho's hand rising to her lips as a bit of soju sprays out. Again, she feels that twinge of envy at their *newness,* how Somi and Hajun are so unweighted, unanchored, by the past. They are as fresh and young as the first morning of spring, both of them.

"It's not even February," Somi wheezes in reply to the smitten Hajun. "It's autumn."

He blinks dreamily at her. "Will you be my . . . pumpkin, then?" *Kissed by the Mafia Cowboy* is spread open on his chest. Somi grabs it and playfully swats at him with the raunchy novel.

Kisa swallows hard as she turns to Seokga. Despite the festivities, the god looks exhausted, holding on to Hwanin's foot as the child floats in the air to stare up at the fairy lights. As Seokga looks back at her, there's a question in his eyes she's not yet ready to answer. Here, on the highest deck of the SRC *Flatliner,* she's as far away from the elevator as she can be, and she doesn't want to think about it.

Kisa quickly pours herself another shot of soju, grabbing the bottle from the small table between Somi and Hajun before walking to Seokga. "So," she says, studying the rim of her glass, "we solved the mystery." The novelty of it hasn't quite worn off. They *did* it.

(Didn't they? What if . . . *Oh, no.* She grimaces. Kisa knows herself to be a terrifying overthinker, and she *mustn't* overthink this. Just because she was, well . . . somewhat occupied . . . during the last hours of its investigation doesn't mean that her brain can slide off and question if the conclusion is right. *Stop it,* she tells her overactive mind. *It is over. Stop searching for what-ifs when there aren't any.*)

"We did," says Seokga, somehow managing to look and sound solemn while holding on to a flying baby's chubby foot.

"And I get to reincarnate," Kisa adds, trying to sound as cheerful as she knows she *should* feel. But after all of this . . . the spa, the banmal, the baby, the bed . . .

She's not cheerful. Oh, she's not cheerful at all.

"Yes," the god replies, averting his eyes. "You do."

A moment of silence falls between them. Behind them, Somi and Hajun are laughing. Seokga's eyes slide over Kisa's shoulder and soften. Hajun is laughing hard as Somi reads him a passage from the book, wiggling her eyebrows salaciously.

"I didn't realize it before, but Hajun reminds me a bit of Hyun-tae," he murmurs. "Before we knew that Hyun-tae was really Eodum." When his gaze drifts back to her, as if to see if she'll agree, Kisa's heart breaks a bit.

"I don't remember," she reminds him gently.

Seokga swallows, eyes falling. "Yes. I know that." Above him, Hwanin giggles in delight as he touches one of the tiny lights. Kisa watches as Seokga gently tugs him back down to rest in his arms.

"Seokga..." Suddenly, Kisa's throat is tight. "Seokga, I...I've had a really wonderful time with you this trip, and...and I'm glad that—that we met, even here..." It's felt as if she's lived more with him than she ever did while she was alive. So much laughter. Nude swims in a cold cavern. The way he looks at her makes her feel like she's still living.

It's not a research project anymore.

It hasn't been for a very, very long time.

Kisa's voice trails off as Seokga's expression hardens, rather than softens. He's still not meeting her eyes. "You're a great friend," she says desperately, wanting him to look up at her, and perhaps wanting so much more than she is determined to allow herself.

He laughs, but it's not an amused laugh. It's something hoarse and tired. "Yes," says Seokga. "A great friend."

The bitterness in his voice stabs at something deep within her. "I..."

"I'm tired, Kisa." Seokga hasn't looked at her again. "I'm so—tired."

—she'll leave—just like—Hani—won't—find—again—so—alone—so—tired—

It's as if the breath has been knocked out of her as a deep blue color crawls down the red thread, cold and lonely and heavy with grief. She reaches for him, needing to—comfort, to help, but he steps away. A small smile curls his lips, but it's barely more than a flicker of bittersweet longing before it's gone. "Tell me something," he whispers. "If we'd had more time..."

"Yes," she whispers before he's even finished his sentence. "Yes."

Joy and heartbreak race across his face. "Would you have?"

She swallows, wiping away an errant tear. When did she start crying? Hajun's and Somi's bright laughter is a world away as she nods. "I know I would."

"I can't ask you to stay," he breathes, "can I?"

Kisa closes her eyes. A cold underworld wind runs its clawed fingers through her hair.

"Not here." Not on this ship. Not in this world of death and sorrow.

Perhaps her earlier fear was unfounded. That if she allowed herself to—feel for him, she would run from reincarnation. Yet here she is, feeling so very *much* for this god who is not at all what she expected... And here she is, knowing she cannot stay.

Not here. Not here.

"Why did you do it?" His voice breaks. Somewhere far away, Hajun and Somi stop laughing. "Why?" Her eyes flutter open as his free hand cups her face. She leans into his touch before she can stop herself.

"Why what?" Kisa breathes up at him. There's such terrible anguish in his eyes as he shakes his head.

"Nothing," he whispers, but his thoughts don't lie like he does.

—*why did*—*she*—*jump*—

Her heart gives a terrible twist as she lurches away. Is that what he thinks? That she jumped from that roof, hurling herself into the night sky like a baby bird who'd not yet learned to fly? She presses a shaking hand to her mouth as her thoughts drift back to that spring night all those years ago. With effort, she manages to stuff her rising grief into a box just as she failed to do in the elevator, and turns to the logical part of her mind to calm herself. Of course he would think she jumped. No person in their right mind tempts fate by sitting on the edge of a skyscraper.

"Kisa?" Hajun is rising unsteadily, arm around Somi's narrow shoulders for support. "Kisa, are you okay?"

"What did you say to her?" snaps Somi, stomping over to Seokga and practically dragging Hajun with her. "It's Kisa's business whether she wants to reincarnate or not, and you have no—*hiccup*—business telling her otherwise!" Her face is blue with indignation, and Kisa feels a surge of fondness for the gumiho, even as she shakes her head at her.

"Seokga didn't do anything wrong," she tells her quietly. "But I've been—keeping something from him. From... all of you." Pained, Kisa meets Hajun's eyes. She knows what he believes, and she's never tried to tell him otherwise, thinking a lie by omission wasn't so bad if it made the broken boy feel less alone. She doesn't want to tell them what happened that night on the roof. But friends, she thinks, taking them in—the gumiho, the idol, and the god—confide in one another. And this might be one of her last chances before the cruise ends and she leaves for the DAR queue. She takes a deep breath. "That night, I didn't fall. I didn't jump." Kisa clutches her shot glass so hard that it could shatter and she wouldn't be at all surprised. "I was pushed."

CHAPTER TWENTY-SEVEN

KISA

FOR A TERRIBLE MOMENT, nobody speaks. Hajun is frozen, dazed eyes beginning to clear as he stares at Kisa, who trembles under the similar stares of Somi and Seokga. Even Hwanin begins to make a soft, sniffling sound, bottom lip trembling as he buries his face in the crook of his brother's neck. Nervously, Kisa clears her throat. "The roof was my sanctuary, and I won't pretend that I didn't understand the dangers of sitting alone up there like that... There was an approximate ninety-seven percent chance of falling. I just... I needed it. I hadn't gotten help, like I should have, so I-I used the roof." She hates how weak, how pathetic, she sounds and avoids their eyes. "That night, I was exhausted. I was... well, I certainly wasn't in a good place."

The memory of that exhaustion, the kind that went deeper than her bones, threatens to send tears spilling down her cheeks. Kisa blinks rapidly. "I was on the edge, staring down at the city. Seoul. It was always so beautiful at night... I didn't realize that I wasn't alone up there." Her heart begins to pound and her palms begin to sweat, black spots beginning to overtake her vision as panic claws at her insides, much like the way it did in the elevator.

This is why she does not think of that night. Her voice is so unbearably thin as she tries to rush past the worst part, as if speed can force away the flashbacks that seem to lurk always just outside the edges of her consciousness, needing only one reminder of her murder to infiltrate her mind. Captain Lee's killing had sent her over the edge, and Kisa fights not to fall from it again as she blurts out: "All of a sudden, there was a hand on my back, pushing me into the air . . . And then I was falling . . ." Her vision swims—

It all happens so fast. Kisa doesn't even have time to open her mouth, to scream a plea to her goddess.

For in an instant, her body is sliding off the roof and she is for a perfect, brilliant moment, weightless and hovering over Seoul. But then gravity grabs her by the ankle and tugs her down, yanking her past rows and rows of gleaming glass windows all stacked upon one another, laughing as it hauls her toward the ground in a perfect swan dive.

Kisa closes her eyes.

It's over soon enough.

—but she manages, through a force of sheer will, to stave off the inbound panic attack. She's already made a complete fool out of herself in the elevator, and thinks she may die (again) of humiliation if she sinks to the ground and enters another comatose-like state of panic in front of her friends.

"I'm sorry I didn't tell you," Kisa whispers to a stricken Hajun. "I'm sorry I let you think for so long that I jumped. It was—it was *wrong* of me, I shouldn't have—" She breaks off as he lurches forward and envelops her in a hug, a warm embrace. Hajun's trembling as he holds her tight. Face buried in his shoulder, Kisa clutches him close and holds back a torrent of tears as he kisses the side of her head.

"That's—*that's* why you don't like it when people touch your back, or stand behind you," he whispers. "Isn't it?"

Kisa cringes in his arms. "Y-yes."

"*Why?*" Hajun chokes out as he finally steps away, eyes pained. "Why did they . . . ?"

"I don't know," she rasps honestly.

Hajun wobbles slightly on his feet, and Somi darts forward to help him. When the gumiho meets her eye, Kisa sees that Somi is also on the verge of tears. Something passes between the two women then, as Kisa remembers her ruined claws. Some sad solidarity between two dead women who met their ends through violence and unspeakable pain. Kisa feels a bond knot between them, an invisible force connecting them—almost like the Red Thread of Fate, but one of sisterhood.

Somi's face crumples and Kisa knows that she feels it, too. Somi's hand reaches out and takes one of hers, squeezing tight. "I'm so sorry," the gumiho whispers, and Kisa knows she's apologizing for much more than what happened in this lifetime.

Kisa wants to whisper back that Somi can tell her story, too, that Kisa will comfort her with as much fierce empathy as Somi's showing her. But now, with Somi swaying unsteadily from drink, just isn't the time.

One person has not yet spoken. The trickster god is deceivingly silent as he stands with his back against the night, but his green eyes glow like a predator's in the darkness.

"Seokga?" Kisa asks quietly, letting go of Somi's hand.

The god does not reply. Fear skitters down Kisa's spine as the air thickens with a power so acute that Hajun's hair stands straight up in the air. Goosebumps erupt down Kisa's arms and legs. The shadows of the ship seem to deepen, to darken.

"Seokga," Kisa tries again as pure rage, hot and black, shoots down the thread. Cautiously, she steps before him, placing one hand on his hard jaw and gazing up at him beseechingly. "Look at me."

His eyes remain fixed on some point in the distance. Behind her, Somi shifts nervously and Hajun darts forward to grab Hwanin from his brother's arms.

"*Look at me,*" Kisa repeats, and this time her voice is hard, brooking no room for debate. Her fingers tighten around his chin as his eyes slowly move down to hers—clouded with rage and something that is quite distinctly bloodlust.

"Who," he growls, and there is such unfathomable fury in that one word. Seokga's nostrils flare as she remains silent. "*Who.*"

"I don't know," Kisa replies calmly, although inside she's anything but. "I never saw a face, Seokga." She's spent seven years wondering who had sufficient enough motive to send her plummeting to her death. Every single time, she's drawn a blank—a rare phenomenon for Kisa, who typically possesses heaps upon heaps of theories for anything and everything. It's just that, well—she didn't have many friends at all, but she had even *fewer* enemies. The closest she came was her rival at school, Kim Dae, who—despite their competition—had never been anything but coolly polite to her. Part of her wondered if it was her stepmother, but while the woman was cold and disinterested, she wasn't cruel. And her half-sisters, although they hardly knew her, still tried to make conversation with her at the rare and awkward family gatherings. "I'm not . . . I'm not sure I'll ever find out."

His chest is rising and falling in an uneven rhythm. "I will find them," Seokga breathes, barely audible. "And I will kill them for what they have done to you. I swear it on all that I am."

—they—hurt—her—they—killed—killed—they'll—pay—make—them suffer—

Kisa scans his eyes for a moment more before turning to Somi and Hajun, hand falling from Seokga's jaw to his chest, where his heart slams against her palm. "Take Hwanin for the night," she tells them. "Please."

Hajun's head bobs in a nod. "I, uh, think that would be best," he says, hair still standing straight off his scalp as Seokga's power pulses through the thick air. Hajun quickly hurries off with the god-child, but Somi hesitates.

"Kisa," she says slowly, "are you sure you don't want me to stay? He looks... angry."

"Go, Somi," Kisa urges, hair whipping in another dark wind. "I'm safe with him." She knows it, deep within her bones. Deep within her soul. There is *trust* between them, perhaps an inexplicable sort, yet it is why he is the one she told about her deepest dream of Okhwang's library, why it is him that she can fall asleep next to, why it is him that she will swim—*nude,* for the gods' sakes—with in a spa.

No, Seokga will never hurt her.

The other woman looks distrustful, but reluctantly follows Hajun off the sundeck anyway, after one final concerned look over her shoulder. Kisa turns her gaze back up to Seokga. Her head barely grazes his chin. "You're losing control."

Illusions flicker in and out of sight, a miasma of bewildering visions. Low-hanging storms churn into formation, angrier than the one he conjured for her in the bedroom. Leaves fall from the sky, oranges and reds turning to dark ash as they hit the ground. A pair of wine-brown eyes—Kisa's eyes—flicker within the storm clouds before vanishing a moment later, replaced by a red, nine-tailed fox that bounds through the leaves toward a new illusion... a stretching shadow monster that opens its maw and devours the fox whole.

A burst of rain-tinged wind lashes through the air as the storm illusion returns, sending Kisa stumbling back from Seokga. Between them, the clouds darken and thicken until she cannot see him anymore through the lashing wind, falling leaves, and the red fox—which has returned to scamper around the deck, laughing almost maniacally.

"SEOKGA!" Kisa screams over the thunder, not afraid for herself, but for her god. The red thread is shaking in panic. She can barely see the deck anymore: The floor has turned to the tops of city buildings, pinpricks of light in a dark sky. It's as if she's standing above a nighttime New Sinsi as she surges forward, diving through the storm, hands stretched out for Seokga . . .

But she never reaches him. Instead, she plummets into another illusion.

He's sitting at a desk in a grimy precinct, hunched over a pile of paperwork. Kisa stands some length away, separate from the scene, yet feeling somehow . . . part of it. Seokga's dark hair falls into his eyes as he concentrates, only looking up when polished-pink, oval nails curl around the edge of his cubicle divider.

"Good morning," a woman greets cheerfully, waggling her fingers at him. *She's beautiful,* Kisa thinks with an ache. Blown-out brown hair, slender curves, and angular wine-brown eyes that precisely match Kisa's own. *Hani,* she realizes with a cold start. *That's—me.*

"You," Seokga snaps icily. "What do *you* want?"

Hani preens, batting her eyelashes. "Haven't you heard? I'm your brand-new assistant."

The scene changes, shifts as the illusion-work unravels and is rewoven. Hani is striding through the precinct doors with an iced coffee in her hands and colliding with a cross-looking Seokga. Kisa stares. This Seokga is unfamiliar to her. There is no hint of the tenderness that seems to show itself only when Seokga looks at her. Only ice.

"I suggest that you watch where you're going," the cold god snaps and then everything is changing once more. There are bodies: a dead gumiho with black veins, followed by a haetae slumped in the middle of an alleyway. She watches it all, Somi and Hani, the bargain offered by Hwanin, the frantic pursuit of an escaped witness on Geoje, hot chocolate and strawberry egg buns in the morning. Kisa laughs, tears silently streaming down her cheeks, as the god and the gumiho tackle each other in a bamboo forest, as they share a tender kiss at the behest of a sly yojeong, and her riddle.

Dok-hyun's framed attack on the precinct. The race back to New Sinsi. Kisa's cheeks heat as she watches Hani and Seokga in the car, on the stakeout—but she can't stop herself from memorizing the exact way Seokga's breathing hitches and his head falls back as Hani's hand—*her* hand—slips into his pants...

Then they're dancing in a club, underneath the flashing strobe lights. Kisa stares in envy at the way Hani moves so freely, the confidence she carries as she dances against Seokga. She's never moved like that, not in this life. She furiously scrubs away a tear, hating herself for hating Hani. Hating herself for hating herself.

It's almost a relief when Eodum descends on the club.

And all of a sudden, they're in a bed, tangled in the dark sheets. Hani is laughing as Seokga kisses her neck, as he bites softly on her ear. Kisa shivers as the god and the gumiho come together for the first time, unable to look away from Seokga—the softness of his expression as he gazes down at the gumiho, at the chiseled hardness of his body, the small birthmark he has just above his navel.

The Dark Days, and the warehouse. "I swear on Hwanung, god of laws and kept promises, that the sun will shine on us both once again." Kisa is there for all of it, caught in the swirl of rapidly shifting illusions, stumbling from cars to cafés to penthouses to grocery stores with plague demons to the warehouse where it all ends. The gumiho lies on the ground, weak-limbed, breathing shallowly as she blinks up at the god. "Seokga," Hani whispers, one of her ruined hands fumbling in her pocket. "This world will... see the morning dawn again." Blood leaks from her mouth. "I need you to know," she whispers, "that it wasn't all . . . a lie. I . . . promise."

"Hani," Seokga whispers. "Just close your eyes."

Kisa sobs with Seokga as Hani uses his hand to plunge the dagger into her heart. She sobs still as Seokga defeats Eodum, as he bursts through the Okhwang throne room and begs his brother to save Hani.

It's when the god is sipping a hot chocolate outside of a Creature Café that the red thread appears for him. Kisa clutches her hands to her mouth as he smiles, a pure, brilliant thing that fades as the illusion disappears, draining away to reveal him. Seokga.

He's slumped against the railing, holding his head in his hands. Gone is that beautiful smile, the hopeful god with eyes full of dreams. "Kisa," Seokga whispers. "I didn't mean to—to show you all of that." The storm breaks. The fox vanishes. The leaves dissipate into ash on the wind. Seokga's eyes are tortured and lined with silver as he looks up at Kisa. "I'm so—I'm so sorry."

All that he's gone through, for her. She never knew. She never asked, afraid to draw too close to him—like a moth to a flame. But now, it's as if all her carefully confined emotions spill out from the filing cabinet, toppling to the ground of her mind.

Oh, they're a mess.

Such a beautiful, daunting mess.

"Stop it, Seokga," Kisa whispers, voice ragged. "You really, truly, have *nothing* to apologize for."

"You were right. I lost control," Seokga rasps. "Hwanin . . ."

"He's with Somi and Hajun." She's stepping toward him, then kneeling down and smoothing a sweat-drenched strand of hair away from his face before she realizes what she's doing. "Seokga . . ." Kisa swallows back more tears. "Seokga, I wish I were her."

His eyes widen, and he grabs her hand from his forehead. "Kisa, you're—"

"I'm not... I can't dance, and I hate hot chocolate. I'm not—confident like her. I'm not *fun* like her. But I wish I was. I can't imagine how it must feel..." Kisa shakes her head, drawing in a shaky breath. "I can't imagine how it must feel, searching for her and finding me instead."

"Who told you?" Seokga demands. "Who told you that you're not—?"

"I've never been to a club. I've never had a boyfriend—I've no idea how to give anybody a, well, erm, what Hani did in the car—" Kisa's cheeks burn and she clamps her mouth shut, mortified. Seokga is staring at her like she's a complete imbecile.

"Kisa," he says slowly, as if struggling to wrap his head around it, "do you mean to say you truly believe that after thirty-three years of endless searching, I could find you wanting in even the slightest way?" Seokga's green eyes are almost hazy with confusion. "Because of your *inexperience*?"

"Erm," she replies, wishing she could disappear forever. "When you say it like that, it sounds rather ridiculous, doesn't it?"

"Because it is." Seokga shakes his head, and there's a glimmer of a smile on his lips again. "Kisa, I have wanted you before I even knew you. It wasn't your dancing, or the way you touched me, that made me fall in love with you the first time. It was your bravery, your intellect, your complete loyalty to your friends. You posed the Ship of Theseus question to me. I know my answer. The parts that are important—the parts that I cherish, that bravery, intellect, and loyalty—are still the same. And perhaps I needed... Hani first. To show me the path to *you*. It took me time to realize that, but, Kisa—you're not so different from who you were in your past life as you think. As I recall, you still seem to have a thing for my 'arse'..."

She groans in embarrassment.

"You're perfect, Kisa," Seokga says. "And I want, very badly, to kiss you."

"But you won't," she guesses, voice feather-soft, disappointment churning in her stomach.

"'Just friends' is a terribly restrictive label," murmurs Seokga, staring at her lips. "It's already beginning to chafe."

Kisa tucks a strand of hair nervously behind her ear. "We never had it on paper... We never swore it on Hwanung... Agreements can be, ah, modified..."

"Loopholes can be found," the trickster god agrees, eyes sparkling with something like mischief. Kisa's face heats as he reaches for her. Seokga's lips curve into a smile as he—in one smooth motion—tugs her onto his lap. Kisa stifles a small yelp of pleased surprise. Her legs bracket his, and this close to him, she can count each and every one of his beautifully long lashes. Heat pools low in her stomach as his right hand skims up her back, coming to rest on the nape of her neck—but not before he tugs, gently, on one of her curls. "Promises can be broken."

"Spoken like a true trickster," she replies, voice humiliatingly breathy. But Seokga's perennial rasp is huskier than usual, too, and his eyes darken as Kisa lowers her head so her nose brushes against his. Atop him, she *feels* his shiver, his gasp. The way his right hand spasms, the way his left one trembles as it finds her waist, the barest hint of skin peeking out underneath the hem of her scrub top. Her lips are so close to his. Seokga's breathing is uneven. Her curls flutter with each of his shallow exhales.

"You're going to break my heart again, aren't you?" whispers her god, staring up at her.

"I don't know," Kisa murmurs.

She knows the right thing to do would be to *stop* gazing at his mouth, stop feeling this soft glow of desire. To slide off his lap. He deserves more than she can ever give him. But he's looking at her like she hung the moon, and his thumb is tracing hesitant circles on her bare hip, and he smells like pine and soap and coffee and she can't stop staring down at his lips, can't stop her heart from pounding with a BPM that can't possibly be healthy...

There's only a centimeter between them, yet it feels like a mile. Perhaps fifty miles, Kisa revises, as longing twists in her chest.

"I don't know," she whispers again, her strained voice sounding tortured even to her own ears.

"Should we find out?" Seokga's words are smooth, calm, but his hope shoots down the thread like an arrow shot straight to her heart. And his hands, oh, how his hands are trembling on her.

"I'd like to," Kisa breathes before leaning that extra centimeter forward and pressing her lips to his.

"Am I, um, doing this right?" Kisa asks nervously sometime later, perched halfway over Seokga on his bed, the two of them having stumbled into the suite after the fairy lights had been shut off on Deck 10. "Is there, er, a certain sort of... angle... you prefer?"

Seokga stares up at her with swollen lips and a sated, dreamy expression that's mingled with amused disbelief. "Kisa," he practically purrs, "stop overthinking."

With a gentle tug, he guides her head back down to his, and her mind obediently shuts off with the next tug of his teeth against her lower lip. His hands roll down her spine almost reverently, and she shivers in delight as they slip underneath her scrub shirt, resting just above her hips. Her skin suddenly feels terribly hot, and she finds herself wishing she was wearing nothing at all. Desire aches within her, and it's hotter, more molten, than any late-night longings she's ever felt before. An embarrassing noise escapes her lips as Seokga deepens the kiss and with extraordinary gentleness, rolls them over so he now lies atop her.

The feeling of him resting between her legs is almost too much to bear. Kisa wraps her legs around his narrow hips and gives in to pure instinct, running her hands through the silken strands of his dark hair and pressing up into him, arching her back until she's certain he can feel the frantic *thump-thump*ing of her heart. She shivers as his mouth pulls away from hers, glistening sinfully before his lips press into the side of her neck. *Neck kisses.* Who could have known that something so simple could feel so wonderful? No anatomy book ever suggested... *oh*...

Kisa is a trembling mess beneath his teeth and tongue. When Seokga's hands tug questioningly at the hem of her shirt, she nods almost frantically. Yes. *Yes.* Nerves swarm in her belly as he gently lifts the shirt over her head, but they're the good sort of nerves, she supposes. The kind that has her making embarrassingly incoherent sounds as her head falls back and Seokga's lips trail a path toward her cleavage, one finger sliding a bra strap from her shoulder. Kisa squirms under his mouth, wanting more, and shakily unhooks the clasp. Seokga's eyes darken with lust as she drops her bra to the floor next to the bed. Underneath his gaze, her nipples peak in desire and she bites her lip as Seokga stills, his breathing shallow.

Has she gone too far, too fast? She's never done anything like this before. Perhaps that's why she's been so quick to bare herself to him, having (to a bit of her own disappointment) died without ever being intimate with anybody. Kisa hesitates.

Or perhaps Seokga's remembering Hani's perfect breasts... Kisa's are smaller, and she's fairly certain that they might be a bit, well, uneven. She was only following what her body longed for, but maybe she should have waited...

"Fuck, Kisa," her god whispers, head dropping forward. "You're perfect."

—she's—everything—

She flushes in pleasure at the praise.

"Kisa," he continues, "I don't know . . . if I start, I don't know if I can stop . . ."

"So don't stop," she tells him, barely recognizing the huskiness of her voice. She wants it all, tonight. Before the cruise ship resumes its course, before she's faced with an impossible decision.

"Are you sure?" the god asks, and she realizes he's trembling with restraint, the veins in his arms standing visible as he holds himself up above her. The red thread between them is shaking with anticipation, and as Kisa gazes up at him, it carries her red lust down its length toward Seokga.

"Just go slow," she whispers, and he nods, his expression so tender as he closes his mouth against one pointed peak and *sucks*. Kisa's entire body tautens like a bow as he bites the underside of her breast with an almost contradictory tenderness and plays with the other, squeezing and pinching as he kisses her stomach. "Wait," Kisa whispers as his fingers dip underneath the hem of her pants. "You first."

Seokga freezes and then smiles, a bit smugly. When he tugs off his own dark sweater to reveal the hard, toned muscle underneath, Kisa's mouth dries out completely. She can't resist dragging her hands down his chest, just as she wanted to do in the baths. Seokga closes his eyes underneath her touch and shivers. Her eyes drop to his pants, to the straining evidence of his arousal, and—remembering how Hani did it in the car—tentatively reaches forward to drag her hand across it. "Could you," she croaks before clearing her throat, flushing blue, "could you, um, show me how . . . ?"

His eyes flash open.

"I like to learn," she reminds him in a whisper, and shakily pushes him back as she rises to her knees, undoing his zipper. There's really no graceful way for an aroused man to shed a pair of stiff, dark jeans and the underlying underwear but Seokga manages—although Kisa suspects, with fond amusement, that there may be a bit of illusion-work involved. When the length of him springs free, Kisa's breath catches in her throat. He's long and hard, and she feels a surge of excited anticipation as she waits—breathlessly—for instruction.

When Seokga fists himself, his eyes become heavy-lidded. Kisa watches ravenously as he slowly strokes himself from the base upward. "Like this," he pants. "I like it—like this."

Kisa edges forward, replacing his hand with her own.

"Tighter," Seokga pants, eyes fluttering shut. Kisa does as he asks, and as she strokes him hard but slow, she admires the way a flush crawls up his neck. "Good—that's good . . . Kisa . . ."

He barely protests as she pushes him onto his back, leaning over him. She's gotten quite good at this quite quickly, she thinks proudly, loving the way he groans underneath her touch. Perhaps it's all the romance books. She stares down at her hand, and—on a whim—replaces it with her mouth.

His hips buck underneath her in surprise before quickly stilling. "Kisa," he groans as she gazes up at him. His hand finds her head, and he gently holds back her hair as Kisa makes a few educated guesses about what is, precisely, the best way to go about this. Within moments, Seokga is panting and groaning, twitching in her mouth, other hand fisted in the sheets. "*Kisa,*" he gasps. "If you don't stop, I'm going to—"

Kisa blinks innocently up at him.

—*fuck—fuck—fuck—*

She sees why they call it the "little death," now. It's as if he falls apart, tortured in some exquisite, erotic way as if the pleasure is pain and he succumbs to it as a warrior might fall on the battlefield. Feeling rather pleased with herself, Kisa swallows and wipes her mouth with a finger, utterly satisfied to see Seokga reduced to a limp, panting figure beneath her, cheeks flushed pink. He reaches for her, and she lies beside him, resting her head on his chest, while he wraps an arm around her.

"You're a quick fucking study," Seokga mumbles into her hair, and she laughs.

—can barely—fucking breathe—she's—perfect—came so fast—like a fucking—teenager—embarrassing—

"Perhaps it's some muscle memory from my last life," she jokes, and he chuckles, an exhausted, sated sound. His fingers trail down her stomach, lazily slipping past the waistband of her pants. A moment later, all hints of his weariness are gone.

"You're lovely," he murmurs, and Kisa trembles in pleasure as Seokga, suddenly intent, peels off her remaining clothing and gazes down at her in worship. "Let me touch you," he begs.

"Yes," she sighs. Her blood sings as he drags a finger down her folds, as he swirls the small nub at the apex. Their roles quickly reverse, for Kisa is the one panting and moaning now as Seokga kisses her *there*. His tongue coaxes the most humiliating noises from her, and he doesn't stop until she's climbing that peak and falling off, thighs shaking as he holds them open. She scrabbles in the sheets for purchase as she comes back down, Seokga only pulling away when she is thoroughly and utterly spent. His lips gleam and he looks incredibly pleased with himself as she draws him in for a kiss. Seokga's length prods gently at her as Kisa nips at his bottom lip.

"Please," Kisa begs.

—gods know—I can never—say no—to her—

CHAPTER TWENTY-EIGHT

SEOKGA

He's terrified of hurting her as he hovers over her, inside her, letting her get used to the feeling. He's sheathed to the hilt, and trembles with the effort of remaining still. Kisa's face is flushed and her eyes are dilated so much that they are nearly black as she gazes up at him.

When she shifts against him with a wordless plea, Seokga slowly, so slowly, begins to move, rolling his hips against hers until she moans in pleasure. Kisa gasps as he finds their rhythm, and Seokga could lose himself forever in the feeling of her. Pleasure gathers in the base of his spine, and Kisa's begun to pant, too, gripping his ass in her hands as she pulls him forward (and she's looking very smug about it, too—he's aware that he really does have a great ass).

A part of him not lost to pleasure is terrified of what comes after this. He's given himself to her so completely . . . only for her to leave. He knows she'll leave. He's certain that she knows it, too.

But if all Seokga can ever have are these fleeting moments, he'll take them. Damn it, he'll take them and hold them close to his chest on the lonely nights, the nights when he knows he is utterly alone in the world. He'll forever remember the sound of Kisa's soft gasps, the look on her face when she comes undone.

He'll forever remember that, for a brief time, he had her.

The god and the gwisin spend the rest of the night curled up together, flipping through their raunchy romance books, laughing with as much heart and soul as they ever have.

When they fall asleep later that night, Seokga refuses to let go of her, burying his face in her mane of curls, arms looped around her slender waist.

"CAN YOU HOLD HIM?" *Seokga roars, wind whipping through his hair and robes as he braces against its onslaught, barely able to see four feet in front of him where Hwanin is braced atop their father, holding him down to the cave's slick, jagged rock that rises at least twelve feet in the air, nearly brushing the stalactites above. His brother's only response is a guttural shout of pain.* "Yeomra's chains!" *Seokga screams as Mireuk unleashes a bellow of rage, the cave quivering with his power.* "Can you secure them? Brother!"

Eyes tearing from the violent gusts, Seokga staggers up the rock, head pounding from the effort of maintaining the illusion. For the Hwanin atop Mireuk is a distraction, a cleverly woven illusion that is taking its toll to uphold. "BROTHER!" *Seokga shouts again, and this time it's a signal to the Hwanin who stands next to him, hidden underneath another illusion.* "NOW!"

As Mireuk thrashes, the true Hwanin lurches forward, knuckles white as he grips Yeomra's skeletal chains in his hands. All they need is an opening to slap the bone-white bonds around Mireuk's wrists—Yeomra's magic will do the rest, tying Mireuk down to the rock forever more. Seokga holds his breath as the true Hwanin rips past his illusioned self and, with a great cry of rage, captures his father's wrists in the skeletal shackles. Panting, he stumbles back as the shackles expand, clicking like old bones as their chains meld into the rock. The ankles are next, Yeomra's death magic duplicating the bonds on the Mad God's wrists onto his feet. The wind abruptly stops, and the cave is silent—so silent, the only sounds the rushing of the river above, the faint drip-dripping from the stalactites overhead. But only for a moment.

Seokga and Hwanin both flinch as Mireuk screams, the truth of their betrayal finally evident. They lured him here, to this cave underneath the Seocheongang River, under the false pretense of a bit of "family spelunking" (it had been Seokga's genius idea, of course) only to commit unspeakable treason. Hwanin's hand reaches out to grip Seokga's as Mireuk twists and thrashes in murderous fury, unable to access his magic through the bonds, which Yeomra crafted from the bones of prisoners who never, ever escaped.

"It's useless, Father!" Seokga shouts. Blood leaks from his nose into his mouth, and his fine, dark green hanbok has practically been torn to shreds. "There is no escape!"

Mireuk roars again, and there is no trace of sanity on his father's formerly handsome face as it twists and contorts. This is the problem with being a creation god—the curse of insanity comes with the unspeakable power. Hwanin staggers, leaning on Seokga's shoulder, as the two gods watch their father and former emperor thrash against his confines.

"It could have been patricide!" Seokga is screaming, fury coursing through his veins like molten lava. Centuries of humiliation, of rejection, flash through his memories. That fucking flower-growing contest. "It could have been patricide, you fucking bastard—"

"Seokga," Hwanin rasps. His brother hasn't fared any better than he has. Half of Hwanin's long black hair has been singed off, and even his immortal healing strengths have yet to smooth out the mottled bruises on his face, the split lip, and his missing front tooth. "It's over. We . . . we must go. Come, Seokga . . ."

But Mireuk's roars have turned to laughs that send chills running down Seokga's spine. "Seokga," Mireuk spits, eyes glinting in the darkness. "Seokga, my son."

Hwanin is tugging insistently at his robes, but Seokga remains still, baring his teeth as he glowers at his father.

"You can free me, Seokga," Mireuk says, and Seokga fucking hates how Mireuk has suddenly, conveniently, remembered that he has a second son only under these

circumstances. "*Free me from these bonds and all will be forgiven. My son, my son. It's not too late to do the right thing . . .*"

"Fuck off," Seokga hisses, angry tears smarting in his eyes. His rage goes deeper than the crimes Mireuk has committed against humanity. He feels like a child again, rejected by his idol at every turn. "You will stay here, Father, for all of eternity. You will become little but a desiccated corpse, sustained only by the smallest deliveries of the worst fucking foods." *The cave has been enchanted by Jacheongbi, who can wield control over agriculture, to force-feed Mireuk enough to keep him from dying. An unnecessary precaution, since if Mireuk were to reincarnate as a baby, the baby would find itself in the chains as well—but the thought does not sit well with the two brothers.* "And I will never think of you again."

Mireuk's smile is bloody and wet. "Oh, you will, Seokga," *he promises, laughing again.* "You'll think of me every day . . . You can leave me down here for as long as you want, but I'll always be with you." *He coughs, blood dribbling down his chin.* "Do you want to know why I've always hated you?" *The Mad God sniggers.* "Because we're the same, Seokga . . . The very same . . . You're no better than me, boy, and time will tell . . . Oh, yes, time will tell . . ." *As Mireuk begins to laugh once more, Hwanin yanks Seokga roughly back to Okhwang.* "You'll be back, boy!" *Mireuk roars as the two brothers vanish.* "You'll be back!"

"*It's over,*" *Hwanin gasps as their feet hit the tiles of the throne room.* "*It's over.*"

"*Yes,*" *says Seokga, wiping the blood from his nose and attempting to return Hwanin's smile.*

But even in the heavenly palace, his ears still ring with the sound of his father's crazed laughter.

And it never fades, not even through the centuries.

It never fades.

Seokga jerks awake with a start, drenched in a cold sweat. It takes him a moment to reorient himself, to remember that the woman lying in his arms is Kisa, his Kisa. Trembling, Seokga buries his face back in her hair, only to jerk away with an angry hiss as his phone rings. He snatches it from the bedside table, furious at whomever has decided to call him at such an ungodly hour and risk waking Kisa—but pauses.

ANNOYING AND MURDEROUS NEPHEW, the caller ID reads.

Hwanung. Snarling, Seokga disentangles himself from Kisa, and locks himself in the bathroom. Before he can think better of it, he's answering the call.

"I'm going to find you," Seokga growls into the phone, "and I am going to disembowel you so very slowly—"

"Uncle..." Hwanung's voice crackles. "I didn't do it. I *swear*. I didn't kill the captain; I didn't kill my father. I was framed. Someone—someone framed me."

"Where, exactly, are you?" Seokga continues, leaning against the door and envisioning how he'll reap his bloody revenge. It's most entertaining.

"You're not listening to me!" Hwanung cries, and his desperation sounds real enough that Seokga pauses. "*I didn't do it!*"

"Then why did you run?" Seokga growls. "Only the guilty flee. I should know."

"Because," pants Hwanung, "I was afraid. I heard what was broadcast over the ship, but I wasn't *there*! I was on Deck 9, looking for *you*, because my father hadn't been returning my calls. I thought you might know where he was. This is the longest we've ever fought and I was worried... It was my voice on the speaker, but it wasn't me—but I know how you fucking work, Uncle, and it's 'kill first, ask questions later.' I ran because I was afraid. Part of me thought it was *you*—and part of me still thinks it is—but you're all I have. Please, Seokga, help me. I know I've been horrible to you, but you have to believe that it wasn't me!"

Seokga grips his phone and glares at his reflection in the mirror. "I'll remind you of what you said the last time we spoke," he spits.

"What?" splutters Hwanung.

"Your allusions to the murder, you whimpering ninny, weren't as subtle as you thought."

"What the fuck are you talking about?" Hwanung cries. "I was angry at my father, and you told me that he was crying and napping! At the time, I didn't take that to mean he was a *baby* again... I thought he regretted our fight!"

"And your statement that you didn't plan on giving the throne up anytime soon?"

"I don't even remember *saying* that!"

"Give it up, Hwanung. I know about Soo-min," Seokga snaps. "I know all of it. Now, I'll ask again: Where are you hiding?"

There's a beat of confused silence. "Soo-min?" Hwanung asks carefully.

"Don't play dumb," Seokga snarls. "Lee Soo-min. The woman you had an affair with, the woman Hwanin didn't approve of. You went to couple's therapy with her. Dr. Jang told me everything."

The line is silent until Hwanung, very slowly, says: "I went to couple's therapy with Ungnyeo." Seokga freezes. The immortal bear-shifter is a far cry from Soo-min. She and Hwanung have been on and off for centuries, even after (accidentally) having a son together—Dangun, who founded Korea's first kingdom. "I don't know anybody named Lee Soo-min. I never have."

Something awful is beginning to prod at Seokga's mind. He takes a thin breath through his nose. "Do you have any proof?"

"Ungnyeo will corroborate it," Hwanung says desperately. "Call her, Uncle. But if Dr. Jang lied to you, that means she's part of it. She *knows* I never brought in Soo-min. And—" He starts breathing heavily, as if realizing something of great importance. Sweat slides down Seokga's bare back. "I saw her. Today. She was the one who told me you were on Deck 9. She walked with me as far as Deck 8."

Deck 8. Where the bridge is. But it doesn't make any sense. Dr. Jang said that Hwanung had slipped away—

"Heejin is involved. She has to be. She framed me—"

Seokga's head is swimming, and he feels as if he might faint.

"—is there a jangsan beom on the ship?" his nephew is demanding. "They mimic voices. There *has* to be a jangsan beom because I swear—on *me*—that I'm innocent!"

To swear on Hwanung is the deadliest oath one can make. For Hwanung to do it now... Seokga's throat has long gone dry. The satisfied feeling of having closed a case drains away from him. "If you're lying to me, nephew—"

"I swear *on myself* that I'm not!"

Shit. Fuck. Shit *fucking* shit. Somi is right. Seokga is an awful detective. Chief Shim would be so disappointed. He can feel him rolling in his grave. "Stay hidden. Stay down. I'll call you back soon." Before Hwanung can reply, Seokga is ending the call and stumbling out into the bedroom. "Kisa," he says urgently, "Kisa, wake up—"

He cuts off short.

The bed is empty. The lights are on.

And the door is wide, wide open.

CHAPTER TWENTY-NINE

KISA

H‍ER SPINE STIFFENS. As it begins, Kisa sucks in a shallow breath, tasting something bittersweet at the back of her throat. It reminds her of her stepmother's fixation with anti-aging creams. She stares down at the city below, heart thumping. It all happens so fast. Kisa doesn't even have time to open her mouth, to scream a plea to her goddess.

For in an instant, her body is sliding off the roof and she is for a perfect, brilliant moment, weightless and hovering over Seoul. But then gravity grabs her by the ankle and tugs her down, yanking her past rows and rows of gleaming glass windows all stacked upon one another, laughing as it hauls her toward the ground in a perfect swan dive.

Kisa closes her eyes.

It's over soon enough.

But the dream isn't. As Kisa lies broken on the pavement, feet clad in glossy red pumps approach her. Kisa groans in pain as two slim fingers tilt up her chin. "You're missing something," a woman with ridiculously voluminous brown hair and glittering wine-brown eyes tells her, just as beautiful as she was in Seokga's illusion as she arches a slender brow. Hani. "Go back."

"Wait," gurgles Kisa through a smashed face, but she's back on the roof, the dark night of Seoul swimming below her.

Her spine stiffens. As it begins, Kisa sucks in a shallow breath, tasting something bittersweet at the back of her throat. It reminds her of her stepmother's fixation with anti-aging creams. She stares down at the city below, heart thumping. It all happens so fast. Kisa doesn't even have time to open her mouth, to scream a plea to her goddess.

Again, she falls.

Again, Hani appears over her, looking annoyed.

"You figured it out before," the gumiho says then sighs, shaking her head. Her voluminous brown hair shines underneath the lights of the city, in the incoming red and blue flashes of the ambulance. "But you dismissed it, and now you've done the puzzle all wrong. Try again."

Her spine stiffens. As it begins, Kisa sucks in a shallow breath, tasting something bittersweet at the back of her throat. It reminds her of her stepmother's fixation with anti-aging creams.

Reminds her of her stepmother's fixation with anti-aging creams.

This time, when Kisa falls to the ground, her body doesn't shatter into hundreds of pieces. She lands on her feet in front of Hani, who cocks her head. "See? You've cast aside a very large clue, darling. And I'm wondering if you need your eyes checked if you can look at this mystery and consider it correctly solved."

"*No*," Kisa says at the other woman's meaningful look. "It was Hwanung and Soo-min. The two murders are unconnected. They have to be."

Hani rolls her eyes. As the sirens begin to wail in the distance, her pink-polished fingers close around Kisa's nail-bitten ones. "Come with me," she says, tone brooking no room for any argument. Kisa has no choice but to run after Hani into the dark city, racing through the streets that become less and less familiar—the infrastructure transforming from glittering skyscrapers and sleek roads to grungy sidewalks and significantly smaller buildings. They're no longer in Seoul. A cherry blossom floats by the two women as they run, somehow keeping pace with them before veering off toward a shop with a sign reading WEAPONS, WAR ARMOR, AND OTHER WANTS where a blurry, dark-haired man seems focused on breaking the doorknob to allow himself entry.

"Where are we?" Kisa asks, not recognizing the new city.

"New Sinsi."

That can't be true. This looks *nothing* like New Sinsi, nothing at all. "Are you sure? I—"

Hani grins over her shoulder at her. "This is *my* New Sinsi. Welcome to the nineties, Kisa."

"How—what—*how* is this possible?" Kisa splutters as Hani drags her down a seedy alleyway toward a dilapidated apartment complex. "It shouldn't be—I shouldn't be able to remember what New Sinsi looked like in the nineties. My mind shouldn't be able to—to generate such *sharp* images, not like this. Everything about this . . . is defying the laws of dreams." For instance, the world remains the same even when Kisa looks away for ten seconds. It's completely fascinating from a scientific standpoint, the suggestion being that past lives might resurface through unconscious dreaming, but utterly baffling from Kisa's personal perspective.

"Right," Hani snorts as she pushes open a battered-looking door and ushers Kisa inside. "But what you seem to be forgetting is that my mind is your mind, and your mind is my mind . . . regardless of whatever 'Ship of Theseus' bullshit you tote around. You're me. I'm you . . . But with much better taste in clothing."

"Are you really here? Or are you just my . . . my unconscious?"

"Why can't I be both?" Hani ushers Kisa into the apartment, which looks as if a small hurricane has blown through it. Mass-market romance books are strewn all over a lumpy-looking couch, and the kitchen is stuffed to the brim with bags of junk food. "Make yourself at home," the gumiho offers, clearing off the couch with one dramatic sweep of her arm. "It's ours anyhow."

Kisa slowly sits next to Hani on the couch. Something has wedged itself in between the couch's back and its cushion—she rummages behind her to pull out the same yellow, dog-eared copy of *Kidnapped by the Time-Traveling Highland Pirate-King* that Somi gave to her.

"You really should have taken better care of your books," Kisa can't help but tell Hani, who shrugs.

"It's my favorite," Hani replies and grins. "I took it everywhere, hence the questionable state."

"'Questionable'? It's falling apart—"

"Chapter fourteen is *especially* good. But you know that already." She grabs the book from her, flips open to a random page, and begins to read . . . Or *pretends* to read, as Kisa realizes a moment later. There's no hint of Elsie and Finlay's scandalously delicious scene. Instead, there's: "'And so Kisa and Seokga unwittingly convicted their story's two scapegoats . . . while the true murderer's plans remained fully intact, and their nefarious goal came closer and closer to fruition . . . What a couple of morons . . .'" Hani shuts the book with gusto. "Do you think it ends on a cliff-hanger? I hate cliff-hangers."

Her head is pounding. "There was evidence," Kisa says, although she's not sure if she's trying to convince herself or Hani. "The loudspeakers on the cruise, they broadcast everything."

"Kisa," Hani says, pinching the bridge of her nose, "at twenty-two, you're far more intelligent than I ever became even with hundreds of years underneath my belt . . . And yet you're so dumb sometimes that it physically pains me. *Think*, Kisa. Claws. Voices.

Sneezing. The bittersweet and the fall. You have something you haven't read yet. I'd suggest you give it a peek soon." Hani leans forward, grabbing her hands in hers. "I know you've already figured it out. I can see it in your eyes. And you're right to be terrified. Something huge is at play here. Something bigger than even Eodum."

"We were wrong," Kisa whispers. "We were wrong." It's always been a terribly devastating feeling for her—being wrong. Never has Kisa encountered a more soul-crushing experience than confidently raising her hand in class only to be at once corrected, or receiving an exam back to see she had completely botched a question she'd felt certain about. Worse still was making a mistake in the hospital. Yet in comparison to this, all her past mistakes dim to nothing. The shame is hard to breathe past, and Hani is silent as Kisa buries her face in her hands.

"It's not too late," Hani finally says. "When you wake up in a few minutes, you'll know what to do."

"I need to wake up *now*," gasps Kisa, and concentrates extremely hard, as if it will force her sleeping self to consciousness. The result, she fears, is that she looks very constipated.

"It doesn't work like that, darling." Hani sighs, scooting closer to the panicking Kisa. "You don't remember it, but you've—*we've*—faced the impossible before. And what's the worst that can happen to you? Death? Please. Been there, done that. The stakes are high, but we can overcome them. We have to—for Seokga."

A strained laugh escapes her lips and Kisa turns to look, really look, at Hani. "He loves you," Kisa whispers before she can stop herself.

Hani's expression hardens. "He loves *us*. And we love him."

"I just met him," Kisa rasps, although something about the statement feels like a lie, an excuse to hide behind. Hani stares at her, and Kisa almost recoils at the fury in the gumiho's eyes. She's reminded, suddenly, of Hani's notoriety and flinches in surprise as Hani launches herself upward from the couch.

"You're *not* going to ruin this for us," Hani snaps. "I'm not even going to waste my breath explaining to you that we knew him long before he came onto the ship. I *died* for him, Kisa. *You died* for him. But in this life, what have you done besides lead him along on a literal string?" She snatches the book from the couch and flips it back open. "'Kisa steadfastly denies her true feelings to herself, and is somehow fine with breaking the heart of the god who loves her, leading him on and on and on . . .' It's *preposterous*. I could slap you. If you go into that reincarnation queue, I *will* slap you. 'Squashing,' my ass."

"I don't expect you to understand," Kisa snarls, suddenly venomous. "What it's like on that ship—I'm *exhausted*. I've been exhausted for years."

"Right," the gumiho snaps back. "You're *tired*. Tired of working yourself to exhaustion in school, in the hospital, and now on this ship. But you aren't tired of being *you*. Reincarnation can be a pain in the ass, Kisa, trust me on that. You lose so much to gain so little." She gives her a rather pointed look. It stings. "I'm sure you can think of something that doesn't involve leaving Seokga with a broken heart. You do it a lot, after all. Thinking, I mean. Besides, what if you reincarnate as a slug that somebody sprinkles salt on? So far, you've had all of my karmic punishment. Sorry about that, by the way."

"No, you're not." Kisa's voice is bitter. Hani has, unfortunately, made a rather valid point about the slug thing. And, possibly, about some other things. Truths that she's not ready to face.

"No, I'm not. I had loads of fun being a terrible person." Hani flops back down onto the couch. "Look, Kisa. I understand that you're frightened to fall. What you need to understand, though, is that you already have—in more ways than one. That *ache*, the longing you've felt... Is it a *coincidence* that it lodged itself in your chest the day that the Red Thread of Fate appeared? Don't tell me that you believe in coincidences, Kisa."

"There is no coincidence," she says automatically. "Only correlation. Sometimes causation."

"Exactly," says Hani with a smug glimmer in her eyes as Kisa's mind whirls, cabinets trembling as neatly filed emotions threaten to spill out. For something deep within her has known, for a while, that Hani is right.

That *ache* feels like the pull of a magnet toward Seokga. It is relieved only when he is near.

When they are together.

Kisa swallows hard, hand fluttering to her chest.

"And, darling, just because you're falling again doesn't mean it will end like last time, with a painful impact. There's something you're forgetting... And what Seokga, bless him, is somehow forgetting in the afterglow... is that he's the interim heavenly emperor." Hani smirks as Kisa freezes, heart stopping mid-pound in her chest. "Or he will be, once he returns to Okhwang and sits on the throne for the first time. You can ask him for anything then, within the confines of his power. Living again isn't an option, but there are other things to ask for... As soon as you admit to yourself what you want."

More time.

"You know exactly what you would ask for, don't you?" Hani blinks guilelessly at her.

"You'd still be *dead,* of course, but you'll hardly be able to tell. And there can be so much more to life than, well, living."

"I..." It's as if her throat is attempting to force down a giant pill dry. Kisa digs her fingers into the couch, afraid that she's choking on some enormous truth, some desire that she's not allowed herself to want in full until now. There's a certain air of smug satisfaction radiating from Hani as Kisa curls over herself from the *want* of it.

"Promise me you'll ask, Kisa," Hani urges, suddenly desperate. When she looks up at the gumiho, Kisa sees that there are tears shining in her eyes. Their eyes. "Some stories deserve a happy ending."

It's all she can do to nod. She'll ask. Of course she'll ask.

"Thank you," her past-self whispers. "Thank you." She hesitates. "It's almost time for you to wake up . . . but I would hate myself if I didn't ask about her. About Somi." Guilt shines on Hani's face. "How is she?"

Kisa smiles slightly, thinking of the other gumiho's flirtation with Hajun, boba teas and laughter. "She's found friends. I'm one of them."

"She told you what happened?" Hani looks nervous.

"I forgave her," Kisa replies honestly. "I mean, well, to me—it didn't seem like there was anything to forgive. I don't remember her, or her betrayal . . . It's like it never even happened. I forgave her before she even apologized."

"Because you're right. There's nothing to forgive. Deep down, you've known it. Because it's true." Hani grimaces, fiddling with the corner of the book. "It was our fault from the beginning. She was so young, so innocent. We weren't there for her when she needed us, but Eodum—that fucking demon—was." Her eyes are bright. "I'm glad you forgave her. I'm glad that she's doing well . . ."

"Her claws, though," Kisa cuts in. "They've been—broken."

Hani stiffens. "Broken?"

"She was murdered. I don't know who did it. She doesn't want to talk about it." And she can't blame her for it.

Rage dances across Hani's face like a tumultuous storm, yet she looks as if she might be sick at the same time. "No. Not Somi. Not her claws." Hani stands again, shakily this time. "Somi-ah . . ." she whispers, stumbling to the kitchen counter, where a Polaroid stands in a frame. In the photo, Hani is grinning in a light brown apron next to a younger Somi, whose face is flushed pink with pleasure as their cheeks press together. Kisa watches as Hani's fingertips brush over the photographed Somi. "Find out who," Hani whispers. "Find out who, and then hurt *them*. Just as they hurt her." The apartment begins to blur. Kisa blinks in panic as Hani whirls back around. "You're waking up. Remember what I told you. You need to read it when you wake. The answers are there."

Kisa suddenly feels very light, very insubstantial. "Wait," she cries as she begins to fade. "Will I see you again?" There's so much she wants to ask her, so much she could learn about the phenomenon of past lives, how they might possibly linger in the depths of the unconscious. She can barely see Hani now, but she knows, somehow, that the gumiho is smiling.

"I'm always here, Kisa," Hani shouts back, laughter in her voice. "We share the same soul! Fuck your Ship of Thes—"

She wakes with a gasp, the sheets sticky with her sweat. The bed is empty next to her, and a sliver of light from the bathroom seeps into the dark bedroom, followed by the low murmur of Seokga's voice. He must be calling another irate god, who's demanding to know what exactly happened on the SRC *Flatliner*.

Remember what I told you.

Kisa's body is pleasantly sore with new aches as she hurries out of bed and slips on her underwear, then Seokga's sweater, swiping it from where it lies in a puddle of soft fabric on the floor. It's huge on her, practically a dress. Breathing hard, Kisa rushes into the sitting room, where she's stashed the stolen journal underneath the settee's thick cushion. Grabbing it, Kisa returns to the bedroom where she flicks on the lights and—not bothering to sit back down—opens the journal and begins to read.

The first entry is dated in 2018. The handwriting is the long, elegant script of an older woman, but Kisa has always been a fast and adept reader. As she skims, her stomach drops as if she's on a roller coaster, flying down from the highest peak. Clenching the sides of the journal, her hands begin to shake and Kisa leans against a bedpost for support. For a moment she can barely make out the next sentence, the journal quivering underneath her unstable grip. It's only with an excruciating effort that she stills them enough to continue unraveling the horrible, damning truth.

Faster and faster she skims, the pages fluttering rapidly as she makes her way through the contents, barely aware of how her skin has turned clammy, sweat pooling at the base of her back. Kisa's eyes have begun to burn and strain as she reads and reads, puzzle pieces falling into place with horrible, nauseating thuds and clicks.

When Kisa reaches the end of the journal, she has to force down a surge of bile. Everything is here. *Everything*. All of her suspicions and all of her questions answered in that innocuous, looping font. "Seokga," Kisa rasps, but she doesn't stumble toward the bathroom, where the god's voice is rising in agitation. She knows what he will do, overcome with rage, and they mustn't yet show their hand. Instead, she's lurching to the door and into the hallway.

Somi. She needs to find Somi.

The ship is silent and dark as Kisa races down into the bowels of the ship, skidding to a halt outside of the room she shares with Hajun. Frantically, she pounds on the door, ignoring the muffled groans of Hajun and the angry wails of Hwanin. She knocks until a bleary-eyed Somi yanks it open, looking peeved. Her annoyance falters as she takes in Kisa.

Somi smirks through slightly bee-stung lips that are sure to mirror Kisa's own, and brushes her short, mussed hair behind her ear. "Is that Seokga's sweater?"

"Somi," Kisa pants, thrusting the journal into her hands. "Your killer. It was a jangsan beom."

The gumiho flinches, eyes widening. "How do you—"

"It surprised you with its attack," she presses on. "But you fought back so viciously that it had no choice but to break your claws. It hadn't meant to do that. *You* were supposed to be this mystery's scapegoat, Somi—*you*. She knew you'd bribe that jeoseung saja and get on this ship. But things didn't go according to plan. You lost your claws. You couldn't take the blame."

Somi suddenly looks much younger than her years, and very scared. Behind her, a groggy Hajun, shirtless and mussed, looking as if he's survived a tornado yet loved it, comes to the door. "What are you talking about?" Somi demands, but there's a slight waver to her voice.

"Kisa?" Hajun asks in concern, voice thick with sleep and confusion. "What's happening?"

"It was never Soo-min or Hwanung," she rasps. "All along, it was—" Kisa cries out as the ship lurches beneath her feet, a terrible, sudden motion that sends her flying to her knees. Somi hits the ground next to her, and Hajun shouts in alarm as Hwanin begins to wail even louder somewhere in the room.

"What was *that*?" Somi gasps, struggling to her feet—only to be thrown down once more as the ship bucks again.

Hajun staggers out into the corridor, protectively holding Hwanin to his bare chest. Somehow the idol manages to remain upright even as the floor rocks with sharp motions. "We need to get to the upper decks!" he shouts, grabbing Kisa by the arm and hauling her up. "Go!"

She falls over and over as they hurry down the corridor, scraping her knees, bruising her arms. Somi catches her, saving her from a nasty fall down the stairs. The two women hold on to each other for support as they climb higher and higher, finally emerging onto the tenth deck, the normally peaceful sundeck. Kisa and Somi rush to the edge, staring down at the waters below... Where ineo have swarmed the boat, webbed hands pressed against the sides, fanged mouths stretched in wide, wicked smiles.

When the ship gives another lurch, this one hard enough that the lounge chairs rise in the air before slamming back down onto their sides, Somi yanks Kisa away from the edge. Kisa staggers right back to the rail, desperate to understand what the ineo are doing...

"The anchor!" Kisa cries. "They've broken the anchor!" Suddenly the ship is moving, pushed through the waters of the Seocheongang by the swarm of mermaids.

"*What the fuck is happening?*" Hajun shouts, narrowly avoiding tripping over one of the sliding plastic lounge chairs. "What are they *doing?*"

"The prison," Kisa gasps, holding on to Somi to steady herself. "They're going to push the ship toward Mireuk's prison—"

A bestial roar shakes the walls of the ship.

"*What was that?*" cries Hajun.

"*That,*" whispers Somi, fear scraping in her voice like sandpaper, a wind whipping through her hair, "was a jangsan beom."

CHAPTER THIRTY

SEOKGA

SEOKGA BURSTS ONTO the tenth deck, having frantically followed the red thread through the bucking ship—and he has no idea what the fuck *that's* about, but it can't be anything good—to its highest point, where Kisa stands too close to the rail, hands gripping the cold iron as she shouts something to Somi and Hajun, who stand behind her. They're all in various states of undress, and Seokga is no different, his chest bare like Hajun's. He couldn't find his sweater quickly enough.

"KISA!" Seokga roars as he realizes the ship is *moving* again, speeding through the waters with a dangerous sloppiness. "GET BACK FROM THERE!" Leaning heavily on his cane, his right leg aching from his sprint from Deck 7 to Deck 10, Seokga limps as quickly as he can to Kisa and practically hauls her away from the drop. The river sprays their faces as the ship veers a sharp right, and Seokga hits the deck hard, cushioning Kisa's fall with his own. Her bare legs tangle with his, and her elbow presses into his stomach as the deck rises up to meet them. He gasps in a breath as Kisa scrambles up to stare down at him, her curls whipping in the violent winds.

"It's Dr. Jang," she shouts over the wind. "I read her journal! All of this has been her, all of it! From the very beginning, years before now!" Her small hands grab his to pull him up. "She's not a shaman, Seokga—she's a jangsan beom!"

As if on cue, an enraged roar resounds from somewhere beneath them. The Red Thread of Fate is glowing black and pink and blue and purple all at once, their tumultuous emotions mixing in the chaos. Seokga wishes he could protest, but it's true—all true. Hwanung's call, Kisa's suspicions... This case was never closed. "*Fuck!*" Seokga snarls.

Another roar. This one closer.

Overhead, thunder booms somewhere in the deathly sky.

"*She killed me!*" Kisa screams, stumbling back toward Somi and grabbing the gumiho's hand. There's so much more than anger in her scream—there's fear and hatred, too. It cleaves Seokga's heart in two before it is mended by fury. Hot anger, as molten as liquid gold, fills in the cracks with a deadly rage. That rage shoots down the thread, burning black, an inky stain on fate.

"She shoved me from the roof, Seokga—*she* was the one who did it! Her lotion—Dermatrick's—I smelled it a moment before I fell! She found me before you did, knowing I was yours, knowing I'd be sent to the ship! And she killed Somi, too, knowing your history with her and intending to use *her* as a fall person, but when Jang went too far and Somi lost her claws in the battle, she had to shift methods and chose Soo-min instead!"

Seokga leans heavily on his cane, sulfuric rain lashing down on the ship. He can barely hear Kisa over the screams of the guests below and the churning storm, but he can hear enough. Oh yes, he can hear enough. His fingers have begun to twitch in the very same way they did all those years ago before he tortured Eodum to death. Staggering, he makes his way over to Hajun, where Hwanin is screaming in fright.

Kisa is drenched by now, rain soaking her hair and his sweater as she continues to shout, voice cracking and breaking over the thunder. "She killed Hwanin! He was never supposed to come with the two of you on the cruise—she had to take matters into her own hands! She followed him to the I-95 after the party and he panicked—the bright light was his first reaction and his second was to teleport to *you*! But he never got that far, only to the stairwell where we found him. In a fit of rage, Jang ripped out his heart during the teleportation, in the corners between space, which is why we never found any sign of a struggle!"

Hwanin cries and reaches for him, burying his small face in his brother's chest as Seokga grabs him from Hajun's stricken grip.

"She mimicked Soo-min's voice when Somi was hiding in the closet, she mimicked her and Hwanung's voices on the intercom after luring Hwanung onto the ship when he called her to ask about his father! And you, Seokga—" Kisa resembles a goddess of wrath as she stands on the deck, fists clenched at her sides, wind and rain failing to move her as if she is a marble pillar. "She's been manipulating *you* for *years*! Posing as your therapist, prescribing you medication that blocks your ability to read minds! Your meds aren't anti-depressants, Seokga, they're *power suppressants,* made from blacklisted ingredients!"

Any help you've received in your life has been double-bladed.

A quietness fills Seokga's ears. A deadly calm before a storm.

"Stop," he whispers. He's heard enough from Hwanung, from her, to lay any doubts to rest. She can stop now. But Kisa isn't done, the words flooding from her like a horrible tsunami, washing over him as he drowns.

"And all this talk about your father!" Kisa staggers back to the rail, where she points a trembling finger to the river beyond. The ship, to Seokga's growing horror, has veered past its original course, toward the riotous waters where red waves crash over jagged rocks and a narrow pass between two towering black moun-

THE GOD AND THE GWISIN

tains is vaguely visible through a dark mist. Seokga's blood turns to ice in his veins. He knows that gap. Bound God's Pass. Beneath those waters in the gap, his father lies, imprisoned with skeletal shackles in an underwater cave. "She killed the captain to take control of the ship! She wants you to free the Mad God—"

"Kisa," Seokga breathes in terror, eyes latching on the webbed hand gripping the rail behind her. "Kisa—BEHIND YOU!"

She lurches away just in time to avoid the cackling mermaid, who pulls herself up over the rail and falls onto the ship with a pike's teeth smile. Ineo on Iseung never looked so monstrous, but they never swam in hell waters, either.

"Oh, no, no, no, *no*," Hajun is screaming, half-hiding behind Somi, who's shouting some panicked expletives as more and more ineo crawl onto the deck, and as another roar shakes the ship . . .

. . . and a white tiger bursts onto the deck with a ravenous snarl.

No, not a tiger.

The jangsan beom. It's a hulking monster of bulging muscles underneath long, coarse black-and-white fur, and a dripping muzzle pulls back to reveal yellow, jagged teeth. The creature's eyes are a pale, vicious gold stained red—from Hwanin's light, Seokga realizes as he snaps his cane into a sword with his free hand. Dr. Jang had begun to wear sunglasses after that fateful night, sometimes even bumping into furniture, after Hwanin had panicked on the I-95 and released his divine, almost blinding, light. A low growl erupts from the jangsan beom's throat as the hordes of ineo, crawling forth on their hands, shepherd Seokga and his companions closer together.

Somi chokes, her hand flying to Kisa's. "*You!*" the gumiho cries, and Seokga has never heard Somi's voice ripe with so much pain and terror.

He remembers her reaction to his list of four-clawed creatures in the trashed security room. *That leaves a samjokgu, a bulgae, or a jangsan beom,* he'd mused, and chalked up Somi's subsequent show of fear to the fox-eating dog. But it was never the samjokgu she was afraid of.

Seokga takes a shallow breath as he recedes deep, deep into himself—far enough that when the tiger shifts into Dr. Jang Heejin, he feels nothing. Cold. He has made himself cold, just as he did before his coup, during the days after his fall.

Seokga can see that her eyes, now without sunglasses, are stained with the same red as the tiger's. But her vision seems to be perfectly fine as the old woman takes in the scene, mouth tightening.

"I should have realized what a liability you'd be," Jang says, narrowing her eyes at Kisa, whose fear skitters down the red thread. "Was it the lotion I dropped? Or the journal you stole?" Her voice is so different from the one he has come to know. This nasally, pinched voice must be her true one. No longer does it remind him of Mago.

"*Both,*" spits Kisa venomously.

"I suppose it doesn't matter," is the sweet reply. "Everything that needed to happen already has." Jang turns her eyes on Seokga. The woman has the audacity to fucking smile at him. "This wasn't the way I wanted you to find out, dear. It must be an awful shock." Her voice has changed again, becoming sweeter, more like his mother's.

Seokga has suffered so many betrayals in his lifetime.

From his father to Hani, his story is a fractured mess of broken promises and lonely sufferings. This should not hurt as much as it does.

But oh, how it aches.

The hours spent in Jang's office, confiding in her thoughts—emotions—he had never had the courage to share with anybody else. The time he broke down in front of her as he spoke of Hani's death. The way Dr. Jang had pushed the box of tissues toward him. Session after session, growing to trust the voice that at times reminded him so strongly of his mother, Mago... All of it fake. Seokga feels the cold rain on his face and the unsteady ship beneath his feet, Hwanin sniffling in his arms, but he is not truly here. He is somewhere far away, alone in the ether.

"In about fifteen minutes," Jang says when he fails to respond, "the ship will reach Bound God's Pass. I'd like you to come with me, Seokga. Your father has wanted to see you for a long time. He misses you and what could have been."

An ineo cackles and snaps her teeth toward Kisa's ankles. She cries out, and that horrible sound is the only reason Seokga is able to pull himself up from the distant reverie he sank into.

"Think about what we've discussed in our sessions, Seokga," Jang says kindly, lacing her fingers together. "All the issues that stem from your relationship with your father can be healed. He wants to start again, like you have... And you, Seokga, can give him that. I know he would be eternally indebted to you."

"Don't listen to her, Seokga!" Kisa cries. The mermaids hiss, edging closer, and Kisa falls silent.

Seokga pauses, and slowly tilts his head as he looks at Jang. Sensing she's got his attention, Jang presses forth. "Your brother, Hwanin, could never understand how much a person can change. Especially your father. It's why I had to kill him, and I'm truly sorry about that. But you, you can understand. You changed during your punishment, just as Mireuk has."

"How do you know my father?" Seokga asks softly, shifting his brother in his arms.

"By visiting his prison, of course." Dr. Jang smiles beatifically. "There are those of us who are still loyal to him. He fashioned our rightful home, Gamangnara. The almighty creator is the only one who can reopen it after what you did. On the anniversary of the

Dark World's fall, we visit your father underneath this river and pay our respects. My first visit to him was some, oh, some fifty years ago. I was young then, and homesick for a place I'd never known. The home of my ancestors, lost to me. Locking a realm has its consequences, you know." There's a flicker of rage across her face but it quickly vanishes. Seokga pretends he hasn't seen it. "But Eodum went about it all wrong. Violence isn't the answer."

"Oh, that's rich," Somi snaps, kicking her bare foot at a grinning mermaid. "You're just Eodum 2.0 and—"

"You're a murderer," Hajun bursts out. "You're sick—" He cuts off as a mermaid wraps sharp-nailed fingers around his ankle. Somi stomps on her head and the ineo snarls, but backs away, as if waiting for Jang's signal.

"What are *you* even getting out of this?" Somi demands of the mermaids. One of them, missing an eye, smiles.

"Mireuk has made us many promises." Her voice is as wet as the slippery gills on her neck. "The humans killed us, and so they will suffer when the Mad God returns to his throne..."

Dozens of tails thump in agreement, scales and fins pounding down with gusto.

Jang holds her hand up for silence. "This plan has been many years in the making, Seokga. I apologize for how much manipulation it required. I didn't take any joy in killing your soulmate, but—knowing her karmic punishment from her past life would be to serve on this ship—it was the only way I could ensure you didn't leave the cruise mid-voyage should you have figured things out sooner and been less... amenable. Everything had to go perfectly."

"How did you even know who I was?" Kisa demands, and Seokga cannot tell the raindrops apart from the tears coursing down her face. "Where to *find* me?"

Jang sighs and glances at Seokga. Her expression is almost...

pitying. Something plummets in Seokga's stomach. Something breaks within him, irreversible in its damage. "Seokga called me," she says.

Kisa lurches back as if she's been struck, her shock and pain flaring down the bond, hurtling like bullets into his chest. Seokga struggles to remain standing, even as every part of him longs to sink to his knees and atone. The final betrayal slices him down to the core in one of the most exquisite, terrible agonies the immortal god has ever known. It had been Jang that he'd dialed with shaking hands as he raced through New Sinsi, following the red thread to Kisa—who'd still been alive, at that point, still living and breathing in the world above. *Seoul,* he'd gasped out to the therapist. *I think—it's leading me to Seoul.*

"When I first started treating him, Seokga told me that Hani's reincarnation would have distinctly unique eyes. That always came up, almost every single session, for thirty-three years. Wine-brown eyes, this. Wine-brown eyes, that. He'd go on and on about them, sometimes for forty-five minutes at a time, describing the color down to each individual hue. So when he called me on the day that the Red Thread of Fate appeared . . ."

"Kisa," Seokga rasps. "Kisa—"

She shakes her head, a tear spilling down her cheek as she holds his gaze.

—it's not—your fault—didn't—know—how could—you—know?—

"Earlier that year," Jang continues, but he barely hears her over the roaring in his head, "I'd visited the Magical Maternity Unit at Seoul's Shamanic Hospital. My gumiho daughter-in-law was in labor, bless her, and needed an emergency C-section at the last minute. One of the doctors there, well, the eyes were a match, but I wasn't sure. It was too . . . convenient. But when the red thread appeared, and Seokga confirmed it was leading him to Seoul, I didn't see the point in wasting any more time. Reaching you before he did wasn't much of a challenge as I had the precise directions rather than a fickle thread. From there, it was easy. All I had to do was kill you, confirm you had been stationed on the *Flatliner*, and manage to get Seokga on the boat, as well. The latter part took a bit of time—seven years, actually—since I had to wait for Seokga to *truly* run himself ragged. Every time I mentioned taking a break, he fled before I could even finish the sentence, scurrying off to Poland or Jamaica on yet another expedition. Finally—after *Antarctica*—Seokga was finally tired enough to come along without finding a way to squirm out of it... Although he did complain. A lot."

Everything Seokga touches falls apart. *Everything.*

"I know how much that must hurt to hear." Jang turns back to Seokga with a sympathetic half-smile. "I know, Seokga, that you're blaming yourself, but you don't need to. Mireuk has the power to create a new story for the both of you. Free him, and he'll reward you. Even as heavenly emperor, there are things you cannot do for Kisa. You simply aren't strong enough. But your father is the most powerful god there is. He might even be able to bring her back to life. Erase it all."

Seokga inhales shakily, still fighting not to let his knees buckle beneath him. Even on the throne, with all the heavenly powers, he would not be able to bring Kisa back. No god can. He should turn away, but he still finds himself asking in a hoarse whisper: "My father. Has he... spoken about me?"

"Oh, yes," says Jang, and Seokga slowly moves toward her, hanging on to her every word. His guilt and pain war with his insatiable curiosity. "He wants badly to start over. He wants to be a father. He wants his son." Jang smiles as she stretches her hand out to Seokga, the other gesturing to Bound God's Pass, looming in the distance. "I promise you, everything you have ever wanted is just beneath the surface. Will you join me? For yourself? For Kisa?"

He wants to be a father. It's everything Seokga's ever wanted to hear. He groans, squeezing his eyes shut. Such pretty promises, wrapped up neatly in a bow. The temptation is a squirming, wriggling thing inside of him. To be the worthy son this time. It all fits so neatly into his fantasies, his dashing rescue and the gratitude—the love—he might receive in return. Slowly, Seokga passes Hwanin to Kisa, who takes the child with an alarmed expression.

"Seokga..."

When she leaves him, he'll be utterly alone. As it was before, so it will be after.

Unless.

Unless, unless, unless.

His eyes fly open.

If there is one thing that Seokga has learned from his years of trickery, it is that there is always an *unless*. Perhaps even multiple. Another offer to make, another path to take. So he steps forward as the ship pitches once more, thunder roaring overhead as demons swoop through brilliant strokes of lightning—and takes Jang Heejin's hand.

It's warm and slightly calloused, wrinkled with age yet still somehow smooth, as if subjected to copious amounts of creams and powder. Seokga squeezes it gently, staring into Jang's crow's-feet-lined eyes rimmed with red. "There's just one more thing I want," he murmurs.

"Anything," she replies, practically beaming. "Oh, Seokga, you don't know how happy this makes me."

"I want you to know"—Seokga bows his head closer to hers—"that you made a mistake. All of this, it just might have worked—if you hadn't killed Kisa."

Jang's eyes widen. She tries to jerk away, but Seokga holds tight.

"And what's more . . ." Seokga draws his sword up with his other hand—and plunges it through the tiger-shifter's heart. "You can never out-trick a trickster," he spits.

Triumphant, he waits for Jang to crumple to the ground.

She does not.

Jang sighs, looking down at the sword in her chest. "I wish you hadn't done that. It makes things so much more complicated."

What in the fucking seven hells? Seokga gapes at her, withdraws his sword. And plunges it back into her. Nothing. Jang Heejin looks bored. Around him, the ineo are laughing, the sound like the sea hissing and bubbling in the heat. Kisa's alarm surges down the red thread.

—blue—it's blue—all along the blade—blue blood—she's—

Slowly, Seokga looks down at the long blade of his sword. Sure enough, blue blood drips from it, slow and thick.

"I killed myself the first day here," Jang informs him as he feels his own red blood drain from his face in shock. "Hung myself with the room's curtains and re-formed as a gwisin. I kept my heart but threw my body overboard." With a horrible drop of his stomach, Seokga remembers the dragging sound outside of his room the first night. The woman who insisted she heard a "splash." "Except the heart. For me to remain on the ship, that particular organ needs to, as well. It's hidden somewhere safe. Please remove the sword, Seokga. It's a bit uncomfortable."

"You should at least be in pain," Kisa whispers, sounding both terrified and fascinated. "You should be in *debilitating* pain—I don't understand how—I have patients who come in for scabbed knees . . ."

"I've done what they can't, through years of preparation for this very moment," Jang says smugly. "Separated my consciousness from the memory of having a body and what *should* happen when

I'm stabbed. I've realized that death is death, and once I'm dead, flesh wounds won't do anything. It's an enlightened state of being. Mireuk will allow my ghost to wander the planes of Gamangnara forevermore."

"How did you separate—that's *impossible*—I've tried, I can't even..." Kisa seems to realize she's coming dangerously close to displaying admiration and abruptly shuts her mouth.

Jang smirks. "Now where were we?" she asks Seokga as Bound God's Pass approaches in the distance. "Oh, yes. I was about to revert to using *force*."

CHAPTER THIRTY-ONE

KISA

THE TIGER GROWLS as it launches into the air, claws outstretched for the trickster god, who's currently recovering from a nasty-looking crash into a pile of fallen pool chairs. It is, reflects Kisa as she dances out of the ineo's clawed reaches, awfully inconvenient to no longer have Hani's powers. She learned how to fight at NSUMD, of course—studying the art just as much as she studied anatomy, or history—but she's never been in a real fight and, most of all, has never been expected to battle while *carrying a child* . . .

Her feet are bare as they hop over thrashing tails and swiping claws. "Shh," Kisa urges Hwanin as he wails in her ear. "Everything is all right, everything is perfectly all right—" She looks around desperately for Hajun, who seems to have constructed a mountain out of plastic lounge chairs and is balancing precariously at the top, swinging a rolled-up towel at the ascending mermaids. *Well,* she thinks.

Perhaps everything is not all right.

"My fox bead doesn't work down here!" Somi shrieks, running around in circles, much like Kisa. "What am I supposed to do?"

"Fox form!" Kisa yelps.

"Without *claws*? Fox teeth aren't very large—"

There's a flash of green on the opposite end of the deck, and Kisa sees that Seokga has shifted into a giant panther. The cat's emerald eyes flash as he launches toward Jang, and Kisa can't hold back five quick sneezes. *Cats.*

"KISA, I'M SORRY!" Hajun wails, jumping from his mountain. "I CAN'T DO THIS!"

"TAKE THE BABY!" Kisa screams, shaking a strong hand off her ankles. It's like a game of American football as Somi races by, grabs Hwanin, and presses the child into Hajun's arms as he sprints for the door. "HAJUN! LOOK FOR JANG'S HEART!"

"AND THROW IT INTO THE RIVER!" howls Somi, stooping down to punch a bloodthirsty ineo in the face. The mermaid howls in surprised agony.

"Go with him!" Kisa cries as she narrowly dodges another mermaid.

"I'm *not* leaving you!"

The ship bounces as the currents become more treacherous. Kisa nearly falls on her face but quickly saves herself. "Two pairs of eyes are better than one!" she manages to gasp out as Somi hurries to her, and the two women press their backs together. The ship tilts again, Seokga's abandoned sword sliding toward them. Kisa snatches it up, the heavy hilt somehow feeling as if it belongs in her palm. In any other circumstance, she'd pause to admire the exact sheen of the moon-harvested silver and perhaps take a few mental notes on its weight and density, but there's quite positively no time for that.

"Where would her heart even *be*?" Somi shouts as red water sloshes over the sides of the boat—reaching even its highest point. Bound God's Pass stands tall and menacing in the eddy of red, washing tides. Kisa sucks in a panicked breath as, down the deck, Seokga struggles beneath Jang's claws—the tiger atop the panther.

A flash of green, and now the panther is a small mouse, escaping from beneath the terrifying creature before shifting into a snarling, massive grizzly bear whose weight causes the deck to groan.

"Kisa? Where would her heart be?"

"I-I don't *know!*" Kisa yells as she swipes Seokga's sword through the air. The mermaids hiss as the sword cuts flesh. It seems as though *they* haven't yet mastered the art of realizing they don't need to feel pain. The deck is slippery with river water, and as it tilts precariously, Kisa and Somi hold tight to each other. Seokga and Jang tumble toward them, a rolling mass of claws and fur.

It's only narrowly that Somi and Kisa manage to lurch out of the way, followed by the bloodthirsty ineo. Jang and Seokga crash into the deck's Hawaiian-style bar, wood splintering beneath them followed by broken bottles and the distinct smell of alcohol. Somi darts toward the mess and snatches up a long piece of glass, its sharp edge glinting as she wields it against the mermaids. It cuts into her skin, too, but the gumiho doesn't seem to care as she launches herself toward a grinning cluster of mermaids.

The injured ineo throw themselves from the deck, heading for the waters below with angry screeches. Kisa's made decent progress against them, but she can feel herself slowing as she remembers the footwork she learned in her academies, the exact way to sweep a blade.

Where would Jang hide her heart? Kisa pants through her teeth as she scours through all the possibilities. An organ like a heart can't risk being found by a guest. Jang's room would be an obvious answer, but some instinct tells Kisa that the jangsan beom would never have admitted to hiding the heart "somewhere safe" unless she was certain it wouldn't be found. Her bedroom is too obvious.

Mentally, Kisa curses the CEO for making this ship so bloody big. Where is he anyway? Surely he would notice the chaos unfolding on his pride and joy?

The heart, the heart. The heart . . . *Oh, no.*

The ship lurches to a halt right underneath the looming archway of Bound God's Pass. Kisa's heart rises into her throat as she stares up at the dark, wet stone. Beneath them, within the rushing red waters, is Mireuk's prison.

She whirls back to the ineo, but they're grinning at her as they slip through the gaps in Deck 10's railing, disappearing into the waters below with small splashes. Seokga's bear is roaring as he swipes at the tiger with massive claws, only for her to ignore the way pain should erupt down her furred chest.

How do you win against an opponent who can't die and can't feel pain?

You restrain them, thinks Kisa desperately. But there are no ropes that could ever possibly hold down the monstrous jangsan beom . . .

"SEOKGA!" she screams in terror as the tiger closes its maws around the bear's middle. Not enough to kill—Jang *needs* Seokga for whatever comes next—but enough for Seokga to roar hoarsely in pain. The sound of it cuts Kisa to the bone. She lunges toward the two beasts, but Somi's hands wrap around her middle, dragging her back.

"You'll get hurt!" Somi cries in her ear as Kisa fights to escape.

"I'm *DEAD*!" Kisa screams with so much fury that Somi falters, grip slackening enough for Kisa to escape. Tears burn in her eyes as the green-eyed bear falls, shifting into Seokga, whose red blood leaks from the deep gouges in his bare waist. They've not yet begun to heal.

No. *No.*

She races forward, only for the tiger to whirl and send her flying backward with a punch of its paws. Kisa sobs in panic, climbing to her feet as the tiger reverts back into Jang, who smiles nastily at her in triumph as she gathers the limp god up in her arms and climbs the rail. Her gray hair streams behind her in the wind. Somewhere above, a demon shrieks in pleasure.

The red thread gives Kisa a harsh yank, adding to her momentum as she rushes forward, intent on stopping Jang before she can bring Seokga to the waters below. The bond between Seokga and her has never felt so strong... Kisa can swear that it becomes heavier around her finger, somehow, as she rushes forth...

Only for Jang to jump over the rail and disappear into the water below, dragging Kisa's god with her.

She skids to a halt. *Jump!* her mind screams at her, but she can't make herself do it, can't make herself fall...

Not again. She can't—she *cannot* fall again. Kisa trembles like a baby bird, staring helplessly into the river below, seeing not the churning water but the bright lights of Seoul, the midnight trains winding far below on their dark tracks, the neon signs advertising new albums and soda and all the trivial little things she would give anything to experience again blinking cheerily up at her.

"Do it," she whispers to herself, furiously scrubbing away a tear. "Just *do it*."

But she can't.

And she doesn't.

Until the gumiho appears next to her, breathless and panting. She grabs Kisa's hand, and she's no longer alone on the skyscraper's roof. She's with Somi. She's with her friend. "We go together," Somi says softly.

"T-Together," Kisa agrees hoarsely. Palms sweating, Kisa follows her up to stand on the rail, legs trembling. She feels sick but Somi's grip is warm and comforting, strong in a way Kisa must be, as well.

"One, two—"

"Three!" Do it. Just *do it*.

With a deep breath, the two women jump from the highest

deck and plummet hundreds of feet into the waters below—holding hands the entire time.

The water is icy cold, enveloping Kisa in a frigid blanket as she sinks down, bubbles streaming up around her. She opens her eyes, lungs burning, but she can't make anything out save for the blurry cloud of bubbles and the red thread, swirling around her in dizzying loops. To her depthless relief, Somi's hand is still in hers, although through the bubbles she cannot see her.

A terrible sensation overcomes Kisa, and Kisa has no idea which way is up, or which way is down. She flails, panicking, lungs burning—and her free fist closes on instinct around the thread . . .

To find it *solid* in a way it was not before. Thicker, too. Like a rope . . .

What . . . How . . .

Surprise has Kisa momentarily forgetting she can't breathe. The thread curls itself into an arrow, pointing downward, followed by what looks—vaguely—like a thumbs-up sign. Kisa nods, and—with slowly steadying hands—begins to follow the red thread toward Seokga, pulling herself and Somi down its length.

I do not need to breathe, Kisa tells herself firmly as her chest aches with pain. *I am dead. I do not need to breathe.*

Her lungs seem to think the opposite. She has, she guesses, about one minute before she blacks out and is utterly useless to anybody. The red thread flexes underneath her, and as Kisa becomes weaker, wraps itself around her waist.

There's a split second before Kisa is being dragged down and pulling Somi with her. The thread hauls her this way and that, descending all the while. Kisa closes her eyes—and only reopens them when the thread drags her across something rough and hard... And the pressure of the water disappears. Kisa's eyes fly open.

They're in a cave—a cave that is somehow *empty* of the frigid river water. She sucks in a deep breath, and next to her, a drenched Somi does the same. Finally able to breathe, Kisa climbs to her feet and the red thread unravels itself from around her.

The cave is dark, stalactites hanging from a damp, slick ceiling. Kisa's bare feet, once the adrenaline wears off, will feel every sharp stone that digs into her flesh. Clusters of stalagmites rise threateningly from the cave's ground, leading farther and farther into inky depths. Behind her, the cave's entrance gapes like a hungry mouth. Scarlet water pushes up against it but seems to be blocked by magic of some kind.

Kisa's hand closes around the red thread as it places itself in her palm. Yes, she thinks, it's definitely solid. What brought on the change?

She gapes as the thread rises into the air and arranges itself into cursive letters. DESPERATE TIMES, DESPERATE MEASURES. LET'S GO, KISA.

When she fails to move, it arranges itself into a sort of angry emoticon. HURRY UP!

"I *knew* you were sentient!" Kisa hisses, wishing she had her notepad to record this absurd development. "I knew it!" The implications of this are nothing short of *astounding*...

GLOAT LATER. HURRY NOW.

"I would hope so," snaps Somi, looking offended. "I have a brain."

"Erm..." Despite its new solidity, Somi still cannot see the Red Thread of Fate binding Seokga and Kisa. "Not you," she whispers, but the thread is already tugging her farther into the cave. "This way. Come on."

The cave transforms more and more the deeper they venture

into it. The sharp, flat surface riddled with grime beneath them gives way to stairs formed from slippery, jutting rock leading into an inky abyss below. Kisa keeps one hand on the slimy cave wall and one hand on the thread as she and Somi quietly pick their way downward. The air is heavy here, thick and sulfurous, damp when it hits their lungs. There is also the faint smell of unwashed body, which only grows stronger as the makeshift stairways end at the bottom of a cavern with three dark tunnels.

"Which one?" Somi whispers.

The thread stretches down the second. Kisa gestures toward it, but hesitates. There *must* be traps. No prison ever comes without them. Seokga's sword is at the top of the SRC *Flatliner,* and Somi's claws are broken and useless. All they have with them are their wits.

The two women edge cautiously into the second tunnel. Kisa half-expects some sort of demon to jump out at them, but instead, they're met by—the CEO? Her heart lurches in her chest as Yeomra emerges from the darkness, eyeshadow glittering even in the depthless shadow.

If he's with Jang . . .

But Yeomra shakes his head, ever so slightly, raising one pale finger to his lips.

"Good of you to finally show up," Somi snaps.

The CEO ignores the irate gumiho, stepping closer to Kisa. "Seokga is unconscious," he whispers. "When his wounds heal, he'll be forced to untie his father."

"Can't you do something about Jang?" Kisa demands, but it sounds more like a plea. "Send her into one of the hells?" Even if Hajun finds Jang's heart and throws it overboard, it's no use now. Jang is off the ship.

"I can," whispers Yeomra, "and I will. But that's not the problem. Seokga is."

"No," she vehemently insists. "He's not a willing participant in any of this—"

Yeomra's black eyes flash. "You don't understand the influence Mireuk has over Seokga. It's the reason Jang singled Seokga out of all the other gods. Even though he'll fight against it, Seokga will still do anything for his father if it means being loved by him. Don't you know what we call him in Okhwang?" He leans forward, as if to deliver the killing blow. "We call him the Lonely God."

"I know that." She glares, even as pain fractures her chest. *The Lonely God.* "I also know that you're underestimating him. He fought Jang on the ship, and he was the one who imprisoned Mireuk in the first place."

Yeomra rolls his eyes, and Kisa dearly wants to punch him. "He was able to fight off Jang because Mireuk wasn't present. He relied on the strength of Hwanin to get through imprisoning him. The Mad God is manipulative, and once Seokga is in front of him, all the fight will drain the fuck out of him. If Seokga tries to free his father, it's a Divine Crime against the pantheon and all of humanity. Worse even than his coup. We need to extract him before he wakes up. I'll take Jang. The two of you take Seokga. We clear?"

Kisa clenches her jaw. "Fine," she snaps.

"Crystal," says Somi.

"Let's go."

The tunnel is long, riddled with murky puddles and stale, stagnant air. Kisa exchanges fearful glances with Somi as they follow Yeomra through its length. When it finally ends, Kisa presses a hand to her mouth. Another cavern looms beyond, a ravenous maw with a tongue of rock—on which a man is bound with chains that are, nauseatingly, the exact color of human bones. It's the shackles that catch her eye first, but when she realizes *who* they bind to the protruding rock, Kisa feels a terror that is unlike anything she's ever felt before. Her bladder threatens to loosen as she stares at the Mad God, clinging close to the shadows, sticky sweat pooling on every inch of her trembling skin.

The Mad God. Mireuk. Creator of life and, later, the sufferings that come with it. Rape. Murder. The gruesome and the horrifying. He lies spread-eagle on the rock, his face almost as skeletal as his chains, so gaunt and haunted. His matted black hair is long, tumbling from the rock and spreading on the ground below. There is a stench of waste, of a long-drawn death, that permeates the air now, mingled with the horrid reek of a body that has gone unwashed for centuries upon centuries upon centuries. Her throat works, and then she's pivoting to quietly vomit all over Yeomra's heavy black boots before she can stop herself. The CEO fixes her with a look of great disgust and betrayal.

Beneath the cavern's tongue, Seokga lies, a crumpled heap. Above him stands Jang, a maniacal gleam in her eyes as she stares up at Mireuk. "*Your Majesty!*" she cries, and although she's still clad in her ridiculous Hawaiian set, she somehow manages to be as terrifying as she was in her tiger form. "Your son! I have brought him here, to you. Your freedom is imminent!"

"Ah . . ." Mireuk's voice is not the thunderous, powerful thing Kisa expected. It's little more than a reedy rasp, hoarse from disuse. He does not sound like an all-powerful deity, nor does he sound like the mortal realm's most dangerous villain. Mireuk sounds *weak*. "Jang Heejin. You've done so well, my little tiger."

Jang beams. "Anything for you, My Emperor."

"You'll be well rewarded, as promised." Mireuk licks his lips. "Wake Seokga."

"*Now*," whispers Yeomra, and before Kisa has the chance to do so much as tense, the death god is lunging out of the tunnel. He's like an arrow shot straight for Jang's heart. With a startled cry of surprise and rage, Jang shifts into her tiger form, leaping away from Yeomra's outstretched hands, which hold a pair of shackles similar to the ones binding Mireuk.

"Go, go, *go!*" Somi urges, and together they sprint for Seokga's crumpled heap. On the slab of rock, Mireuk is silent, but Kisa knows in her bones that the god's clouded eyes are watching her acutely as she bends over his son. She does not like the weight of his stare, as if he is not threatened at all by her presence, but merely impassive: like he's watching an ant futilely crawl up a wall moments before being smushed. Kisa swallows in fear as she hooks her arms around Seokga's armpits.

"Fuck, he's heavier than he looks," pants Somi as she tries to lift Seokga by his feet—but a heartbeat later she's crashing into a cavern wall, having been struck by a snarling Jang. Yeomra is shouting something from the other side of the cavern, claw marks ripping across his face as he stumbles back to his feet, but the jangsan beom has turned her murderous gaze on Kisa. She hears nothing as Jang's hot breath steams onto her face.

"Kisa," the tiger sneers, yellow fangs glinting. "Give up."

Yeomra is still shouting, and if Kisa were to look at the death god, she would see that his hands were raised toward the stalactites and that, swirling upward from the dark ground, skeleton soldiers are forming, crawling to their feet with rictus smiles. She is unable to move, however, as Jang's yellow, red-stained eyes narrow at her. In her arms, Seokga stirs.

"Put him down," the tiger demands in Jang's voice, looking bored.

Slowly, eyes on the red thread—which has urgently arranged itself into a crude but understandable pictograph, an instruction—Kisa obeys. Jang licks her chops, smiling in the way only an apex predator can.

A moment later, at the thread's urging, Kisa launches into action, fueled by adrenaline and *anger*. Hand gripping the now-solid string, Kisa leaps over Seokga's body. Jang swipes a clawed paw at her, but Kisa jumps to the side, winding the Red Thread of Fate around the tiger's outstretched leg. The thread does most of the work, snaking around the furred limb, but Kisa is still panting in concentration as she continues the binding.

The jangsan beom has reared onto her hind legs, giving Kisa a perfect opportunity to dive beneath her stomach, looping the red thread around the furred and muscular waist. Angry, rancid spit sprays her as Jang twists, but the red thread holds tight around the monster's body. Even when Jang, evidently pulling a trick from Seokga's book, shifts into her smaller human form, the red thread holds still. Kisa watches in satisfaction as the old woman topples to the ground, unable to move.

She jumps about a foot in the air when a skeleton clicks over to her, bending down to admire her handiwork. Yeomra follows, looking both impressed and annoyed as he waves a hand, dissipating the veritable army of skeletal soldiers he apparently summoned at one point during the chaos. "Nicely done," the CEO says, but Kisa's too exhausted to even bloom under the praise as Yeomra reaches forward and snaps a pair of bone shackles around Jang's waist. The red thread unwinds itself from the old woman's body and arranges itself into two thumbs up.

"*Ughggrgrg,*" Somi groans, drawing herself up to her feet and rubbing her head as she staggers over to stand next to Kisa. "That was . . . awful . . . I'm seeing double, no, triple . . ."

Yeomra yanks Jang to her feet and smiles unpleasantly. "Do you prefer the Hill of Knives or the Chop Shop?" he asks. "Choose wisely—it'll be your home for all of eternity."

"Why not send her through all seven hells?" Kisa asks, the words colder on her tongue than any words she's ever spoken before. She grabs Somi's hand and holds tight as she stares down their murderer. *Find out who, and then hurt them. Just as they hurt her.*

"Over and over, until you reincarnate her as a useless, helpless slug—with all her memories—that somebody salts? Then start the process all over again. And again, and again, and again."

"And again," Somi adds, voice hard, squeezing Kisa's hand in her own.

Jang pales.

"Huh." Yeomra looks slightly awestruck. "Do you have any interest in working in our Torture Department?"

"Do it, Yeomra," a new voice rasps. Yeomra's eyes widen in panic and Kisa whirls around to see Seokga, standing with a slight pitch forward, green eyes glimmering. "I'll be the one pouring the salt."

CHAPTER THIRTY-TWO

SEOKGA

THE FIRST THING he sees through his blurry, black-ebbed vision is Kisa. His Kisa, standing in the cold cavern, drenched to the bone. Seokga nearly falls to his knees in relief. *She's alive,* he thinks, before the sickeningly icy knowledge that she was dead before he ever met her sets in.

The second thing he sees is Jang, struggling in skeletal shackles, defeat written all over her face. He smiles in satisfaction, even as he holds a hand to his still-bleeding side.

The third thing he sees is his father.

Sprawled on the rock where he left him so long ago.

A *living corpse,* he thinks as he stares at his father. Dirty, skeletal, gaunt. His black eyes are coated by a dull film. Seokga's stomach twists inside of him, and he tells himself it's only the pain of Jang's bite. Thanks to the incline of the rock, Mireuk is perfectly able to see him, as well.

"My son," Mireuk says, cracked lips stretching into a bloodless smile. "You came."

"*Fuck,*" Yeomra breathes, freezing on the spot. Jang smirks.

The enormity of seeing his father for the first time since his imprisonment is like a sudden death to Seokga. His airways work and fail before he can finally find enough breath to compose himself even though he is falling apart on the inside.

"Hello, Father," Seokga finds himself somehow managing to sneer. The pain in his side has receded and his whole body has gone numb. "You're looking... terrible." He sways on his feet slightly, saved only from falling as Kisa darts toward him. Her presence steadies him.

"Ah, Seokga," Mireuk says with a sigh. "I've missed you. All this time, the things I have regretted..." His eyes slide to Kisa. "And this must be her, mustn't it? She's pretty. I see why you like her."

"I'm not freeing you," Seokga grits out between his teeth. "Your crimes against humanity put you here, and here you shall *stay*, Father." A glimmer of pride spans down the bond between him and Kisa.

"You think me so incapable of change," the Mad God whispers mournfully. "I could prove you wrong. I could undo all of it, if only these shackles were to come off... A world without pain. I could do that. Take it all back..."

"*Bullshit,*" Seokga snaps. The madness in his father's mind is not the sort that can be treated or empathized with. They tried. For so long before imprisoning him, they tried. All it led to was death and destruction.

"I can turn back time... You can save Hani... or save Kisa... whomever you prefer..."

Kisa stiffens next to him.

—manipulative—he's—goading—Lonely God—said—Yeomra—can't—need—leave—now—now—now—

At his sides, Seokga's fingers twitch. Kisa watches them until she cannot.

"This will help you, too, Seokga... Don't pretend it will not..."
All the issues that stem from your relationship with your father can be healed.

He wants to start again, like you have . . . And you, Seokga, can give him that. I know he would be eternally indebted to you.

"My son, my son." Mireuk's bloodless smile grows. "Don't you want that?"

You love him. I think that you would still do anything for him.

"I do," he rasps before he can stop himself. He can feel Mireuk's influence encroaching on him like a fungus. His head aches with the effort of withstanding it.

"Seokga, please," Kisa begs. "You can't listen to him."

"You and I are so alike, Seokga," Mireuk whispers. "Misunderstood at every turn . . . All you have to do is untie me, son, and we can prove them all wrong."

"Seokga," Yeomra warns, voice dark. "Don't. You *know* what your penance will be."

Do you mean to say that a part of you doesn't still long for his approval? Doesn't wonder about what would happen if you earned it?

"Listen to *me,* Seokga," Mireuk says. "Don't listen to him. Come here. Unchain me. Do what your brother could never do . . . Be better than Hwanin could ever be."

"Seokga," whispers Kisa, grabbing his hand. "Please . . . don't do this. I'm begging you—"

You love fully and completely, only to have it returned in less than half.

"Son . . ." Mireuk licks his lips weakly. "I love you. It would break my heart . . . if you wasted my love."

I love you.

I love you. I love you. I love you.

How long has he waited to hear those words?

Seokga takes a deep breath. And lets go of Kisa's hand.

He'll have to let her go eventually anyway.

"SEOKGA!" Yeomra roars, but with a flick of his wrist, Seokga has created an illusion of unbearable pain for the death god.

Yeomra falls to his knees as Seokga, chin held high, eyes holding his father's, ascends the rock on which he lies.

"*No!*" Kisa cries, scrabbling after him. But Seokga is faster.

The first set of shackles are smooth under his hand. Seokga smiles down at his father as he rips them from the stone, shattering them into nothingness. Mireuk's grin turns monstrous and wicked as his arms, and then legs, are freed.

The Mad God rises . . .

. . . and realizes he cannot.

From where he stands, illusioned invisible at the base of the rock, Seokga waves an indolent hand and dismisses the Seokga that stands above his father. Dismisses the illusion of broken chains, revealing that the skeletal shackles are still firmly in place on his father's wizened wrists and ankles.

"*NO!*" roars his father, straining against his bonds. "*NO!*"

The illusion hiding himself, the true Seokga, from sight is the next to dissipate . . . followed by the pain grounding Yeomra. In Seokga's opinion, the bastard deserves it for consistently failing to notice what's going on in his own godsdamn realm.

"You villains. Always falling for the same tricks," Seokga says in mock boredom, brushing invisible lint off his sodden pants as he looks meaningfully at Jang, and then at his father. "When will you learn? It's utterly pathetic. If you're going to be evil, you might as well be halfway good at it."

Above him, perched on the rock, Kisa grins down at him. She doesn't look at all surprised as she hops down. "How exhilarating," she gasps. "I was never much one for theater—or improvisation, at any rate—but I think I pulled it off, don't you?

"You knew?" splutters a pained-looking Yeomra.

"I see him for who he is," she replies, pointedly cocking an eyebrow. "No matter if he's illusioned or not. I told you that you underestimated him."

Seokga has never loved Kisa more than he does in this moment.

"I'm sorry," he murmurs, swaying on his feet. "I should have listened to you about Jang. I-I shouldn't have called her..."

"No," Kisa says firmly, lurching closer to him and cupping his face in her hands. "Don't blame yourself for it. For any of it. My death is not your fault. It's *hers*. And I don't blame you for not wanting to think she had it out for you..."

"Seokga," his father pants desperately, "think of all I can give you... that we can give each other..."

"No, thanks," says Seokga, leaning into Kisa's touch. It's all he'll ever want. All he'll ever need.

Mireuk's face contorts into the vicious mask that Seokga remembers. "I will hunt you to the ends of the earth... I will burn your mother's verdant hills and plains with scorches of wildfire... I will *pull the veins from your skin and tie them together*..."

"That's not completely anatomically possible," Kisa points out, beaming at Seokga. Her eyes are sparkling, and damn it, if his heart isn't swelling full to the point of bursting. Tenderly, he wraps his arms around her. Embracing her is like gasping that first breath of sweet air after drowning. Seokga buries his face in her mane of coffee curls, squeezing her tight.

"I love you." She doesn't need to say it back. She doesn't even need to feel the same. He just needs to say it. "I love you, Kisa."

He's not hurt when she pulls back slightly. The time that they've had, he will treasure forever. The two of them got a second chance, and that's more than many can ever ask for.

So when Kisa smiles tenderly at him and whispers the words

back, he's sure he's misheard her, or has found himself in an illusion of his own making.

"I think I might love you, too," she murmurs.

"*SEOKGA—*" Mireuk roars.

"Goodbye, Father," Seokga says, turning away. And he doesn't look back once.

CHAPTER THIRTY-THREE

SEOKGA

THE STRANDED SRC *Flatliner* is somewhat lopsided as Seokga, Kisa, and Somi reappear on the tenth deck. He glimpses his fallen sword and snatches it up, reverting it to a cane and leaning heavily on it, glad to once again have the support for his right leg. Yeomra has gone to the seven hells to imprison Jang and free Soo-min (offering her a reincarnation deal in exchange for her suffering). The death god is also sending out a team of reapers to find the lost soul of the murdered Captain Lee.

"Hajun!" Somi gasps in worry, and hurries with a panicked desperation across the slanted deck toward the door. She only falls twice in her haste before she disappears.

Kisa laughs softly beside him, and he turns to her, memorizing her blue-flushed cheeks and shy smile. "I mean it, you know," she whispers, and when she reaches up to gently brush a strand of his wet hair from his eyes, Seokga thinks he just might die. "I know the answer to the Ship of Theseus question now, Seokga, and I . . . I was *wrong* before. I love you because for my soul, loving you is like breathing. It's all it knows how to do. It's all it wants to do, and it's *dangerous,* almost . . . I would plunge into hell's river for you . . .

I would face the *Mad God* for you. Because I love you, Seokga. In this life and the last."

"Kisa . . ." He fumbles for words, but he cannot catch any. There are no words in any language that can adequately describe what he feels for her, what it means for him to hear her say that. As if taking pity on his struggles, the red thread glows before sending a *rainbow* of emotions sparkling down its length toward Kisa, whose eyes widen. Blue, red, yellow, pink, purple, green . . . All in varying shades, all beautiful. All breathtaking.

"I know," she breathes, "*I know.*" And then she is kissing him, running her hands through his hair, pressing her body against his. Her lips are so sweet against his, and when her nose bumps against his Seokga wonders if he has found in Kisa a religion outside of his own to worship.

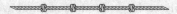

Hwanin screams as his small hands reach for Seokga in the sick bay, where the medicine cabinets are completely strewn across the floor and the lightbulbs flicker haphazardly above. Seokga feels like screaming himself as Hwanin wipes his snotty nose all over his bare chest, but finds himself cradling his brother close, an unspeakably soft emotion rising up in his throat and choking him. Hwanin screams and screams, as if enraged with Seokga for leaving him.

"I'm sorry," whispers Seokga, and he's apologizing for so much more than the baby understands. "I won't leave you again." Hwanin looks up at him with teary, watery blue eyes and reluctantly falls silent before closing his eyes and sinking into an exhausted doze.

Hajun and Somi are currently locked in a passionate embrace—and have been for some time. Seokga and Kisa exchange fond glances as the other couple whispers soft declarations to each other, Hajun staring down lovingly at Somi and playing with a strand of her short black hair.

"I think," murmurs Kisa, standing beside him, "that it's time to ask Yeomra for another favor." He doesn't protest as her hand slips into the pocket of his pants and pulls out his waterlogged—yet somehow undamaged—phone and sends off a long message to Yeomra.

As if hearing her for the first time, Hajun breaks his embrace with Somi (but for no lack of longing, thinks Seokga) and rushes over to pull Kisa into his arms. "I'm sorry," he says as Kisa hugs him back. "I couldn't find the heart."

"It's okay, Hajun," Kisa says, a smile in her voice. "Jang has an eternity of torture in front of her. She won't be returning to the ship regardless. But I'm sure Yeomra will have his jeoseung saja scour the ship later and dispose of it." Seokga silently agrees. Mainly because Yeomra is undoubtedly revolted by the fact that a bloody organ is lying about somewhere on his pride and joy, smelling of rot and gore.

Sours the image of the underworld's esteemed *"ultimate vacation cruise ship."*

"Good." Hajun wipes his eyes as he steps back. "I never trusted that old lady. I knew it all along."

"Please," scoffs Somi, though she looks amused. "You barely even met her."

"Are you insinuating that my detective skills aren't all they're made out to be?" Hajun places a hand dramatically on his heart. "Ouch—"

"Oh, stop," the gumiho snickers, trailing a hand down his chest. "You have other uses that you excel at . . ."

Hajun blushes deeply and stutters something in reply as Seokga tries not to gag.

His phone buzzes in Kisa's hands, and her soft joy spreads down the thread as she reads a message, then looks back up at Somi and Hajun. "I have something for you," his Threaded says, "if you'd like it." Wordlessly, she hands the phone to Somi, whose eyes grow to the size of saucers as she reads.

"Tell him yes," Somi blurts as Hajun reads over her shoulder.

"Yes!" the idol half-pants, half-gasps, looking unsteady on his feet. "Yes, yes, yes." He laughs as Somi leaps onto him, like she's climbing a tree. Kisa's eyes sparkle as she finally turns the screen to Seokga.

Seokga: Somi & Hajun deserve more time together. Would you consider letting Hajun stay on the SRC Flatliner for as long as he wants—as a guest—before entering the reincarnation queue with Somi?

Yeomra: Rich of you to ask me that after illusion-ing me to think that my insides were in a blender. I hate you a little. Next time I see you, expect a slap in the face. Maybe a fist.

Seokga: This is Kisa, actually.

Yeomra: That explains the better spelling. Yes. Fine. In thanks for his help, Hajun can stay on as a guest with Somi as long as he wants. The ship will be repaired soon.

Yeomra: Any favors to call in for yourself?

Seokga: Only one ... But I think
I'll ask Seokga.

Yeomra: Any thoughts about that position in the Torture Department?

Yeomra: ... hello??

"What's your favor?" Seokga asks, utterly uninterested in the rest of the text exchange. Kisa hesitates, suddenly looking shy. He chooses to ignore that behind her, Somi and Hajun are devouring each other like starving animals. Seokga looks only at Kisa, at her blue-blushing cheeks and hopeful, wine-brown eyes.

"Well ... you're heavenly emperor now ... or you will be, at least until Hwanung comes back ..."

Seokga shrugs, rubbing Hwanin's back as he shifts in his sleep. "Interim heavenly emperor for the interim heavenly emperor for the interim heavenly emperor ..." Hwanung will return soon, and Hwanin is only emperor until their mother, Mago, awakens.

"Still," Kisa says with a little smile, "I want to ask *you* for this."

"So ask," he breathes, certain he's about to die from the anticipation. "Ask while I can give you anything in the world."

She does.

Eyes bright, Kisa leans forward to whisper her wish in his ear.

CHAPTER THIRTY-FOUR

KISA

"I DIDN'T KNOW goodbyes could hurt so much," Hajun whispers as he stands with Kisa on the newly repaired tenth deck of the SRC *Flatliner,* his eyes filled with tears. Kisa tries to smile at her friend, but her face crumples as his does.

"Me, neither," she whispers, pulling him into a tight hug. His soft black T-shirt, so different from his usual stiff scrubs, wrinkles under her embrace. "You'll have fun, won't you? Don't let yourself miss me too much." She feels him nod.

"Thank you," he whispers. "For everything."

"You deserve it all, Hajun," Kisa replies, holding him tight, breathing in his cinnamon cologne. "For as long as you want it." She allows herself to hold on to him for a few moments longer before she slowly, gently, steps away.

"Kisa," Somi says, and the dam of emotions in Kisa breaks again as the gumiho steps forward, dark eyes unusually glassy. Somi's short hair flutters in a morning wind. "I guess this is goodbye—for real, this time." Her red-lined lips tremble and her knuckles shine around the handle of a suitcase. "I'm glad we could do it over. I'm happy, so happy, that we can part as friends."

"Me, too," Kisa says, scrubbing a tear away. "Somi... I need you to know that what happened last time was never your fault. Hani never blamed you, and neither do I. For what it's worth, I'm—*we're*—sorry, so sorry, for everything." As Somi shakes her head, Kisa practically drags her into a hug. Somi hesitates before wrapping her arms around Kisa and squeezing her hard enough that she nearly gags.

"You'll visit?" she asks as Kisa struggles for breath.

"Yes," she wheezes. "Of course. As long as you're here."

"Good," Somi sniffles, stepping away. Hajun grabs her hand, looking worriedly at the crying gumiho. "If you don't, I'll be forced to take some drastic measures."

She believes it. "You'll know where to find me," Kisa replies, and she can't help but to smile as her friends nod, their faces softening.

"I want you to have these," Somi says, giving her the suitcase. As Kisa's brows raise, Somi bends to unzip a portion, giving Kisa a glimpse of *dozens* of battered romance books packed together. "They were yours to begin with, and they should be yours at the end, too."

Kisa's eyes blur with tears. "Oh, Somi," she whispers. "Thank you."

The gumiho smiles, even though she's still weeping. "I think they'll make good additions," she says. "Don't you?"

"Definitely," Kisa chokes out around a sob.

The red thread around her little finger—no longer substantial, and back to its regular thinness—gives an insistent tug before shaping itself into a clock. TICK, TOCK, it tells her in looping red letters that are distinctly impatient.

Right. She takes a deep breath. Seokga is almost here, having left the previous night to sit on Okhwang's throne as interim-

interim-interim heavenly emperor (as he calls it) and bring Kisa's wish to fruition.

She felt it happen, the exact moment her soul was unbound from the SRC *Flatliner* and bound to another place instead. A sort of lightness in her body that she forgot could *exist,* a feeling of vast potential—that she was about to go home.

She forgot what that felt like.

"Be happy, Kisa," Hajun whispers as the Red Thread of Fate quivers in joy and Seokga appears out of slightly undulating air to take his place next to Kisa. Just his presence beside her sends Kisa's heart thumping quite a bit more loudly than before.

"I will," she promises as she takes Seokga's hand. She already is.

The last things she sees on the SRC *Flatliner* are Somi's and Hajun's small, teary smiles before the world disappears around her . . .

. . . and re-forms into a world smelling of old paper and ink. Kisa bites her lip to contain her shout of joy as she takes in the worn mahogany walls crammed with yellowed scrolls and leather-bound volumes, spinning around on the dust-covered, uneven planks of the well-trodden floor to stare at the precariously balanced towers of books that nearly scrape the domed ceiling hundreds of feet above. It is a maze of literature, a forest of forgotten books. The book towers are the trees, the softly falling motes of dust their leaves, illuminated by grimy windows from which sunlight—real, pure, dazzling *sunlight*—streams. Bats hang from the darkness-obscured wooden beams above, and moths flutter from book to book, as if they believe themselves to be nectar-drinking butterflies. The forest stretches on and on, growing deeper and darker through narrow corridors and swooping staircases that look rickety at best. Despite the cold, despite the stagnant air, the Heavenly Library is the most beautiful thing Kisa has ever seen.

She turns to Seokga and presses a shaking hand to her mouth.

His green eyes glimmer in both hope and concern. "I told you," he says. "Cold, dusty—"

"And messy," Kisa agrees, but she's smiling, joy blooming in her chest. "It's nothing that the Dewey decimal system and a crackling fireplace can't fix, really."

"I have to admire your tenacity," he murmurs, drawing closer. Her breath hitches. "But are you sure, Kisa, that this is where you'd like your soul to be bound?"

For a gwisin must always be bound to one location or another, whether it be the place of their death, an active haunting site, or a point in the underworld like the SRC *Flatliner*. Without a binding, a gwisin will wander. They may wander for centuries without becoming lost to themselves or the physical worlds, but wander long enough and it will happen.

Seokga's binding will be gentler than Yeomra's. She will be able to dance in the sun, or visit her friends atop a rushing underworld river, but eventually, she will always be called back here. Here, to this new world. Her forest of forgotten books.

Kisa knows that there are stars in her eyes as she takes in the library, as she *feels* the secrets surrounding her like a shimmering blanket. There is no telling where the Heavenly Library ends. It is an entire realm in itself, and one in which she is content to stay. "Oh, yes," she whispers. "This is *home*, Seokga." Her fingers brush over his lips. "With you."

—*I love her   so much—can barely breathe—Kisa—Kisa—Kisa—*

As the morning sunlight streams into the library and envelops the god and the gwisin in its shimmering glow, Kisa presses herself up to her tiptoes and kisses Seokga with all of the deep, endless love that swirls within her soul.

Somewhere, far away, the god of laws and kept promises smiles. For an oath has finally been fulfilled.

EPILOGUE

SEOKGA

A LONE CHERRY BLOSSOM is carried away on a soft breath of wind, swooping and soaring through New Sinsi's bustling streets and past glittering skyscrapers. It flutters by a Creature Café, where coffee roasts and pastries bake, rising and glistening with pearls of sugar in ovens. The cherry blossom is content to roam New Sinsi until it flutters delicately to the ground—but something peculiar happens first.

Perhaps the sudden gust of wind is summoned by one of the wind deities—Yeongdeung Halmang, or one of her wily sons—or perhaps it is simply one of those spring gusts that carry with it the recent memory of a winter storm. Whatever the case, the cherry blossom rises up, up, and *up,* floating far above the mortal realm and into the heavens where it finds itself flying toward a dark forest where heavenly maidens wash their wings in a burbling brook, and where a small wooden palace sits nestled between the maples and oaks. Through the narrow crack in the dark door the cherry blossom squeezes, escaping into a world that is so much bigger than it appears on the outside. A new sort of forest, where the trees have transformed into scrolls and fluttering pages and the soft, mossy ground into a smooth, yet uneven, floor.

The breath of wind, with one last exhale, sends the blossom fluttering deep through the stacks, too fast to note that each vast section has been meticulously organized by an expert hand. There is everything from tattered, raunchy romance novels to historical tomes the size of a small horse. Yet the blossom sees only the small cottage nestled peculiarly in a bookish grotto, encircled by swirling shelves. It has a thatched roof and a small green door, and the cherry blossom is just as confused as a cherry blossom can manage to be as it finally comes to rest atop the cheery welcome mat outside.

WELCOME! greets a jaunty but messily embroidered scrawl.

KEEP OUT OR ELSE, reads a much spikier font below.

A moment later, the door swings open. Seokga the Trickster steps on the fragile blossom as he ventures into the library's depths, hiking three miles for the specific book its librarian requested.

Hwanin giggles as he sits atop Seokga's shoulders, small hands stretching out to brush against the spines of books. His older brother smiles.

They're in the Dark Stacks now, where the light from the Shallow Stacks' window doesn't permeate. He and Kisa have done an admirable job cleaning the Shallow Stacks toward the front of the library from its snow-like piles of dust and pest infestations, but back here, it's as wild as ever. Mushrooms sprout from cracks in the floorboards. Bats rustle up above, and there's a small demon population inhabiting the Deep Stacks of the library.

More than once, he and Kisa have ventured into the Deep Stacks armed with a sword and a large baseball bat, respectively, only to find themselves sprinting back to the cottage. (It had been a gift from Samsin Halmoni, who apologized to Kisa with such emotion that one would think *Kisa* was the goddess. The closest thing to an apology that Seokga received from her was something that might have been a remorseful smile if he squinted.) Seokga doesn't even want to know what resides in the shadows past the Deep Stacks—the *Deepest* Stacks. Kisa has hypothesized that there just might be a coven of witches, and is quite eager to meet them. Seokga, considerably less so. Whereas shamans draw their magic from the gods, witches draw their powers from demons like eoduksini.

The Dark Stacks are oddly silent, save for a faint chittering that sounds suspiciously like a minor plague demon. It's a relief when Seokga finds the book he's looking for and can turn back before the foul thing causes Hwanin to come down with a cold. The cottage's small windows glow with candlelight, a welcome sight in comparison to the Dark Stacks.

When he slips through the door, Kisa jumps up from her desk in excitement, hurrying to grab the heavy tome from his hands.

"Oh, this is perfect!" she cries in excitement, and he watches like a man in love as she flips reverently through its pages. The red thread forms into little hearts as he gazes at her.

"Stop that," he mutters to the scarlet string. Its fully revealed sentience has, quite a few times, made Seokga wish it was possible to strangle it. Yet Kisa has theorized it only becomes truly solid during times when its Threaded partners are in mortal danger. The most Seokga has been able to do to the again-insubstantial thread is swipe at it in annoyance.

HEHEHE, is the amused reply, written out in taunting loops. *SHAN'T.*

So dazed by Kisa and distracted by the bond, Seokga barely notices as Hwanin—with a mischievous, toothless smile—rises up into the air.

Kisa rushes back to her desk before one of the windows, where a laptop (stolen from a Samsung store in Seoul, courtesy of Seokga) sits open and blinking, a massive document filled with text awaiting her return. That beloved notebook from her time on the SRC *Flatliner* lies open, her messy hand detailing everything from the red thread's first appearance to her discovery of its sentience. She sets the new tome on the one scarce inch of free space on her desk, eyeing it reverently. Seokga peers over her shoulder. The header on the left page of her ever-open Word document reads, *Fate's Thread*.

A delighted squeal has Seokga whirling around. Hwanin is currently doing somersaults in midair, much to the weariness of the trickster god, who cannot for the life of him coax the little menace down. "Hwanin," he tries, only for the child to snicker at him, rolling into the small kitchen, brushing through the dried flowers hanging from the rafters, which Kisa uses to make the baby's food. He grimaces as Kisa comes to stand next to him.

"He'll come down eventually," she says, watching Hwanin as he hovers over the small, round dining table.

Seokga rather wonders why, for the life of him, he ever desired what others describe as "domestic bliss" as Hwanin begins to shriek, as if horrified to find himself in the air, despite it being *his own doing*. Brothers. After some fumbling, he manages to drag Hwanin down by his big toe.

"You monster," Seokga murmurs, kissing the top of Hwanin's head. The baby squirms happily as Seokga turns back to Kisa. "How's the book coming along?"

"Just about as well as it was this morning." Kisa sighs, running a hand through her curls. She's wearing one of his sweaters and he'll never get used to the joy he feels at seeing her out of those scratchy SRC *Flatliner* scrubs. "We might have to try and venture out into the Deepest Stacks tonight . . . There's another reference I need."

Seokga grimaces.

Kisa grins. "Don't tell me you're frightened . . ."

"Never," he mutters as Kisa steps forward, smoothing out the crease between his eyebrows with her thumb.

"Poor little god, so scared..." Her kiss is soft and sweet, casual in a way that has Seokga's knees weakening. Whenever she kisses him, simply because she *can* and she wants to, he wonders how his wicked soul ever came to deserve this. "We can always ask Hwanung to come along with us again."

Seokga grimaces, remembering the one disastrous Deep Stacks expedition they had with his nephew. He still has not recovered from the music Hwanung chose to blast on his portable speaker while Seokga and Kisa fought off a horde of chubby, salivating baegopeun gwisin. He couldn't concentrate with heavy rock in the background, and had ended up nearly getting his leg chomped off. "Please, Kisa, no—"

He cuts off as there's an abrupt knocking at the door of their small cottage. Kisa's surprise flares down the thread. Hardly anyone visits the cottage in the library, save for Hwanung's biweekly visits where he stomps into the cottage in his ridiculous studded boots and treks in mud, dust, and other grime along with a dramatic exhaustion and complaints of how "being interim emperor is so tremendously hard." Seokga never has much sympathy for him. But Hwanung visited two days ago, which means whoever's at the door, it's not his nephew.

"I'll get it," Seokga says, tightening his grip on his cane.

"No, I will," Kisa retorts, pushing past him.

"I have the *sword*—" Seokga tries to step in front of her, only for Kisa to nimbly trip him with one of her feet. He staggers to the side, irate.

"*I'm* the dead one," she tells him over her shoulder, and before he can formulate an argument to that unfortunately logical statement, she opens the door.

And freezes. Her back stiffens and her shoulders rise as the red thread between them flares purple in her growing panic and alarm.

In a flash, Seokga scoops Hwanin up from the floor and staggers to stand behind Kisa's shoulder, transforming his cane into a sword with a flick of his wrist.

When he sees what lies beyond Kisa's slender shoulder, Seokga nearly drops both his brother and sword in shock.

A woman with skin the color of spring leaves and hair no less dark than the richest soil stands on their welcome mat, dressed in a simple brown hanbok. She's yawning, as if having just awoken from a long slumber, stretching her arms out as her lips part. In her hands is a glossy magazine.

SEXY SEOKGA'S SORDID TELL-ALL! the bubbly pink headline reads, followed by a rather unflattering photo of the trickster god glowering down at a camera in a dimly lit broom closet.

"Mother?" whispers Seokga, hardly daring to believe it.

Her eyes, as green as Seokga's own, crinkle warmly in the corners. "I don't suppose," says Mago, goddess of the Earth, rightful empress of Okhwang, and Seokga's (no longer) slumbering mother, "that you'd like to tell me what this is all about, Seokga?"

SEXY SEOKGA'S **SORDID** TELL-ALL!

THE SECRETIVE TRICKSTER GOD SPILLS THE BEANS

Godly Gossip's EXCLUSIVE Spring Issue

by Suk Aeri, editor in chief

My, my, *my*! When an opportunity presents itself to you all wrapped up in a pretty bow, what choice do you have but to take it? That's what we at *Godly Gossip* did this past autumn when a certain sexy trickster god played right into our hands. ~~With a bit of blackmail,~~ He was more than happy to answer the *burning* questions that we've puzzled over for years!

We at *Godly Gossip* are thrilled to finally present the answers to you in our extra-special spring issue! Be warned: The contents of the following interview are **extremely hot**! Please be advised to handle them with caution . . . Or don't. Dive right in and find out what dirty little secrets Seokga (former not-god, longtime winner of *Godly Gossip*'s Hot-but-*Not* award, and everyone's favorite green-eyed devil) has been hiding from us!

. . .

NOTE: Names of the interviewers have been **redacted** for **anonymity**.

Interviewer 1: We at *Godly Gossip* would like to thank you for sitting down with us today—

Seokga: Fuck off. You and I both know why we're here. Go on, ask. Before I lose my patience.

Interviewer 1: Fine. Do you wear a toupee?

Seokga: Do I wear—no. I don't wear a *toupee*.

Interviewer 2: Fascinating. Here's a good one. Seokga, you have a *long* history of being an asshole.

Seokga: Thank you.

Interviewer 2: Our readers would like to know to what extent you would say that "pretty privilege" has saved you from being fed to an eoduksini by the pantheon?

Seokga (*smirking*): A vast extent. But what the pantheon understands—even if they deny it or forget it half the time—is that all things require balance. My nature brings that balance.

Interviewer 2 (*sarcastic*): Is that why you break into security rooms and destroy them? For "balance"?

Seokga: I'm going to treat that question as rhetorical.

Interviewer 1: It was. The next one is: Is it true that you got plastic surgery to enhance the size of your pecs? Our readers have noted that they seem unusually large and, in their words, "hard. Very, very, hard."

Seokga (*spluttering*): No! Honestly. How inane. These questions do little to endear your readership to me. A bunch of bumbling *bimbos*—

Interviewer 1: Did you really date an elderly dog-walker?

Seokga: I have been trying to tell you people for years that I *haven't*—

Interviewer 1: In that same vein, what's the most inconvenient place you've been turned on?

Seokga: Fucking hells. In a bamboo forest near a horde of hungry ghosts, I suppose.

Interviewer 1: Would you like to elaborate on that?

Seokga: No.

Interviewer 2: Have you ever... you know... in animal form?

Seokga (*aghast*)**:** You're sickening. *No.*

Interviewer 1: Do you have any dirty kinks you've been keeping secret?

Seokga (*pained*)**:** I... used to... like to have a... mirror nearby.

Interviewer 2: For yourself?

Seokga (*glaring*)**:** Maybe.

Interviewer 1: Is it true that in 2000 you attended a TLC concert and cried during "Waterfalls"? The photos were so grainy that nobody could tell if it was you or an overemotional mortal man.

Seokga: ...

Seokga: Yes. That was, unfortunately, me.

Interviewer 2: Do you still have vivid fantasies of power? If so, do you have any plans for world domination anytime soon?

Seokga: Interesting that you ask . . .

Want more *sizzling* questions answered? Sexy Seokga's SORDID tell-all is continued on pages thirteen to twenty-four!

ACKNOWLEDGMENTS

I would not be where I am today without the unwavering support of my family. Mom, you're arguably Fate's Thread's biggest fan. Thank you for cheering me—as well as Seokga, Hani, and Kisa—on each and every day with your unparalleled enthusiasm. This book is dedicated to you for a reason. Thank you to my father, who is the bearer of annoyingly sage advice. I truly wish you weren't right so often. It's exasperating. To my brothers, thank you for your unapologetic authenticity and steadfast friendship. 할머니 and 할아버지, thank you for your love and support—as well as for all the delicious Korean food. Grandma, Grandpa, thank you for your endless cheer.

I'm blessed to have an incredible literary agent, Emily Forney, who has been with me every step of the way for years now. Emily, to say that I appreciate everything you do for my work would be a massive understatement.

It seems that I'm just surrounded by fantastically talented Emilys. A huge, huge thank-you to my editor, the singular Emily Archbold, who is a complete joy and wonder to work with. Here's to more adventures to come!

Del Rey has been an amazing publishing home and is full of folks who have done an incredible job getting *The God and the Gwisin* out into the world. Thank you to my copy editor, the eagle-eyed Madeline Hopkins. Thank you to my spectacular marketing team: Ashleigh Heaton, Tori Henson, and Sabrina Shen. Thank you to Meghan O'Shaughnessy and David Moench in PR. Thank you also to Madi Margolis, Scott Shannon, Keith Clayton, Julie Leung, Alex Larned, Pam Alders, Michelle Daniel, and Paul Gilbert. To designer Belina Huey and artist Sija Hong: You have my eternal gratitude for creating such beautiful covers for this series. Thank you also to Ralph Fowler, who made this book's interior so stunning.

Across the pond is another fabulous team that I am incredibly grateful for. Thank you to Molly Powell, Sophie Judge, and Kate Keehan at Hodderscape, as well as to Kuri Huang, who illustrates the gorgeous UK covers. Thank you also to Anissa and the lovely team at FairyLoot.

To Serena Nettleton—my best and oldest friend, my sister in all but blood—thank you for your wonderful companionship and for inspiring me each and every day. I love you more than words.

Kamilah Cole, please accept this as my official apology for "killing" Hwanin. I know how dear this silver-haired god was to you. All I can say is, "Oops?"

Finally, to all of the readers who have supported Fate's Thread: Thank you, thank you, thank you. None of this would be possible without you.

As we reach port, it's finally time for us to disembark from the SRC *Flatliner*. I sincerely hope you enjoyed your stay upon this "ultimate vacation cruise ship" (Yeomra's words, not mine), and that we'll meet again soon on another whirlwind adventure.

ABOUT THE AUTHOR

SOPHIE KIM is a #1 *Sunday Times* bestselling author with a penchant for writing stories about mythology, monsters, mystery, and magic. Her work includes young adult novels such as the Talons series and critically acclaimed books on the adult spectrum such as *The God and the Gumiho*.

sophiekimwrites.com
Instagram: @sophiekimwrites

ABOUT THE TYPE

This book was set in Requiem, a typeface designed by the Hoefler Type Foundry. It is a modern typeface inspired by inscriptional capitals in Ludovico Vicentino degli Arrighi's 1523 writing manual, *Il modo de temperare le penne*. An original lowercase, a set of figures, and an italic in the chancery style that Arrighi (fl. 1522) helped popularize were created to make this adaptation of a classical design into a complete font family.

DISCOVER MORE FROM
DEL REY &
RANDOM HOUSE WORLDS!

READ EXCERPTS
from hot new titles.

STAY UP-TO-DATE
on your favorite authors.

FIND OUT about exclusive
giveaways and sweepstakes.

CONNECT WITH US ONLINE!
◎ ⨍ 𝕏 @DelReyBooks

DelReyBooks.com
RandomHouseWorlds.com